THE NEAR DEATH EXPERIENCE

JOHN ELLSWORTH

Life is but a dream

— Eliphalet Oram Lyte (1842 - 1913)

He tried to tell us that the animals could speak. Who knows, perhaps they do. How do you know they don't? Just because they've never spoken to you...

— John Denver

Now we see but through a glass darkly—

— Apostle Paul

*For Stuart Hameroff and Roger Penrose
Let's all stay entangled*

1

In the end, the breast cancer won. Took her away.

Which left Thaddeus with four children, two horses, three dogs, a barn teeming with half-feral but plump cats, and a law practice.

Plus, friendships from one end of the country to the other.

One of those friends, Christine Susmann, came to Katy's memorial service. She stood at Thaddeus' side and slipped her hand through his arm as he stood praying. He would later tell Christine that he didn't know what he was praying for or who he was praying to. He was just praying, as there was nothing else to be done.

She was gone. He had lost her.

He went back home that day and drew the kids close around him. They were Turquoise, Sarai, Parkus, and Celena. Christine made lunch for them all. Then Thaddeus and Christine took them out to the barn and saddled six horses. They took a ride into the Coconino National Forest, following Forest Service roads for a mile before heading into the aspen grove on the south side of the San Francisco Peaks. The air grew very cool and very clear as they climbed from 6,000 feet to 8,000 feet. Sweatshirts were shrugged on as the horses moved north.

Three miles in, they stopped; the adults spread ground covers and gathered the children into a circle. The horses stomped and grazed on a rope line nearby. Sweeping winds rattled through the autumn golds and yellows of the aspen while tall ponderosas wailed in the swirling tumult of winds beneath the fleeing cumulus clouds.

A smoked oyster tin was opened, and crackers passed around.

"Your mother loved these," Thaddeus said, biting into a pair of oysters on a Ritz cracker. "I'm doing this to remember her."

The three smaller children declined the offering. But Turquoise, now twenty-one and a first-year student in the University of Arizona's School of Veterinary Medicine, accepted an oyster cracker and chewed silently, looking off into the trees. Her cheeks were laced with tears, and she backhanded them away several times as she chewed.

A backpack was opened, and soft drinks passed around. They still retained enough refrigerator cold to satisfy. Three Orange Crushes, one Diet Coke, one Pepsi Light, and a Dr. Pepper.

There was very little talk, and the smaller children, for once, seemed content to remain with the adults and just be nearby rather than dashing off into the forest for a game of tag as they usually chose to do.

Thaddeus leaned back on the ground cover, supporting himself on his elbows. He was wearing gray ropers, blue jeans, a black T-shirt beneath an unbuttoned RL denim shirt, and sunglasses pushed on top of his head. He occasionally would lose it and brush away tears very openly and without any attempt to hide his pain and sorrow. He was thirty-two years old and wracked with a lost love.

"All right," he said at last to his family and Christine. "Let's all tell one thing we remember most about Mama. Sarai, you can go first."

Sarai was seven, and she was usually given to squirming, but just then she was still and thoughtful. She sat cross-legged, watching her horse pulling clumps of grass and chewing as he swatted away flies with his long tail.

"Mama made me chicken noodle soup when I was sick. She read books to me. She heard my prayers at night. And I love her. And I miss her, and I'm going to be with her when I die."

Thaddeus nodded. His gaze came to rest on Parkus, their adopted son, now six.

"Parkus, what about you? Do you have something to say about Mama?"

"I love you, Mama," he said. "I wish you didn't go."

"Fair enough," Thaddeus said. "Now Celena?"

She was nine and beginning to notice the world around her. A microscope was set up in her room and there was a constant succession of slides passing beneath its monocular eye: pond water, bugs (wings were her favorite, for their translucence), hair and fibers (Thaddeus wondered: would she work CSI?), drops of blood, horse feces, fingernail clippings—an endless stream of samples revealed a hidden world to her inquiries. Beneath the window that looked south from her bedroom, there was a reflecting telescope with a three-inch lens where she was able to type in the name of a star cluster or constellation on its keypad and watch as the finder located the target before she peered into the heavens. Secretly she believed she might see her mothers (there had been another) if only she kept looking hard and long enough. She said simply, "She told me she loved me, and I believed her. I loved her back. I miss her, and now Daddy cries a lot. I wish he would be okay."

She didn't look at Thaddeus as she said this. It was shared more as a secret about someone than a statement of fact, and she clearly wasn't sure how it would be received.

"Daddy loved your mom," Thaddeus said and squeezed his daughter's hand. "And you're right. Sometimes I do cry. It helps me express my grief."

"But it scares me when you cry," said Celena, her eyes welling up. "What if we lost you, too? Then we would be orphans again."

They had lost their birth parents to a terrible set of incidents back in Illinois. Celena remembered her parents well and was still tormented by their deaths, even though Thaddeus and Katy had spent endless hours trying to love them back to health and peace.

Christine spoke up. "I would never let you be orphans," she said. "I would immediately be there to help you."

Celena heard this, but Thaddeus could see it didn't register with his child. The notion that there might be yet another substitute parent in her life was just too much to contemplate even. She didn't respond.

"Well, I promise I won't leave you, Celena—any of you. I'm your dad, and that's not going to change. We have one more. Turquoise?"

Turquoise was intently feeding cracker crumbs to a line of ants and watching them bear away the unexpected gifts to God only knew where. She nodded and looked up at Christine. "You've always been there for us—especially for my dad, Ms. Susmann. Thanks for saying that. About my mom—she and I are of the same Navajo clan. She was my mom, but she was my sister too. We understood each other better than anyone will ever understand me. She rescued me and gave me a life. Now she's with Grandfather and is happy. I'm glad she doesn't hurt anymore. That's all. Can we ride now?"

Thaddeus raised a hand. "Your mother's final instructions to me do not fit with tribal customs. She makes no excuses."

Then Thaddeus sat upright.

"I'm ready to ride," he said. "Does anyone else have anything to say?"

Eyes met his and they all said the moment had passed. The talking was concluded.

The family plus Christine mounted up and swung the horses north. They fell into a line, Turquoise leading and Thaddeus bringing up the rear. Christine was just ahead of him, and he watched as she gracefully sat on her horse and let it pick its way along.

He wouldn't take his eyes from her the rest of that afternoon.

She felt his gaze upon her back. She was glad her presence gave him some peace.

Higher up the side of the mountain the little procession went, feeling the wind, searching the crystal blue sky for signs, beating back the tears or allowing them to flow, safe enough with the other riders to give the feelings their rein.

At 9,000 feet they rode into a meadow surrounded by an aspen grove. At this altitude the aspen branches were bare, and the sky was a heart-wrenching purple blue, a great canvas stretched over their world, which seemed, at that moment, to be holding everything together and in place, as the mother was no longer there to do that. Thaddeus stepped down from Coco and reached into his backpack. The earthen urn was opened, and a puff of white dust rose up. He made eye contact with each of his children and waited until he was sure they understood what was happening. Then he climbed back up on Coco and lurched forward into a gallop, turning the urn on its side and issuing a long white banner of ash until the setting free was done. Then he turned and silently walked his horse back to the others. Without a word he urged Coco between them and headed back down the mountain. This time, he led the way and the children understood as best they were able. He would lead; they would follow.

Thaddeus had known the ride would be restorative.

From her deathbed, Katy had made him promise to do this.

Then they were to let her go and move on with their lives.

He blinked hard against a new flow of tears as he recalled this. Blinked hard and leaned forward and patted Coco's chestnut neck. The horse was more than willing to take him away from his grief and loss.

Now if he could only allow it.

2

NADIA TURKENOV WAS A JOYLESS, tight-fisted woman who had saved every dime she ever earned. And she was lonely: more than anything, she wanted to see Henri, her deceased husband. She wanted to see him and cry in his arms like the hurt little child she was. Only she would never tell anyone that because she wanted to be seen as strong and unyielding, as someone beyond the tender years of sweet love.

She had been hurt when she was young, terribly hurt. Which left her with a life not worth living, in her view. Hers was a life that was about going through the motions almost as an automaton: getting up three days a week and heading off to work; climbing on the treadmill on her days off and spending an hour on the spinning rubber while trying to burn off the angst that followed her everywhere; paying lip service to the remaining members of her family—all while expending more energy at covering up than actually living.

It was Monday morning, and she was already into her workout. The treadmill was at 5 and she was slowly jogging now. On her lower torso were the Capri leggings; on her upper body was a tank top, made of the same stretchy material as the leggings. Her long, auburn hair was damp and pulled back in a ponytail. Long strands of hair lay plastered across her forehead like a series of commas. Her profile was soft and delicate, but her mien was forever screwed up into a scowl as if she had just told someone off. Which was too often the case.

Nadia punched the UP arrow, and the machine went to 6. Her pace increased, and she settled into a comfortable jog. She looked around her office, dreading the waste of time it would mean to bring order out of its chaos. Her nursing bag was sprawled across her wood desk, its top unzipped, left there after the weekend's sixty home health visits she had made as a very busy home health R.N. The remainder of the desktop was taken up with plastic-wrapped IV pumps, bandages, syringes, unopened medications of all description, and the usual accoutrements of the working nurse, including stethoscope, electronic thermometer, and blood pressure cuff. She preferred the old style cuff with the Velcro sleeve; it was good enough for nursing school where she had learned on it, and it was good enough for the real world. Besides which, it was paid for. Which was always at the forefront of Nadia's thinking. How best to save a dime.

She was fifty years old and had a vault full of dimes saved up. Not actual dimes, of course, and not actually in a vault. She had managed to save $1.1 million by returning to school at the age of thirty and becoming a nurse. She lived frugally; her apartment consisted of a small living room with a couch, recliner (her back demanded it after forty-hour stints over the weekend), and coffee table. Off to the right was her bedroom and small bathroom en suite, while straight ahead from the living room was the galley kitchen that actually was separated from the living room only by an island; and off to the left was her office/workout room, where she maintained a locked cabinet full of drugs and medical supplies that had been issued for current patients. Against the far wall of the office/workout room, she kept her desk and treadmill. There was a small closet as well, which usually was stuffed with nursing scrubs and utility belts she had taken to wearing for she liked the expediency of scissors, tape, and other implements at her waist where she could quickly put her hands on them. While putting a pump into Mrs. Roosevelt's IV line, there was nothing quite as handy as the roll of tape which hung from her utility belt. She swore by it and wished she had come up with the idea and been the first to the patent office. But she hadn't and so she had to keep on keeping on, visiting patients Fridays, Saturdays, and Sundays.

After her three workdays, the rest of the week was hers. She had two children, several siblings, and both parents were still alive and very active in the Russian Orthodox Church on Howard Street. She spent as much time with family as she could stand, which most days was limited to five minutes on the phone or putting in appearances for lunch or dinner or even attending her siblings and their children when they were ill.

Albert Turkenov was her son and at twenty-six he was a failed hustler. He worked as the used car manager for the Flagstaff Chrysler-Dodge dealership, or, at least, that's what he had told her last Thursday. Deep down she suspected he was just one more salesman working the bullpen. Anastasia Millerton was Albert's twin, and she was in her fourth year of medical school at the University of Arizona. They didn't talk much anymore, mother and daughter; there had always been a discomfiture between them, unexplainable by either woman, though mother guessed it was because she had been unwilling to pay for Ana's college or med school expenses, while daughter guessed it was because mother disapproved of the child who went to medical school when nursing had been good enough for the mother. Truth be told, they had never actually come right out and discussed the chasm between them and maybe never would. Anymore, it was the last thing on Nadia's mind. Family exhausted her, and she tried to keep it up on a shelf, next to the Aspirin.

She punched the treadmill up to 7. Now she was breathing hard and in a full long distance runner's gait. Her mind slipped away from conscious control as she ran, and she began yet another useless review of her life. She tread lightly around her memories of Henri, the man who had made life bearable and even wonderful, but who had succumbed to pancreatic cancer in his early forties. Tears came to her eyes as she remembered his perfect smile and his eyes opening first thing in the morning and searching her out and him whispering that she was the best thing that had ever happened to him. Henri was a financial failure—wait, she couldn't say that, exactly. He was just underserved by any motivation to achieve financial success. He had worked maintenance at the kids' high school. Not even that: he was a janitor. He swept floors and emptied trash cans. Which had been fine; Nadia was motivated enough for all of them. It was she who had amassed a small fortune while still putting healthy, hot food on their table and providing a four-bedroom ranch style while the kids were still at home. On Henri's death, the home had been sold, and the kids had gone off to college. Albert had dropped out after one semester; Ana was a senior.

She pulled the white towel from the treadmill's display board. She rubbed it hard across her wet hair and patted her face and neck, then ran it up and down her bare arms. She checked her pulse rate by placing two fingers on her right carotid and focusing her eyes on the digital display. Anymore she would count the beats to ten, multiply by six, and have a fairly good idea where her heart rate was. In fact, better than fairly good: perfect. Medicine demanded no less, and she did all things medical better than most.

Twenty-two minutes to go. She inclined the platform two degrees and felt her heart rate immediately increase. Good, she thought. This is my maximum burn.

With her right hand, she reached and retrieved the TV remote from the treadmill's basket. She clicked on a local channel and saw the graphic for *Good Morning, Flagstaff*, which was a local Flagstaff broadcast that played during the five or ten minutes they were cut away from *Good Morning, America*. The man on camera was quite good-looking, she thought; she slipped on her headphones.

"—And this went on for six days. On the seventh day, I awoke. Everyone had thought I was gone, up until that moment. In fact, the morning I came out of the coma, my wife, and the medical team were discussing removal of my life support. They were going to let me pass peacefully."

The camera swung away to the young, blond host.

"Well, that's the most amazing story I think I've ever heard,

Doctor Sewell! And let's see, you wrote a book about your experience?"

The medical man leaned back and grasped his knee between his hands. It was a very Ivy League kind of cool move; Nadia thought, and her mind imagined he was a grad of some acclaimed medical school back East.

"I did write a book. *The Doctor Is In...Heaven* is the title."

"Had you ever written a book before?"

"I had authored several dozen papers that went on to be published in some very fine medical journals. I have four articles on neurosurgery in the *New England Journal of Medicine*. But a book? Never. And I never in my wildest dreams had ever imagined I *would* write a book."

Nadia reached forward and leveled out the incline. It was making too much noise with her feet flopping against the tread, and she wanted to hear what the doc had to say.

"Well, Doctor Sewell, without giving away the whole book, can you walk us through a little of what heaven was like?"

Nadia felt a shock roll down her spine. Heaven? What *Heaven* was like? Had she just said that?

He smiled, releasing his knee and coming fully upright. Nadia liked his posture and saw how confident he was. It occurred to her: this man might be the real deal.

"Well, for me, there wasn't a bright light and heavenly music. When I died, I found myself in a grassy meadow, beside a stream of the clearest water I'd ever seen. I watched my reflection in the flow and then realized someone was behind me. I turned to see, and there were my deceased parents. Their arms were spread wide to welcome me. They came near and surrounded me with love."

"Did you say anything? Did they?"

"It was funny. No words were necessary. Thoughts were just instantaneously exchanged."

Nadia reduced the speed to 5. This was worth hearing.

"And what did they say to you?"

"Lots of things; it's all in my book. But the main thrust of it was that I was loved more than I could ever imagine. And that they had loved me since before the beginning of time."

"Did you see anyone else you knew?"

The doctor lifted a blue mug with GMF emblazoned in gold letters.

"I did. I saw my grandparents. And my favorite aunt."

"What did they say?"

"Tears of joy, Nancy. Happy tears."

"And the book is?"

"*The Doctor Is In...Heaven.*"

"Well, that's all the time we have now. Our thanks to Doctor Emerick J. Sewell. We'll now rejoin *Good Morning, America*, right after this."

A Pep Boys commercial came on, and Nadia clicked the remote. The TV screen went black.

Nadia quickly hit the down arrow and the treadmill slowed and slowed and finally rolled to a stop. She stepped off and went straight to her desk. Her laptop was open, browser up. She went to Amazon and immediately ordered *The Doctor Is In...Heaven*, for her Kindle.

She didn't even bother to shower first. She was going to sit around in her sweat—something she had never allowed before. But she didn't care; this couldn't wait to get the full story about his death and trip to heaven. She fired up her Kindle and began reading.

First the foreword. She had been right; the doctor was Ivy League. Harvard Medical School. Of course. He had had that confidence, that charm, that certainty that others would like him if only they got to know him. So Ivy. Board Certified in Neurosurgery and a second certification in psychiatry. Are you kidding me? She thought. How unusual, but how impressive! The credentials were certainly in place.

But how upset the East Coast medical community must be with the man! He had flown over the cuckoo's nest, what with this story. Or fable. Or fairy tale. Whatever it was. Died and went to heaven? *Seriously*? She'd see about that. She'd read on and find the loopholes in his story, and she'd debunk his claims herself. It took one medical professional to judge another. And she was ready. She tore into the book with her claws and fangs ready to shred the guy and his tale.

So where, she wondered as she read, did the memories of heaven and dead family come from? She twisted the cap off a bottle of water and jumped back into the book. She hadn't found it yet—the logical fallacy—but she would. She was the nonpareil investigator: the lie would reveal itself...and soon now. On she read.

At noon, she looked up. Her sweat had dried and more than two hours had passed while she read the neurosurgeon's book. The back matter of the book consisted of his medical chart—his file, his doctors' and nurses' notes and records and brain scans and reports. Plain as the lines in your palm. The man had been comatose and without brain activity for four straight days. And he had returned with an amazing tale of his journey to heaven and back.

Nadia finally stood and began peeling off the workout clothing. It was time for a shower.

She opened another bottle of water and took it into the shower with her. The giant shower head pummeled her with water, and for a moment she had the feeling she was being baptized but that only made her laugh. She had never been a churchgoer, despite her parents' encouragement and despite their having dragged her to the Russian Orthodox Church during her childhood. None of it had stuck, and she simply didn't believe any of that old religious junk. It held no sway over her; she laughed at believers and shunned them.

But how would she reconcile what Dr. Sewell had clearly experienced in his journey to heaven, with her longstanding belief system of denial? She toweled herself dry in the shower, stepped out onto the bath mat, and studied herself in the steamy mirror. She still had a firm body, despite the years and the child-bearing. She attributed her physique to working out and working very hard at a physically demanding job. Plus she stayed active around Flagstaff. There were hikes, and there were long excursions on her backcountry skis when the snows inevitably came and stayed for months. All done alone, distanced from the world around her while she went through the motions and wondered why none of the experiences had ever evoked any feeling in her. Not awe at seeing some of the most beautiful country in the world as she made her way through forests in hiking boots or clamped onto backcountry skis, and not humility, as the towering mountains provided perspective for her life. She felt nothing and she had come to find that feeling nothing was its own kind of exhausting.

So, she decided right then and there, nude before the wide glass mirror, to follow in the doctor's footsteps. Yes, she would give it one last try, a medical experiment that would ground her in some belief system that would make her life worth living: she would journey near death and see for herself what near-death would reveal.

She shocked herself with the thought. She went into her bedroom and dressed in baggy blue jeans and a T-shirt that featured a skier in a Telemark turn. But the leaf had been turned over. She had made a decision and, in Nadia's world, decisions once made were never reversed.

She went to her locked supply cabinet and spun the lock. Right-left-right-right-left. The numbers clicked, and the door swung open.

Her fingers traced along the wrappers of the medicine bottles. She was looking in particular for a certain pain reliever. Enough of that should do the trick. Enough of that should render her unconscious to the point where she might have a near death experience for herself.

She selected the bottle with great care. She considered her body weight and the normal dosage for the drug. Then she doubled it. But that wouldn't be enough to take her away to the level of unconsciousness she wished to attain. So she doubled it yet again.

Now there was another preparation to be made. The preparation of a letter to be read by whoever found her if she happened to overdose and didn't make it back. The thought was less than frightening for Nadia. She was realizing, as she made her plan, that she had been done with the world long ago. Going through the motions of living was no longer good enough. It was time for a deeper experience and the possibility that she might not make it back held no fear for her. At least not enough to make her stop and reconsider.

So she wrote and printed a letter of explanation. It said:

If you find this, I am probably dead. Please don't be upset if I am because I was bored with living anyway. I was tired of life and until you live a life like mine you probably won't understand.

Dr. Emerick Sewell has a book called The Doctor Is In...Heaven and I have taken pills to try to get to where he was when he had his journey into heaven. I'm following his medical advice on what happens. Did I get there? If you're reading this, you'll probably never know. But I will know.

This is my life and it's a choice I have made. Am I selfish? Maybe, but I don't care. My kids have their lives and they are happy. I've lost Henri and my life is no longer valuable to me anyway, so don't mourn. Just let me go.

Nadia.

She then added a PS:

All of my money shall be used to create a scholarship called the Henri Turkenov Nursing Scholarship at Northern Arizona University. No money should go anyplace else. Thank you.

Nadia

It was signed with her scrawl and was left in her lap as she sat back in her recliner and downed her pills with a water chaser. Which was when she realized: she had no last will and testament. She leaped up and went back to her laptop and printer. She re-wrote the letter, this time with a p.s. that said, simply, *I have my money in Bank of America. Phoenix branch on Camelback. N.*

Armed with the new, revised letter, she went back to her recliner. She felt the pills beginning to take effect and hurriedly plopped into her chair. Again, the letter was left resting in her lap.

She closed her eyes and placed her arms inside the armrests.

A deep breath. Another.

While she waited.

3

Six months earlier, Thaddeus Murfee had accompanied his wife Katy to the oncologist in Flagstaff.

"I'm sorry to have to tell you this," the oncologist said, his eyeglasses perched on his forehead and his arms folded on his chest as he sat at his desk. "I have reviewed the scans. The cancer has progressed to the right hip, the thoracic spine and lumbar spine, and the skull, right occipital region."

"Which explains my headaches and backaches," Katy said.

"Which explains your pain, certainly," said the doctor.

Thaddeus stirred in the seat beside his wife. He was the only non-doctor in the office, but he was ready to meet the challenge head-on. They were already several steps ahead of him, but he had no way of knowing that.

"So what's indicated, Dr. Jurgens?" he said. "Radiation? Chemo?"

The doctor's eyes never left Katy's eyes.

"Neither. I'm afraid we've run out of options."

Thaddeus came fully upright. "Then we need a second opinion."

"I wouldn't blame you for that, Mr. Murfee. I can recommend several docs in the Phoenix area who I am sure would review the case. My nurse will give you the short list on your way out."

Katy shook her head. "I don't want that, Honey. I'm a doctor, and I know what 'no options' means. I don't want to spend my remaining time driving back and forth from Flagstaff to Phoenix."

"Then I'll do it by myself," Thaddeus said. "I'll see him myself and report back to you. I'm not done fighting."

She touched his hand. "Then you'll be away from me, and I don't want that either. I want you and the kids close by."

Thaddeus slumped back in his chair. He said nothing. His head came forward, and his chin rested on his chest. He took a long, shuddering breath. There were no words.

"How long are these things, usually?" Katy asked.

"Six months, give or take. Maybe even a year. Maybe only one month. But I would call it six if I were you."

She turned to Thaddeus. "See? We do have some time yet. There's so much we can do."

He nodded. "Absolutely. There's so much we can do."

Although he had no idea where to begin. Right then, he only wanted to take her in his arms and never let her go. Maybe that was where he should begin.

"All right," he said at last. "I think I'm beginning to see what you two are seeing."

"That will be best," said Dr. Jurgens. "Our tumor board here at the hospital has carefully reviewed this case. You are receiving the benefit of the best thinking of many excellent physicians, Thaddeus."

Thaddeus shook his head. "Please. You don't have to convince me."

"What he means, is that—" Katy began.

Thaddeus laughed. "What am I ever going to do without you around to explain to people what I mean?"

He said it with the greatest love possible, and she knew it. So did Dr. Jurgens, who chuckled.

Thaddeus stretched out his arms and stretched his legs. It was sinking in, and he was visualizing his role. He would be supportive, loving, and patient. He would also need to learn about participating in palliative care for the terminal patient; something he had always thought was maybe fifty years down the road where it would be Katy caring for him. But it wasn't. This was it, telescoped fifty years ahead, and he was to be the caregiver, not Katy.

"So," said Dr. Jurgens. "Let's talk about pain management."

"Please do," said Katy. "It would be nice to make the backaches and headaches hurt just a little less."

"We can do much better than that. We can make you comfortable right up to and including the end."

"A course of medication all thought out and tested," she said.

Dr. Jurgens nodded. "That would be correct."

"All right. What do I need first?"

"First will be a home health nurse. She will be there at first just for med management. Her role will change as your health diminishes."

"Understand."

"You will eventually need round-the-clock help from these nurses."

"Okay."

"My nurse has some providers you can contact. Your insurance will cover any of them. We've already confirmed that."

"Thanks," said Thaddeus.

She drove them home.

"I want to do the driving, make the beds, load the dishwasher, cook the dinners as long as I can. I am going to live while I can."

"Can't argue with that," Thaddeus said. "But I do think we should make a trip to Phoenix and, at least, check in with another doctor. It's your life we're talking about here."

"Thad, I know Dr. Jurgens. Everyone says he's the best. Impeccable credentials. Mid-sixties, been around forever. The Medical Center has the latest scanners money can buy; the radiologists are all board certified in the group managing my care. Another doctor isn't going to change the fact that the cancer has spread. All the second opinions in the world aren't going to change that."

"I know that. That much we agree on. But I'm not in agreement that there are no treatment options for what we're looking at.

Different clinics are beating cancer every day. Think of the Cleveland Clinic. I'll fly you over there. Or Johns Hopkins. Or Scripps. Or Mayo's. We can go anywhere in the world, also. Let's at least think about it."

She gave a long sigh and moved her hands on the steering wheel. Staying within her usual manner of discussing things with Thaddeus was becoming difficult. She had pain, and she didn't feel like arguing, much less discussing anything at length. She gritted her teeth anyway and decided to give him some room for movement.

"All right. We'll take one shot. You get online and make your calls, do what you think is best, and we'll get a second opinion. In a way I guess I owe you that."

He smiled and touched her thigh. "You owe *you* that."

TWO WEEKS later they had visited with none of those first named health care providers. Thaddeus had learned that the best in the country in cancer care was reported to be the University of Texas MD Anderson Cancer Center in Houston. So early one morning Katy drove them to Flagstaff Airport, and they took the Gulfstream to Houston. The appointment was at noon, which they made easily. Katy had refused a full workup with new scans and tests. Instead, she agreed only to a chart review by the world-renowned staff.

When they were done, Thaddeus was silent as they took a cab back to the airport. He stared out the window at the lengthening afternoon shadows and felt very lonely. His left hand found Katy's hand, and he clutched it. Tears came to his eyes, and he blinked hard and concentrated on how her hand felt just then. He wanted never to forget that moment when they were together and when he was holding her, the inevitable now confirmed by the best second opinion available in the United States.

"I'm sorry I made you come here," he said when he had forced himself to rejoin her in the moment.

"You didn't make me. I agreed," she said. "And I won't say I told you so. It is what it is, and you needed to hear it for yourself."

"Thanks for doing it. I mean that. I've taken you away from the kids and your house for a full day. I promise not to do that again."

"And I promise not to let you," she said with a laugh. She withdrew her hand but immediately reached across and patted his hand before he could move it away.

His face turned to concern. "How are you feeling right now? Would you like to get some of Houston's fabled Mexican food?"

"Nope. I want a roast beef sandwich on the plane, and I want to stay up all night watching the kids sleep. I really do."

"Then I'll stay right up with you. Is that okay?"

She slowly nodded.

"I wouldn't want it any other way, Thad."

4

ALBERT TURKENOV WAS DRIVING across Flagstaff to see his mother, Nadia. It was Friday morning, and Nadia hadn't checked in with work to begin her three-day home nursing duties. So the registry had called Albert, who was listed as next of kin.

He was behind the wheel of a brand new Chrysler New Yorker convertible with the top down and the wind whipping through his long hair. Wraparound sunglasses shielded his gray eyes from the mid-morning sunlight, which was always harsh at the altitude of Flagstaff with so much less atmosphere at 6500 feet to soften the sun's rays. He checked himself in the rearview on the windshield: teeth free of any bagel bits; three-day growth of beard in keeping with the current style; hole in earlobe where the earring went in after he came off duty at night from the auto dealership and before he began hitting the bars in search of Miss Right; perfect smile looking back at him as he put on his new car salesman's face—it was all there. He was top salesman so far that month and had been top salesman three months previous.

The drive from his side of Flagstaff to his mother's side was only fifteen minutes, but for Albert Turkenov it was a drive that always felt like a march to the guillotine. His mother hated him; he was sure of that. She hated him for so many reasons: he had barely graduated high school, had dropped out of college before semester one was concluded; had failed miserably with three very nice women his mother had approved of; a bankruptcy at twenty-two. And he had lied to his mother about his position at the dealership: he wasn't a sales manager, he was a lowly salesman. At least, that's how he viewed it. His father would have maintained that no employment was lowly, but Albert wasn't his father. Besides, it was more that he had lied to his mother than anything else. Why was that? He wondered. Why did he lie to her? For her part, Nadia had tried to embrace him no matter what was going on. But Albert could tell that her efforts were forced, that there was no real mother-son bond between them. Unconditional love wasn't who she was. There were terms and conditions with her; always had been.

Eyes fixed on the road, he continued his thoughts. Mother, Nadia. Why hadn't she reported to work that morning? Was she sick? Had someone broken in and strangled her to death? He put both of those thoughts out of his mind immediately. No, she was probably just asleep, having forgotten to set her alarm or just blowing it off—which wasn't even in her vocabulary, he knew: Nadia didn't ever just blow things off. She was super-responsible and always right in anyone's face who might make the mistake of hassling her. A real tiger. So where the hell *was* she?

He turned north on San Francisco Street and went up past the hospital, where he took the second left. Down two blocks and there, at the far end of a residential street, was Nadia's apartment complex. He parked beside her Corolla and headed for the stairwell. His mood was growing darker the closer he came to actually being with her. His stomach flip-flopped when he acknowledged she might ask him about work. She should have been a lawyer, he thought. She was great at cross-examination of her family; always had been.

At the top of the stairs, he entered the hallway and went left. Three doors down and he paused outside 206. He slowly raised his fist. He expected her to respond immediately to his knock. She always responded immediately. So he rapped his knuckles on the wood. He waited. He rapped again. "Mom?" he shouted at the door. "You awake in there?" He waited several minutes, but no sound could be heard from inside. For just a moment, he was relieved: maybe he wouldn't have to face her after all. But that relief immediately dissipated. After all, she might be in there sick or injured. So he did the next best thing: he went back downstairs to the manager's office. He explained his visit and his mom's non-answer, and Susan Norbert jumped up to follow him back and let him inside his mother's home.

Susan turned her key and motioned Albert to pass by, which he did. She waited at the door. He disappeared into a side room. Then she heard a yelp—a cry for help.

"My God, call 911! She's unconscious!"

Susan whipped her cell out of her pocket and made the call. In under a minute, she could hear the sirens nearing.

What Albert had found was his mother, sitting upright in her recliner, her arms inside the armrests, with a yellow page in her lap with printing on it. Her eyes were closed, and she didn't appear to be breathing. He felt for a pulse on her neck and couldn't find one. Immediately he was breathing hard and without any idea what to do. He found himself wishing he'd taken one of those community courses on CPR so he would be able to try to revive his mother.

"Ma'am," he called to Susan, "Do you know CPR?"

"No. I know the Heimlich Maneuver is all."

"Great."

Closer the sirens came, and soon they were in the parking lot and the crew was running for the stairs as Susan called to the medics from the upstairs landing.

The standard procedure had them arriving with oxygen and a defibrillator. The first one in, a woman dressed in the black pants and black shirt of the Flagstaff EMT corps, immediately placed a stethoscope on Nadia's chest. Close behind her came a short blond man with a graying goatee. He edged in beside the female and muttered something to her that Albert couldn't make out.

The female EMT shook her head. "Nothing," she said loud enough for Albert to hear. He immediately understood: there was no heartbeat. Then the two EMTs turned to the third one in, a Hispanic man lugging the defibrillator; a huge commotion broke out as Albert's mother's T-shirt was ripped open and defibrillator paddles placed against her chest.

"Charging," said the Hispanic man. "Charged. Clear!"

All hands pulled back as the paddles delivered their jolt of electricity into Nadia. Her upper torso lurched upward a good six inches but then flopped back, still lifeless.

The female listened with her stethoscope. She shook her head.

"Clear!" said the Hispanic man and he shocked Nadia again. Again the female listened.

Meanwhile, the second man was preparing a syringe of a clear liquid. When the second shock produced no result, he inserted the syringe into Nadia's chest and injected epinephrine directly into the heart muscle. Again the woman listened. Then she raised a hand.

"Something," she said. "Very faint."

And at that moment a second EMT team arrived and pushed a cart into the room. Nadia was loaded on and rushed from the room.

Albert followed helplessly behind. He didn't see Susan lock the door behind them once everyone had cleared out. He didn't give a second thought to the note he'd found in his mother's lap, but it was carried along by the EMTs and now attached to her hospital file.

Ready to be examined by cooler minds.

5

Dr. Emerick Sewell was still on his book tour. This time, he appeared on *Good Morning, L.A.* and he was answering a question from his host, a young woman. It was two days after Nadia had swallowed down her overdose of narcotics so that she might experiment with near death and see for herself.

"So, Doctor, please amaze us with something we don't know about the near-death experience."

Dr. Sewell smiled his increasingly famous smile at the young woman.

"Did you know that among quantum scientists there is a growing number who think human consciousness is located inside microtubules in the brain?"

"I didn't know that," she said.

"Did you know that these scientists believe this consciousness, upon death, leaves the microtubules and goes back into the greater, universal consciousness?"

"No."

Dr. Sewell nodded solemnly.

"As a neuroscientist who has experienced what death is like, this information supports what happened to me. My consciousness left my body and took a little trip."

He was smiling, sure of himself and happy, for he'd received news from his publisher just an hour ago that his book was number two on the best-seller charts and headed for number one. Momentum was gathering and propelling his book to greater sales figures every hour. He had been told the *Good Morning, L.A.* viewership was more than one million so he was sure the morning's brief appearance would sell a boatload of books itself.

"Took a little trip? That's an interesting way of putting it. My gosh, you went to heaven!"

"That I did."

"Can you tell our viewers what heaven looks like?"

"Well, it looks like it does here, except the light isn't from a star. The light is from God."

"How do you know that?"

The doctor nodded. "In heaven, there are some things you just know. Knowledge just appears in your mind with a certainty that doesn't question it."

She looked straight into the camera and said, "Tell us what God said to you."

"He told me I was loved from before the beginning of time."

"And what did you tell God?"

"I told Him thank you."

Both host and guest laughed and smiled at one another. It was a great response.

The show broke away for a commercial. The host turned to her makeup artist and allowed her forehead to be sponged and her lip gloss to be renewed. The doctor sat smiling in his chair until his tour manager came out and bent down to whisper to him. Then a look of concern crossed his face.

"You're sure of this?" the doctor whispered to his manager.

"Just got the call. The woman left a note with your name in it. She said she knew you were a doctor, and she was acting on your medical guidance."

"Good heavens!"

"I know. I've got a call into our lawyers."

"For the love of God! She OD'd because of *me*?"

The tour manager shrugged. "That's what I'm told."

"Well, what about it? Surely there's no liability to my readers just for telling my story?" He was frustrated, sitting fully erect and defensive as if expecting to be jumped at any moment.

The manager looked very concerned. "Maybe, maybe not. You *are* a doctor, and it's to be expected that some people might take your message as medical advice. It's not unforeseeable. Legal is asking how this book got past them, as we speak."

"Oh, my God!"

6

IN FULFILLMENT of her final semester of hospital duties before she would receive her M.D., Anastasia Millerton was paged by the general switchboard and immediately responded. A general switchboard page was very unusual for a mere student in the grand hierarchy of all things hospital. Anastasia hurried into the hall and returned the call on her cell phone. She was told to call her brother, Albert Turkenov. She made the call, got a muddled stream of words from her brother regarding her mother's hospital admission in Flagstaff, and ten minutes later Anastasia was roaring out of Phoenix's Good Samaritan Hospital's staff lot on her way to Flagstaff. Her husband, Jack, had given her the Volvo she was driving as a present at the start of her senior year. "You need to look successful, now," he had said, although she was still looking at years of residency before the money flow would change directions. But she graciously accepted the car from her husband, a CPA, who knew all about tax write-offs and who assured her the car would pay for itself with "deductions against income," whatever that meant.

She entered the freeway northbound just beyond Nineteenth and floored it. The speedometer swept up to eighty-five where she pegged it, thinking she could explain the illegal speed to any traffic cop, since she was still wearing scrubs and was, in fact, responding to a medical emergency.

Truth be told, she was very apprehensive at the interruption in her hospital shift. Albert hadn't been very clear about what the hospital admission was all about, but, knowing her mother, she knew it wasn't some imagined or fleeting pain. No, her mother—the nurse—was the last one who would have wanted to spend time in a hospital with its staph germs and exhausted workers. Which was why she worked home health: it allowed her to avoid hospitals and be her own boss. Anastasia knew all this, and so she was taking the trip very seriously.

But as she went north on Interstate 17 her apprehension increased. Her mother would be confrontational, angry and upset that Anastasia had left her training to visit. Mother was never a person to put family or feelings before the responsibility of holding a job or attending school. She just wasn't like that and Anastasia, as she passed the Prescott turnoff, just wasn't ready to hear the condemnation.

She pulled open her glove box and retrieved the hidden box of cigarettes. With the hidden Bic. She lit one and put the sunroof back. Air streamed inside the car, toying with the hair she kept short to reduce the time it took to climb from her cot at the hospital and respond to a page. She inhaled and blew a long cloud of smoke into the slipstream. Her pulse quickened as her heart responded to the nicotine. She knew all about the physiology of cigarette smoke and how deleterious it was to one's health, but, frankly, she didn't give a damn. The closer she got to medical school graduation the less she was allowing herself to be herded around like a cow in a feed lot. Cigarettes were her way of rebelling. She was someone her mother had less and less sway over.

In Flagstaff, she drove up to the Medical Center and almost parked in doctors' parking, but instead chose the visitors' lot.

The elevator took her up to the ICU and she quickly located her mother's room. Albert was there and he turned and nodded to her. She approached and put a hand on his shoulder. Together they studied their mother, unconscious and connected to a ventilator for life support.

"Let's go in the hallway for a sec," said Anastasia.

Once outside, she could talk in a normal tone. "So what the hell, Al? What's going on?"

Albert shrugged. "They don't know. They're doing tests right now. One of them said it looked like a drug overdose."

"*Drug* overdose? Seriously? *Nadia*? Huh-uh, that's never gonna fly!"

"I know," said the son. "They just don't know Nadia."

"Besides, why would she ever do such a thing?"

"One of the EMT's showed me the letter she left. It said she was experimenting with near death?"

"Holy shit!" cried the sister. "Near death? She's not that stupid, Albert."

"I don't know. I know she hasn't been happy."

"She hasn't ever been happy, *really* happy."

"Not since Dad passed away."

"She misses him."

"No doubt. Maybe it was an experiment."

"Highly doubtful. Do you have the note?"

"No, they gave it to the nurse."

"So it's in her chart. I would like to see that."

"Good idea."

Back inside the suite, Anastasia went to her mother and touched her hand lying at her side.

"Mom? Can you hear me? It's Ana."

No response.

"If you can hear me, please move your eyes."

No response. Albert shook his head. "I don't like this," he whispered.

Anastasia nodded and backed away. "Let's do this in shifts," she whispered. "I'll stay until midnight, then you come in and wait and I'll grab a bed in the doctors' lounge. I'm beat. Thirty hours without sleep when they called me."

"Okay, if that's what you want. But I can't go home and sleep right now. I think I'll just go back to the lot and peddle some cars."

"You should do that. She doesn't need us both here. Besides, you need to pay your rent. You've got to earn while you can, little brother."

"There's always that."

Just then Uncle Roy Underwood came bouncing into the room. He was Nadia's younger brother and he owned a used furniture store on the east side. The specialty was used appliances and oak furniture. He was wearing a Hawaiian shirt and gray slacks with black NB sneakers. His silver eyeglasses were hung around his neck and his eyes were full of fear.

"Jesus," he said to the siblings, "what's up with Nadia?"

"Outside, please," said Anastasia, and she steered her uncle into the hallway.

"I dropped everything when Albert called me."

"We don't know much yet. I just got here myself."

"I don't know," said Uncle Roy. "I don't like all that crap they've got her hooked up to. That doesn't look good. You're the doctor, Ana. How's it looking to you."

Ana folded her arms across her ample bosom. "Way too soon to know anything, Uncle Roy. They're doing blood work right now. Then we'll know something."

"Is it a heart attack? Stroke? It looks like a stroke to me. Did anyone check?"

"We'll just have to wait for the blood work. That's the key."

"All right. Well, I've been concerned about her anyway, before this."

Ana moved her head to the side. "Concerned? Why's that?"

He leaned closer and said confidentially, "I'm concerned there's something with her finances."

Ana leaned away. "You mean she needs money?"

"No, no, no, not that. I think there's lots of money squirreled away someplace. Which makes me wonder if maybe someone was trying to get her to move money around and so they gave her drugs."

"My, a conspiracy theory? Already, Uncle Roy? You usually come in later with those."

The stout little man shrugged. "I'm just saying. We need to give this some thought."

"We need to give her finances some thought?" Ana was feeling uncomfortable. The first vulture had arrived and was sniffing around his sister even though she hadn't gone anywhere. She wondered where he might be going with this. Then she found out.

"Hey, she can't look out for herself right now. We've gotta do it for her. Maybe she needs a conservator. I'm willing to serve."

"Oh, please, let's find out what's going on before we get into that kind of stuff."

"I'm just saying...."

Her uncle's comment came as no surprise. Nadia had been the successful sister, the one who was able to put money away. Uncle Roy, conversely, had always struggled with money. He had run several businesses into the ground and had lost a house to foreclosure, yet still fancied himself just short of a genius when it came to money and business. Anastasia sighed. She had hoped Nadia's siblings wouldn't find out their sister was comatose. It would only get worse as they came out of the woodwork, not better.

"Well, we'll keep that theory in mind," she told her uncle and returned to the suite.

7

Four months ago the disease had revealed itself externally. Katy's face thinned out and her skin turned white—a far cry from the normally brown skin of her Indian heritage. Thaddeus watched these changes with alarm. Of course he wouldn't ever mention any of it to Katy, so he kept it bottled up.

He drove her over to see her grandfather, Henry Landers. Henry was 104 years old and now lived in a reservation nursing home. Katy was paying for it; Henry was beloved by all of his children and grandchildren and any one of them would have done anything they could to help. But Katy was the one with the resources to keep Henry warm and well-fed in the nursing home.

They pulled into Kayenta (*Tó Dínéeshzhee*) south of Monument Valley, for Katy to see him one last time. The home was called *Diné Rest*, *Diné* meaning, loosely, "the people" in Navajo.

They found the old man in his room, at his desk, reviewing a map of the Four Corners area.

"I'm going to take a trip," he said when Thaddeus and Katy came in.

"Where are you going, Grandfather?" asked Katy.

"I'm going to the Grand Canyon and I'm going down in to say

hello to some of my Havasupai friends there." The Havasupai was a tribe that made its home in the bottom of the Grand Canyon. Katy had visited there before and vaguely knew of some connection between her grandfather and the elders of the tribe.

"And when will you be going?"

The old man straightened up. "Did you know they took away my truck? I'm no longer allowed to drive."

"That's all right, Grandfather. I'll drive you there."

"When can we go?"

"Soon."

"No, I need a date."

"How about next Friday? I can come for you Friday morning."

"I'll be waiting. How long will we stay?"

"We'll stay overnight. I'll make reservations at the Canyon."

"I'll be ready."

"So, Grandfather, how are you getting along?"

"I miss my sheep. I miss my hogan. I miss my truck. Other than that, things are going beautifully."

"Well, I'm sorry we had to move you here. But we were worried about you all alone in your Hogan."

The old man smiled. "What, afraid I might die and you couldn't be there to save me? How old do I have to get before people just let me dry up and blow away? I don't want to be saved. I want to go home."

Thaddeus spoke up. "You know, Katy, I think Henry's right. I think he should get to live in his hogan if that's what he really wants."

"See?" Henry beamed. "Listen to your husband, Granddaughter."

Katy moved across the room to the rocking chair. She sat down and began rocking forward and back. She considered Henry. She considered her own situation. She was doing exactly what she wanted in her last days; why shouldn't he get to do the same?

"You know what, Grandfather? We're going to take you back to your hogan."

Thaddeus smiled. "I couldn't agree more."

Henry painfully arose from the table and limped to his granddaughter. He took her face in his rough hands and looked deep into her eyes. "I knew you had your mother in you. Do you know what? I even had a vision about you."

Katy smiled. "Now I would love to hear about your vision. But first let's get you out in our truck and on our way."

"Where's your truck, Henry?" Thaddeus asked.

"Gone. They sold it."

"Never mind. We'll stop in Flagstaff and buy you a new one. A man should have his truck," Thaddeus said.

So they did. They stopped off in Flagstaff and bought Henry a new silver Chevrolet pickup and then headed west on I40. Thaddeus led the way; Henry and Katy brought up the rear, Katy driving the new truck, much to Henry's chagrin. She argued with him and said the only way it was going to happen would be for her to drive him on the interstate highway. Henry resisted at first but then saw her mind was made up. He relented and agreed to her driving. When she and Thaddeus were again out of his life, he planned to immediately drive east to the Grand Canyon and visit his friends. Let her have her way, for now, he cautioned himself. Then you get your way.

"So what about this vision, Grandfather?" she asked as they rode along.

"I was at the Hopi snake dances in Prescott."

"This was recent?"

"Maybe one year ago. I was in the grandstand watching the dance. Suddenly I had a vision of you, Katy, when you were a young girl. You were standing on a beach when the sun was coming up. You were maybe six or seven years old. Your husband, Thaddeus came to be by you. He was grown up, but you weren't. You spent the day with him on that beach. Kite flying, making houses in the sand, collecting seashells. Then you went away."

"Where did I go, Grandfather?"

"Into the water. You walked into the ocean."

"So I—I died?"

"That part I don't know. But I don't think you died. I think you just went somewhere else. With your ancestors, maybe."

"That's beautiful, Grandfather. Thank you for telling me that."

"It's a good one, yes?"

"It is a good one."

Henry patted the dashboard. "I love this truck already. I'll make a stake bed for moving my sheep around."

"You're getting more sheep?"

"What good am I without my sheep to look after? I will drive up to Bud Yellowmexican's ranch and buy more sheep."

"Do you need money?"

"I have money. They made me sell my old sheep, remember?"

"How much do you have?"

"Not too much to get into trouble with women and liquor. But enough to buy my sheep back."

"All right, Grandfather. As long as there's enough but not too much."

Henry looked out the passenger window.

"They lost my Stetson when they took me to the home."

"We can get you a new Stetson."

"I can go to Kingman for that."

"All right, Grandfather. I'm sure you know best."

"I'm sure I do."

"Do you still have your driver's license?"

"I hid that in my boot. Of course, I still have it. It's good four more years. That should be enough."

"In four years you'll be a hundred and eight. You still plan to be driving?"

Henry patted the dashboard once again. "As long as this one's still running, I'll still be driving."

"Fine. Look out, world."

"Yes, look out."

8

Uncle Roy hired the law firm of Wang, Harley, and Mitter, of Flagstaff. Milbanks Wang was the progenitor of the firm and had formed Uncle Roy's corporation when the used furniture business got underway.

Wang was a fourth generation American, who preferred Mexican food to Chinese. He owned a cattle spread by Williams, Arizona. He was raising a herd of whitefaces, one thousand strong. Wang preferred the wide open spaces of his ranch to the confines of a law office any day. But the law office supported the hobby ranch, so it was a necessity. Wang was five-ten, heavily muscled, and wore his hair in a flattop and his suits two sizes too large because, like his love for wide open spaces, he also needed suits that gave him plenty of room. Confinement of any kind was abhorrent. His key practice area was criminal law. But he also knew how to see the dollars in a situation so, when Uncle Roy appeared in his office with news about his unconscious—but wealthy—sister, Wang didn't hesitate.

"You're smart to come here," Wang told Uncle Roy. "Your sister does need legal protection."

"She needs a conservator?"

"Exactly. With that much money in the Bank of America in Phoenix she needs active conservation of the corpus."

"Corpus?"

"The money."

"So what do I need to sign?"

Wang held up a hand. "Not so fast. Tell me about the other members of the family. Any kids?"

"Two. A ne'er-do-well son and a daughter in medical school in Phoenix."

"The son. Does he have business sense?"

Uncle Roy laughed. "Not in a thousand years! He's already been through bankruptcy and he's not even twenty-five years old yet."

"That sounds hopeful. What about the daughter?"

"That might be a little stickier. She told me her old man's a CPA. She said if anyone was going to manage her mother's estate it should be her husband."

"But her husband is not a blood relative. Arizona law would prefer a blood relative."

"There's some good news," said Uncle Roy. "No, he's a son-in-law, this one."

"But the daughter? What about her taking it on?"

"She already told me no, she was too busy with her fourth year of med school. Evidently, she all but lives at the hospital. Besides, she's down in Phoenix."

Wang nodded slowly. "Any siblings besides you?"

"We have a brother Marshall and a sister Abigail. Marshall lives in Iowa and Abigail is somewhere on the East Coast. I don't think anyone knows where. She married and moved away thirty years ago."

"So what about Marshall?"

"He's sixty. Had a stroke a couple of years back. Doubt that he'd have the wherewithal."

"So I'm hearing either you or the daughter. Would that be about right?"

"That's what I'm thinking. How long before you can have papers for me to sign?"

"We can have conservatorship papers by first thing tomorrow. Let me turn you over to my paralegal. She'll get the particulars and get to cracking with the documents we'll need. Now. Do you have twenty-five hundred dollars?"

"What for? I thought you would bill the estate?"

Wang smiled. "I certainly plan to do that. But for now, until we get you appointed, there's no estate to bill. You'll have to pay me to get this thing off the ground, Roy."

"I'll have to sell some furniture at cost. I can have it by tomorrow."

"Fair enough. We'll be ready at ten o'clock. Come by anytime after."

They shook hands and agreed that ten o'clock would work just fine.

9

ALONG WITH THE lawsuit against Dr. Sewell came the letter Nadia had written before she swallowed down the pain meds. Dr. Sewell, living in L.A., read it one night in his home. The next day he flew to Flagstaff and went to see the woman who was suing him.

As he drove up the hill on San Francisco Street, approaching hospital parking, he pulled the letter from his shirt pocket and scanned it again:

If you find this, I am probably dead. Please don't be upset if I am because I was bored with living anyway. I was tired of life and until you live a life like mine you probably won't understand.

Dr. Emerick Sewell has a book called The Doctor Is In...Heaven and I have taken pills to try to get to where he was when he had his journey into heaven. I'm following his medical advice on what happens. Did I get there? If you're reading this, you'll probably never know. But I will know.

This is my life and it's a choice I have made. Am I selfish? Maybe, but I don't care. My kids have their lives and they are happy. I've lost Henri and my life is no longer valuable to me anyway, so don't mourn. Just let me go.

Nadia.

There it was in black and white: *Just let me go.* He pursed his lips and let out a low, soft whistle. He understood what she meant. Knew exactly what she meant. *Just let me go.*

He reached in the back seat, found his stethoscope, and draped it around his neck.

At the visitors' desk just inside the front doors, he flashed his medical ID—from another state—and was immediately provided with the room number of Nadia Turkenov.

On the elevator ride upstairs he kept his eyes on the blinking floor numbers, avoiding eye contact with the two orderlies who were transporting an elderly woman on a cart. He looked at her out the side of his eye just for a flash and realized she was probably forty-eight hours from death. He was a neurosurgeon; he knew these things.

On Nadia's floor, the doors whooshed open and out he stepped. He was wearing slacks, a yellow shirt, and a blue blazer. Around his neck, the physicians' stethoscope opened all doors in any hospital in the world. He was always astonished at its power: no one asked for ID once they saw the stethoscope worn cavalierly around the neck. It was better ID than anyone could forge and much easier to obtain.

Down the hall he swaggered as if he were in charge, looking for her number.

He stopped just outside her door and listened, pretending to be speaking on his cell phone. Then he moved to the open door of her ICU suite. She was being attended to by a nurse so the doctor waited for his chance. Nadia's chart could be seen hooked to the foot of her bed.

The nurse left the room, giving him a stiff smile as she circled around him and made her way back down the hallway.

He stepped inside and lifted the patient's chart from its hook. It was a fairly thick chart—she had been hospitalized for two weeks now, and he quickly located and scanned over the parts he wanted: the test results.

Clearly, she was comatose and brain dead. It was only a matter of time until the attending physician talked to the family about withdrawing life support. Maybe that talk had already taken place.

He moved to her bedside and looked down.

So. Here lay the woman who was suing him. He studied her face, the high cheekbones, the firm neck, the graceful jawline and spotless hands resting along her sides. A ventilator was in place and breathing for her. He knew that turning it off would result in a fairly abrupt death. She wouldn't breathe and she would be gone in five minutes.

He stole a look at the door and reached down and took Nadia's hand in his own. He stroked the back of her hand with his fingers, all the while studying her face. He knew there would be no reaction to his touch and there was none. Her expression remained unchanged, her eyes didn't flutter or appear to register any nuance beneath the eyelids, and the hand itself neither returned his caress nor shied away.

The woman was already dead, for all intents and purposes. It was only a matter of time.

Holding her hand, he stood upright and closed his eyes. He remained like this for several minutes.

Nurses passed by the room in the hallway, spotted the stethoscope around his neck, and assumed one of her treating physicians was making rounds.

Silently he stood and concentrated while at the same time quieting his own mind. If she wished to contact him by thought, he was ready. He turned off his mind and waited, receptive and open. Hoping against hope that her spirit would speak, he was not surprised when he heard nothing. You usually didn't, especially where you'd never known the person and had a relationship while they were conscious. Which he, of course, had not.

He opened his eyes and gently replaced her hand on the thin blanket over her.

Turning to the foot of her bed, he replaced her chart.

He faced her then and his hands opened and clenched as he looked helplessly at the woman in whose failed consciousness he'd played a part. The lawsuit was clear in that respect. She had watched him on TV; she had read his book. Based on his reassurances while he was selling books on his publisher's book tour, he had represented spiritual matters in such a way that she'd decided to have a look at the other side for herself.

He felt it was his fault. His shoulders slumped. He grimaced and turned away, beaten down, and crossed to the door. As he exited her room, the same nurse returned.

"Good evening, Doctor," she murmured in passing.

He only nodded and stood aside. He had seen what he had come to see. He checked his watch. His return flight would be made in time.

On the flight high above the California desert, the doctor peered out his window.

What would happen next was written in the stars already. As certain as the constellations, the universal consciousness had already welcomed Nadia Turkenov.

She was gone.

Now to tell the body.

10

Thaddeus Murfee was working out of his home office when the call came from the heavenly doctor's agent.

"Mr. Murfee, this is Peterson Lambre in Hollywood, California."

"Yes?"

"I'm the agent for a physician by the name of Emerick Sewell. You've heard of Dr. Sewell?"

"Can't say as I have. What's up?"

"We've received a letter from an attorney in Flagstaff. Milbanks X. Wang. Heard of him?"

"Sure, I know Mils. What's up?"

"Evidently he is the attorney for a Mr. Royal Underwood. Who is the conservator for a woman named Nadia Turkenov. Any of these names mean anything to you?"

"Nope. Should they?"

"No, and that's a good thing. They're not and haven't ever been your clients?"

"No."

"Well, this lawyer, Mr. Wang, is making a claim on behalf of the Estate of Nadia Turkenov for the sum of ten million dollars plus future care."

"Does your guy owe it?"

"We don't think so."

"What's it based on?"

"My client, Dr. Sewell, had a medical event. An infection in his brain. During the time, he was comatose he died and went to heaven. And then came back to write about it."

"Sure he did," said Thaddeus. "I'm sorry, but you've lost me right there. This sounds to me like a wild ass scam, Mr. Lambre. Not interested."

"Wait. Let me tell you the rest of it."

Thaddeus looked at his watch. He had told Katy he would take her into town for a vegan lunch on San Francisco Street. There was a place she loved. He'd give the guy three more minutes before politely hanging up.

"You've got three minutes, Mr. Lambre."

"My client is a graduate of Harvard Medical School and is board-certified in neurosurgery and psychiatry."

"So he didn't start earning until he was probably forty years old. Too bad."

Lambre ignored the comment. "He fell ill and was admitted to the best hospital in Boston, where he stayed unconscious for about six days. During that time, according to the brain scans, my client was medically brain dead."

"No brain wave activity?"

"No brain wave activity."

"What was the diagnosis?"

"An infection of the lining of the brain."

Thaddeus knew his medicine from previous medical malpractice cases. "Pneumococcal meningitis? Was that it?"

"You'd have to look at the records. I think so."

"So what happened? How'd he come out of it?"

"That's the strange thing. The doctors had given up. They had recommended to the family that life support be withdrawn. On the morning the ventilator was to be unplugged, the patient suddenly opened his eyes."

"Residual damage?"

"None. It was amazing. He went from total brain death to total consciousness without deficit in the blink of an eye."

"So what's Attorney Wang's claim about? How is your doctor involved with Wang's client?"

"Well, that's just it. He's not. But what Wang is claiming is that his client's sister, this Nadia Turkenov, saw my client on TV, read his book called *The Doctor Is In...Heaven*, and decided to pop some pills and try for a near death experience herself."

"Holy shit. Why would she do that?"

"Dead husband. Lonely. Desperate. Hell, who knows why anyone does anything? Long story short, she wanted to have a near death experience. Hoping to talk to the dead, I guess."

"My God."

"Hey, I just represent people. That doesn't say anything about what I do or don't believe. It's a business."

"Still, what a crock!"

"That's right. So she evidently OD'd on something. She's a nurse. And she's still in a coma and the family is mad as hell at my client for giving bad medical advice."

Thaddeus came upright at his desk.

"Bad medical advice? They're claiming medical malpractice for—what, a near death experience? Like your guy recommended it?"

"I don't know. But we're taking it seriously. His publisher is up in arms and threatening to pull my client's inventory from the shelves. We can't let that happen, Mr. Murfee. My client has an amazing story to tell and he should be allowed to continue telling it without threats from people like this with dollar signs in their eyes. Can you help?"

"Why me? I'm up here in Flagstaff. Your guy is L.A. Based."

"Nadia Turkenov is in your hospital. Her brother, the conservator, has a used furniture store in Flagstaff."

Thaddeus shook his head. "You know, I have to be honest. I'm very skeptical about the whole near death thing. I don't believe in stuff like that at all."

"How can I convince you? It wouldn't mean you would have to

believe. Just defend someone who does. Would you review the medical records if I sent them to you?"

"I don't know. My own wife—"

He had started to tell the man about Katy and how sick she was when it suddenly occurred to him that information about death and dying might be exactly what Katy needed to hear right now. After all, she was dying and she had no hope for anything beyond death. Katy was a fatalist. She had no religious faith and didn't want any. Still, what if something like this gave her some hope?

He knew he would regret it...but. He fought back his words of skepticism and said he would review the records. The Hollywood agent told Thaddeus he would have the records the next day and hung up.

Thaddeus sat back at his desk. From this position he could look straight out at the San Francisco Peaks, perhaps two miles off, where the aspen groves made their run up the side of the mountains, up and up until the tree-line, where the green cover thinned to gray and the volcanic mountainside emerged and ran on up to the snow-line where the snowcaps began. He knew he would take her ashes there when she passed away. He knew that's where she had chosen to come to rest. Four months ago, she had been told she would be dead in six months. Which meant she had maybe sixty days left. He winced and turned away from the sweeping vista. Even now, she was upstairs, slowly taking her bath and getting dressed for their lunch date. Had never quit fighting it, and he was proud of her for that. And he loved her more than ever for that.

He would ask her to review the records with him, for she was a doctor too. Who knew where that might lead?

But more than anything, she demanded to stay active.

Maybe this would be a chance to do that.

11

"I'M TELLING YOU, Murfee, I think what hustlers like us oughta do is just rob a frigging bank and get it over with!" said Shep Aberdeen. Shep was a stout, muscular man from Durango, who practiced criminal law and raised whiteface cattle. He was all of six feet, with brown hair kept long in back, rimless spectacles, and very white, very even teeth. He was a stroke victim, but the paralysis had been all but overcome and his speech was clear as ever.

Thaddeus had stopped by his old friend's office on North Agassiz following a Monday morning court appearance. Thaddeus had just asked Shep what he thought about a snake oil case like the near death experience doctor. Shep had replied they might just as well rob banks as take on those kinds of cases.

"So I take it you're not a near death believer?" Thaddeus said.

"My great-great-great grandfather sold glass beads to the Indians in Massachusetts. I've got a rich vein of the con running through me. But near death experiences? What the hell does that even mean?"

Thaddeus spread his hands. "Believe me, I'm trying to get my head around it too. But the guy's selling a shitload of books. He's number one on the bestseller lists."

"Sure he is. Everyone wants to know what heaven looks like. Shit, even I do." Shep slumped behind his kidney-shaped desk, cut from ironwood and inlaid with mother-of-pearl. To his left was the flag of the United States; to his right the state flag of Colorado—Durango transplant that he was. Shep took off his eyeglasses and pinched his nose. He was drinking from a Starbucks cup and puffing a Winston from a hard pack, one of four packs scattered across the ironwood.

Thaddeus leaned up to the desk. "Well, he's moving books. But here's what I want to ask you since you've lived around here forever. How is a northern Arizona jury going to view a doctor who says he died and went to heaven? We're pretty conservative around here, right?"

"Damn right. Blue as hell. Your man has a tough row to hoe. You asked for my advice, so here it is. I'd turn the damn case down. It's a hot potato. I wouldn't touch it. Besides, life's too short. Look at it this way: your wife's very sick. She needs you more than the snake charmers need you. Let him find someone else to get this lady's case dismissed. You don't need this, Thad."

"Funny you should mention Katy. I told her about the case and she went all doctor on me. She wants to see the guy's medical records. So they're sending them to us and she's going to review."

"Sort of keeping her hand in, is she?"

"Something like that. Besides, I thought it might hold some... interest for her. Given her prognosis. No, I'm saying that wrong. It sounds opportunistic of me and it's definitely not meant to be. I'm just at a loss about what else I can do for her and so I figured this might be a chance to let her look at a spiritual approach that might be interesting to her. Or hopeful. Or hell, I don't know!" Shep's eyes never left the young lawyer's eyes even when they filled with tears.

"You're trying to give her hope. Even false hope. I get that."

"No, no, no, no. Not false hope. I'm just—it's just—well, maybe it is false hope. The truth is, I don't know what the hell to think about it. But this much I do know: she's chomping at the bit to see the guy's records. So that's something."

Shep leaned back and stabbed his cigarette out in the amber ashtray. "I don't know how I would act if I were in Katy's shoes. Maybe

I'd still need to feel I was useful. I don't know. But if she's chomping at the bit then what the hell. Go for it."

"That's my thinking. We'll at least go over the records. So, if I do decide to jump in, I'm thinking I would like to associate you on the case."

"Me? What the hell for? You've done damn well around here without me. Took our friend Angelina Steinmar to trial and won that one. Took that Turquoise case and won that. You're two-and-oh without me, son. How about if I just make myself available for you to bounce things off of? That do it for you?"

Thaddeus grinned. "I would really appreciate that, Shep."

"Then you've got yourself a bouncer, little friend. Shake on it."

The two men shook hands across the desk. Shep then sat back and eyed his friend with barely concealed curiosity.

"So tell me, Thad. Have you read this doctor's book?"

"I started reading it online."

"Does it stack up?"

Thaddeus shrugged. "That's just it: stack up against what? I don't have any experience with near death. Nobody does. But I Googled it and there's a shitload of information out there. There are websites full of stories who say they died and came back to tell about it."

"No lie?"

"Yes, and I mean *lots* of them."

"What do the doctors say about it? Hell, they see death every day. They oughta have some kind of news for us."

"That's where I'm at right now. It gets very complicated, Shep. Have you heard of quantum mechanics?"

"Quantum what?"

"It's the measurement of very small things. We're talking very small. Anyhow, the physicists in this area of physics, some of them think human consciousness exists inside microtubules in the brain."

"Whoa up, Hoss, you're losing me here. Micro what?"

"Small cells in the brain that have a certain helical structure."

Shep half-smiled. "Sure they do."

"Let me go on. These scientists believe that human consciousness is linked to universal consciousness, so when we die our consciousness leaves these microtubules and returns to the universal consciousness. At least, I think that's what they're saying. There's lots of math and formulas that make zero sense to me."

"Not my circus, not my monkey," said Shep. "I wouldn't be telling a jury this kind of stuff. You'd lose them on the first turn around the track. Keep the focus on whether this Nadia woman had a legal right to try something she read in a book and sue the doctor if it didn't work out as she hoped. Keep it simple, stupid."

"Agree. I'm just telling you some of what's out there. Anyhow, Katy's reading all this stuff now as fast as she can get her hands on it. There's a guy named Rachmanoff and another guy named Penrose. She's read everything she can find by these guys. Then there's another doctor, a woman, who died and went to heaven."

"Thad, I need to get back to work. Your stuff is making me dizzy."

Thaddeus laughed. "No, the damn cigarettes are making you dizzy, Shep. How in the hell do you justify smoking after you've already had a stroke?"

Shep smiled and crossed his arms over his chest. "Let's just say I've already had my own near death experience."

"What about it?"

"What about what?"

"Did you see heaven on the other side?"

"Heaven is a field full of whiteface cattle on an inky blue sky autumn day. That's as close as I ever hope to get."

"I hear that."

"Guys like us, we don't go to heaven. We go to court. Later, little friend."

"Later, Shep. And thanks."

"You've got it."

12

THE RECORDS ARRIVED in two stuffed transfer file boxes. Thaddeus lugged them inside from the porch and manhandled them into his office. He called upstairs to Katy and let her know the records were awaiting her. Wearing loose-fitting jeans and a Stanford sweatshirt, she came into the office ten minutes later.

"I'm groggy," she told her husband. "Just had my Demerol about a half hour ago."

"Are you up for this?" he asked.

"Uh-huh. How about grabbing me a cup of coffee? That will help the scales on my eyes."

"You've got it. I've got the boxes open if you want to shuffle through."

"Mmmm."

She came around to his desk chair and lowered herself down, steadying herself with the armrests as she performed the almost exhausting task. Anymore, a shower required a thirty-minute nap after. A trip downstairs required preparations and pain meds, followed by a nap on the sofa in Thaddeus' office, where she kept a comforter.

Thaddeus returned with two mugs of steaming coffee. Black for him; cream for Katy. He arranged her mug where she could easily reach it from his chair and went around to the side chair for himself.

"Well?" he said. "How do we start?"

"*We* don't. I do."

"Oh. All right, then, you go through and tell me what we've got? Do I just sit here?"

"No, you skedaddle up to the office for the day and let me read."

"No, I'm staying with you."

"Then stay right here. I love having you in the same room."

"And who is going to do your bidding if I give you some time to read?"

"The service will have a nurse here at ten o'clock. I'll manage until then."

"If you say so. But you know I hate to leave you without help."

"This is not just a request."

"It's an order. All right," he said and pushed up from his chair. "I'll just take my coffee and go."

"Please do. And change out of that damn NAU sweatshirt. You've had that on all week."

"Understand," he said with a smile. "Actually, I was planning a shower first."

"That would be nice. You smell like a men's locker room."

"How would you know what a men's locker room smells like?"

"You don't want to know. It has something to do with the men's football team, though," she said with a chuckle. "Maybe I'll tell you sometime, when you're in the mood for titillation."

"TMI, lady. I'm outta here."

"Just as well. Now, hush."

She reached into the box with a Roman numeral one on the side and pulled out the nearest manila file. She opened and began reading.

Fifteen minutes later, when she looked up, Thaddeus could still be heard upstairs, making his preparations for the office.

She leaned back and smiled. The kids were all in school and she would be alone until about ten. In a way she was apprehensive about being alone for ninety minutes until the nurse arrived. But in another way she was excited to think she could still manage time alone.

It was empowering and exciting, what had once been mundane.

∽

THADDEUS HAD REPLACED his Mustang with a Dodge 3500 4x4 with crew cab and Cummins diesel since coming to the ranch. It had the trailering package so he could move horses around when he took the kids to Colorado for a week of riding and camping. He smiled as he drove toward Flagstaff. Those had been the best times he'd ever had, him, Katy, Turquoise, Celena, Sarai, and Parkus. The trailer hauled eight horses, which included two as pack horses, and everyone's tack and camping gear. Given that they now had four kids, Thaddeus had foregone bucket seats up front for a bench seat, where Parkus would ride and play his never-ending electronic games.

As he neared town, Thaddeus punched in the speed dial for Katy. She took the call.

"It's me. How are you doing?"

"Well, I'm still alive, so there's that."

"Yes, there's always that," he said with a sigh. Anymore, she hated when he asked how she was. But it totally set him off. He loved her, damn it, and if he couldn't stay close to her, then what? He was hurting too; but, as he thought through it, he decided to let her have it her way.

"I'll tell you how I'm doing if anything has changed," she promised. "You don't have to ask me over and over all day." He had agreed, but now he violated that basic principle of communicating with a dying wife. It was just something he couldn't not do.

"I meant, how are you doing with the records?"

"You did not, Thaddeus. You wanted to know how I'm doing, doing."

"You're right. How are you doing, doing?"

"Don't ask. It's not pretty. But I'm upright and reading. It's pretty amazing so far, what Dr. Sewell went through."

"Can you tell me any of it?"

"Let me finish up with the boxes, then we can talk."

"I'll just have to wait. Patience was never a strong suit with me. Please remember that."

"How about this? I'll call you at noon and then we'll have coffee and talk again when you get home at five?"

"You'll be taking your afternoon nap?"

"Of course. Thaddeus, I'm honestly okay. The pain meds give me a good bit of freedom from the pain. They make me groggy, yes, but other than that I'm basically still the same old girl."

Sure you are, he thought. Sure you are.

"So give me a slice of what's to come."

"Well, Dr. Emerick Sewell was forty-four when all this happened. He woke up in his house one morning in San Diego with a terrible headache. And his back hurt as well. He got up, went into the bathroom, and fell off the toilet onto the Spanish tile floor, face-down, passed out. He finally came around and crawled back to his bed. His wife heard none of this. He pulled himself up and sat on the edge of his bed, trying to stop the room from spinning. When it wouldn't stop, he stretched out on the bed and immediately fell back asleep. That's where I am so far."

"Amazing. Any idea what was wrong?"

"Just guessing, there was something systemic. Some kind of infection, maybe."

"Well, keep reading."

"And I'll do that if you'll let me off the frigging phone."

"Goodbye," he said and clicked off. He slammed his fist against the steering wheel and yelled, "God damn it! Doesn't she ever stop to think how *I* feel too?"

He roared into town and took San Francisco south three blocks, then east toward Agassiz and his law office.

He parked and sat in his truck and counted to one hundred before he went inside.

Katrina was busy at the front desk, wearing her headset and listening to dictation. She doubled as receptionist/word-processor, plus writing her master's thesis in criminology. She was tall, red hair and very pale face which caused her red lip gloss and dark blue eyes to pop, as he'd heard her telling a paralegal one day. "My skin is so pale, any color just pops," she had said. It had stuck with Thaddeus, for whenever he looked at her, he checked to see if her lips and eyes popped. Most often, they did. She was beautiful and smart and married to Ronnie Van Walten, a lineman for Arizona Public Service.

"Morning, Kat," Thaddeus said. He paused to pick through the unsorted mail on her desk. She immediately reached out and covered the mail with her hand. "Me first," she said. "Office protocol in case there's ever a question about what came when and who opened it. Let me date stamp it and then you can have it."

He shook his head. "Actually, I don't even want it."

She frowned. "I didn't think so. Why don't you go on in your office and sue someone? I'll do the mail."

"Give it to BAT. I don't want it."

BAT—Billy A. Tattinger—was Thaddeus' key paralegal, the man who made Thaddeus' legal world keep spinning on its axis. He was a black man whom Thaddeus had salvaged from jail and a rough life on the streets. Helping him get cleaned up from drugs and alcohol, he'd then hired the guy to work a restaurant in the casino Thaddeus once owned. The man had performed so well that Thaddeus had moved him into his law practice and sent him for paralegal training. BAT was heavyset, bearded with clear frame eyeglasses, happily married, now with two children, and loyal as the sunrise. He never failed Thaddeus and was low maintenance, which Thaddeus greatly appreciated and always required, busy as he was with clients and cases. And now, Katy.

Passing by BAT's work carrel just outside his own office, Thaddeus asked him to join him in the office in five minutes. Without looking up from his keyboard, BAT nodded.

Thaddeus entered his office, sat at his large, marble top desk, and reviewed his calendar for the day—a useless act, as his staff had cleared just about all appearances except the most necessary, given that Thaddeus was spending his days with Katy.

Nothing on the calendar and that was just fine.

He crossed to the wet sink and placed a K-Cup in the Keurig. The machine hissed and dribbled coffee into Thaddeus' favorite mug before ending its run with a loud scraping sound, presumably as the water reservoir emptied itself out. Even the most minor things about his environment were noticed anymore, he thought; a dying wife will do that to a man.

He returned to his desk and BAT came in and sat across from him. Football and weather were discussed. Then Thaddeus got down to it.

"We've got a doctor who wrote a book. And a comatose woman who read that book. What have you found out about medical malpractice where the injured person isn't a patient?"

BAT shook his head. "Everything is telling me there needs to be a duty owed by the doctor to the claimant. A legal duty, such as one created by the doctor-patient relationship. I haven't found anything that says there's a duty when the doctor writes a book, someone reads it and gets hurt somehow. Where's the nexus?"

Thaddeus nodded. "Agree. Where's the nexus? On the other hand, are we about to get our ass handed to us and make some new law we don't want to make?"

"That's the other side of the coin. There's always that possibility."

"But it would seem to me the doctor would have to expect that the book would be followed by people in the course of treating some ailment or other. Isn't the issue whether or not the use to which the book was put by the reader was reasonably foreseeable?"

BAT nodded. "Now you're using the common law language of negligence. I like that and I think it's a good way to analyze our facts. By the way, what are our facts?"

"Dunno. We just got the records and Katy insisted on going through them before us."

"How's she doing?"

"She's dying, BAT. That's how she's doing.

BAT was suddenly crestfallen. He looked like a little boy who had been chided by a parent for doing something evil.

"I'm sorry," Thaddeus immediately said. "I shouldn't have taken it out on you."

"Naw, that's all right, Thad. I've got broad shoulders and you need to vent."

"I need to go out back of my house and shoot my pistol at Coke bottles."

"That works. Better some target than me."

"I know. Again, I'm really sorry for being such an asshole lately."

"You're not an asshole, Boss. A little sphincter, maybe, but not a full-blown asshole."

"Thanks, BAT."

"By the way, have we heard anything about the woman who OD'd? Is she still alive? Comatose?"

"I believe comatose, but I haven't heard. I need to call up Mils Wang and see what I can find out."

"Do that," said Thaddeus.

"By the way, a court order came in last evening on the heavenly doctor's case. I picked it up from our box at the courthouse."

"What is it?" Thaddeus took a long drink of the coffee, steeling himself for official news from the court down the street that actually controlled his life no matter how well he surrounded himself with staff.

"Judge wants to see all counsel in her office this Friday. Status conference."

"I might send Jonas."

"No, she specifically says in the order that Thaddeus Murfee *shall* appear—not *may* appear—in person. Jonas ain't gonna get it done."

Jonas was actually Jonas P. Hawk; a third-year trial lawyer Thaddeus had hired straight out of UCLA Law School. Jonas was aggressive—maybe overly—but he was currently responsible for covering all of Thaddeus' court times. Except this time the judge wanted Thaddeus personally. He sighed; it couldn't be good.

"All right. I'll be there. But diary Jonas for the hearing too. Judge needs to get accustomed to seeing him on the case. We'll finesse my way out."

"Since he'll be the one trying it?"

"No, when it goes to trial that will be me."

"What about meeting the client? Date been set?"

"Yes, I think sometime later this week. I'm waiting for his agent to call."

"His agent. Good grief. A celeb."

"Yes, a celeb."

"Well, here's hoping he's not so Hollywood that he turns off our little jury over here in northern Arizona."

"It is so hoped, BAT."

"Amen. Hey, can I ask you something personal?"

"Sure."

"Did you ever get your money back from the guy who set up Sarai's kidnapping?"

"Nope."

"Are you ever going to?"

Thaddeus drew a deep breath and contemplated. His youngest daughter, Sarai, had been kidnaped during her infancy. Thaddeus had eventually hunted down the man who took her and he had taken the guy out. However, the real force behind the kidnapping was still at large. Every day he felt the urge to hunt down that guy too, but so far had not done it. Finally, he said, "Hadn't thought much about it lately. Why you asking, BAT?"

"It just rankles me. That cost you three hundred million. You can't just let it go, I hope."

"Now's just not the time. I've got too much going on out there," he made a motion with his hand indicating he was speaking about his home life. BAT understood.

"Would you consent to me doing some background on the guy? Start looking around for him?"

"Consider my consent given."

"What's the guy's name again?"

"Lincoln Mascari. Last known whereabouts Skokie, Illinois."

"Mob guy."

"Sure. Local boss. He headed up one of the four Chicago families."

"Heavy in the drug trade."

"That he was. Probably still is."

BAT stopped making notes. "Do you want to hazard a guess where he is now?"

"I'm thinking Sicily."

"Jesus."

"That would be my best guess. Why?"

"That's sort of what I was thinking. Do you mind if I spend a little money on some skip tracing help? Maybe buy some information out of Interpol?"

"Be my guest. Let's cap it at five grand to begin. That do it?"

BAT whistled affirmatively. "Indeed, it will, good sir."

"Then go for it." Thaddeus' face broke into a broad smile. "Now that you brought it up, I *do* want my money back."

"Is that all?"

Thaddeus flushed. "BAT, you're an astute observer of things Thaddeus. That isn't all, you're right. I would also like to see the guy fermenting in the ground. Or at the bottom of the Atlantic Ocean."

"Maybe the two of us could make that happen."

Thaddeus' eyes narrowed. "What are you saying?"

"How about cutting me in if I help run this guy to the ground?"

"How much we talking?"

"I don't know. Twenty percent of the recovery?"

"If you can live with ten percent, you've got a deal. But this means you do the workup on your own time."

"Not a problem. I've got Internet at home. High speed."

"Then get it done."

"What's our play?"

"I'm not above flat-out stealing my money back out of his bank. Something high-tech."

"But you want up-close to take him out as well?"

"Let's pretend you never said that," Thaddeus said, his voice low.

"But you get me up close and then turn your back. I do have a score to settle with the guy who kidnapped my baby and left her alone in the desert to die. I suppose we haven't finished up yet."

"So get back to your gun range, Boss."

"I'm on it, BAT. Already there."

13

THADDEUS DROVE to the Flagstaff Airport to gather up Dr. Emerick Sewell, who was flying in that noon from San Diego. Southwestern flight, running on time, swooping low over the pine trees just off the end of the runway, and flaring and rolling along the asphalt. Thaddeus watched all this from the side of the airport where he kept his own aircraft. Then he went inside the terminal to meet and greet his client.

He was last off, a middle-aged man wearing khaki trousers, white shirt, blue blazer, and green and white striped tie. On his feet were tasseled loafers; Thaddeus would have expected no less from the Ivy Leaguer: the look was perfect and was exactly what Thaddeus had predicted to Katy.

They exchanged names and shook hands.

Thaddeus watched his new client as he waited at the luggage carousel for a large, black bag. One of about fifty exactly like it. The man was tall, maybe six-one, and weighed in at about one-eighty. He wore long tousled brown hair with blond sun streaks (time at Pacific Beach?), no hint of beard stubble, a gold wedding band and a black onyx class ring with the crimson Harvard "H" engraved on the stone, and a smile that was disarming and charming. He knew you were going to like him; there was that assumption in his manner, and Thaddeus found that he did, in fact, immediately like the guy. He appeared harmless, and as they talked on the drive through town and headed north toward the mountains, Thaddeus learned the guy really had no ax to grind and was welcome as a stream of water burbling through a mountain meadow and equally innocent. He sincerely did not understand why someone like Nadia would file a lawsuit against him when in truth all he had done was come back from the other side bearing good news. The best news. "News that would change the course of human destiny," he said, replaying for Thaddeus the feelings he had known upon awakening from his long coma. "I was certain I had been returned not as a prophecy but as an affirmation. The deal was struck: God loves us and has sent me back to share the news."

"I can see why you might believe that," Thaddeus said. He had read the book and found the doctor's enthusiasm engaging. However, he found he still had his guard up and was taking everything the doctor said about his supernatural experience with a huge grain of salt. In fact, he believed none of the supernatural aspects but was fairly confident the medical reportage of the doctor's illness and unconsciousness was accurate enough. He had no doubt about that part of the story. The problem was, Thaddeus observed to Katy that night, was how the medical part of the story so nicely dovetailed into the supernatural part of the story. "Confidence in the medical encourages confidence in the supernatural," said Thaddeus.

Katy nodded, as she had now studied all the records and had spoken with the doctor when he arrived around two o'clock that afternoon.

"I'm Katy," she had said with her hand extended. "Stanford and Chicago."

"Emerick," said the doctor with a charming smile, "Harvard eighty-eight. So happy to meet you."

"Come in. Thaddeus will get us some refreshments while we talk. Do you mind, Thad?"

"Of course not. What's everyone want?"

The Near Death Experience

After Thaddeus had departed for the kitchen, Katy and Sewell talked families for five minutes. They were treading water until Thaddeus returned, knowing he would demand to hear it all from the top.

At last he returned with two Diet Cokes and one black coffee.

"All right," said Thaddeus, sitting next to Katy on the sofa in the family room, "let's cut right to the chase, if you don't mind, Dr. Sewell."

"Please call me Emerick and I'll call you Thaddeus."

"Thad is fine."

"Well, I've been sued by a woman who claims she read my book, as I understand it."

"Right, the family has taken the position in the complaint that your story was prescriptive—meaning you were holding out to her and others a form of medical procedure in your story."

Sewell shook his head and crunched ice from his Coke. "Preposterous, eh?"

"Definitely," said Katy.

Thaddeus studied his new client closely and said, "Maybe we're getting ahead of ourselves. It would be good to discuss how the law views books written by physicians. There's quite an interesting slant on it."

"Which is?" said the friendly, Ivy doctor.

"The law looks at medical writings in at least two ways. On the one hand, there is the historical view, in which the law says that anyone can write and tell a story and ask people to believe it. But on the other hand is the prescriptive. This view says doctors can also write books that offer medical solutions to medical conditions. These writings are loosely termed, 'prescriptive,' in that they offer prescriptions for sick people. Not prescriptions in the form of medication, either, in that narrow sense. It also includes prescriptions in the form of lifestyle change, changes in thinking, attitudinal, and all of the stuff you'll see in the medical aisle at your typical Barnes and Noble. There are hundreds of such books published every week, all of them offering a cure for some sort of a condition of some sort. That's your prescriptive writing and, yes, such books can create a legal relationship between author and reader."

"You're serious?" said the doctor, pausing in mid-chew on a melting shard of ice. "That's amazing!"

"And you've maybe never heard it before?"

"Not at all."

"This is becoming known as negligent publishing. Negligent publishing refers to published material that ends in a reader's harm or injury. This type of claim should be of particular concern to physicians," Thaddeus said. "For example, if a doctor writes a book on dietary advice that leads to a reader becoming ill, a negligent publishing claim could arise. Even though you have no patient-doctor connection with readers, you certainly have a duty not to be negligent in what you're writing about."

"Why didn't I see this coming?"

"Because we're doctors, not lawyers," Katy said. She meant to placate the doctor and he nodded his agreement at her.

Thaddeus, watching their tacit agreement, was unsurprised. In his experience, most physicians usually were amazed upon learning they might have done something in the practice of medicine or public speaking or writing that could result in legal consequences. Thaddeus knew that doctors just often didn't think in those terms, which was maybe a good thing, as you didn't want these most important members of society to be hamstrung when discussing your health and possible treatment modalities or medication regimens. Sadly, the other side of the coin was that because of the choices available to physicians in the practice of medicine, which was still more art than science, legal implications lurked behind every bush. That seemed to be the legal posture in which Thaddeus found his new client. He felt sorry for the guy, too, because he knew that claims like this didn't just up and walk away. They required tenacious in-fighting and stressful months and even years of pushback. The man's life had dramatically changed and he realized very little about that fact. It would be up to Thaddeus to help bring him up to speed on these things, which would also, much to Thaddeus' dismay, begin to dissuade the doctor from his very Pollyanna view of the world. He was about to learn what a really nasty place it can sometimes be . Say sayonara to innocence, Thaddeus thought.

But what he hadn't counted on was the doctor's commitment to his new work.

"God has sent me to tell the world about His love. He will protect me against all who would do me harm. I have no doubt of that, believe me. Thaddeus, you're part of my mission. I can feel it."

Thaddeus blushed. "I don't feel a part of anyone's mission. I'm just a lawyer up here in Flagstaff doing my job. It just so happens Ms. Turkenov lives here and I do too."

"I can see God using you in my work. And what about you, Dr. Murfee, what's your take on all this since you've read my records?"

Katy nodded. "I'm totally fascinated by what happened to you. Your brain activity was absolutely non-existent when these incredible visions came to you. We have immutable proof of that in your brain scans. So what happened to you? And how did you recover so fully from the terrible infection that rendered you comatose for a week? I have lots of questions."

"Most medical professionals do come away from my records simply stunned. No one's ever seen anything like it. I was truly dead and came back. They were within an hour of removing my life support when I suddenly opened my eyes."

Katy stirred on the couch, shifting her position and moving her legs up under. She took a drink from her Coke and fixed her eyes on the doctor.

"Do you—would you mind telling me about the vision itself?"

"Vision? It wasn't a vision. It was an actual experience. I died and went to heaven."

Katy nodded. "All right. Experience. Would you mind telling me about that?"

"Sure." Dr. Sewell drew his arms back along the armrests of his chair. He stretched out his legs and crossed them. His head went back and he looked up at the ceiling, gathering his thoughts.

"Many near death experiences or NDE's share a common pattern.

The patient's heart stops beating and a bright light appears, a tunnel, music, and bright light and maybe God. You can find that kind of NDE all over the Internet. Entire websites dedicated to those stories. But that wasn't me."

He paused and again looked up at the ceiling. He was gathering memories of the most important event in his life.

"I lapsed into a coma and vaguely, vaguely, vaguely knew I was a body in the ground. I was in muck and dirt and damp—wet—and I couldn't breathe. Three inches above my face was solid rock. It prevented me from moving. If I even took too deep a breath, my chest pressed up against the rock and I was restricted. I couldn't roll onto my side. And it was loud, angry noise. Have you ever been inside an MRI machine when that terrible banging begins? That's what this was like but a thousand times louder. I could not only hear the banging I could feel it along the entire length of my body. This condition persisted for something like forty hours. I knew I was in hell. But then something funny happened. I saw music. It came in the form of raindrops coming out of the rock and as the drops hit the mud around me, they sounded a musical note. The music grew and swelled. It became symphonic, then it became heavenly and I found myself aloft, flying on a filament, moving through clean air with dappled sunshine all around, green fields, murmuring brooks, and I looked beyond me and realized I was traveling on a song. The notes were sweeping me along and it was a song I hadn't heard since childhood when someone was singing me to sleep."

"Goodness," said Katy. "My mother used to do that for me."

"Exactly."

"Can I say something?" Thaddeus asked. He wished he could go upstairs and take a shower then retreat out back and work with his horse. This had become all too much. But neither did he want to dampen the conversation with his obvious discomfort with what was being said.

"Sure, Thad," said the doctor, "what's up?"

"Are you all right, honey?" Katy asked.

Thaddeus slowly nodded and came upright on the couch.

"I just remembered I have a call I need to make before four o'clock. I'm just going to climb upstairs and take care of that. Will you excuse me?"

"Sure," said Dr. Sewell. "Actually, I've probably been talking too long anyway. I could stand to grab a shower and freshen up."

"No!" said Katy resolutely. Then she heard the sound of her own voice and pulled back a notch. "I mean—would you please continue with your story. You're in the air, moving through—was it heaven?"

"All right," Thaddeus said. "Excuse me."

Thaddeus stood and headed for the stairs. He could hear the doctor's voice continuing with his drama as he hurried up the stairs.

Actually, there was no one to call. He just wanted to lose the suit, change into jeans and boots and a T-shirt and go see Coco.

Which he did.

Coco was loose in the corral and saw him coming. He walked up to the gate and lowered his head, eyeballing Thaddeus as he unlocked the gate. The horse knew. They always knew when it was time.

Thaddeus let himself inside and seized Coco by the halter.

"C'mon, Buddy," he said. "Let's go brush you. Then we'll lunge you and maybe have a short spin around the property."

The property he was referring to was fifteen hundred acres of PJ —piñon and juniper.

Coco let off a shuddering whinny and followed Thaddeus into the barn. There they connected, hand to brush to coat. Inside the huge house, perched on the side of a mountain, Katy and the visitor continued with the visitor's journey to heaven.

For his part, climbing aboard Coco and walking off onto the land was the same thing for Thaddeus.

A journey to heaven.

And it was all Thaddeus had ever wanted.

Now if only Katy could find her own way. As he rode by the windows, he could peer inside the floor-to-ceiling windows of the family room. A glassy figure that he knew to be Katy on the couch could be seen small and helpless inside the house on the mountain.

He said a silent prayer that she would connect with something greater than herself and that it would take her the rest of the way.

For he was exhausted at that point. Almost too exhausted to continue on with her.

But he swallowed hard and fought back the tears.

He would never let her know that.

And Katy, watching him pass by fifty yards below, would never let him know that she already knew.

She returned her attention to the doctor. It was more than she had ever hoped for.

Heaven was real and waiting for her.

Now she only had to summon up the courage and go there herself. Or maybe it didn't even take courage at all. Maybe it just took her letting go.

She watched Thaddeus disappear off-stage. She looked past the doctor out to the swell of the mountains and up to where the peaks disappeared into the clouds.

And she knew.

It had been right in front of her all the time. All she'd had to do was accept.

So she did the next indicated thing.

She let go and let God.

14

Anastasia was so wrapped up in her final year of med school that she handed off her mother's estate questions to her husband, Jack Millerton. Jack was a sole practitioner CPA in Chicago and he felt that Uncle Roy—Nadia's lowlife brother, as Jack referred to him—had picked Jack's pocket by managing to get himself appointed as Nadia's conservator.

"Talk about the fox in the hen house," Jack told Anastasia one night. They had just finished dinner in their French Provincial dining room, paid for and deducted on their tax return by Jack. He fancied himself a great curator of fine art and furniture, all of which began life in his professional office where it was appropriately deducted on the corporate tax returns, but which, after only a short appearance on that professional stage, quickly found its way down to his home for personal use—a use definitely not allowable on Jack's 1120S return. But Jack, in his usual sneaky pattern, didn't really give a damn. He figured that if the IRS came snooping around, he'd simply move the furniture back up to the office for the duration of the siege then move it back home again. Simple, tidy, and totally illegal.

But that was Jack, as Anastasia told her friends.

"Fox in the hen house?" said Anastasia. "Would you rather that *you* were in the hen house?"

"Well, it makes a helluva lot more sense. Do you want a used furniture guy managing Nadia's million bucks or do you want her CPA son-in-law who has ethical restrictions placed on him by the state CPA licensing board?"

Anastasia had to fight off the laughter. Ethics? She thought. *What* ethics? Like most professionals burdened with ethics, Jack was all too quick to trot his ethics out when they would benefit him. Otherwise, they were never mentioned—or followed.

But Anastasia was true blue—or, more apt, she was not quite ready to eject Jack from her life yet; not until she had her M.D. degree under glass and on the wall. Nadia's pill popping had come at a bad time: that was the bottom line for Anastasia. And another thought crossed her mind increasingly: if Nadia happened to die from her OD, shouldn't she, Anastasia, be ready to take her cut of the estate soon after? She figured that with Uncle Roy standing between her and a few hundred thousand it would be hell to get him to turn loose of her money. So maybe it would be best to see husband Jack standing in the gap rather than Uncle Roy if Nadia nosedived.

"I would rather have you, Baby," Anastasia said. She placed her forehead against Jack's forehead and then kissed him. "Always rather have you."

Jack took a drink of his Wild Turkey.

"Exactly. I say we go in with a petition to revoke Uncle Roy and have me appointed. Base it on malfeasance. You know Roy's two weeks late with the initial inventory of your mother's assets? Two weeks! Give me a break!"

"He is? Two weeks? No, I didn't know."

"I'm calling my lawyer. This has gone on long enough. You're next-of-kin and you should know before Uncle Roy what assets Mama has. What the hell!"

"Yes, call that lawyer. I'm behind you on this, Jack. You know I always count on you for this kind of stuff."

"I know you do, Baby. I know you do. We'll have a petition to revoke on file this week. I can promise you that."

And so he did. Friday afternoon, Federal Express delivered a certified petition to revoke conservatorship based on four acts of alleged malfeasance. It was signed by Jack under oath and notarized. The clerks at the Coconino County Clerk of the Court's office sniggered when they saw it come in. Uncle Roy's lawyer—Milbanks Wang—visited the court several times a week and reviewed the file himself—in itself billable hours, useless as they were. He would be apoplectic when he discovered the interloper had sullied his clean court file with some accusatory petition to revoke. The clerks could hardly wait to see his expression go from chipper to obscene. For Milbanks Wang was known for his rages and public meltdowns whenever he didn't get his way. This development held great promise for the bystanders in the Clerk's Office.

Sure enough, at four p.m., here came Attorney Wang to review his precious file with its promise of huge legal fees. Expecting to find the same old nothing new in the file, Wang was civil and courteous and even said "Thank you" when the clerk handed over the file. Then everyone watched out the corner of an eye.

It soon erupted.

"Holy shit! Who filed this?" Wang demanded of the clerk who had given him the file.

"I—I—did."

"Well, take it out! Immediately."

"Mr. Wang, I can't just un-file something. That wouldn't be legal."

"I'm the lawyer! I say what's legal and what's not. I say take it out!"

"Let me get the Clerk."

The deputy disappeared into a back office and reappeared moments later with Nancy J. Reardon, an extremely confident and competent black woman who outweighed the lesser Wang and would have crushed him in at least two out of three falls in the wrestling ring.

"Sir, are you having a problem out here?"

"Problem? You goddam right there's a problem. Your helper filed this perjured petition in my case!"

"Well, it's a properly formatted, properly signed pleading which self-identifies as having been signed under oath both by the petitioner and by his attorney too. I have no choice but to file such a document in *my* file."

"*My* file!"

"Well, actually it's the court's file. Neither yours nor mine."

"*My file!*"

The Clerk sighed and pressed her massive bosom against the filing counter.

"Look here, Mr. Wang. You can always file a motion to strike the pleading and take it up with Judge Gabberts. I would encourage you to do that. But I'm not removing that document from that file and if you do it I'll have the sheriff arrest you."

"On what charge?"

"Destruction of public property. Interference with an official act of an elected official. Theft. Perjury before an elected official. Do you want me to continue?"

She had her gaze screwed down tight on him now. Wang perceived the first round had been lost. Or maybe was a draw.

"I'll be back this afternoon with a motion to strike the pleading."

"We close at five, sir. You have fifty minutes left."

Wang spun on his heel and leaped from the office.

Superior Court Clerk Nancy Reardon watched him go.

"Blowhard," she whispered to her deputy. "Close five minutes early today, Cynthia."

"You sure?"

"Did you hear me?"

"Yes, Ma'am."

When the doors were bolted shut at 4:55 that afternoon, there had been no subsequent pleading filed.

Neither did anyone pay any attention to Wang's bullheaded pounding on the door glass two minutes before five when he arrived with his paperwork.

THIRTY MINUTES LATER, Wang was arguing with the nurses over getting to see Nadia Turkenov on his visit to her hospital room.

"She is my conservatorship," Wang warned the nurse, Molly Potter, who blocked his entrance into Nadia's small, glassed-in suite.

"Sir, I couldn't care less. You aren't family so you don't get in."

"But I think my client, Uncle Roy, is in with her."

The nurse turned around and looked.

"Her daughter and her husband Mr. Millerton are in with Ms. Turkenov. Are they your client?"

"Certainly not. But they will want to see me."

"Then when they come out, they can. You are welcome to wait at the end of the hall in the visitors' area. There are soft drink machines, microwave—"

"No, no, no. That is Jack Millerton in that room and he is guilty of perjury. He filed papers in my case and I *must* talk to him!"

"And you shall. Just not in my patient's room. It is not a conference room. It is the ICU room of a very sick hospital patient. Family only, Mr. Wang!"

Wang head-faked the nurse and stepped around her. Up to the window, he scurried and rapped the glass with his knuckles. Both the woman and man inside looked up from the patient. They studied Wang, who was now motioning them outside.

Jack Millerton said something to Anastasia and went around her. He stepped into the hallway.

"You're Jack Millerton!" cried Milbanks Wang. His voice was accusatory and threatening. Jack took a step backward.

"Who the hell are you?" said Jack.

"I am the lawyer for Uncle Roy."

Jack's eyes narrowed. He scrunched up his face and moved a step closer to Wang.

"You're the sombitch who beat us all to court. Bastard!"

Wang stepped back. He hadn't counted on the CPA closing the

gap between them. Encouraged, Jack closed the space between them again and Wang moved back again.

"You filed that pack of lies today!" cried Wang. "It's all perjury and I'm going to see to it that you serve time in prison for what you've done."

"You do that. In the meantime, I'll have you disbarred!"

"For what? I haven't done anything."

"I rest my case. You're two weeks late with the inventory. That's malpractice, bub. We're suing you personally next week. Malpractice insurance paid up? Goddamn well better be!"

Wang's hands clenched and unclenched. He wasn't sure about the insurance, and the malpractice threat rattled him not just a little. Did he owe these people a duty as clients? Or did he just owe a duty to Roy? Or maybe Nadia, too?

"Please, we need to talk about what's best for Nadia," said Wang, abruptly turning his horse around midstream. "That's all that really matters here."

"Goddam right. My mother-in-law—"

Wang had suddenly had the best idea of the day and it stopped Millerton in mid-sentence.

Said Wang, "How close are you to that Phoenix lawyer who filed for you?"

Jack paused. He was about to attack from a new direction, but he paused instead. The question just posed was a very good question.

"I'm not married to him. I've used him before on tax audit cases."

"So he's not even really an estate lawyer?"

"I guess not."

"Then we should talk."

"About what?"

"About working together."

"Really? And just how does that work?"

"I dump Roy and take you on. I've read your petition a dozen times. It makes some good points. Roy has been less than diligent in getting the inventory on file. Are you ready with an inventory, by the way?"

The Near Death Experience

"No, but I could be. By Monday, with your help."

"What do you say we meet tomorrow and talk this through?"

"What time?"

"Nine a.m."

"Where?"

"Bank of America building. Three-oh-four."

"See you then."

"Mr. Millerton. I wouldn't mention our little talk to your wife."

Jack looked at his wife and looked back at Wang.

"Who said I was going to?"

Wang smiled. "Nine a.m. then."

"And the lawsuit against the devil doctor. Would I be in charge of that as well?"

Wang looked Jack over. He nodded, a gleam dancing in his eye.

"You would."

Jack smiled. His chest swelled with glad anticipation.

"That's the whole mission. To make a case against this charlatan and hit a huge payday."

"Agreed," said Wang. He stuck out his hand.

They formed their grip and shook.

The deal was made, it only remained now to clear away the debris (Roy) and drive ahead.

15

Lincoln Mascari had done his genealogy. When one was living in Sicily under blue, cloudless, Mediterranean skies, one had time to do one's genealogy.

His paternal great-grandfather, Salvatore Paulo Mascari, and grandmother Pietra Gaetani were married in Termini Imerese in 1879. His grandparents were married in 1910 in New York City. They were Giuseppe Mascari and Helena Gaito. His parents were married in 1937 in Chicago and he was born in Skokie in 1950. He was the eleventh of eleven children and he swore up and down that being the youngest is what had made him the meanest, for he was. Additionally, there was a world of brother and sisters, of course, like all good Catholic families. And there was a greater universe of cousins, nieces, and nephews, the majority of whom he had never met. Nor would he ever meet them, not since he had fled Skokie and returned to the birthplace of his great-grandparents in Termini.

Like many Sicilian men returned from Chicago and New York, Lincoln Mascari had a secret.

A secret about his money. A secret that would have to remain a secret at all costs, because the money that Mascari had arrived in Sicily claiming as his own was actually money he had extorted from

Thaddeus Murfee. In return for the safe return of Murfee's baby daughter, Mascari had received from Murfee a wire transfer of three hundred million dollars. It was money that Murfee had been awarded in court against Mascari, and it had come from the sale of a certain Las Vegas casino the court had transferred from Mascari to Murfee in satisfaction of that court award. The way Mascari saw it, he had only taken his money back. Money that was his in the first place. It honestly never occurred to him that Murfee might be seeing it differently.

Every morning at seven o'clock, Mascari went down to the docks and walked along the sidewalk, smelling the salt air, the scents pouring out of the holds of the oceangoing vessels at moorage, and the abundance of fish markets along the way. He was so taken with the return to his roots that he had even returned to the Church of his youth and was once again actively practicing his faith. And so after walking for an hour, he then appeared at the daily eight o'clock Mass. Mention of the extortion of Murfee's money had never pierced the panel separating priest from penitent during any trip to the confessional. In fact, it was buried in Mascari's brain so deep that he had forgotten all about it and presumed everyone else had, too. No, in his confessional, Mascari stayed on the safe topics: lust of the eyes, yelling at the wife, cursing at the butcher, cheating at Friday night poker: minor sins that were just bad enough to demand dogged Hail Marys. And so Mascari was repentant but shunned going so far as sackcloth and ashes. And shunned going so far as returning Murfee's money to him. Or asking forgiveness of the young lawyer for kidnapping his two-year-old baby girl, taking her out into the desert north of Las Vegas, and abandoning her there in a fallen-in shack without water or comfort, to die.

It had taken him a full year to hide. Which included time to cover his tracks. There was new identity: Zurich. There was plastic surgery: Geneva. There were banking ministrations complex enough to make even the Cayman officials lose track. There was travel around the globe under three different names claiming three different nationalities claiming three different hairstyles, disguises, and backgrounds.

The final goal had always been Sicily, of course. But no one ever came to Sicily directly from Chicago. It just wasn't done.

Before ever entering Sicily, Lincoln Mascari had taken care of one last little problem: his name. It was changed by using the names of his forebears Salvatore Paulo Mascari and Pietra Gaetani. His new name was Salvatore Paulo Gaetani. All driver's licenses, passports, official documents and banking documents were changed to reflect the new identity. At last, Lincoln Mascari felt safe.

There was, however—as there always must be—one loose thread in all this. That thread was in Palermo—100 miles west of Termini, at a lawyer's office. His name was Edoardo De Filippo. "Edoardo" loosely translates to "keeper of the richness," and it was this role to which Edoardo had been born, raised up, and trained. He was a Sicilian Mafia lawyer, a man surrounded by bodyguards, and the overseer of great wealth not his own. He had taken the oath of *omertà* and if he traded on any client's secret he could expect to be suddenly and mercilessly killed, but not before watching his attackers first kill his wife, his children, and his children's children right before his eyes.

But there was a tell. There is always a tell. Unlike the understated grays and blacks of his Sicilian neighbors, Edoardo's wardrobe ran to the light greens, soft blues, luminescent oranges, and daring yellows of the Italian fashion world. He was a fashion peacock and kept not one but two walk-in closets for himself inside the five-hundred-year-old house he shared with his wife and quartet of children.

It was this colorful plumage that would prove to be his undoing. That and a change of name.

16

THE COURT SET its first status conference in *Conservatorship of Nadia Turkenov v. Emerick Sewell* for eleven a.m. Friday. Thaddeus was ordered to attend, not his associate.

Boomer Magence arrived at 9:20 a.m. from L.A. Boomer was larger than life, and came into the airport wearing a $3000 Valentino Newman suit with French cuffs and diamond cufflinks, a $500 navy silk tie with a diamond pen, and Italian sunglasses that Thaddeus was sure they weren't selling at Walgreen's. The famous Hollywood lawyer brought along his associate attorney, M.J. Jones. Jones was more caddy than lawyer, scurrying after the baggage as Boomer swept Dr. Sewell into his arms and embraced him, air-kissing both sides of his head Continental style. Thaddeus was then introduced by Sewell to Boomer, who took little notice of Thaddeus because Thaddeus was only involved in the case at all, in Boomer's view because Boomer wasn't licensed to practice law in Arizona and needed local counsel so he could appear *pro hac vice*. Thaddeus had been selected by Sewell's Hollywood agent as local counsel. Upon seeing his new co-counsel, Thaddeus groaned, knowing how rural juries in Arizona would be immediately put off by such puffery. After bags had been retrieved, they loaded into Thaddeus' SUV and headed back to town.

They seated themselves at Thaddeus' desk at the office.

"As I understand, Mr. Murfee, you practice in both Chicago and Flagstaff?" said Boomer.

"Correct. We're eventually going to be free of Chicago and all cases will then originate in the West."

"I don't follow that. Chicago's where the money's at. Seems like damn poor planning, to me. Dear," said Boomer to Katrina, who had arrived from the receptionist's desk to lend a hand, "do you suppose you could rustle up a mocha latte for me?"

"There's the Starbucks on the corner," she said to Thaddeus, "should I leave the phones and go down there?"

Thaddeus said he thought BAT could handle the phones while she ran the errand. He rolled his eyes at her when no one was watching and she understood. Tom Terrific would be catered to, she understood, but just so far. She had seen Thaddeus rain down on visitors who overstepped before. She hurried out to the elevator.

"Where were we? Oh, yes, your leaving Chicago. Well, never mind. I just received a letter from Physicians' Mountain Mutual Insurance, our good doctor's malpractice carrier. They are going to defend the case, but with a reservation of rights."

Thaddeus frowned. "May I see it?"

Boomer Magence handed over the letter. It was a serious development in the case, for a reservation of rights letter was an insurer's notification to an insured that coverage for a claim might not apply. Such notification allowed an insurer to investigate a claim without waiving its right to later deny coverage. Thaddeus read on. The insurer was using the reservation of rights letter because all the insurer had so far were various unsubstantiated allegations in the complaint and, at best, a few confirmed facts.

"This isn't good, Dr. Sewell," Thaddeus said to his client, and then explained what it meant and what it might portend: that the carrier could at any moment jerk the rug out from under him, stop paying his lawyers, and claim a situation where there was no insurance coverage.

"But do I still have insurance?" asked the doctor.

"Dear man," said Boomer, "I'll sue them for you if they get out of line. Not to worry."

"Well, it's actually a little more serious than that. Of course, Mr. Magence can sue them, but in the meantime you would have to pay your lawyers yourself and there would be no insurance to cover your loss if the other side did prevail against you. It's not a welcome development at all."

"Are you still willing to serve, Thaddeus?" said the doctor.

"Sure I am. We can always work something out."

"But I would have to bow out," said Boomer laconically, drumming his fingers on the desk. "I wonder what happened to my mocha latte?"

"We've got about ten minutes to get over to the courthouse and get situated," Thaddeus said. "I suggest we walk across the street now."

Boomer sighed. To M.J., he said, "You wait here. When my drink arrives, bring it right across the street to the courthouse. Room—"

"Judge Raul Mendoza's court. Third down on your right, second floor."

"Yes, sir," said M.J., acting as if this was the daily routine he had signed on for. Which, in fact, it was. Thaddeus wondered if the man ever practiced law—probably not, not from within the shadow of Tom Terrific.

The men walked across the street. It was early May and there was still a chill in the air. But overhead the sky was crystal blue and the mountains shimmered in the north, still snow-capped, still visited by nighttime snows and howling winds, while down below, there in Flagstaff, mere mortals enjoyed milder weather.

∽

RAUL MENDOZA HAD RUN for governor in the last general election and was still licking his wounds from the thrashing he had received at the hands of the Phoenix candidate, one Lemuel Goddard, a Republican, who had carried all counties. Mendoza had won his hometown of

Flagstaff, Democrat though he was, and now vowed he'd never run for public office again. The lawyers cooled their heels in his outer office while Judge Mendoza hovered over his desk, clearing away new filings and dictating minute entries for Edwarda to keyboard and distribute. He was a dour, middle-aged Basque, descended from three hundred years of shepherds who still toiled in the high valleys and plains of the Coconino and Kaibab forests. He wore progressive eyeglass lenses which forever had him reaching for coffee cups that weren't precisely where the lenses said they were, so it wasn't uncommon for the files that crossed his desk to be stained with coffee spills and cigarette ash from the Camels he chain-smoked. The courthouse—and his office—was a non-smoking building but, as Chief Judge, Mendoza had entered a special order for his own office, allowing smoking within the Judge's chambers.

Edwarda came into the Judge's office and shut the door behind her.

"Quite a crowd out there. One of them is some important dude out of L.A."

"Good. I'm not quite ready."

"Yessir."

"Five minutes, then send them in."

"Yessir."

Five minutes later, they clamored into the office without further ado. Boomer immediately took a seat in front of the judge and Ellen Roddgers took the other one. Ellen was a solid citizen in Thaddeus' view; a competent, outspoken attorney who didn't suffer fools, especially misogynist lawyers who dared cross her. Boomer knew none of this, of course.

"Okay," said Judge Mendoza. "We're on the record in my chambers. First some housekeeping. Ellen, you're representing who?"

"I'm here for Roy Underwood."

"And he is—"

"He is the younger brother of the ward, Nadia Turkenov. Roy has received a petition to substitute conservators filed by Jack Millerton, his niece's husband."

"And who has that case?"

"You do, Your Honor," said Milbanks Wang, the lawyer for Jack Millerton in his effort to unseat Uncle Roy Underwood.

"And you represent who?"

Milbank leaned forward dramatically. "As of this moment, I represent Nadia Turkenov in her lawsuit against Dr. Sewell. I am representing her through the conservator, Roy Underwood, but I'm trying to substitute in Jack Millerton for him. Jack is a CPA and—"

"Whoa, hold it," said the Judge, leaning away from the throng in exasperation. "You're telling me you're representing two clients with competing interests? Isn't that a conflict of interest, Milbanks?"

"Technically, yes, I supp—"

"Naw, I think it's more than technically, Mil. I think you've got an ethical thing going on here that you need to straighten out before we can proceed with you involved. For the record, I'm going to show the ward, Nadia Turkenov, as being unrepresented at today's hearing. You'll not be asked to speak on the record again, Mils. Not until you come back to me with an agreed order involving your two clients. Ms. Roddgers will, of course, be involved as she also appears for Roy Underwood although you're still, technically and legally, representing him by order of the court appointing him to serve as conservator. Either the first one agrees to stay and the second agrees to bow out, or the first agrees to bow out and the second agrees to stay. We need that for you to proceed."

"Let us take them into the outer office and hash it out, Judge."

"Be my guest."

"Roy and Jack? Would you come with us, please?"

"I don't think so," said Roy. "I need to stay here and represent my sister. Ms. Roddgers is gonna help me now."

"The judge just said you can't speak on the record," said Milbanks Wang.

"No, he said *you* couldn't. He didn't say anything about me."

"Tell you what, Roy," said Judge Mendoza. "I won't take any action regarding your sister until her rights are secured by a sitting conservator. So you're free to go out and discuss this matter with your attorney and Mr. Wang. Who is also your attorney."

Roy swelled out his chest. "Wang is not my attorney. Not after this!"

"Well, go talk to your ex-attorney, then. This needs to be resolved."

Roy stood and glumly followed Wang and Millerton and Roddgers out of the chambers. At which point, Boomer Magence rolled his eyes at the judge and said, "May we get on with it?"

Judge Mendoza leaned forward. "And who might you be?"

"I'm the attorney for Dr. Emerick Sewell, the defendant in the lawsuit we're here on."

"I don't have an entry of appearance for you in the file. Only from Mr. Murfee. Good morning, Thaddeus. Be right with you."

"Good morning, Your Honor. Mr. Magence has brought along a motion to appear *pro hac vice*. Maybe he can hand that to you now."

With a flourish and a flutter, Magence handed over his motion. "Signed, sealed, and delivered," he said.

Judge Mendoza took the pleading and placed it face down on his desk without reading.

"So you think Dr. Sewell needs two lawyers on his case? Are you licensed in Arizona?"

"No, my motion goes into all that."

"Well, what makes you think that a lawyer who knows nothing about Arizona law and procedure would be helpful in an Arizona medical malpractice case in my courtroom?"

Thaddeus felt his limbs warm up a degree or two. Judge Mendoza was known to bend over backward to help deserving litigants, no matter who they happened to be. But out of town—much less out-of-state—lawyers were not given quite the same freedom as local counsel were given. Thaddeus could see that Magence had his work cut out for him. And he was glad for that. He had decided on the walk over that he didn't want the guy on the case at all and worried that Magence could only hurt the doctor's presentation in front of a local jury. The guy was a liability and Thaddeus was hopeful the judge would disqualify him.

"What makes me think I would be helpful? Judge, do you know anything about my eighty-five-and-oh jury trial record in Los Angeles County?"

Judge Mendoza sat back and folded his arms on his chest. "Do I know about your record? No, and I don't really give a damn about your record. I'm concerned about your record in Arizona courts and you, sir, have none. Mr. Murfee, is Mr. Magence essential to your defense of this case?"

Thaddeus was suddenly thrust into the middle of it, something he had hoped to avoid.

"Essential? I don't know. I'm sure he would be helpful."

"You sound less than enthusiastic."

"Your Honor, I only met Mr. Magence just this morning. I've never seen him appear in front of a jury or even a judge. So in all honesty, I'm afraid I'm not going to be much help."

"Put it this way, then, Thaddeus: do you want him on your team?"

Boomer Magence swung around and stared daggers at Thaddeus. While he did, the judge continued.

"And what about the defendant himself, Dr. Sewell? Do you want this man defending you in an Arizona court when he's never appeared in Arizona and definitely isn't licensed in Arizona?"

"I—I—"

"Of course, he does, Your Honor!" said Magence in his courtroom voice. "Plus his insurance carrier signed off on me."

"Judge," said Thaddeus, "there's a reservation of rights defense."

"I see. So the insurance company doesn't even know yet if it's going to extend coverage. Doctor, do you understand what this means?"

"Uh—I think so."

"It means you might wind up owing a barrel of money to the claimant Mrs. Turkenov and owe a barrel of money to your lawyers—two of them, or three if the lawyer who evidently is accompanying Mr. Magence this morning is also assigned to the case."

"M.J. Jones, Your Honor," the caddy said from the side of the room. "I'm not actually submitting bills on the case, Sir."

"Very well. That's good to hear. So here's what I think we're going to do here. I think we're going to allow Mr. Magence to appear in my court in this case but only as a non-participant. He will not be allowed to speak or file pleadings in the case. He will sit at counsel table during trial, but only as an observer. Does this work for you, Mr. Murfee?"

"Yes, Your Honor," said Thaddeus, relieved that Magence would be muzzled. At least, there was that.

"And what about you, Dr. Sewell. Does this work for you, keeping in mind that I don't even have to allow him in my courtroom at all?"

"It works for me. Judge, I'm sorry this has even happened and is taking up your time. I don't think I've done anything wrong."

"Well, this isn't the time or place, Dr. Sewell, though I appreciate your need to tell me. That's just fine."

Just then, the outer door opened and Milbanks Wang with Uncle Roy and Jack Millerton and Ellen Roddgers re-entered the small office.

"Yes, Mr. Wang? Is there a decision?"

"Roy Underwood and Jack Millerton have agreed to share the conservator's duties, Your Honor. They propose a joint conservatorship. Ms. Roddgers will stay on the case and assist me."

Ellen Roddgers scoffed. "More accurately, Mr. Wang and I will share the legal representation of the co-conservators. Not the same as assisting him."

"How very Solomonic," said the judge. "Can't cut the baby in half so we'll take the whole baby. I'll allow that."

"Thank you, Judge," said Uncle Roy.

"Thank you, Your Honor," said Jack Millerton, not to be outdone.

"Yes, Judge," said Attorney Wang.

"All right then, we have the parties sorted. Except the gentleman sitting in the rear on my couch. Are you here in some capacity, Sir?"

Albert Turkenov blanched. He had hoped he wouldn't have to speak. But at this point, he had begun to think that maybe he, too, needed an attorney. It wasn't that he didn't trust his sister Anastasia, but he was beginning to think he didn't trust her husband, Jack, who had just weaseled his way into co-representing Albert's mother, Nadia. Albert thought of his mother, unconscious and hooked up to a dozen tubes up at the Medical Center, and his face felt hot. He was worried about her and now was very worried about her assets, as he sat and watched the maneuvering here this morning.

"I am here because Nadia Turkenov is my mother," said Albert. "And I'm wondering if I should be one of her conservators, too."

"All right," said the judge. "Has Mr. Wang contacted you at all about the conservatorship?"

"He served the papers on me."

"Did you get a chance to discuss those with a lawyer?"

"He told me I didn't need to."

"When did he tell you that?"

"When I called him. I called him and asked why he was using Uncle Roy instead of me, Nadia's son. I'm in business and I know about my mother's assets and stuff. It seemed to me I should have at least been contacted first."

"Indeed," said Judge Mendoza. "So what did you do when he said you didn't need to talk to a lawyer?"

"I didn't talk to a lawyer. I trusted him. Except I think that's wrong. I need a lawyer too. I mean Uncle Roy has one—rather, two; my sister and brother-in-law have one, but I don't have one. Why don't I have one? Who's looking out for me?"

"That's the question, Sir," Judge Mendoza said to Albert." He sighed and lit another Camel from the embers of the last one. He inhaled mightily and exploded in a coughing fit that all but rattled the window in his small office. "I think we're going to continue this matter for one week so Albert Turkenov can consult counsel. Any objections to that?"

"Well, I object," said Boomer. "I've made a trip all the way from Los Angeles today. I don't think we should stop at this point. He's had plenty of time to consult."

"You have no standing to speak on the record, Mr. Magence, so we're just going to ignore you."

Which was the wrong thing to say to Boomer Magence, a man who wasn't accustomed to being ignored, not ever.

"Ignore me? How can you say that! I'm sitting right here and I'm a lawyer and I have associated local counsel!"

"Did you not hear my earlier order, Sir? Your *pro hac vice* petition was denied. You are not admitted before this court. All right, everyone, anything else?"

"Then I'll report you to the Judicial Ethics Committee!" cried Boomer. "I'll have your black robe before I'm done!"

Judge Mendoza reached beneath his desk and hit the panic button. Then he said nothing but he returned Boomer's glare. Minutes later, four burly deputy sheriffs burst into the office. Their guns weren't drawn, but they were definitely ready to rumble.

"Officers, please remove this gentleman right here. He refuses to obey a court order and I feel threatened by him."

The deputies went immediately to Boomer and each grabbed a limb. Bodily they carried Boomer out of the room. In the outer office, he was placed on his feet and cuffed. The largest deputy returned.

"What do you want done with him, Your Honor?"

"Just take him out to the sidewalk and turn him loose. But explain to him that he is never to return inside this courthouse. If he does, I'll hold him in contempt and throw his butt in jail."

"Gotcha," said the deputy, and spun on his heel.

The remaining attorneys and litigants waited for the judge to catch his breath. Inside, Thaddeus was smiling. The last thing he wanted was that blowhard negatively impacting Dr. Sewell's Flagstaff jury. Good riddance, he thought.

Dr. Sewell sat with his head bowed, chin on chest, studying his long surgeon's fingers. He shook his head and broke the silence.

"That was unnerving," said the doctor. "I'm sorry that happened, Judge. I won't bring him into your courthouse again."

"Not your fault, Dr. Sewell. The law business is often tense and people lose it. Water under the bridge. All right now, we need to take up the matter of the joint conservatorship, so I'll move from the negligence case to the conservatorship case. Has everyone received notice of the petition for joint conservators? No? Then that's the first thing needs to be done. Give all family members and other interested parties notice of the proposed change. Once this is done, let me know. I may set it for hearing at that time and I may grant or deny the petition *sua sponte*. Is that all for now?"

"What about discovery deadlines on the negligence case?" asked Thaddeus. "Shouldn't we set that up?"

"Good question. Yes. Let's complete all discovery four months from today. Which puts us at October nine. Is that enough time everyone?"

Everyone acknowledged that would be enough time.

"Then we're in recess. Thank you, everyone."

One by one the litigants and lawyers filed out of the judge's office. The talk was subdued, following what all had just occurred with Boomer Magence. Thaddeus imagined he would never see the man again, and that was just fine.

17

BAT visited Interpol in Sicily. He spoke with Leonardo Nobilio, who told him how, recently, Interpol had arrested one of Sicily's most wanted criminals. Vito Asuncion Reynaldo was arrested and sentenced in Palermo to nine years in prison for external collusion with the Mafia. Reynaldo, who was the subject of an Interpol internationally-wanted persons Red Notice, was arrested in Bangkok 30 March by Thai authorities with the support of Interpol's Fugitive Investigation Support unit and Sicily's State Police. He had been returned to Palermo for trial and sentencing. There had been plea negotiations and the nine-year sentence resulted.

BAT listened to Mr. Nobilio explain all this at his office in Palermo overlooking the city square. BAT made his notes and then followed up with questions.

"Tell me, Mr. Nobilio, the name of the attorney who represented Mr. Reynaldo in the proceedings here in Palermo."

A slight, balding man with a thick mustache covering all of his upper lip, Leonardo Nobilio scratched his jaw, "Why not?" he said to no one. Then added, to BAT, "The lawyer is Edoardo De Filippo. He is known as *Lu Tacchinu*, which loosely translates to *The Peacock*, for his taste in clothing. Very show-offy. His office is here in Palermo.

While the file is sealed for the sake of our security personnel, please remember that you did not get this man's name from me. He is widely known as the Mafia's key legal representative here in Palermo, so if you were a regular in our city you would have known this and if anyone asks, you can ascribe your having Edoardo De Filippo's name to common knowledge. Do we agree?"

"We do," said BAT. "And let me thank you for that. Is there anything else you can share with me? Has this Lincoln Mascari crossed your radar yet?"

"No—no one by that name. Is there a picture we can run through our database?"

"No. But if I provide pictures, will you help me?"

"Definitely. Better yet, if you can provide fingerprints. Many of these hoodlums will pay hundreds of thousands for plastic surgery and change their looks totally. But their fingerprints—most never agree to that most excruciating pain. So I would begin there, with fingerprints rather than photos.

"I'll do that very thing. Thank you, Mr. Nobilio."

The man waved him off. "It's nothing. We are always ready to accommodate the good guys."

BAT grinned. "Thanks for seeing me."

"We knew about it when Mr. Murfee's three hundred million dollars entered Zurich. But after it went to the Caymans it was reshuffled and moved from there to Hong Kong in a thousand smaller pieces. We lost track or we would be able to do more for you."

"Zurich to the Caymans to Hong Kong? That probably wasn't the end of it, either."

"Definitely, would not have ended there, you're right."

"Well, thank you again."

BAT extended his hand and the two men shook. He then left the office.

He found a telephone book in his hotel room and quickly located the offices of Edoardo De Filippo. A twenty-minute cab ride from his hotel took him to the address. It was a street level office with a carved black door and windows with drawn curtains. He turned and looked back across the street and found what he was looking for: a downtown flophouse with very cheap rooms for rent by the week, day, or even hour. He headed over.

He waited for sunrise in Arizona and then called Thaddeus from his new room in the flophouse.

"I need another body over here," he told Thaddeus. "Someone we can trust with our lives. Literally, because these people are the real thing."

"Let me make a call or two. I'll get back."

∼

THADDEUS DIALED her number and waited. It was an hour later in Chicago and she would probably already be in her office.

"Chris? Thad."

"Thaddeus! I was just thinking about you and Katy. Are you all right?"

"I'm all right. Katy is slipping every day."

"I'm so sorry. You must be at wit's end."

"I am. Can't sleep. Don't want to eat anything. I've lost ten pounds, but I'd never tell Katy. It's killing me."

"I know it must be. I'm so sorry, Thaddeus."

"Thank you. Look, the reason I'm calling. There is a very bad man living overseas. BAT is over there having a look around for him. And we need help. Not just any help, either. We need someone we can trust with our lives and the lives of our families."

"Will we take your plane or mine?"

Thaddeus felt the tears come into his eyes. This one was a keeper.

"Let's talk about that."

Their conversation continued for another ten minutes on the scrambled phones. When they were done, it was all a neat, wrapped package and Christine herself would be in the air that afternoon.

∼

THE FRONT DESK paged and told him a Ms. Gulfman was there for him. Christine was quickly let inside the unremarkable hotel room by BAT. They hugged.

"Deserter," she said, for BAT had recently worked for her in Chicago.

"Still pissed at me?"

She smiled and laughed. "You are impossible to replace. Did anyone ever tell you that before?"

"No, no one ever told me that. But it's damn nice to hear."

"Well, you are. So what do we have going on here in Palermo?"

"There's a man."

She sighed. "There's always a man. What's he done?"

"Kidnapped Sarai."

She inhaled sharply and her back stiffened. "*That's* who this is? Wonderful! Do we know where he is?"

"No. We don't know what he looks like or what name he's using, either."

"Which makes it a bit more of a challenge but hey, I love challenges. Where do we start?"

"I've got a room across the street from the Mafia's Palermo lawyer."

"So our guy needs a lawyer?"

"We don't know that. We can only hope he does. But I think he's already used the lawyer."

"Well, sorting through people who come and go in the guy's office—that could take years before our guy shows up. There's got to be a better way."

BAT spread his hands. They were sitting at the small dining table at the curtained window in BAT's room. They had called out for coffee and pastries, which soon arrived, and they made their selections. Soon, they were chewing Sicilian pastries, and sipping cappuccinos. The friends were thoughtful and unspeaking.

Christine wiped her mouth with the linen napkin.

"Okay, so. How do we find a man with no known name, living

who knows where, wearing a surgically altered face? How do we even know that he's in Sicily?"

"Because all Chicago mobsters flee to Sicily. They just do."

"Okay, so we go online and get access to the records of all Sicilian courts. Then we search for Lincoln Mascari."

"Why would we do that?"

It was her turn. "Because all Chicago mobsters, when they flee to Sicily, change their names. You with me?"

BAT's eyes brightened. "Exactly! But how do we get access to Sicilian court records?"

Christine nodded. "I have some friends in Slovakia who can gain access to any computer system in the world. For a price."

Without waiting, she dialed a number in Bratislava from memory.

"Jozef? Ama Gloq calling. I need your help with a name."

Two hours later, Christine's cell phone vibrated. She answered.

"Okay, yes. Let me write that down."

She wrote three words on a sheet of hotel stationery. She held it up for BAT:

Salvatore Paulo Gaetani

"Can you help with an address for this man?"

More writing.

"All right. My office will transfer fifteen thousand USD to you tonight. Thank you, Jozef."

She clicked off and turned to BAT.

"The court record was sealed, but that proved no problem for our intrepid helpmate."

"So Lincoln Mascari is now Salvatore Paulo Gaetani?"

"Exactly."

"Do we have a location?"

Christine smiled. "My, you want the moon itself, don't you, BAT?"

"I do," he said and returned her smile.

"Termini. One hundred miles east."

"What else?"

"I have the street and house number. If they're still good. They were when the name was changed. They may or may not still be."

"Well, shall we find out?"

"Can I take a shower first?"

"Go for it. I'll see if there's a Starbucks down on the street. I know how much you need that stuff."

"BAT," she cooed, "how sweet that you haven't forgotten!"

"How could I? I kept you cranked on French Roast for two years by myself. I'll be back."

"I'll be ready by then. I won't be long."

"Later."

18

He would later say that, on his third visit to Nadia's room, he felt her soul rub against his like a friendly cat. At that moment, he opened himself to her. She spoke as one speaking across the universe yet close by, it felt.

She told him her body was always cold in the bed. She told him the nurses were rough with her when they turned her. And that her children would argue about money back and forth across her blanketed form. But most of all she missed the light. She didn't have to tell him which light it was, he would later say. He already knew.

He asked her how he could help.

Just set me free, she asked him. She wasn't pleading with him, patient to doctor. She was speaking as his equal, soul to soul.

When he recounted these things later, at the jail, Dr. Stoudemire —the jail psychiatrist—rolled her eyes and the corners of her mouth curled into a small smile. Or grimace. Outside the open door where he was being held while he met with Dr. Stoudemire, he heard his words whispered back and forth and stifled laughter.

So Nadia told him what she needed. He replied that he would talk to her family and see. He thought surely they would let her go.

But she wasn't so sure.

She had made a handwritten will and left it inside her desk at home. She had made it right before losing consciousness; it was only three lines at the end of her goodbye letter. But it left all of her money to a nursing scholarship she had created in the name of her beloved husband, Henri. All of it. The children had found the will when they created the inventory for her estate and they didn't want anyone to see it because they would get nothing if she died.

That's why they wanted her alive. There were huge conservator fees while she was alive. Her estate could even invest in their business schemes. There was no one who would object.

They wouldn't set her free.

Dr. Sewell would later tell the police it was at that moment he had promised to help her.

Sure, they said. Sure you did.

19

Dr. Sylvan Glissandos found both children with Nadia when she made her rounds Friday evening.

"What does all this mean, Doc?" said Albert, indicating the tubes and machines connected to his mother. "Are you going to be able to bring her back?"

The doctor shook her head.

"There is no one treatment that can bring your mother out of her coma. Treatments can prevent further physical and neurological damage, however."

"Like what are you doing?"

"Well, first I'm making sure she isn't in immediate danger of dying. The tube you see going into her throat is a ventilator. It does her breathing for her."

"She can't breathe on her own?"

"We don't know, so we ensure it. That's why we have her hooked up, to be sure she gets the oxygen she needs to stay with us."

"What else can be done?" Albert asked. "Is her insurance paying for everything she needs?"

"Insurance isn't my concern. So far I've gotten everything I've ordered. That much I can tell you."

"Such as?"

"CT scans and EEG. EEG is a test we do to test the brain's electrical activity."

"What does that show so far?"

"Well, there is no activity."

Anastasia took her mother's hand. "Meaning she is brain dead."

"Meaning that, perhaps," said the doctor. "Your mother is alive but there is little chance of regaining consciousness, Albert."

"But there's still some slight chance? Enough to keep her alive?"

"We can always have hope," said the doctor.

"What else?"

"Well, I've tested for meningitis by tapping her spinal fluid. No problems there."

"Who was that in here moving her arms and legs when we arrived?"

"Your mother gets physical therapy. This prevents long-term muscle damage. Again, the insurance company has made no objection and these are pretty standard precautions so far. She also receives electrolytes to help regulate body processes."

"What's the yellow tube down there?"

"A tube in her urethra to carry away urine. That's non-stop."

"Oh my God," Albert said, and his eyes clouded over. He began wiping tears with his shirt sleeve.

Doctor Glissandos laid a hand on Albert's shoulder.

"There, there, Albert. You just let it out. Mama might even hear you. That could only help let her know how much she's loved."

At that moment, Anastasia swore she saw her mother's eyelids flutter. But she didn't say anything. She knew that such movements could be involuntary. Still, it made her think her mother might actually be hearing them. So she began speaking softly into her mother's ear. No eyelid movements resulted.

The doctor left to resume her other rounds and just minutes later Jack returned with two coffees. He handed one to Anastasia and kept one for himself.

"So, our lawyers are talking?" said Jack.

Albert shrugged. "Guess so. I haven't heard from Ms. Roddgers."

"Wang called me. They've about got it all worked out."

"Am I going to be a conservator too?"

Jack looked away, thoughtfully considering how he might answer. "Not exactly."

"What's that mean? I either am a conservator or I'm not."

"You're going to be conservator of her person while Roy and I are conservator of her estate."

Albert's eyes narrowed. He looked at his brother-in-law with great suspicion.

"Meaning, you get her money and I get her?"

"Well, we don't *get* the money. We just take care of it."

Albert nodded. "Uh-huh. Sure."

"Hey, you can only have so many conservators, Al. Mr. Wang figures two is enough."

"And who appointed him Mother Superior?"

"Well...no one did. He's just trying to help all of us."

"This the same Wang who told me I didn't need a lawyer? That one?"

Anastasia turned from her mother and placed her hands on her hips.

"Look, you two," she said. "How about if *I* act as conservator of the person *and* the estate. Albert, you trust me and you obviously don't trust my husband."

"What about Mom's brothers and sisters? They tell me they want Uncle Roy for their part."

"They don't have a part. Nothing of mother's belongs to them."

"What if she dies?"

Anastasia shuddered and strode right up to Albert and locked her face inches away.

"That's our mother there, stupid. Don't say stuff like that. What if she's listening?"

"Sorry, Mom," Albert said foolishly. "I didn't mean it."

"Good God," said his sister. She stepped back. "So how about *I* do it?"

"Don't forget the goddamn will. The scholarship gets it all if—you know."

"Well," said Jack, "there are already expenses of administrative, legal fees and conservator fees. My time is valuable. I expect I have a hundred hours on the case so far."

"What! A hundred hours? For what, jacking off to pictures of hundred dollar bills?"

"Fuck off, Albert," cried Jack. "That's totally uncalled for!"

At which point Anastasia seized the arms of both men and steered them out into the hallway. She closed the door to her mother's room.

"Honest to God!" she cried. "How in the hell can you? Albert, if she dies, we get nothing. What about that don't you understand?"

Albert shuffled his feet and tried to avoid his sister's stare-down.

"I understand that if I were conservator I would get paid too. Isn't that better for everyone?"

Anastasia looked at Jack. "What about if her estate invested in your business? Would that satisfy you?"

"Maybe it would. I don't know. Maybe it wouldn't, either."

"All right, then you be conservator! Misappropriate her money if that's what it's going to take to shut you the hell up! Or buy yourself a new car! Only please shut up about it!"

Albert sniffed. "I'll call Ellen tomorrow and tell her we've decided that I should be the conservator."

"Hold on," Jack said to his wife.

"Jack—"

"What the hell, Jack, this isn't between you and anyone. This is between my sister and me!"

"But I'm the CPA!"

"Creepy. Pissant. Asshole. CPA to you!"

Jack doubled up his fist and took a swing at Albert. It caught him in the side of the throat. Albert staggered and came back with an uppercut. Miraculously, it connected with Jack's glass jaw. Jack crumpled to the floor and his eyes closed.

"Concussion!" shouted Anastasia. "You gave him a concussion!"

"Nurse!" Albert called to the nursing station just down the hall. "This man fainted."

"Like hell! This man hit this man!"

"But he swung at me first," Albert told the young nurse who was running to them. "He swung first!"

"What happened here?" the nurse asked. She turned and shouted back to the nurses at the station. "Someone call security!"

"All right, I'm leaving," Albert said, and he ran for the elevators.

"You better run, you bastard!" cried his sister. "We'll see you in court!"

Jack came around when the nurse broke a smelling salt under his nose. He clambered to his feet and leaned against the wall.

"Head hurts."

"There, there," said Anastasia. "I told you he might lose it. That's Albert. I warned you on the way here. But oh, no, you have to be Mr. High and Mighty CPA. What is it about those three letters that sharpens your lead anyway? What is it that makes your dick so hard you'd swing at my brother?"

"Head hurts. I need an X-ray, Nurse."

The second nurse to arrive, an older woman wearing her hair inside a net of some kind, placed the back of her hand against Jack's forehead.

"He's hot. We need a CT scan. Come with me, Mister. We need to go downstairs and get you admitted to the ER."

"Oh, shit," Anastasia said under her breath. "Oh, shit."

"Now there's no way I'm stepping down," Jack said. "I'm the conservator and Roy and Albert are going to have to sit on it. I'm not giving another inch!"

"We'll see about that. First let's get the CT scan and then we'll go somewhere quiet and talk it through. Come on, Jack."

"That's better. Talk nice to me, Ana. My head is throbbing."

"Please stop saying that. They'll admit you if you keep saying that."

"Well, it *is* throbbing."

"CT scan," said the woman with the netted hair. "Stat."

"Stat," said Jack, looking back over his shoulder as he went off with the nurse.

Anastasia stayed behind. She wanted to check on her mother and make sure none of what happened had reached through to her.

"Stat," she said. "Stat."

20

IT WAS an early day in summer when Katy saddled up Charley, her paint horse, and left the ranch. She was wearing Wrangler jeans, a light sweatshirt, and a Patagonia shell which, in the righthand pocket, carried a copy of Dr. Sewell's book, *The Doctor Is In...Heaven*. It was time for some serious reading and Katy didn't wish to be interrupted. She had loaded up on as much Demerol as she thought she could ingest and safely navigate the forest on her horse. And in her lefthand pocket were two more doses, just in case. Her cell phone was next to her book. It was turned off. This was a ride that Katy had made many times before, though never alone.

She was riding against her nurse's wishes. The older woman had raised holy hell when Katy told her she was going horseback riding. "Your spine is full of cancer," she clucked. "You'll break your fool back if you fall off and then where are we? We'll have to put you down!"

Katy shook her head and swung a leg up over Charley. The mount was more difficult than she remembered from her last time several months ago. Things popped and clicked up and down her spine and in her hip where tumors were eating away bone and growing every minute of every day. She tried not to think about the tumors in her spine as well; there were several. Enough! Her mind shouted. Just get off where you can read your damn book!

She and Charley began the climb up the mountainside at the foot of the San Francisco Peaks at about 7200 feet ASL. Her journey would take her up to about 11,200 feet. She knew that at 10,000 feet pilots were required to use oxygen inside their cockpit and, with a slight chuckle, she wondered whether the FAA would ever get around to regulating horseback riders and hikers who chose to ascend above the same altitude. Katy was not a big fan of governmental regulation as she had practiced medicine long enough to feel the crush of regulatory paperwork and HIPPA rules that, in the end, simply bled time away from patient care.

Charley wanted to stop and browse grass along the way. Katy kept her knees sharp in his shoulders to let him know she disapproved, nudging him onward.

Two hours later she was sweating and felt weak in her legs and hips, which she ascribed to the cancer. But still she urged Charley ever higher up the mountainside. It had been an incredible ride so far, and she realized that she had come here to say goodbye to the forest and mountains. She knew that she would never feel capable of making the ride again. In fact, even now, it was a tremendous challenge as the Demerol was definitely wearing off and she was definitely feeling more pain as she rode along. She considered another dose of the pain medicine but decided to wait until she reached her meadow.

Charley was a trail horse that Thaddeus had picked up from a riding club. He had wanted very tame mounts for the family, and Charley and Coco and the kids' horses were exactly that: long-term veterans of trail rides. They very easily picked their way through the ponderosa forests of Coconino County. It would be rare for Charley to be thrown off his normal gait and familiarity with the route he was to take.

Halfway up, cumulus clouds gathered overhead and it began raining. Thunderclouds rolled and rumbled and lightning flashes struck the peaks of the mountains. Katy moved underneath a 200-foot ponderosa and pulled up the collar on her shell. She reached inside her jacket and retrieved her bush hat from the inside pocket and snapped the cap open. It was large for her head and settled on her ears, which was fine, as it was now drizzling hard enough the cap was keeping the rain off her face. A steady stream began rolling off the brim of the cap and pattering harmlessly off her shoulders. She thought this would be as good a time as any for a snack, so she retrieved a Dr. Pepper and a tin of smoked oysters from her saddlebag. A handful of crackers, decorated with smoked oysters, was munched and chased down with Dr. Pepper.

She felt a chill run along her spine and thought it was the cooling air that had come with the overcast. Maybe it was, but she also felt the pain from her cancer hammering at her bones and wracking her head with excruciating pain. It felt as if alien fingers were probing her body and poking hard at the sore spots. She realized she had gone too long without her pain meds, but, damn it, she had been enjoying her ride and was even imagining she had been cured and was riding out to celebrate her freedom from pain and medication. It hadn't paid off; the pain had definitely run ahead of the meds and was now making her pay. She opened a dose pack and swallowed the meds. Dr. Pepper pushed them down her throat and she leaned in the saddle and put her head against the tree. She shut her eyes and waited. The pain was unrelenting, so she decided to ride on, figuring the activity would help get her mind off the pain until the pills overtook it. She nudged Charley onward and he resumed his climb. The rain was still coming down.

Twenty minutes later they made the meadow, and the clouds retreated. It was suddenly bright and sunny and the light beams were dazzling and the air warmed fifteen degrees. Katy unzipped her shell. She removed the bush hat. She shrugged out of the shell and laid it over her saddle horn and waited for it to dry. She turned and tucked the bush hat into her saddlebag.

Five feet ahead, a Black Rattlesnake slithered up out of its hole, seeking the warmth of the sunlight. It had been caught out in the rain and was returning to where it usually sunbathed. The Black

Rattlesnake was a common rattler in the Coconino National Forest. Usually, they were heard before seen and could be avoided. But not this time.

She moved Charley ahead and his right foreleg came down within inches of the Black Rattler's head, causing the snake to coil and rattle aggressively. Charley immediately rose up on his hind legs, pulling his front legs away from the threat, and in the ensuing tilt Katy was thrown off the back of her horse. She hit the ground hard. The impact knocked the wind out of her lungs and she lay in the grass and dirt gasping for air. Charley stepped ten paces to the right and dropped his head, the snake forgotten. He began browsing the grass.

Katy's breath returned and she moved to sit up. But she could only come up off the ground an inch until an excruciating pain slammed her back against the dirt. In an instant she knew: the spine had shattered when Charley bucked her off. There was no doubt in her mind, and she closed her eyes against the pain.

She tried rolling onto her side. She figured she would push up from there if she were going to manage any movement at all. But as she rolled, her legs stayed behind. They refused to move. She blinked hard, fighting back waves of pain and fear and she willed her legs to move. Nothing happened. The messages sent from brain to leg had been severed when the bones in her spine shattered. She was paralyzed.

On her back, unable to move, her phone in her jacket twenty feet away with Charley, she looked up at the sky and cried out for help. Yelling was all she had left, though to whom she was yelling she had absolutely no idea.

She tried calling Charley. He had never trained to the whistle or spoken name, so he ignored her, chomping the deep grass around his legs.

"Please, Charley," she pleaded. "Good boy. Come to me, Charley!"

Charley didn't waver in his quest for the delicious wild grass of the sunny meadow. He wandered even further off.

But one thing she knew beyond all doubt: Thaddeus would come for her. He would know.

Over the next hour, she watched as the clouds again gathered, and a cold, bone-chilling rain began pattering then pouring. She was instantly soaked. The shakes took her body and drove the pain to ten. Her thin sweatshirt was all but useless. She wrapped her arms across her chest and shut her eyes against the downpour. Within minutes, the rain was roaring down the mountainside in dancing rivulets of icy water. It ran up to the side of her face and entered her ear. She lifted her head off the ground and shook it from side to side like a dog. The water flowed back out of her uphill ear and she could hear again.

For what good hearing did. All around her, there was only chaotic noise between the lightning, thunder, rushing rivulets of icy mud and winds that never stopped at this altitude.

Her core heat was dissipating rapidly. She knew that when it was gone, she would go into shock and die. It was only a matter of time now.

She loosened her arms and lay them down beside her in the mud. Arms were useless to try and hold heat in.

She shut her eyes, clenched her hands into fists, and waited.

21

As Katy lay drifting into shock, attorneys Ellen Roddgers and Milbanks Wang were meeting with their clients, Uncle Roy Underwood, and Jack Millerton. They were sitting around the conference table in Wang's office, a table that did double duty as a coffee table and conference table. It was bounded on two sides by two love seats and on the other two sides by wingback chairs. Attorney Roddgers had one of the wingbacks and had placed her file before her on the table. It was closed. Attorney Wang had the other wingback and he was sitting with an ankle over a knee, drumming his fingers anxiously on the file in his lap. Uncle Roy was sprawled on the white brocade love seat, dressed in slacks and a short sleeve white shirt with black clip-on necktie, while Jack Millerton was elaborately spread out in the black love seat, his CPA's case lovingly beside him with its raft of papers, files, and books at the ready. He was poised to do some serious business this morning, just waiting for Wang to turn him loose on his new co-conservator, Uncle Roy.

More than anything, Jack wanted Roy to take a backseat to him. Roy, more than anything, wanted Attorney Roddgers to carry his water, to actually get down and fight for him, but he wasn't convinced she had that talent. Wang just wanted to get the whole mess over with. But, he needed some quick money to fund his injury cases and it looked like he could grab some fees out of Nadia's case without much trouble and quite soon. Still, he was beginning to regret he'd ever gotten mixed up with the squalling family and the exotic lawsuit against a doctor who had faced death and won. It wasn't your typical medical malpractice case like the brain damaged babies he preferred to represent in their lawsuits.

Round two, Wang thought. Here we go.

"All right," said Wang. "We have a petition for co-conservatorship and just this morning Judge Mendoza signed off on it. We need to decide which of you two gentlemen is going to walk on point for the conservator's lawsuit against Dr. Sewell. Uncle Roy? I would suggest it be my client, Jack, because of Jack's familiarity with the law. Would that be agreeable?"

"I think—" Uncle Roy began but Attorney Roddgers shushed him with a raised hand.

"We believe both men should walk the point, as you put it. Roy Underwood is a long-established businessman and knows his way around balance sheets and income statements as well as anyone."

"I take exception to that," said Jack Millerton, CPA. "Familiarity with one's own records in one tiny facet of business does not a CPA make. In that regard, yours truly is the pro. It should definitely be me."

"Wait a minute, I'm flashing on something here," said Uncle Roy. "The one of us that does it, he gets paid extra, am I right?"

"His hourly would be paid and if he's instrumental in prosecuting the civil action, why then, yes, he would be paid more."

Roy kicked the table then leaned forward and apologized. "I get it! Then I definitely want to be the one to do the suing. It's for damn sure I need the money. Besides, Nadia is my sister. Jack is just a son-in-law. No blood there."

Wang raised both hands. "Why don't we do this? Why don't we have Jack actually sign stuff and sit with me in court at the trial, subject to Roy reviewing everything. That way Roy gets his hours and has his say-so, but we still keep it streamlined with one main conservator for the litigation. And as far as additional hours, Roy, I'm sure your attorney and I can find other duties that can be assigned to you that will keep your billables up with Jack's. Fair enough, son?"

Roy's head bobbed side to side. "I think so. I think that sounds pretty darn fair."

"By the way, Roy, how is your sister?" said Wang as an afterthought.

"No change. Sleeping and drooling. Drooling and sleeping. She's getting bedsores even though they move her every hour. Some of it's pretty nasty looking stuff."

"And what about your wife, Jack; how is Anastasia doing?"

Jack sniffed. "I'm really the one you should be asking about. I've had to personally set up the accounting system for the conservatorship and no one's even told me thanks for that. Took all weekend, I might add. Twenty-some hours."

"What about you, Ellen?" said Wang. "Any luck with the bar journal ads?"

Roddgers opened her file and peered down at the top paper. She nodded. "I'm running ads in forty bar journals. I'm asking all attorneys with clients who have been injured by Dr. Sewell's book to please contact me."

"Forty," Wang said and whistled. "How much is *that* costing us?"

"Nothing," said Millerton. "I wrote her a check out of the conservatorship account."

"Is that right?"

Roddgers nodded. "That's right. Eighteen thousand dollars for a small ad in each journal. Forty of them."

"Holy shit," said Wang. "Excuse my French. How many responses do we have so far?"

Roddgers leaned back in her chair. It was taller than her and considerably wider. It reminded Uncle Roy of a skit from *Saturday Night Live*, the little girl in the grown-up chair. "So far we have zero responses. But I'm very hopeful," Roddgers added.

"Yes, there have to be other people out there who have been injured," said Wang, who immediately felt stupid for suggesting there were other nitwits out there who might purposely overdose so they could have a near death experience. The whole idea was absurd, but Ellen Roddgers had insisted that if they get more claimants involved against the doctor they could bring more pressure on his insurance company to settle. Wang looked at his watch. Nearly eleven. They had set aside a full hour for this tripe. Well, it was time to move in the direction he had in mind.

"Now here's the next order of business," Wang said. "I think it's time we pay ourselves some temporary fees." Translated: I need money to fund my injury cases right away.

"Out of Nadia's account?" asked Jack Millerton. "Don't we need a court order for that?"

Wang leaned in conspiratorially. "Ordinarily, I'd say yes. But where the key parties are sitting here together and everyone's in agreement, I don't see what harm there would be in doing it first and getting the court's okay on down the road."

"I could use some money," said Roy, always on the lookout.

"Too risky," said Roddgers. "We should ask Judge Mendoza to review a motion for fees."

"Well, I'm lead counsel," said Wang. "And I say we're going to do it. Not much at first. Say, five thousand each. Five thousand for Ms. Roddgers, five thousand for Roy, five thousand for Jack—"

"Plus my time doing the accounting last weekend—"

"Plus your time from last weekend, and five thousand for me. That's only twenty thousand altogether. We've been assigned the important task of taking care of one-point-two million bucks, so I think we need to keep ourselves paid up. It's an awesome responsibility."

"Well, show my continuing objection," said Roddgers. "But I sure as hell won't turn down Jack's check. Jack?"

"I can have them by this afternoon. The checkbook's right here." He pounded the side of his CPA case.

"Then it's done," said Wang. "Come by at four o'clock. We'll have the checks ready."

"Sounds great," said Uncle Roy. It was going to be a good weekend. There might be enough to pick up a used bass boat with a trolling motor and eighty horse Evinrude for out at the city lake.

"I'm sending out a letter that I disagree," said Roddgers. "So don't be surprised."

"But you will swing by for your check?" Wang confirmed.

"Of course."

Jack said, "I'll write the checks then I'm headed down the hill for Phoenix. It's about time to file quarterly returns for my clients and I'm up to here busy." Still, the five thousand was going to take a lot of pressure off his CPA practice that was forever tardy with getting its own bills covered.

"Let's wrap-up. I've got an eleven o'clock," said Wang. Anything to bring this to a halt. He stood without waiting for a response and strode back to his desk. Five thousand play dollars for doing jackshit, he thought. Screw the injury cases. He could pay those bills later. For now, he'd go to Amazon and buy something expensive and utterly worthless. It satisfied his inner child, a bellicose personality his analyst was always encouraging him to honor more. Maybe a short wave radio? His inner child had always wanted one of those.

He couldn't wait for his office to clear so he could pick one out.

22

It had alarmed Thaddeus, the call from his ranch hand. Thaddeus listened, got the gist of what was transpiring, and he called Katy's nurse. The nurse recounted how Katy had doubled down on her noon dose of pain meds. Then she had ridden into the mountains on Charley and was out there during the storm. She must be soaked. But even though she probably was wet, she still hadn't shown back up at home. Thaddeus had just finished up with his client Emerick Sewell, who just happened to be a neurosurgeon. "Come with me!" Thaddeus shouted and dragged the man out of the office. Together they left the office on the run and headed downstairs to the parking garage.

Twenty minutes later they were headed into the forest on Thaddeus' green ATV. They were still dressed in suit pants. Thaddeus had brought along his sat-phone. He dialed 911 on the way out. He figured the sheriff's rescue chopper would probably spot her from the air before he got to her on the ATV.

It was going on five o'clock and shadows were lengthening as Thaddeus veered crazily through the woods. Knowing Katy, she had ridden up to her meadow, which was exactly where they were headed. The steering on the ATV was very tight and sensitive and enabled Thaddeus to keep the throttle full on while dodging bushes and tree trunks. He glanced at Dr. Sewell, who had grabbed a helmet and was holding onto the panic bars for dear life. There were no seat belts, which terrified the doctor even more. "Don't worry, I've got this, Doc," Thaddeus reassured him, yelling over the rushing wind and whine of the engine.

"I'm not worried about you! I'm worried about these low-hanging branches. They could pop your head right off your shoulders!"

"Keep ducking! You're doing great!"

On and on they roared, both of them keeping lateral lookouts for any shape resembling a horse or a human. So far, though, there had been nothing, just an endless green pastiche of pine boughs and black trunks and swatches of blue sky overhead. Then they drove to the edge of the rain storm. There was nothing to do but keep going. The water was stinging their faces and slapping them around, but still Thaddeus kept the throttle open. "I've got clothes your size back at the ranch!" Thaddeus yelled. The doctor only nodded, hanging on, white-faced and praying out loud.

Thaddeus considered this with a jolt, the praying. He'd never had another man around him praying who wasn't a priest or a politician running for office. But what the hell, he thought. It sure can't make it any worse than it already is.

Then up ahead they could see through the clearing to the other side of the final hundred yards of forest. But no Katy, no horse, not at first.

Thaddeus raced the ATV to the edge of the clearing then backed off the throttle. Now they were crawling.

"Stand up, Doc. Time to take a look around!"

Dr. Sewell, still clutching the panic bar, stood and surveyed the vista before him. He was first struck by the beauty of the place, the serenity, the pulse of the wild place. His sharp eyes continued their sweep across the meadow. Then he saw it. A horse, standing at the far right edge of the field. Dr. Sewell poked Thaddeus' shoulder and motioned with his head. Thaddeus swerved and off they bolted toward the horse.

"I know that guy," said Thaddeus. "That's Charley, Katy's horse."

Charley looked up to watch the approaching ATV, a machine he'd seen hundreds of times and which was neutral in his mind. There was no fear.

Thaddeus jumped from the throttled-down ATV and ran up to Charley. He pulled Katy's shell from the saddle horn. He riffled the saddlebags and found her hat. Wet. She would be nearby.

His heart ached as he turned and looked back across the meadow. She was out there somewhere, down, probably injured and in tremendous pain. He shook his head, for he expected the worst, taking into account the degeneration of her spine and hip as the cancer devoured her. "Oh, my God," he said. "Oh, my God!"

The two men hopped back on the ATV and began working the meadow back and forth like a lawnmower. Dr. Sewell stood to watch and Thaddeus drove, his heart aching, afraid that the next part in the meadow grass would reveal her limp body.

"Hold it!" cried the doctor. "I think I heard something!"

Thaddeus immediately throttled back and they jolted to a stop as if hitting an invisible wall.

"There!"

"I hear it too," cried Thaddeus. "She's yelling my name!"

Dr. Sewell jumped from the machine and broke into a sprint. "Bring the ATV, Thad. We're going to need it."

Thaddeus followed hard on the heels of the running doctor. Thirty yards out, the man's hand shot up and he made the universal cut-throat sign. Thaddeus shut down the ATV and jumped off running.

She was spread-eagled on the ground. And she was a mess. Her short hair was matted with mud, her face stained and streaked where the flowing water and mud had changed her skin color to a tannish tint. Her lower half was twisted at a desperate angle from her upper half and Dr. Sewell again held up his hand.

"You're hurting, Katy, I know," said the doctor. "Please do not move."

Thaddeus dropped to his knees and put his face against Katy's. He remained there while the doctor began feeling her from the bottoms of her feet north. Then he pulled up the cuff of her jeans, revealing her ankle and shin. Withdrawing a ballpoint from his shirt pocket, he projected its tip and jabbed it into her shin—not hard, but hard enough to elicit a response. But there was none. He jabbed again. "All right," he said, "tell me when you feel this." He jabbed a third time. A fourth. Switching legs, he repeated the test. Nothing on either leg. Thaddeus watched all this, his heart in free fall. He was beside himself with grief and panic.

"I'm so cold," she moaned, fighting hard to stay awake. "Please get me up off this mud!"

Thaddeus looked down at the doctor, who shook his head.

"We need to leave her right here until that chopper arrives with a back board. She can't be moved without it."

"Thaddeus, I'm so cold."

Thaddeus was wearing his barn jacket, which he slipped off. Then he lay down beside her, stretching out fully along the side of her body, following her contours, and placed his warmth against her chill. The doctor covered them with the barn jacket, and he took the opposite side of Katy and did the same thing.

"Do you have any meds along?" asked Thaddeus.

"In my jacket. On the horse, if you can catch him."

"The jacket's on the ATV," said the doctor. "Be right back."

He returned seconds later, holding out the dose pack for her to see. "Can you swallow without water?"

"Yes. Give them to me please."

Dr. Sewell ripped open the dose pack and placed the pills in her mouth. She swallowed hard, choked, coughed, and swallowed hard again.

"Okay. I got 'em down."

Both men resumed pressing their bodies against her.

Ten minutes passed while Katy was nodding off with the new load of Demerol in her bloodstream.

Thank you God, Thaddeus thought.

Then the beating blades of the chopper could be heard. Dr.

Sewell jumped to his feet and wildly waved his arms at the bird. But there was no need: the chopper had them spotted and swiftly set down a safe distance away. Two burly EMTs ran toward them with a back board.

"I'm a neurosurgeon," said Dr. Sewell to the two men. "Her back is broken. She's paralyzed."

They nodded and began the touch-and-go of moving her onto the backboard. All four men were needed to bear as much of the weight without distance between hands as possible. Katy was unconscious the whole time. Thaddeus panicked. Was she even alive?

The EMTs hurried her to the helicopter.

"You coming?" said the husky Hispanic man. "*Vamanos!*"

"We're both coming. We'll leave the ATV, Doc."

"Sure."

The husband and the doctor clambered aboard and the chopper rotated off the ground. Immediately its skids were at treetop and the pilot brought its nose around for the Medical Center's helipad.

23

SHE TRIED OPENING HER EYES, but they didn't work. Faint glimmers of distant light filtered through her eyelids, but a scene wouldn't reveal itself. A faint electrical hum of a pump and monitors came from somewhere above her head. She twisted her head from side to side and tried to speak. "Unh," she managed. "Unh."

She tried her eyes again and they finally opened. It was dark in the room. She twisted again and saw poles and hanging plastic bags and tubes inserted at different points on her body. At just that moment she realized there was a tube in her throat and that the heaving, whooshing sound was a ventilator breathing for her. As a doctor, Katy had heard the sound many times before and it became clear to her: a hospital room, probably ICU.

Her lower back cramped, but there was little pain. She tried wiggling her toes and had no sensation of movement. Then she tried her legs; again, no sensation. A word came into her mind, but she knew it was worthless trying to speak. The breathing tube allowed no words from her.

She heard the drip of the IV in her left arm. It was inordinately loud, like a bass drum pounding. She knew she was hyper-sensitive and that was probably brought on by the meds. Pain med, she thought. And who knew what else?

Then she remembered. Charley, the paint horse. The Meadow. The rain.

She started crying and closed her eyes to staunch the tears. But still they came, a silent, tearing wail that couldn't be heard.

Hours later. Opening her eyes again, she looked for the nurse call button. Her hands patted the bed on either side. No button, no way to tell them she was awake.

Once again, she closed her eyes.

The IV did its work and she began lifting from the earth and floating blissfully through a ripple of soft morning sunlight.

Then she was out.

∼

SOME TIME LATER—WHO could say when—her eyes opened again. She could sense movement in the room as staff came and went and tube lights were shined into her eyes. Voices came near and moved back. Occasionally a hand or hands would hold one of her hands. Words would be uttered over her. A prayer. A man wearing a white collar. Another man, one she knew. He came near and kissed her forehead.

Thaddeus. The name came to her.

She tried to reach up to him, but he faded into the wall and was gone.

Tears came again. They were salty and hot as they found her mouth. The pillow beneath her head became damp.

It would be so easy to just let go and leave. She could feel her spirit bouncing against the shell of her body, straining to free itself. But she resisted.

It wasn't time.

∼

THREE DOCTORS in white frocks were peering down at her. They had worried looks on their faces and were talking low among themselves. One of them she recognized: Dr. Sewell. He said something and the other two doctors—a man and a woman—nodded and said something back. Then light beams entered her eyes and she felt someone breathing against her face as they peered into her eyes. The light flicked out and she was left with an afterlight that darted about as she moved her eyes.

"Nothing surgically to be done," Dr. Sewell's voice said.

"She *must* be stabilized," said the woman doctor.

"For the love of God, do something," a third voice pleaded.

Thaddeus. That was Thaddeus.

He was there for her.

24

Sicily - Late Afternoon

CHRISTINE STAYED in one place for too long.

They made her while she was parked across the street in a black Alfa Romeo. Her camera was directed at them when the taller bodyguard suddenly looked up, looked right at her, and pointed. Christine slumped down in the bucket seat, but it was too late: they had seen her. She realized what it was: the sun was directly behind them and she had been shooting into it. The lens flare had caught the guy's eye and drawn his attention right back along the barrel of the camera.

The taller bodyguard ran for his motorcycle. The smaller, olive-skinned man began running toward her. His hand reached inside his suit coat as if to retrieve a gun. Christine threw the car into reverse, spun the tires backing up, came forward in low gear, and squealed around on two tires as she made a U-turn and headed up Viscounti Street, going the wrong way on a one-way.

Within minutes, the taller bodyguard was on his Ducati and coming up behind. He wasn't wearing a helmet and in the rearview Christine could look directly into his eyes. His face was a mask of rage and yet his riding was controlled and certain. Her heart fell; the motorcycle would easily overtake her and he was undoubtedly armed. A mafia crime boss like Lincoln Mascari would allow no less.

Panicked and eyes darting ahead looking for an escape, Christine suddenly twisted the steering wheel hard to the right and the black car went up onto two tires as she came around the Hotel Termini. Its long, white scalloped fence and spraying fountain passed out of her field of vision and then she saw it ahead: an alleyway leading off to her right. She immediately braked full-on and the motorcycle behind her turned sideways as both brakes locked up and the machine skidded toward her, coming up close, resting right beside her bumper. She thought she heard it make contact but couldn't be sure.

She tromped on the gas and skidded into the handicap parking slot closest to the hotel's kitchen entrance. She slammed it into park, and darted for the door. The Alfa Romeo was left running, the key still dangling from the ignition. Christine couldn't have cared less: she was running for her life and knew it. If they managed to capture her, she knew she would give up Thaddeus if they tortured her. She had been tortured before and couldn't go through that again. So she ran.

∽

CHRISTINE AND BAT had located Lincoln Mascari in Termini by paying out substantial sums of cash. In the end, it was one of his own men who gave him up, though Mascari would never know about it.

The Chicago mobster, transplanted to Sicily, was living on a sloping promontory looking out over the ocean. Framed like the bow of some magisterial ship, the massive windows built out over the waves had seduced him. Mascari loved the windows at sundown, when he would stand before them with his mistress, both nude, champagne flutes in hand, allowing the rays of the setting sun to turn their brown skin golden in the evening glow and then dark and darker as sunset turned to night. By then their lovemaking was completed, the Demi bottle of champagne drained, and the cooks had appeared upstairs to prepare another enchanting French meal—

Mascari's favorite food—and to serve aperitifs. Dressed in robes and sandals, the lovers would stroll out onto the veranda and watch the groundskeepers light the gas torches around them and down along the walkway to the beach. His arm around her waist, her head against his shoulder, he was totally unaware that he was being watched from an adjacent home where the owners were in Rome and the intruders were accomplices of Thaddeus Murfee. For Mascari had kidnapped Murfee's daughter at one time, though the girl had been located and returned to her parents essentially unharmed. But during that episode, Mascari had made an enemy for life, which he had known, and he had fled to Sicily with Murfee's money. Along the way, he had purchased a new face and a new identity to avoid the retribution that would otherwise run him to the ground and leave him dead. Murfee was known to the Sicilian mob for his payback; several of their number had already lost their lives to the avenging lawyer.

Christine and BAT traded off at the spotting scope every hour. That night, when the fawning couple stepped out on the veranda, it just so happened that it was Christine's eye at the scope. While she couldn't be sure—due to his plastic surgery and the flickering gaslight—that it was Mascari, the sources they had bought and paid had reassured them. She decided that she would take what photographs she could and post them to Thaddeus' online account. He would be able to have his technicians review them and confirm whether Christine had found their target.

One thing they knew: the grounds were crawling with security—and not just any security. These were made men, Mafiosi who would stop at nothing to protect their meal ticket. Sawed-off shotguns were the norm and the premises were fenced and monitored 24/7. Whenever the target came and went, it was never just one vehicle making the move. Three—and sometimes four—vehicles came and went at once, windows blacked out, so Christine was never certain which she wanted to follow. As it turned out, she memorized the license plates and, over the ensuing days, followed them in turn. She cracked the code: Mascari had defeated his own system: he had a favorite. A black Mercedes driven by the tall bodyguard who made no effort to hide the shotgun and sidearm he wore whenever he drove. It was he who would eventually spot Christine and give chase. The bodyguard's name was Giuseppe Rele and he was the nephew of Lincoln Mascari. He had followed Mascari from Chicago to Sicily.

∾

INTO THE KITCHEN SHE RAN, and she heard, outside, the thump of the motorcycle and the sudden whine of its engine accelerating as it was dumped on its side still roaring. Running footsteps could be heard, and Christine ran down a service way and into a room with prep tables and huge ovens preparing dinner for the guests of the hotel. At the far end of the room, where the double doors endlessly swung in and out, hulked the smaller bodyguard in the black suit, the only person in the entire room paying any attention to her. He crouched as she ran toward him, ready to do battle. Four feet from his grasp. Christine suddenly left her feet, kicking her left shoe at the man's throat, catching him across the epiglottis, and causing him to tumble backward as she literally leaped over him and crashed through the swinging doors.

Ahead was a small hallway that opened onto the dining room. Off to her right was an open linen closet. She jumped inside, retrieved an apron, and swept it around her body, covering her shoulder to knee. In one spinning motion, she picked up a large circular serving tray and pushed back through the swinging doors she had just come out of as if she were just another waitress coming inside to pick up another dinner. As she stepped in, the tall motorcycle man pushed by her and continued his chase. She let out a huge lungful of air. Just as she contemplated: he hadn't been close enough to view her features; he had only known that it was a woman he was chasing. Not only that, he hadn't even known what she was wearing.

Christine retraced her steps to the back door, dropped the tray and stripped off the apron. Then she was outside and nearly free. Incredibly, the Ducati bike was still down with its engine racing. She darted to the bike, pulled on the hand caliper to release the clutch, and stood it upright. The bike outweighed her, but Christine could lift almost 200 pounds, so she leveraged it upright with her arms, back, and legs. Mounted on the seat, she spun the bike on its rear wheel and dug out of the parking lot.

Three blocks away she began paying attention to the color of the traffic lights. Up until then, it had been an all-out sprint. She relaxed somewhat and felt her way through the controls on the bike. The combination of fast throttle cam, poor fueling, and light flywheel made the throttle feel snatchy and more difficult to control. But it would do. She decided to keep the bike and ride it out to the house. From there she and BAT could decide what to do about the killer next door.

25

Dr. Sewell pulled into the hospital parking lot and left his rental in doctors' parking. It was just after six o'clock and he guessed that Nadia's visitors, if any, would be having supper and he might be able to steal a few minutes alone with her. He only wanted to pray over her.

The elevator doors opened on the second floor. Dr. Sewell stepped out and looked around. He was wearing a light sports coat, black slacks, and a nondescript necktie. He had a stethoscope draped around his neck. The duty nurses were gathered around the nurses' station. Dinner was being served by the cafeteria staff, the cart rolling slowly down the hallway as dinners were passed to those able to eat normally. Dr. Sewell strode confidently by the nurses, who ignored him, and continued to Nadia's room. He entered and paused.

It was dimly lit, the green and yellow LCD points of light from the monitor panel and ventilator glowing to indicate all was well.

But after he had glanced through the newest additions to her chart he knew all wasn't well. Brain scans indicated a complete failure of brain stem activity. The woman was medically dead. He walked up to her and squeezed her toes though the light blanket.

"Hello, my dear," he whispered. "I'm going to pray for you and would like for you to speak to me if you want."

Of course, there was no response. He crossed to the head of the bed and looked down at her.

"God, bless this child," he whispered.

The prayer continued.

When he had concluded, he went deeper inside his mind and, as was his practice, took the steps he deemed necessary to open his consciousness to hearing from her consciousness.

Thus, he stood, eyes closed and slowly breathing when Albert Turkenov and Ana Millerton suddenly entered the room.

"Hey, Doctor," said Ana. "How are we doing tonight?"

Dr. Sewell opened his eyes.

He shook his head. "She's gone, you know."

"Maybe not," said Albert. "We're hoping for a miracle."

"You're family?"

"Children. Who are you?"

Ignoring the question, he said, "Can I be totally frank with you?"

"Please do, doctor."

Dr. Sewell drew a deep breath. "Brain stem activity is totally absent. You'll not get your miracle at this point."

Anastasia stepped forward.

"Who are you?" she asked. "You're *not* one of her doctors, are you?"

He smiled and shook his head.

"No, I'm the doctor you're suing. I'm Emerick Sewell."

Albert moved closer.

"What the hell are you doing in our mother's room? I'm calling security!"

"No need for that. I'll leave quietly. Truth be told, I was praying for your mother."

"You should be, for what good that does," said Anastasia, her voice tight and angry. "You scam artists and your prayers. You can all go to hell!"

"All right, I'll leave. But first, may I ask you a question?"

Anastasia grimaced. "Can we stop you?"

"I just want to ask, why haven't you withdrawn her life support? I'm sure your doctors have explained the futility of keeping her body alive."

Albert stepped closer, his fists clenching.

"As if our family is any of your goddamn business!"

"You died and went to heaven and came back? I've read your stupid damn book. Doesn't that make you, of all people, think there might be hope for our mother?" asked Anastasia. She folded her arms across her chest and challenged the visitor.

"Totally different presentations, your mother and I. My case was just about as hopeless but something was different. I was supposed to come back."

"But you weren't brain dead."

"In fact, my doctor had just recommended to my wife that life support be withdrawn. She had agreed."

"But you woke up instead," said Anastasia. Her face was gathered in a frown. Dr. Sewell knew she was ready to do battle. Talking sense to her appeared to be out of the question, so he tried to step around. She sidestepped, remaining directly in his path. "Not so fast," she said. "We're not done here."

"What else would you like me to say? I'm more than willing to discuss."

"Why don't you tell your insurance company to pay our claim? Why fight us? Your book is misleading and caused our mother to follow the worst advice ever given by any doctor in the history of medicine."

"That's not my decision. I don't have any control over my insurance company."

"Sure you do. You can tell them what you want and they have to give strong consideration," Albert said suddenly. "There's a legal duty they owe you," he said, drawing on his one semester of academic training where he'd completed a business law course.

"I don't know about that, Albert. I only know what my lawyers tell me. But I can ask. That I can and will do. You have my word on that."

"Sure we do," scoffed Albert. "Just like my mother had your word on her chance to visit heaven. Pure bullshit, Dr. Sewell!"

The doctor edged around Anastasia, but now Albert was blocking him from leaving. He stopped, realizing they weren't done. So he decided to take the initiative.

He asked, "Why won't you let her go? I'm getting the definite feeling there's money involved here. Am I right?" He knew it was a risky thing, broaching the key subject head-on. But they had left him no choice except to question their motives as he had been told by Thaddeus that her will left all her money to charity, so the kids had a financial interest in keeping her alive.

"That is not open for discussion. Our mother's finances are off-limits for you. Our mother's case is off-limits to you. In fact, why don't you just leave? I oughta call security on you anyway, bastard," said Albert angrily. However, he did step aside so the doctor could pass.

"I'm sorry about your mother," Dr. Sewell said, walking to the door and pausing before he left. "If I caused her to be in this condition, you'll never know how sorry I am."

"Well, you did, Doctor," Anastasia said. She shook her head. "You really need to print a retraction. That book of yours is very dangerous."

"Food for thought," said Dr. Sewell. "Food for thought."

26

They removed Katy's breathing tube on the seventh day. It came out with a cough and a gasp for air directly into her lungs. Katy lay back and listened to herself breathe normally without a machine pumping air into her. The silence was precious and she said a prayer of thanks. She looked to her left. Thaddeus was there, watching her.

"Hey," he said.

"Hey, yourself." Her voice was an octave lower and gravelly.

"Dr. Sewell is coming in to talk to you."

"He doesn't have to do that. He's not my doctor."

"He wants to. Now that the tube's out, you can ask your questions."

"Let me sleep for now. The tube ordeal was too much."

∼

Dr. Sewell arrived an hour later, and Katy awoke with a start to find him standing at her bedside, examining the monitor on the wall.

He turned to her when he realized she was watching him.

"Hey, Doctor."

"Hey, Doc."

"Katy, I've been a practicing neurosurgeon and I've seen thousands of spinal tumors. They're always excruciating. You must be in terrible pain. Your paralysis is probably taking away some of that."

Katy was flat on her back on the bed, no pillow. The surgeons and neurologists were waiting for the swelling in her spine to subside. Nothing could be done with the swollen tissue so they had immobilized her and were treating only the pain.

"I know," she moaned. "From about belly button down there's nothing. But I'm out of it—meds working."

"You go ahead and be out of it, honey," said Thaddeus from his bedside chair. "Everything is under control at home. The kids are eating and getting to school on time. Homework is getting done. Rooms are somewhat decent. Most of all, we're in your corner."

She grimaced and raised her hand. "Kiss it," she said of her hand. "Make it better."

Thaddeus took her hand and pressed it against his face. Then he kissed it and gently placed it on the light blanket. "Love you, Biscuit."

"Let me update you, Katy," said Dr. Sewell. Your back is broken in several places. They've told you that. Your hip is broken. The plan is to put a plate in there."

"What about the back, doc?" asked Thaddeus.

"For now, no surgery. The treatment of metastatic spinal tumors usually involves a team of surgeons, radiation oncologists, medical oncologists plus diagnostic and interventional radiologists and on and on. The goal would be to manage the pain. In general, extensive surgical procedures involving open surgery are avoided with metastatic spinal tumors."

"Why is that?"

"Because open surgery increases the risk of systemic complications."

The doctor looked at Katy, whose eyes were closed and whose breathing was shallow as if sleeping. He whispered, "It hasn't been proven that survival is extended with aggressive treatment. Especially where expected survival is less than six months."

Thaddeus turned away and looked out the window. He folded his arms across his chest and hung his head, not wishing to turn back around and face Dr. Sewell.

"But here's what we can do. Radiation therapy is effective in shrinking tumors. This can alleviate pain by relieving pressure on nerve roots and the spinal cord. This is what I would recommend when the treating physician lists out your options."

"But that doesn't help her to even sit up does it? I mean, what about it—will she ever have any mobility again?" Thaddeus turned and spread his arms wide as if pleading.

"There's a procedure that involves inserting a needle through a small incision in the back so that a bone cement can be inserted into a fractured vertebra to fill in the empty spaces. This helps stabilize the bone."

"What's that called?"

"Vertebroplasty. It can alleviate pain up to seventy percent if nothing else. Which is dramatic and very helpful in your wife's case."

"So she's never going to walk again. Is that what I'm hearing?"

"Thad, she's paralyzed. I know you know that."

"I know. I'm just—I'm just—" He slumped in his chair. It was more than he could even begin to contemplate. His incredible wife was fading right in front of him and he was powerless to stop it! A moment of panic swept over him and he fought to keep it down so she wouldn't see.

"You just don't want to accept it. That will come too."

"Will she be able to sit up if I help her?"

"Somewhat. No one can say for certain at this point."

Katy's eyes fluttered and she reached for the plastic drinking cup. She was able to raise her head with Thaddeus' help and take two swallows. Then she abruptly fell back asleep.

"We can talk more," said the doctor, "but we don't need to do it here."

He motioned at Katy with his head, and Thaddeus understood.

"Thanks, Doc. You know what? I think I'm just going to sit here with her for awhile. You don't have to stick around."

"No, I need to be getting back to San Diego."

"Well, thanks for coming over. I have a much better grasp of the facts of your case now. And thanks for the help with Katy out there on the mountain."

"You handled that very well yourself, Thad. I was glad to do what I could."

"We'll talk in a week or so."

"Don't hesitate to call me with any questions. Day or night, I'm available to talk."

"Okay. Thank you."

Thaddeus stood and extended his hand and the men shook hands. The doctor gave Thaddeus a warm look. Thaddeus turned away and collapsed into the chair. When he looked up, Dr. Sewell was gone.

Ten minutes later, Thaddeus had dozed off. Suddenly he was awakened by someone shaking his shoulder. He opened his eyes.

"Turquoise!" he exclaimed.

"How is she, Dad?" said his daughter. Her lips were trembling. She handed Thaddeus a thermos of coffee and bent to her mother. "Oh, she looks so innocent."

"She's pretty banged up."

"They said she fell off Charley?"

"Yes. She heard a rattler and the next thing she knew she was on her back looking at the sky."

"Poor baby," said Turquoise, and took her mother's hand. She massaged the palm and fingers, all the time studying her mother's face. "Thanks for sending the plane, Dad."

"What about school? Is this going to mess you up?"

"No," said Turquoise, shaking her head. Her hair lay on her shoulders in two braids and they swung as she moved her head back and forth. "I'm ahead in everything. Besides, I don't really give a damn if it does cause problems. This is my mom and I want to be with her."

"Agree. You can always go to school."

"Exactly. Now tell me about her injuries. Someone said she fractured four vertebrae?"

"They're not exactly sure. They're having trouble getting clear images and don't want to move her much to do it. But she's in a lot of pain, which they're managing with meds. Right now she's either asleep or passed out. Maybe both, I don't know. I think the dose is pretty high."

"The kids are all at home? Who's with them?"

"Katrina from the office picked up her little girl and she's out at the ranch keeping an eye on things."

"Her little one's Celena's age? Eight or nine?"

"I guess. I just know Celena idolizes her. So does Sarai, for that matter."

"What about Parkus? Does he have anyone?"

Thaddeus smiled. "Now he does. You."

"You want me to go out there now?"

"How'd you get here from the airport?"

"Taxi."

"Let me call the ranch. I'll have Emanuel bring the truck and pick you up."

"So you're staying here?" She saw the look on her father's face. "Dumb question. Okay, Dad."

He reached and pulled her down and kissed her forehead.

"I'm just glad you're here," said Thaddeus. His voice was husky and low.

"Me too."

Thaddeus was on his cell phone a minute later, making arrangements.

Turquoise went to the end of the bed and grasped her mother's toes beneath the blanket. She slowly shook her head and tears formed and streaked down her cheeks.

"Why did you have to ride Charley? Now, of all times?"

"Because that's who she is. Fiercely independent even if it kills her."

Turquoise looked at her father.

There was no taking back the words and they both knew it.

27

THE PAIN TOLD her that she was dying. She could actually feel the tumors that had metastasized from the breast cancer and spread in her body. The thoracic spine tumors were the worst: she could find no possible position to get comfortable and sleep. Sleep only came when she was heavily medicated and then it would overtake her and leave her dreamless for a few hours until she would awaken drowsy, drugged, and feeling like she hadn't slept at all.

One afternoon in the hospital she was waiting for the nurse to come around and increase the dosage of the pain meds hanging above and behind her. She clicked the button again. She was angry that help hadn't appeared immediately and now it was five minutes and still no response.

So she shut her eyes and began counting. It was all she had left, counting. Her body could offer no further resistance to the disease that was killing her. Her psyche could spend no more time dwelling on her impending death and dealing with the terror. Her mental state had deteriorated to the point where she no longer cared; she only wanted out of the body that was failing her, the body that had turned her over to the tumors.

So she counted some more. It was a useless act: there was nothing she was counting. She was just counting because there was nothing else.

She shut her eyes.

However much later it was, she didn't know. Maybe a minute, maybe ten. She honestly didn't know.

When she opened her eyes she was at the water's edge, kneeling on the beach, digging with the sand shovel, building a sand castle. She stood up and her belly protruded. Like a child's belly, the belly of a little girl. She felt her arms. They felt like taut rubber; the arms of a little girl. She held out her hand. Yes, said her mind, it was a child's hand.

Which was good.

So she turned back to digging. Every so often she would wade into the surf and fill her bucket. It was her favorite bucket, the one with the bubbly whale on the side. Half-full of ocean water, the bucket was then poured into the trench she had dug around her castle. She had seen something like it on TV. She knew that people with castles kept water around them.

A man came up to her. He looked familiar.

But she didn't know him.

"Hello, Biscuit," he said to her.

Someone had called her "Biscuit" before. But she didn't know who.

She looked up at him and smiled.

"Want to walk?" he asked and held out his hand.

She nodded. More than anything else, she wanted to go with the man.

Together they strolled off down the beach. She cast a long look back over her shoulder. There was no one else to be seen. It didn't occur to her there were no other people. Nor was she worried.

In fact, she felt a great joy come over her as she walked along with the man.

In celebration, she pulled free of him and ran into the surf. Her feet kicked up fleece and foam with each pattering step. The man followed. He rolled his trouser legs up to his knees and began trotting after her. He caught up and seized her by the hand. Together they walked into the deeper water. She lay out in the water and he pushed her by her feet. Then she folded in half and came up laughing. Now the surf was breaking just beyond them and the water was swirling up to her chest. The man's pants were wet and baggy.

"Hungry?" he asked.

She nodded.

They left the water and walked further up the beach to the hamburger shop. It was a square green structure with exterior shutters that were pinned up and open because it was doing business.

She stepped up to the counter and smelled the cooking food. Suddenly she wanted one of each.

"—and a daylong sucker," she finished, after relaying a long list of what she wanted.

The man behind the counter looked at the man who brought her there. He shrugged. "Give her whatever she wants."

She tossed her head and did somersaults across the hot sand. Then she took the man's hand and ran around him, making him spin and laugh with her. Faster and faster they went, spinning and laughing. Then she stepped inside the imaginary circle and gave him a hug. She felt his strong hand in the middle of her back. He was patting her.

The food came and they loaded up with carry trays and headed back toward the sand castle.

~

THE LIGHT ROSE in the sky. The sand was quite hot on her feet. She spread her towel and leaned back on her elbows. The man sat down beside her, she on the towel, he in the sand. His pants were still rolled up and wet up to his waist. He seemed not to mind in the least, which was different from how she knew most adults to behave. Then she realized, she couldn't remember any of their names. But they spoke to her.

"One thousand and four," she said in a strange voice.

"One thousand and four what?" the man said. "Are you counting?"

"—Thousand and eight—"

"You must like to count very much."

The light was just over the ocean and going down.

The man scooted closer to her and took her hand. He looked at the tiny lines in her palm.

"What are you doing?" she asked.

"Committing to memory," he said and continued looking at her hand.

"Do you have a dog?" she asked.

He shook his head. "No dog."

"I have a cocker spaniel. His name is Woofers."

"Woofers. I like that."

"One thousand and thirty-five—"

"There you go again."

The light was setting behind the ocean.

She stood and put her hand on the man's shoulder. He didn't move. Then she smiled and nodded. She turned and began walking toward the sea.

When she felt the water on her feet, the light blinked on and off and on. She continued walking into the sea.

"Oooooh, Did I overdose you?" a voice said.

She struggled to open her eyes.

"What?"

The nurse flicked her index finger against the plastic bag. "This thing isn't feeding. Wait here and I'll grab a new one."

Katy looked at the woman's back as she hurried out the door.

There was no pain. There were no drugs in the line threaded into her hand, either.

"Two thousand," she said, and dropped her head onto the pillow.

She was no longer afraid.

28

AFTER VISITING WITH KATY, Dr. Sewell left Thaddeus alone with Katy.

Dr. Sewell stepped into the hallway and looked both ways. Then he walked down four doors and entered. The patient was Nadia Turkenov.

There was no one else in the room. The doctor studied her at the bedside. She looked frail and, since he had first visited her many weeks ago, her skin had turned ashen, a sure sign, to his eye, that she was not thriving. And, he thought with a shake of his head, who would be? He reviewed her chart quickly; he set it back down, shaking his head.

The ventilator was attached, of course. It was breathing for her, the familiar "Shush-shush-shush of the machine as it delivered oxygen to her lungs. Without the machine, she would die. He knew this and, in studying her and watching, he made a decision.

Taking her left hand in his—he was on the far side of her bed, next to the monitors and pumps—he felt her pulse. It was regular and strong. He lightly stroked the back of her hand with his fingers.

Then he closed his eyes and did not move, still holding her hand. This continued for several minutes.

Finally, he opened his eyes and lay her hand back down beside her on the bed.

At the Medical Center, mechanical ventilators were designed to generate alarms when patients became disconnected or experienced other critical ventilator events. However, those alarms could blend in with other common sounds of the ICU. Ventilator alarms that went unnoticed long enough would result in permanent harm to the patient or death. So FMC had developed a system to monitor critical ventilator events through the hospital network. Whenever an event was identified, the new system took control of every computer in the patient's ICU unit and generated an enhanced audio and visual alert that there was a critical ventilator event and identified the room number. Knowing this, and knowing what would happen if the ventilator failed or were shut off, Dr. Sewell proceeded otherwise.

With his surgeon's skilled hands, he removed the dressing and unplugged the ventilator coupling from the throat of Nadia Turkenov. With his hand, he then mimicked the back pressure against the hose that would exist were the ventilator actually attached to the patient.

Five minutes later, he again felt for Nadia's pulse. It was much weaker.

He repeated another five minutes.

As this was going on, Nurse Charlotte Mendoza approached Nadia's room. She came up to the door and was about to enter when, feeling instinctively at her neck, she realized she had left her stethoscope in the previous patient's room when she had helped a child listen to her mother's heart. Nurse Mendoza turned on her heel just before entering Nadia's room and circled back down one door.

Dr. Sewell sensed someone about to enter, but still he manipulated the ventilator hose so that no alarms fired.

Several minutes later, Nurse Mendoza came barreling into the room. She paused when she saw the doctor there.

"Family?"

Dr. Sewell shook his head. "Just a friend."

"I've seen you here before."

"I have two friends in this hospital. Plus, I am a physician."

As Mendoza's eyes passed from the doctor to the patient, she then realized the ventilator was detached from the patient. She screamed and pushed the doctor aside. Tearing the free end of the hose out of his hands, she reconnected the patient's life support. The doctor backed away and went to the foot of the bed. He watched as the nurse checked vitals. There was no pulse and no measurable blood pressure. That monitor had been shut down, Mendoza realized.

She screamed and re-armed the monitor then hit the panic alarm on the monitor board.

"You did this!" she screamed at the doctor.

"I did. But she's free now. She asked me to set her free! You'll just have to trust me."

She screamed again.

"She's free now."

Security, nurses, and two duty physicians came crowding into the room.

"He did this!" Nurse Mendoza screamed. "This man unhooked this patient from her life support!"

Security grabbed the doctor from behind and handcuffed him. He offered no resistance.

As they surrounded him and checked for weapons, he said to the blue-shirted officers.

"Please. Let me speak with your supervisor. I can explain where she's gone."

"Sir!" said the youngest officer. "She's on that bed!"

The doctor smiled. "No, that's only what your eyes are telling you. Nadia Turkenov is actually gone from here, gone from this room, gone from this hospital. I can explain!"

29

THEY PUT him in an isolation cell. They wanted to evaluate him before introducing him into the general jail population. They explained there was blood testing to be done to make certain he wasn't a threat to the other prisoners: AIDS/HIV and Hepatitis-C. What they didn't tell him was they wanted the jail psychiatrist to evaluate him. As the arresting detective phrased it, he had given some "Pretty damn off-the-wall explanations for what he's done," in unhooking Nadia Turkenov from life support. There was a legal duty to protect the other inmates from a crazy one, and the jailers were taking no chances.

"She asked me to release her," Dr. Sewell told the jail psychiatrist.

The psychiatrist, Nancy Stoudemire, was a humorless little woman all of five feet tall with gray hair she kept pulled dramatically away from her face and gathered in a ball on the back of her head. She gave away no reaction to the neurosurgeon's words. She was cool and she demanded of herself that she be that way.

"She was hooked up to life support, Dr. Sewell. So how did she speak to you?"

Dr. Sewell touched the side of his head. "Here."

"Here? What does 'here' mean?"

"It means she spoke directly into my mind. No, wait, don't write that down! Let me finish before you characterize my response as cuckoo. Her consciousness was waiting inside her broken body for the opportunity to return to the universal consciousness. Her consciousness was frustrated and knew there would be no recovery of the physical body. There had been no brain activity for ten days; her consciousness was aware of this, of course. So, let's just say I was recognized as a kindred spirit when I cleared my mind and invited her to speak to my mind. She accepted."

"And that's when she asked you to set her free?"

"Yes. Exactly that."

"What words did she use?"

"'Set me free,' something to that effect. It was very moving, very impassioned. She also asked me to be her doctor. She said the other doctors hadn't listened to her desire to be set free."

"So, based on that, you unhooked her from life support?"

"Yes. There was nothing else to be said after that."

"Dr. Sewell, please don't take this the wrong way. But I have to ask. Have you been in communication with other voices in your head in the past?"

Dr. Sewell leaned away from the steel table. He shook his head, obviously put off by the intention of the question, the suggestion that he was hearing things like a schizoid personality would perhaps hear things. The old voices coming through the fillings in the teeth, kind of thing. The CIA is talking to me through my radio, kind of thing. But Dr. Sewell wasn't going to allow the staff shrinks to treat him that way.

"Please," said the neurosurgeon. "Please don't try to reduce my awareness to a lowest common denominator such as cuckoo. The words of Nadia Turkenov were real and they were precise. 'Set me free,' she said. Plain as the lines in your palm."

"All right. Well."

The psychiatrist busied herself with note-writing. Her lips moved as she wrote, pausing occasionally to smile across the table at Dr. Sewell.

Then she added, "So, we can say, as a baseline, that you ended the life of the victim because voices told you to?"

"Not voices. Voice. And it's not a voice you hear with your ears. It comes directly into your brain."

"So you don't actually hear the voice. You just receive it. Like a radio."

"But without hearing. These are not aural hallucinations, Doctor."

"No, no, no, I hear exactly what you're saying. Now, have you spoken with a lawyer since this incident?"

Dr. Sewell shook his head. "I haven't spoken to anyone but you and my agent. I called my agent and told him I was in trouble."

"When you withdrew the victim's life support, would you say you knew what you were doing?"

"Of course, I knew. I'm a physician just like you. I knew I was doing what someone should have done before. I was doing what the patient asked me to do as her doctor."

"You knew you were ending her life?"

"Of course. But just the physical body. The consciousness would continue to exist."

"Well, that's probably enough for now. I'm going to recommend that they keep you single-celled at this time. We'll need to follow you for a few days."

"Afraid I'm a threat to others?"

The psychiatrist grimaced. "There's no denying you've already taken one life. Caution is indicated."

Dr. Sewell got up from the table. He went to the wall, placed his forearm at eye height and leaned his forehead into his arm. "Damn, damn, damn. This is going to be hard."

"Going to be hard? What, your case?"

"Yes. I'm in trouble because nobody understands."

"No, nobody will understand."

"It's time for the truth to come out. That's what my trial is going to be about. The entire truth about human consciousness. What happens to us when we die."

"All right. Well, good luck with that, Doctor."

"Please. Don't condescend. There's no need. What I'm talking about is good science."

"No, I sincerely wish you good luck. At this point in time we all need some good news. Maybe you're the one who has the inside track."

Dr. Sewell kept his head planted against his arm.

"Goodbye," said the prisoner. "Thank you."

"We'll meet again in a day or two. One last question. Are you on any medications?"

"Nothing."

"All right. We'll talk later, then."

"Goodbye."

30

THADDEUS WAS asleep in the chair beside Katy's bed when the call came. He looked at his cell and saw the number calling: COCONINO COUNTY JAIL. He stepped out into the hallway, leaving Katy asleep. Before answering, he stretched and yawned mightily. He wasn't sure how long he'd been with her, but he was sure he wasn't leaving her side. Not like she was.

"This is Thaddeus Murfee."

"Thad. Emerick Sewell."

"Why are you calling me from the jail?"

"You didn't see me being dragged out of the hospital while you were with Katy?"

"They were bathing her after you left. The door was closed. What happened?"

"I went down to Nadia Turkenov's room."

"The woman who's suing you? What the hell did you go there for?"

"I've been going there off and on, praying for her."

"Okay. So what happened?"

"I went into my superconscious state and she came to me and asked me to set her free."

Long silence.

"You just told me you went into superconsciousness. That gives me pause."

"What, you don't believe me?"

"Doc, I don't know what to make of you at all. All this stuff about consciousness and going to heaven and now you're into heavy meditation and you were meditating—in her room? Was that it?"

"Sort of. My consciousness was heightened. She came and asked me to free her. She told me I was her doctor now and I was to respect her wishes."

"Ms. Turkenov asked you?"

"Yes."

"To set her free? So what the hell did that mean?"

"I withdrew her life support."

"Hold on. You're not at the jail as a doctor?" He said it as a statement, not really a question. "You're telling me you've been arrested?"

"Exactly. They tell me the District Attorney will be charging me with murder."

"What? You withdrew—never mind. Emerick, I'm here with Katy. You know her situation. I can't leave her to come help you."

"That's why I'm calling. I don't know any other lawyers here in Flagstaff."

"Just sit tight. I'm calling my friend Shep Aberdeen. He's Flagstaff's finest criminal lawyer."

"You're Flagstaff's finest criminal lawyer. That's what my agent told me."

"Yeah, whatever. Look, I'm calling Shep. But remember this one thing: do not talk to anyone there. Not the jailers, not the DA, not the sheriff or detectives, not even your cellmate. Especially not your cellmate. You reading me?"

"I am, Thad. Loud and clear."

Thaddeus hung up and called Shep. Shep showed little interest in visiting with Dr. Sewell, but finally agreed when Thaddeus suggested they might work the case together.

"How would that work?" asked Shep.

"You do the procedural; I do the substantive."

"What the hell does that mean?"

"You do court and motion practice, I'll handle the trial witnesses and arguments."

"Can this guy afford to hire us both?"

Thaddeus chuckled. "He's been a neurosurgeon ten years longer than I've been a lawyer. My guess is, things are looking up at Bank of America."

"All right. I'm still at the office so I'll hoof it down to the jail and put him to bed. Any chance we could both talk to him sometime tomorrow?"

Thaddeus was hesitant. "You know, I just can't leave Katy right now. It's really touch and go."

"What's going on? I hadn't heard."

They discussed the horse ride and Katy's injury. Shep said he would send flowers to the hospital and Thaddeus didn't argue, even knowing that Katy didn't care for flowers all that much and had already made him promise there would be no sprays at her funeral.

He hung up and walked back inside her room.

"Who's that, Thad?" she murmured.

"You're awake. How we doing?"

"Same old same old. Pain, then drugs, then groggy, then sleep, then pain wakes me up. You don't have to ask anymore, Honey. I'm always at one of those five steps."

"All right."

"Was that Turquoise calling?"

"No, just a client."

"They have your cell number?"

"This one does. Emerick Sewell."

"He was checking up on me?"

"Yes. He wanted to know how you're doing. What should I tell him next time?"

"Tell him about the five steps."

"And have you decided on the back procedure?"

"Yes, I want the glue but nothing else. I figure the back glue will take away some of the pain, which will let me take fewer meds, which will let me be more alert around you guys when I get home."

Thaddeus sat in the chair beside her bed. He rubbed his face with both hands, thinking.

"Yes, I talked to Dr. Torres about going home," he finally said.

"When do I get out?"

"He doesn't think it's such a good idea for you to leave."

Silence. More silence.

Then, "Well, that's not gonna happen. I am going home and you're going to take me!"

"I knew you'd understand. That's what I told him."

"Tell me you'll take me home."

"I will take you. Let's get the glue injections in the broken vertebrae first. Then we can go."

"I want the glue tomorrow."

"Actually, they came in while you were asleep. They're doing the glue early tomorrow morning."

"Dr. Tomasik?"

"Yep. He came in too. They're doing four regions in your back. It should only take two hours, he said."

"And then what?"

"Then you have to stay still for twenty-four hours. Then I'll bust you out."

"You damn well better, Thaddeus Murfee. I'll never forgive you if you leave me in here."

He reached over and rubbed his hand against her cheek.

"I'd never leave you here. You want to go home, you're going home."

"I knew you would take me."

"But no more horses. And you have to do what the nurses tell you. I'm serious, Biscuit. No more screwing around."

"I promise. Just get me the hell out of here. I hate hospitals."

"Me too. So. Let's see what's on HBO tonight."

"I'd rather just lie here. Why don't you go home and sleep? Tomorrow morning will be here way soon now."

"No. I'll be staying right here. I don't mind just sitting here in the dark, being near you."

"I'd like that. But there is something I want to talk to you about."

"Oh, God. What now?"

"Don't say it like that. I'm serious, Thaddeus. I need to tell you this."

He sighed. "All right. Out with it."

"After I'm gone, I want you to be with Christine."

"Christine? *Our* Christine?"

"She loves you. I can tell by the way she looks at you."

"Don't even say that! There will be no one else for me."

"Thad, get real. We've got four kids. They need a mother."

"Christine is a lawyer."

"Oh, yeah? Ask her what she'd like. You might be very surprised."

"As in?"

"She just might want to make a home with you. She might be ready. It's been two years since Sonny died and I know she's lonely without a partner. I can tell. Promise me you'll talk to her after I'm gone."

"I don't know."

"Thad—promise me. I need to know you'll do it."

Another sigh. This one deep and long.

"All right. I'll talk to her. But how about my feelings, don't they count too? I'm not sure I ever want to get this close to anyone again. This is incredibly painful, losing you, Katy!"

"Your feelings count. But they're not all of it. I'm thinking about what's best for you *and* our kids. Not what's best for your feelings."

"Well that's a helluva note."

She laughed. "Your avoidance days are over, Murfee. You've got four kids who are soon gonna need a mother. It's up to you to make that happen."

"Let me think about it."

"All right. You do that. You think."

"All right."

31

THE DISTRICT ATTORNEY was a bull of a man named Gary Sanders. Gary was a retired rodeo cowboy who had splintered his pelvis and shattered his knee in a fall from a bucking horse in Wyoming during the summer rodeo circuit. The hip had been replaced along with the knee, and Gary now walked with the gait of someone forever tentative about his balance on the earth's surface. "Every step I take without falling over is a milestone," Gary laughed. Mid-afternoons he could most often be located in his second office, the unofficial one where he ran the DA's office by cell phone out of Kientzel's Grille, a Navajo cowboy hangout on the south end of San Francisco Street. Staff and police alike were turned off by his drinking and carousing, but Gary was loved by the common man and was easily reelected to the office of District Attorney every four years.

The story of the doctor who had removed Nadia Turkenov's life support drifted into Gary's office ahead of the official police report from the Dick Eight squad at the Flagstaff Police Department. Drifted in because Gary's wife worked ICU weekend shifts at FMC as a charge nurse. Sunday night she had told him about the incident and the arrest of the doctor from L.A. By Monday morning, news of the incident was making its way through the coffee shops downtown when the Dick Eight squad finalized its report and dropped it on Gary's desk. Dick Eight consisted of the eight homicide detectives who rotated in shifts on the homicide detectives squad. Herbert Constance was the senior detective on duty Monday morning; it was Constance who hand-carried the report to Gary Sanders and waited patiently in the DA's outer office while the prosecutor read it through.

Then Sanders leaned outside his door. "Connie, come on in."

Constance, tall and lean with a hawkish face ravaged by teenage acne and still bearing the evidence of that derma-turmoil, hurried into the office and took the client chair the cops always took.

"You believe this shit?" said the cop.

Sanders plopped into his high-backed leather chair.

"No. I heard about it last night from Andrea. What the fuck, Connie?"

"I know."

"Who is this guy?"

"He's a doctor who has a book out and he's been all over the TV channels trying to peddle it."

"What's the book about?"

Constance shrugged. "Haven't read it. One of the guys says his wife saw him on *Good Morning, Arizona*. Evidently the guy believes he died and went to heaven. So he's got an inside track on that."

"Sure he does. And this has something to do with cutting off the lady's life support?"

"Yes. He told Dr. Stoudemire over at the jail."

"Great. A visionary."

"A lunatic."

"So he removes her from life support. She was in bad shape to begin with, I take it?"

Constance grimaced. "That's where it gets really flaky. This Turkenov woman was in the hospital because she read the doctor's book and decided to give heaven a try herself."

"Come again?"

Constance spread his hands. "Swear to God. She sees this guy on TV and decides to visit her dead husband in heaven. So she swallows down a half-pound of painkillers and bam! Overdose. That's why she was in the hospital in the first place. Then, to top it off, her kids are suing this Dr. Sewell for medical malpractice for encouraging people to ride the freeway to heaven."

"Whoa, whoa. The dead woman's kids are suing the defendant?"

"Exactly. They set up a conservatorship and filed suit against the doc. They're after him for ten million bucks for putting their mother in the hospital."

"Okay, then he goes to the hospital and unhooks her. Wow."

"Not exactly. He's up at the hospital visiting Katy Murfee. She's dying, you know."

"I heard. Sad. Poor Thaddeus."

"Yes. Anyway, it turns out Thaddeus had been hired to defend the doc on his malpractice case. The doc finds out about Katy and goes up to the hospital to see her. While he's there, he detours down to the Turkenov woman's room and unplugs her from life support. Ten minutes later she's dead. End of malpractice case."

"Not exactly. Now it's a wrongful death case. A better case."

Detective Constance smiled. "That's what we were thinking too. Then one of our city attorneys who's overhearing all this says it ain't so."

"It's not a better case? Why not?"

"Because the doctor's medical malpractice insurance doesn't cover a wrongful death case. It was covering the medical malpractice case, but an intentional act that results in someone's death is definitely not covered by insurance. So now the heirs have no one to collect from if the doc's in jail. Catch Twenty-two."

"For certain. So what are you looking for?"

Detective Constance leaned his chair back on two legs and slapped its frame with his palm.

"Murder One. There was premeditation."

Sanders looked at the bank of windows to his right. His office was on the second floor of the Coconino County Courthouse and he had a partial view of the San Francisco Peaks. Rolling it around in his mind, he finally grunted and turned back to his visitor.

"First degree it is, then. We can always plead him to second."

"That's your call, Gary. Now, what about a search warrant?"

"For where?"

"Well—he was visiting here and staying at Murfee's ranch."

"No reason to search there. Where else?"

"His home?"

"Where's he live?"

"San Diego."

"Our warrant's no good in San Diego."

"Good point. So we just go with what we have?"

"Tell me about witnesses."

Constance nodded and looked up at the ceiling. "Let's see. He admitted the crime to Dr. Stoudemire at the jail. Before that, he told two security officers and I think two nurses, maybe three, at the hospital that he'd removed her life support because the woman's spirit asked him to."

"So maybe four or five people heard him admit it. Sounds like a classic insanity defense."

"Sounds like." Constance made a winding motion at the side of his head. The international sign of crazy.

"Uh-huh, exactly. Crazy as a bedbug. So tell me, was this guy still practicing medicine?"

"Not since he had his own death experience."

"What's he been up to then? Just selling books?"

"Books, videos, seminars. Plus showing up on TV plugging his book. It's a best seller. Called *The Doctor Is In...Heaven*."

"I've never heard of it."

"Yeah, well they probably aren't doing book reviews down at Kientzel's Grille."

Sanders blanched. "No, no book reviews. We've got bigger fish to fry down there." He laughed.

Constance's eyes narrowed. "So when's your wife filing for divorce? She must be sick of your carousing."

"Not open for discussion. All right. Anything else?"

"Nope. Want me to give the file to Mrs. Vasquez?"

"Yes, on your way out drop it on her desk. Tell her I said Murder One."

"Thanks."

"We'll get the calendar set up and send you notice. You're the chief investigator?"

Constance nodded, standing and taking back his file. "Yep. Yours truly. Me and Detective Hemenway."

"Good. See you in court, Connie."

It was Constance's turn. He said to the DA, "What about it? You on this case personally?"

"Hell, yes. Very high profile. We'll have CNN here before it's all said and done."

"Counting those votes already. Between the CNN audience and the voters down at the pub, you're a shoo-in next time."

They laughed and Constance left the office.

32

Lincoln Mascari was a hoodlum but never say hoodlums are dumb. And Mascari was the smartest of the smart. He knew the woman with the black hair in the car across the street had been taking pictures of him and using a telephoto lens to do it. In short, she was interested in his face. Interest in his face was a red flag to Mascari: someone was looking for the previous, unimproved version. Which meant someone was after Lincoln Mascari, and that was never good. Friends knew how to get in touch with him through certain people in Chicago. Enemies had been forever left behind. But the woman with the camera? That was too damn close for comfort to this godfather. So, he did what all good hoodlums do; he investigated his environs. Which is to say, he sent out Sicilian toadies all over the neighborhood trying to locate anyone with an interest in him.

Next door lived the Modiglianis, a family surrounded by mountains of euros from their holdings in merchant ships. Their ships plied all the oceans of the world, primarily delivering olive oil to wholesalers who would move the stuff into restaurants and groceries. Alfredo Modigliani was the *patri*, the senior alpha of the pack. A ranking member of the *Corleonesi*, Alfredo frightened even Mascari, and Mascari knew better than to trouble the man. But it was also known the old man and his family were away, and their house was deserted except for staff that came and went, which provided cover for Christine and BAT as they came and went at night, keeping an eye on their prey after the Modigliani house staff had left for the day.

Mascari's scouts reported back with some terrible news: a white woman and a black man were keeping watch over Mascari from the Modigliani house. Did they know they had been discovered? Of course not said Diego Luchesi, ex-Special Forces from the Italian navy or *Marina Militare*. He had scaled the house on the far side, his ropes dangling from a parapet while he found an unlocked upper window and let himself in. Stealthily moving through the hallways and rooms down to the ground floor, he had watched from the shadows as the woman and man trained their optics on the house and grounds of Luchesi's employer, Lincoln Mascari.

"Should I end them?" Luchesi wanted to know.

Mascari shook his head violently. "Of course not! We must know who sent them. That is the question!"

"How will we do that?"

"You will shadow them. Eventually, they will lead you to their employer."

And so Diego Luchesi was sent out after Christine and BAT, always keeping far enough away that he went unnoticed, his face disguised and altered with wigs and glasses and mustaches and clothing; they noticed nothing.

~

On the morning of May 12, Christine was parked in an Alfa Romeo a half a block away from Mascari's sprawling residence. She was alert and carefully surveying the traffic and pedestrians that came and went. Once, one of Mascari's Mercedes entourages sped by, but Christine made no effort to follow. Mascari's personal favorite, the S550 wasn't included in the pack so she did not pursue.

Mothers with baby strollers passed by in both directions. Joggers came and went. An old man bent low on his walker came down the hill and an hour later came back up the hill. She smiled as he went by, but he looked neither right nor left. "Until the very end," she said to the man though he didn't hear her. "With you in spirit."

At the other end of the block, BAT was parked in a Ford Taurus rental, ready to follow if Mascari drove by in his direction. He had his radio on, listening to the latest Maroon 5 and wishing he had a Starbucks muffin, for his stomach was growling. In his rearview he could see a speed walker approaching on the driver's side. The walker appeared to be drinking from a large paper cup. Billy A. Tattinger paid her little mind; joggers and walkers and baby buggies were common in the neighborhood. He was punching in the search button on the radio when he heard a knock on the driver's side window. He looked up, and there was the speed walker with her drink. BAT rolled down the window and the woman looked as if she were about to speak when she suddenly tossed her drink on BAT and followed it with a blazing cigarette lighter. BAT was shocked at the assault and recoiled in horror. The drink, he realized as he was enveloped in flame, wasn't a soft drink, but gasoline. From waist to head he was covered in shooting flames and he struggled to slap them out, to find something inside the rental car to snuff them out, but these were his last thoughts as he lost consciousness and burned up alive.

Christine heard BAT's screams in her earpiece. She frantically started the Alfa Romeo and squealed away from the curb, making her way up the street toward BAT in her fishtailing car. She leaped out of her car. When she reached him, he sat slumped in his seat--now on fire and burning down to the springs. She watched in horror as her old friend was devoured by the flames. Then she realized she had given herself up by coming to BAT. She desperately looked around for the person or persons she knew would be watching. Running back around to her car, she pushed thoughts of BAT to the back of her mind and realized she was, at that moment, fighting for her own survival. Somehow they had been discovered and their surveillance of Mascari had been found out. BAT's death was the first to come; she would be next, she knew. Extraordinary measures would be required.

It would be necessary for her to leave the country in the fastest way possible.

Falcone-Borsellino Airport was about twenty-eight kilometers west of Palermo. Her own Gulfstream had dropped her off there, along with BAT, but she had sent it away because its registry was in her own name and keeping it at the airport would have been just inviting discovery.

So she headed for Lungomare Cristoforo Colombo and ran the stop sign at the intersection, tearing along West. LCC was a narrow, two-lane road with the seaside off to her left and old rental housing and marketplaces to her right. Watching in her rearview mirror with one eye and advancing with the other, it was a nerve-wracking fifteen minutes until she could make the cutover to SS113. She then raced along Via Giuseppe Navarra Erudito until she gained access to E90, the high-speed roadway that would lead to Palermo.

Her aircraft was on the flight line in Rome and taking off twenty minutes from her panicked call. It would fly directly to Palermo and meet her there. Christine kicked it up to 160 KPH and ran for twenty kilometers at this speed. Then she took an off ramp at Bagheria and squealed into an Espresso gas station/food stop. She told the attendant to fill it and then went inside. She headed towards the rear of the store, where she placed her back up against the pastry counter and began watching the arriving vehicles. Five minutes later she was fairly confident she wasn't being followed. At least not by anyone who had followed her into the station.

She turned and looked over the glassed-in showcase full of treats, including some elaborately glacéed cakes made of almond paste, and a great variety of cookies. Her favorite was the quaresimale, so she ordered a dozen in keeping with looking like anyone else out for a lark that day. She paid for the gas and cookies and headed back outside to her car. Starting the ignition and watching all around, she nosed the little car back behind the station and waited, engine running. No one came up behind, and no one came around from the front. Which didn't rule out that they might be waiting out front of the station, but she was taking every precaution until she was safe aboard her aircraft and out over the ocean on her way home. Then she drove around front and retraced her route back to the freeway.

They came up behind her just beyond Bagheria. It was the black S550 Mercedes that Mascari preferred for himself, judging by the silhouette in her rearview mirror. She kicked it up to 160 KPH and the powerful pursuit car stayed right on her bumper. She then backed it off to 100 KPH and the Mercedes didn't vary, staying right on her bumper.

Great, she thought, they had her. The solar reflection denied her a look inside the vehicle. She had no way of knowing if there was just one of them or six. It was impossible to say. Christine took inventory of her predicament, instantly recognizing they had the benefit of knowing the highway and street system of the area while she was, essentially, lost with the GPS directing her travel.

Traffic flow was increasing as they neared Palermo. Which was a good thing, if she were going to lose them. A quarter of a mile ahead was an eighteen wheeler, and she pulled out and came up behind it. Approaching from the left lane, she saw that it was a double-truck: an eighteen wheeler tanker pulling a second tanker. She swung in behind it and the Mercedes followed suit. After a half mile of close-in driving, she saw an upcoming sign for the next exit ramp. Two kilometers ahead. Now if she could just time it right.

She watched the odometer spin off a kilometer and then she pulled to the right side of her lane of travel. Up ahead was the exit sign. Waiting until she was no more than a half a kilometer from the off-ramp, she suddenly swerved hard left and shot ahead of the truck, shooting across to the right lane and settling in just ahead of the roaring truck. The Mercedes followed in her path, saw it couldn't edge in between her and the truck, and broke back across the left lane. She knew the driver was trying to decide whether he should pull ahead of her or back behind the truck. One thing was for sure: he couldn't stay in the left lane or he would lose her. As he began dropping back with the intention of pulling back behind the trucking rig, the three vehicles came up on the exit ramp, which Christine suddenly swerved onto without warning. There! The truck and the

Mercedes blasted on past the exit ramp as the Mercedes driver just couldn't react in time; he was beyond the turnoff before he even realized she had taken it.

With a scowl and wave as the two vehicles ran parallel for a hundred feet, Christine braked for the stop sign at the end of the ramp, ran through it, and headed back beneath the highway, pulling left and left again, now coming up on the on ramp running the exact opposite direction of her pursuers, back the way she had just come.

Two kilometers down, she took the next off ramp, came back across underneath the freeway, and began picking her way toward Palermo on secondary roads, avoiding E90. For the first time that morning, she took a deep breath and assessed her situation. She leaned back in the seat and smiled. She tried a pastry.

It had occurred to her that Diego Luchesi might have planted a tracking device on the Alfa the same night he had scaled the parapet of the Modigliani house and come inside. But she hadn't been able to locate it if in fact he had.

In parallel from the E90, her pursuers were merely running abreast of her now, although separated by three kilometers of houses, markets, and back roads.

She was never out of sight even when she was.

33

At Palermo, she parked the Alfa in a front lot of a Ducati motorcycle dealer on Via Trapani. Her American Express made her the owner of a two-year-old Ducati sprint bike; thirty minutes later she was headed for the airport on the northwest side of town. Christine knew that once inside Palermo airport she could check-in quickly and discreetly in the General Aviation Terminal, completely separated from the hustle and bustle of standing in the lines of regularly scheduled airlines. They also offered a direct approach to her plane.

Through the fence, she spotted her Gulfstream waiting, just before she turned into the GAT. Once inside the terminal, there was no one in line and she was through the terminal and headed for her aircraft in five minutes. She had made no effort to hide her identity.

Ambrosia Semolina, the captain of her Gulfstream, waited for her at the top of the stairs.

"We are in a hurry, Amby," she told him as she trotted up.

"Aren't we always, Chris?" said the portly, affable pilot. "We're fueled, filed, and ready to fly."

"You're the best."

Kent, the second chair, followed her back to her lounge.

"Hey, K," she said. "Got any coffee?"

"Just made. Let me get you a cup."

"That would be incredible. And a bottle of water."

Kent smiled. He was only too happy to wait on his boss, who he secretly was in love with. And he was greatly relieved that she was safe aboard the aircraft and about to head back to the States.

Christine looked out the window after she had her coffee and the throttles were pushed to the dashboard and held there by two hands. The small runway structures and signs began flashing by as she watched. Then the plane rotated and they were off the asphalt.

Only then could she close her eyes and return her thoughts to BAT.

The loss was huge. She loved the man and knew it was she who would have to report his loss to his wife. She dreaded the visit but knew it was required and knew she wanted to do it herself, in person, of course, as soon as they touched down.

The widow would want his body. Christine would put her law office staff on that. Surely, there would be a way to make a claim and arrange a transfer.

Then she pushed the thoughts out of her mind, drank the last swallow of coffee, and reclined her seat. Kent stopped by with a blanket as he always did and she nodded and smiled as she felt it being arranged for her.

Then she was asleep at 45,000 feet.

∼

THIRTY MINUTES LATER, the aircraft carrying Diego Luchesi blasted through the same air.

The flight plan terminated in Flagstaff, Arizona. Thaddeus Murfee lived just five miles out of town. Luchesi located the lawyer's property on a digital plat map. He also located the public highway that gave access to Murfee's home.

Luchesi gave orders to the pilots to stay onboard until he

returned. It might be an hour, it might be two weeks, he said. He would return and the takeoff could mean life or death.

The pilots understood. They replied that they would remain onboard, fueled, and ready to depart on a minute's notice.

"*Bona partuta*," they told him. Have a good journey.

34

ON THE SECOND day following her vertebroplasty Katy went home in an ambulance. She was lashed down and completely immobilized. Thaddeus followed behind in his Ram pickup and as he drove, he watched the sunlight shafts play through the ponderosa branches on both sides of the road. He was wondering whether Katy could see the same thing; he hoped she could because he imagined it was her last ride anywhere. Thinking these thoughts, he began to cry. All he could think about was Katy gone from his life, the loneliness he would feel and how useless he would be to anyone. Tears streamed down his face as he bit his lip and willed himself to stop. He didn't want her to see bloodshot eyes and tearstained cheeks. He rationalized that the outpouring of feelings was probably the result of being cooped up in the hospital for the last week and getting very little sleep. While Katy had dozed on and on under the influence of her medications, he had sat upright in the padded chair and tossed and turned all night long, snatching fifteen minutes here and there until another sound out in the hallway would jar him awake or until another Invasion of the Nurses flooded into her room so that vitals could be taken, fluid levels checked, and fluid outputs noted. He was grateful they were going to the ranch; he wiped hard at the tears and his cheeks and soon found himself laughing at his foolishness. He thought it was not unlike whistling past the graveyard, his laughter.

At the house, the ambulance driver backed right up across the sprawling front grass and up to the deck that stretched the full width of the home. From there, it was an easy enough move to wheel the stretcher across the wood planks of the deck and up to the front entrance. They came into the entryway, rolled past the formal living room on the left where Katy had meticulously gathered together Southwestern artifacts and art pieces and made a place for Thad to meet the occasional client who stopped by. The first door on the right was a walk-in coat closet and the second door was a large study lined floor to ceiling with books and small sculptures, plus the mandatory big screen TV. Off the back was a bathroom. On the right was a huge stone fireplace with gas log—Katy's requirement as she wanted something that would immediately put out heat after a long winter's day in the outside world.

They rolled her in here, the study, and carefully moved her onto the hospital bed against the far wall facing the door. She was heavily medicated and glassy-eyed and didn't complain even one time. Immediately she was overrun with greetings from five-year-old Parkus, seven-year-old Sarai, and nine-year-old Celena. The kids had been allowed to stay home from school so that Mama could have a meet and greet with her greatest fans. The little ones hadn't been allowed in her ICU suite and so the delight in again having their mother back was infectious. Nursing staff arrived and set about the task of preparing Katy's tubes, hangers, and pumps, as well as preparing charts for her physical functions and medication history. In the midst of all this Katy felt like she was floating in a twilight state, responding to the kids and answering questions put to her by the nurses. Then the stable and ranch workers filed through and welcomed her home. Thaddeus watched all this from a leather recliner in which he sometimes read late into the night. He wondered how she found the energy and will to manage as he watched her ooh and ah over the kids and warmly greet the workers. Well, as warmly as possible, anyway, he thought. Given the circumstances, it was enough.

An hour later, everyone was fed and the kids were back to their daytime play routines, scattered inside and out, and the nursing staff had dwindled down to one onsite nurse working the noon to ten shift. Meanwhile, Thaddeus hadn't left the room and was hanging close by so that he could respond immediately to anything his wife had to say. He realized she was beckoning him closer and he stood and went to her bedside.

"What's up?" he asked.

"You. It's time for you to go to the office and work. We can't pay for this unless you're earning, brother."

He laughed.

"No, I'll be here with you until—well, until you're well enough that I feel good about leaving you alone."

"Thaddeus, that time is never going to come. In the meantime, I need my household to be as regular as possible. You go to work; the kids go to school. The cook cooks, the nurse nurses, the outside people do their thing. I can't have you all hovering around me. It's not enjoyable and it doesn't make me feel better, FYI. In fact, it makes me feel worse. So if you really want to help me feel good, go to your office and be a lawyer. Come home when all the other men go home to their wives."

"No. I'm here with you. If I'm crowding you too much I'll go into my own office and hang out there. But I'm not leaving your side."

"Then take me back to the hospital. I'd be happier there."

"You were unhappy there! You made me promise to bring you home!"

"But it's not home with Mr. Gloom and Doom hanging around. Go the hell to work and leave me in peace. Now. Please!"

Thaddeus stepped back from the bed.

"It doesn't feel right to leave you."

"Then deal with it. I'm not going to argue. Go now. Please."

Thaddeus stepped back to the bed and leaned down. He placed the side of his face against her lips. "Kiss me, then."

She did.

"All right. I'll be home around five."

"Good. Sue somebody. That's always good for your soul."

"Please."

"Now, go!"

He did as ordered. First a quick run upstairs to change and then back down and a quick look in at Katy, who was asleep and breathing deeply. Her sweet face crushed his heart and he thought for several moments that he was going to break down and cry and probably frighten her awake. He stifled a sharp cry, swallowing hard against it, and pressed his hands to his face. "Oh, my God!" he moaned.

Then he forced himself to turn and leave.

Driving east toward Flagstaff, he got the call from Christine. BAT had been murdered. The whereabouts of his body was unknown. But Christine had set her staff to work on recovering him and bring his body home for his wife's instructions.

"I should call her," Thaddeus said. He was driving in stunned disbelief. First Katy; now this? His life was lurching way out of control and for the first time since he was very small he felt very lonely and afraid. "Yes, he repeated, I'll call her."

"I already did," Christine told him. "Marcy and I go way back. She used to help with the kids when BAT was working for me."

"Well, I'm calling anyway. It would be wrong of me not to."

"You're right."

"First, bring me up to date. Have we found the son of a bitch?"

"We have. In Termini, Sicily. Just west of Palermo."

"Under an assumed name, of course."

"Of course. At one point they made me and came on hard. I managed to evade them but I had tipped him off that we were looking for him. He searched the neighborhood around his house and I guess that's how they spotted us. We were running automobile surveillance when BAT got fooled into rolling down his window. That's all I can think of anyway."

"So how did he die?"

"Burned up. They set his car on fire. I saw him slumped and burning as I went by."

"Holy Mother."

"Terrible way to go. Poor BAT. And how I'm gonna miss him. Marcy was inconsolable. She even wound up cursing me."

"We've got to take care of her," Thaddeus said. "I'll make that arrangement this afternoon yet. She needs money and she needs financial security right now, with the kids and all."

"What will you do?"

"I'll take her a check. And I'll make good on BAT's piece of the action when we get my money back."

"About that."

"Yes?"

"I know some guys."

"Isn't it always that way? I know some guys who know some guys who know some guys? All right, what do you have?"

"These guys are good. They're European and there isn't a firewall in the world that hasn't warmly welcomed them inside."

"Have you paid them yet?

"No, I wanted to run it past you."

"Do it, Chris. I want my money back now more than ever. And Marcy gets a piece of it, BAT's share. And you know what else? I want five minutes alone with Mascari. For Sarai and for BAT. Just five minutes."

"I don't know how that's gonna happen. He's heavily fortified, his car travels with three or four others in two separate groups. It's going to be very difficult, Thaddeus."

"But not impossible?"

"No, not impossible."

"When you get back, let's get together and you give me a rendering of his layout. A map. Street names, Google pictures, the whole nine yards."

"We have our own pictures. Remember who you're dealing with, Thaddeus."

"That would include pictures of the new and improved Lincoln Mascari?"

"You'll be glad you have them. He's even lightened his facial skin."

"No way!"

"Way. It's pretty damn shocking. You'll see."

"Okay. Are you coming to Arizona?"

"Got to hit Chicago first, deal with the kids, let them know they still have a mother. Then I'll be out. How's she doing anyway?"

"Shit, Chris, she's dying."

"I know that, asshole. I'm asking if she's in pain."

"No, they're keeping her full of strong drugs."

"Good. Bless her heart."

"Yes, bless her heart."

"Well okay, good buddy, I'm signing off now."

"Roger that."

"Goodbye."

Thaddeus clicked off and hit the speed dial for BAT's home.

"Marcy? Thaddeus. I just heard, Chris told me. I am so so sorry. And I need to see you."

They talked for several minutes then hung up.

He pressed his head back against the RAM's headrest and continued on toward town. Stinging tears filled his eyes and he swept them away with a backhand. They came on again and he rubbed them away again. "My God," he cried out in the silent cab, "have you completely forgotten me?"

35

For three days the dark driver had reclined on the mountainside and glassed the route he would take, memorizing the structures and impediments that might interfere with his coming and going. Now, with its lights killed, the SUV nosed across the two acres separating the Murfee's ranch house from the main highway. Moonlight helped define the passage. The ingress was quiet and sure, dodging around ranch and farm implements and outbuildings with ease.

Lightning snapped just beyond the two-story ranch house. A drizzling rain moved in and within minutes, it was pouring with more on the way. Behind him in the forest, the lightning was flashing and snapping. The rain storm seemed to follow him across the field; a minute later the windshield wipers were running full tilt and the moon was now obscured. But it was good, in a way, for the crash and boom of the storm masked any sound the SUV made as it came on directly at the ranch house.

He peered ahead through the gloom. Lights were burning brightly on all three floors; he would have his pick of windows to take out with the shotgun.

On he came until a lightning flash suddenly illuminated the vehicle against the black backdrop of the mountains and the man knew he might have been made in that brief instant. If anyone was watching.

~

INSIDE THE HOUSE, Thaddeus and Katy were in the study, Katy alternating between a comfortable, pain-killer drowse, and *The Voice*, which Turquoise was watching from the couch. Thaddeus was bent forward at the desk, inspecting client files on his law firm's network. His partner Albert Hightower still had a staggering caseload being tended to in Chicago and the hunt was on for a third trial lawyer to come in and ease the burden. Thaddeus shifted his attention to Flagstaff cases and was relieved to see their files numbered less than fifty. So far.

Katy's eyes opened.

"Do I hear the kids running upstairs?"

Thaddeus looked up.

"Thunder. Storming."

"Hush, mom! I want to hear this girl's voice!" Turquoise cried from the couch. Her voice was half-teasing; she was spending as much time with her mother as possible as her time was finite and Turquoise was well aware of this. The smaller kids weren't tuned in at all to Katy's predicament and so their childhood raced on, willy-nilly, with wild nights on the second and third floors of the sprawling house. Both Parkus and Sarai had playrooms attached to their bedrooms: places they could romp and run and laugh their happy laughs. Celena, nine, was at the other end of the hallway on the third floor, where she had her electronics and texting open for business with her girlfriends from sunup to bedtime.

"Don't hush me," said Katy. "Someone needs to pay attention to the little ones. You two aren't. What are you going to do when—"

"Katy, we've got it," Thaddeus said gently from the desk side of the room. "You can relax about that."

Katy nodded and turned her head away.

Thaddeus stood and crossed to her bedside. He reached and took her hand.

"Let's just let them romp and run while they're little. In a year or two, we can do more officiating. But for now, they're not really hurting anything."

Katy's head turned back.

At just that moment, the lightning flash outside the window where Thaddeus was standing illuminated in silhouette the oncoming SUV. He blinked. Had he actually seen something there? He waited, wishing for more lightning. What in the hell? He thought. Then he decided it was his imagination. No one would be driving across the front pasture. Would they? He returned to his desk and the computer screen.

Two minutes later he stood up from the desk. Something was niggling at him. Something wasn't quite right. He didn't just see things; there had been a vehicle out there. He was sure of it, the more he ran it through his mind.

"Please remain seated," he told Turquoise as he left the room.

Ignoring her father, as was her general first response to either parent, Turquoise kept her eyes on the flat screen. Blake Shelton had just scored a new member for his team.

Thaddeus went outside through the back door. It was pouring, but he didn't mind. He reached back inside, around the corner, up above the door, and unsnapped the AR-15 from its mount. He worked the charging mechanism, loading a round into the gun's chamber. Then he moved to the corner of the house.

He was soaking and shivering when he came around the corner. Lightning strikes were bouncing and jagging across the front pasture. Just as he made the first downspout beyond the corner, he heard a loud roar and knew instantly: shotgun!

His first instinct was to rush back inside and check on his family. Tearing for the back deck, he was up and running inside in four steps. Back through the mud room and kitchen he dashed, crashing down the hall and back inside the study. Turquoise was still seated on the couch, her comforter pulled up around her neck, her face sheet white. Her large eyes were frozen on the missing front window that had extended across the width of the study. All right, Thaddeus thought, and he ran for Katy's hospital bed. The first thing he saw was blood spreading across her sheets. He ripped off the top sheet and immediately was sprayed with arterial blood from his wife's lower leg.

"Katy!" he cried. "Talk to me."

"Can't feel it! Can you believe it? I'm paralyzed, Thad, so I can't feel the wound!"

"All right, just be still."

He immediately whipped off his belt and cinched just above the blood flow. For a moment, the blood lessened, then suddenly increased again. He pulled the belt another hole tighter and this time the flow was staunched. For the most part. When he turned to bark orders at Turquoise, he saw she was already on her cell phone.

"I need to report a shooting at Thaddeus Murfee's home. Yes out on one-eighty. Yes, just past the restaurant turnoff. First road south."

"Good," said Thaddeus, and he pulled Katy's hospital gown up to her shoulders, checking for other damage. Seeing none, he ran for the stairs. Just as he went around the corner, the three younger children came pell-mell down the stairs, running for their dad. The two little ones wrapped around his legs and Celena fell into his arms. Cries and wails filled the vestibule.

"Everyone okay?" he asked, checking them over.

Cries wailed on, cries terrified at the gun shot and the frightening shouts from their mother as she called at them to get on the floor.

"Okay, everyone in the study."

Once they were secure in the study, Thaddeus picked up the gun and ran for the front door.

Without hesitation he ran to the center of the front deck and let his eyes roam over the pasture, looking for any movement. His ears prickled when he heard tires squeal a quarter mile away on the main road. A minute later, headlights flared far to the right as the driver switched on his lights and sped away.

Thaddeus considered giving chase but thought better of it. Right now his family needed him.

He ran back inside to check on Katy's leg.

She was still astonished she'd been shot. She felt nothing and had only heard the blast shattering the window. There had been no warning, she told Thaddeus as her eyes suddenly filled with tears. Nothing.

The kids were surrounding her bed and she was counting noses and feeling each child's arms and torso for wounds.

Then she lay back against her pillows and forced herself to steady down. The last thing the children needed right then was to see their mother crying and losing control. They were frightened enough without that kind of display.

In a strong, steady voice, she said to Thaddeus, "See anything?"

He shook his head. He was bent down examining her leg.

"Ambulance is on the way, with the cops," Turquoise whispered across the room. "Hold on, Mom."

Katy shrugged and gave a half-laugh. "The crazy thing is, I don't feel it. I have no feeling waist down."

"It's just as well," Thaddeus said. "I've pretty much got the blood stopped. I'm going to loosen my belt for a minute."

He did that, and the blood erupted again from the wound in her leg. But it was much less plentiful. He decided she'd probably been hit by one shotgun pellet. However, that one foreign object had obviously nicked an artery as the flow of blood increased until he again tightened the belt. Then it subsided again.

Sirens could be heard at last.

Katy's look caught Thaddeus. She demanded safety for the kids, her face said.

He nodded.

It was time to get XFBI back on the job. These were bodyguards he had ceased using when they had left Illinois.

It was time to call for reinforcements.

THADDEUS DIDN'T LEAVE HOME the next day.

The cops came and went, snapping photographs of the broken glass and damage to the outer wall. They took statements and assured the kids that they were on the job. Thaddeus remained unconvinced. He waited, and by one in the afternoon the first agents from XFBI were onsite. They spoke with Thaddeus. They developed a plan of protection for the Murfee family. There were kids to accompany to school; perimeters to be established; shifts to be manned and weapons to be issued.

"Whatever the cost," Thaddeus told Richard Bolt, his account manager in L.A. "It's worth everything to me."

The initial crew was selected and put in place. Only then could Thaddeus relax and even think about his clients again. Katrina called from the office with messages. These needed to be returned today, she implored him. Top of the list: Dr. Emerick Sewell, Coconino County Jail.

He didn't bother showering or shaving; he needed to speak with Dr. Sewell ASAP.

Their usual lassitude notwithstanding, the gatekeepers at the jail finally had to allow him inside to see his client. Thaddeus swore under his breath at the public servants manning the jail who all too often obstructed anyone who wanted to visit what the jailers considered their own private inventory. Prisoner and family needs and feelings be damned.

He declined help in finding Interview Room A.

His client looked to have aged ten years since being incarcerated. But jail did that to a person, Thaddeus knew, and he wasn't surprised by the man's forlorn look and gray complexion. What should have been an easy remediation for the Turkenov family—turning off the life support—had become, because he had done it without permission, a serious crime. The doctor's kind eyes said he knew this but that he would do it again.

"Thanks for coming, Thaddeus. Sorry if my phone calls jangled any nerves."

"We've been busy at home."

"Is it Katy?"

"Not exactly. Now, let's talk about you. The last time we talked, you told me you went into Ms. Turkenov's room and withdrew her life support because she asked you."

"That's what happened."

"Of course, she was unconscious when she asked."

"Consciousness isn't that easy. Her brain was damaged by the narcotics she ingested and her brain was essentially dead. However, her consciousness was fully operational and communicating *if* you knew how to listen."

"Which you knew."

"I did."

"And I believe you said she asked you to set her free."

"She did."

"You know, Doc, I have a hard time finding any defense in all this. For openers, we tell the jury that you did it. You caused the woman's death. Then we tell them that she asked you to do it. You may not know this, but even if Joe Blow asks me to shoot him and if I do and he dies, I've committed murder. That's your situation. Even though she asked to be released, you didn't have the legal right to do that."

"No, that's correct. I was following a much higher law. A much higher authority gave me permission."

"Well, I don't need to go into that right now. That's between you and whatever religious beliefs you have. But even that doesn't solve your problems inside a courtroom. We see lots of clients telling us God told them to do this or that."

"And lawyers and judges and police officers routinely write those people off as crazies."

"Right. Which brings me to your mental state."

"Shoot."

"Well, for openers, were you under a doctor's care when this happened? Were you taking medication at the direction of your doctor?"

"Cholesterol pills."

"Anything psychotropic?"

"Nope. Can't help you there."

"All right, then have you ever been under the care of a physician on account of mental health concerns or problems?"

"I was depressed in college after Kathy Gray broke up with me. That was resolved with a pitcher of beer and a camping trip with a certain senior cheerleader."

"Did you see any doctor due to that depression?"

"Only at the university student health clinic. The cheerleader blessed me with genital herpes."

"Have you ever been hospitalized because of mental health issues? This is a 'no' I'm guessing."

"You guessed right. No."

"On the day you withdrew Ms. Turkenov's life support. Were you hearing voices that day?"

"Not with my ears. My mind, however, heard her voice. Rather, my mind received her thought."

"Explain that."

"In the realm of nonlocal consciousness, two spirits can communicate."

Thaddeus abruptly clicked his ballpoint. "You know what, Doc? I don't think I'm gonna be able to help you with this case."

The doctor smiled and stood up from the table.

"I scared you off with that one, eh?"

"Pretty much. Besides, my wife's terribly sick and needs me around. More than that, I want to spend my days with her. You've probably got yourself the wrong guy here."

"What if I could provide scientific proof of what I'm saying?"

Thaddeus sat back and adjusted his glasses. His eyes narrowed.

"What if you could provide scientific proof? What, some scientist has a picture of a ghost?"

"Not at all. Have you ever heard of quantum physics, Thaddeus?"

"I read something on *Huffington Post* about that some time back. Don't recall anything about it."

"Well, it's a study of particle physics, long story short. It's about tiny little events, little laws that operate in the physical world totally different from the laws of physics you and I know about."

"Give me an example," said Thaddeus. He was fighting off sneaking a look at his watch.

"Well, in quantum physics a particle can be at point A and over here at point B both at the same time."

"You just lost me."

"It just is. It's a scientific fact in quantum physics."

"Give me something about spirits talking."

"To do that, you're going to have to learn about entanglement."

"I know a lot about entanglement already."

"Not this kind you don't," said the doctor. "This is the kind that keeps consciousness intact when it leaves the body at death."

The room fell silent. Thaddeus debated looking at his watch. But didn't. Didn't because the doctor had just shared something with him that was very important to him and Thaddeus didn't want to disparage it by insulting him with a look at his watch. Instead, he honored the moment, sitting quietly, thinking about what had just been said.

Finally, "When the consciousness leaves the body at death. Is this something a doctor like Katy would know about?"

Dr. Sewell shook his head. "Probably not. But she should. I had planned to open her mind to this science but then this other thing happened and now I can't because I'm stuck in here." He indicated the jail but Thaddeus didn't even hear him. His mind was far down the road, considering how he might spring the doctor from jail so he could take up the notion of life after death with Katy. As for himself, Thaddeus believed in no such thing. But for Katy's sake, he would act as if. If it gave her any hope to cling to, he would act as if. Moreover, he would go so far as to pause his own life and defend this doctor to the bitter end just so Katy would know he was invested in a belief system that had come to give her hope. If it ever came to that. But it was looking like it would not, because the good doctor, the bearer of the good news, was locked away in jail facing a Murder One charge. That was ordinarily not a bailable offense.

Or was it?

He pulled a notepad out of his messenger bag and for the first time that evening began writing.

"Let me think," he told Dr. Sewell. The doctor closed his eyes and set his mouth. He could wait.

Knocks came on the door. Demands that he "hurry up." He stuck his head out and asked what the rush was, that there was no limit on the time a lawyer could spend with a client. This kept the jailers at bay for another hour.

Finally, he had the bare bones of a motion to set bail in a first-degree murder case. It was predicated on the typically common phrases, "ties to the community," and "no prior history of criminal acts," and "not a threat to himself or to others," and the like. But that's where common ended. Common ended because Thaddeus then argued—in his short, handwritten motion that someone would type up tomorrow—that Nadia Turkenov couldn't have been murdered, that she was already dead.

You can't murder a dead person. That was elementary stuff, Criminal Law 101.

But it's what he had been given, the cards he had been dealt.

And he planned to make the most of them.

36

"So you're telling me you failed, Diego," said Mascari over the scrambled phone.

"I am telling you that I have just begun," retorted Luchesi. He was hot and angry; he didn't like being told he had failed. Not at anything.

"So how will you get to him?"

"Through his wife. I will use her to bait the trap for him. Trust me, it is as good as done, Don Mascari."

"I trust you will get it done or I wouldn't have sent you. But it needs to be now. The woman got away and already they are preparing to return with her. Especially now that you torched her companion."

"We will bite off the head of the snake and the body will wither and die. With Murfee gone, there is nothing else to be said."

"I can't argue with that."

"So I take her down. Then he will leave the security of his XFBI guards to come for you. Once he is away from them, he belongs to me."

"He will return with that woman. She worries me as much as him."

"She will be next. After the wife, I will go for her. We will isolate this Murfee, leave him utterly alone and enraged, and then we will strike."

~

THE NEXT DAY found Diego Luchesi in the offices of Peak Home Health, a provider on the west side of Flagstaff. It had taken Luchesi all of two telephone calls to determine the identity of the company providing Katy Murfee's home nursing care. Now he was waiting in the outer office of the Director of Nursing, his bogus resume and forged nursing license in his satchel. He was dressed in chinos and a blue button down with a red striped tie and blue blazer—looking every bit like the home health aide he meant to portray.

The DON showed him inside her office. She was a mid-fortyish woman, heavy around the girth and burned out with nursing, as so many are when they reach their forties and are still caring for the sick and injured. Right now she was wishing she had a nice, secure job in some large corporation doing HR recruitment—anything that didn't require dealing with sickness and death. But, it was what it was and now she had to meet with another possible staff, a home health aide, the position most needed by home health agencies—after R.N.'s, of course.

"Take a seat," she told Luchesi. Her manner was short and curt. He was low on the food chain though high on the needs chain. But she had no stake in the agency other than her salary and it was late in the day; common courtesy was almost too hard to provide.

She reviewed the resume, highlighting two or three lines with her yellow Hi-Liter. She nodded several times and then cleared her throat.

"So you've just moved here from Miami. Are you Cuban?"

"I am. Grandparents were refugees. I am second generation American."

"You have an accent. Cuban?"

"Yes, my grandparents speak no English. They basically raised me."

"Got it. Okay. Says here you've worked at maybe a dozen agencies and you're what, twenty-eight?"

"Twenty-eight. I like to travel and so I've moved around a lot, trying to see the U.S."

"I haven't actually heard of any of these agencies you have listed. Like Topeka? You were there eight weeks? And then on to Omaha? Why Omaha?"

"It came next on the map, to tell the truth."

She peered at him over her half-shells. "What's the weather like in Omaha?"

"I was there in the summer. Very humid."

"Yes, it is. So what are you looking for with Peak? Long-term or are you going to kiss us goodbye after a month or two?"

"I want to put down roots here. I have a girlfriend."

"Oh, you do."

"She is pregnant. We're getting married."

"Well, good for you, Mr. Luchesi. This is a nice town."

"So I'm looking for permanent."

"Well, you have the credentials. Any shift preferences?"

"Graveyard. I'll be taking classes at NAU during the day."

"Good on you! Right now we have several around-the-clocks. Any preference in location?"

"Well, I live on the way out to the Grand Canyon. Anything out there?"

"Yes, we have an oncology patient out on one-eighty. Metastases in her spine and brain. I can get you maybe six weeks there. I'm told she won't last much longer than that."

"Graveyard?"

"Uh-huh. When can you start?"

"Tonight?"

"How about this weekend. We can have your ID badge and computer ready by then. All charting is on our company laptops then uploaded after each shift. Simple. No paper, Mr. Luchesi. What should I call you?"

"Diego is fine. Friday night will be perfect."

"Good. I'm going to give you back to Caroline out front. She'll take your picture and do the intake stuff for your personnel file. So, thank you for coming in. I have a feeling you're going to thrive here."

"Me, too. I really like this town and I'm very excited for this opportunity."

"Come in Friday at noon and we'll get your ID and computer turned over. We start our aides at fourteen. Does that work for you?"

"Fourteen is perfect. Any chance of pulling doubles?"

"Double shifts? All the time. You know, I like you. You're going to do just fine here. Goodbye, then."

"Goodbye."

A headshot was taken by Caroline. It was then sized and laminated onto Luchesi's new ID card.

The ID card he would use to get past her XFBI guards.

37

JUDGE HERBERT HOOVER had spent his life angry at the parents who named him after a dead president of the United States. For what good it did. He sat at his cluttered desk in the Coconino County Courthouse in downtown Flagstaff and read again the motion that Murfee's office had delivered. The judge had agreed to a three o'clock initial appearance and bail hearing, leaving him thirty minutes to prepare. He was a tall carrot-top with thick black eyeglasses as was the style, a light fluff of reddish-blond mutton chops, and extra wide suspenders to help support the suspender holster he wore with his Glock subcompact pistol. He'd been shot at from the street before and the next time, by God, he planned to return fire. Same went for anyone who managed to smuggle a weapon into his courtroom. He was a card-carrying member of an international group calling itself Concealed Carry and he had even paid for a one-million-dollar insurance policy that would cover the aftermath of any non-justified shooting he might be involved in and even covered the fees for an attorney of his own choosing to defend him. He was always prepared for the worst-case scenario, and who wouldn't be, after serving twenty years as District Attorney and ten years as a trial judge? The worst of man's nature was no mystery to him, exposed as he had been vis-à-vis the two public offices.

He finished his second read-through of Murfee's motion and cocked his head back and hooted. "Sumbitch is pushing the envelope, Chuck!" he said to an imaginary Chuck Yeager, the test pilot of the Bell X-1 who always maintained that in flying the first aircraft to break the sound barrier in 1947 he had only been "Pushing the envelope." Judge Hoover had been a small boy when it happened. Yeager was his first hero. Bob Matthias of Olympic Decathlon fame was his second. His third was yet to be named. Given how long he had survived the so-called Halls of Justice, he was even thinking of bestowing the third hero's medal on himself. A passing thought.

Back to Murfee: the judge was seventy-four and prone to mental frolics and detours just like now. He forced himself to continue reading, shutting out the rest of the background chatter his mind increasingly provided.

So Murfee was claiming the woman was already dead, *ergo* his client couldn't have murdered her.

"Genius," the judge said. He played an imaginary foxtrot in his mind and snapped his fingers to the backbeat. "Genius, Murfee. I think you might have won me over just by the creative oomph this motion took."

Ten minutes later, he was sitting atop his own Olympic platform —the judge's high throne in the judge's own permanent courtroom. He pointed an index finger at both attorneys and said, "You two. Are you going to argue this with each other all afternoon or do you want to give me a listen too?"

Thaddeus Murfee and Gary Sanders, the bull of a man who presently served as District Attorney, broke off their verbal fencing match and turned their attention to the judge, who had just then flounced into his seat.

"Sorry, Your Honor," said the litigants' counsel in unison.

"All right, then. Mr. Murfee, I assume that is Dr. Sewell sitting beside you in the ever-stylish Coconino County orange jumpsuit?"

"Yes, Your Honor. This is Dr. Emerick Sewell. Please stand."

Dr. Sewell stood and Thaddeus nudged him over to the lectern between counsel tables.

"For the record, state your name," said Judge Hoover.

"Emerick Sewell."

"And you're a medical doctor?"

"I am."

"What kind of medicine?"

"Neurosurgery."

The doctor's responses were just audible though the courtroom was essentially empty and still.

"And do you understand the charges the District Attorney had brought against you?"

"Yes."

"Well, you've been charged with First Degree Murder. In Arizona, that is a very serious charge that could if you are found guilty, result in your own death. Are you hearing me, Doctor?"

"Yes, I am."

"Good. Now you've availed yourself of one of the finest attorneys in northern Arizona, Mr. Murfee is at your side and he has filed a motion to set bail in your case. First, though, let me take you through the formalities of the initial appearance."

It took another five minutes while defendants' rights were spelled out and legal procedures explained. But then he was finished and the judge sat back in his heavy leather chair.

"Mr. Murfee, it's your motion for bail. Do you wish to be heard?"

Thaddeus slowly nodded. "It would be extremely rare that we would call a witness on a bail motion, Judge Hoover, but I think in this case I want to do just that."

"And who would you call? I see no one else in the courtroom."

"I would call the defendant himself."

"That's even more rare. Are you sure about this, Mr. Murfee? Doesn't this open your client to a barrage of cross-examination from our fine District Attorney, Mr. Sanders, who will, I am sure, bless us with a very thorough schooling in the uses of cross-examination where the defendant is totally vulnerable?"

"It does open him to a barrage. But I think he can handle it."

"Very well. It's your defense. Please proceed."

Thaddeus spoke more to the court reporter, "Defense calls Dr. Emerick Sewell to the stand."

The clerk swore the witness and Dr. Sewell, long and lanky, took his seat on the witness stand.

After the preliminaries, Thaddeus wasted no time.

"Dr. Sewell, what is the medical definition of death?"

"Well, as a neurosurgeon who has testified many times on the subject of death, I would have to say that one of the most common scenarios where death is usually pronounced is when a person is considered brain dead."

"Did you know or have reason to know whether Nadia Turkenov was brain dead?"

"I had been to Ms. Turkenov's room several times. During those times, I had the opportunity to read through her chart, including the brain scans and reports."

"Why did you do that?"

"Why? Because I felt responsible for her being there and wanted to help. She had read my book on my own death experience and had acted on that. I felt responsible."

"I don't want to get into whether you were legally responsible or not for her condition."

"I don't know about legal, Mr. Murfee. I'm speaking to a much higher standard, that of moral responsibility. I felt and feel morally responsible for what happened to her."

"When you withdrew her life support, namely the ventilator, what was your intention?"

"To set her free. She was already dead. The ventilator was doing what she couldn't do for herself. And her condition was irreversible. Her chart is very clear about that. Several physicians had concurred. She was gone."

"Why hadn't the family turned off the machines?"

Dr. Sewell smiled ironically. "Money. Her comatose state meant they could receive money from her estate. Her death meant her estate would go to a charity she was funding. A nursing scholarship."

"So, what you're saying is that you didn't murder her, you didn't end her life. She was already gone when you found her."

"Precisely. It was like I turned off a light switch with a burned-out bulb. Nothing changed. Nothing."

Thaddeus turned to the judge. "That's all for now, Your Honor."

"Mr. Sanders, any cross?"

DA Sanders all but exploded up out of his chair.

"My good doctor, wouldn't you agree that Ms. Turkenov was merely in a comatose state when you found her?"

"No. The word 'coma' is correctly used only when there is a temporary unconsciousness in which brain-stem functions are not irreversibly impaired. That was not the case here."

"But isn't there always the possibility that someone like Ms. Turkenov could come out of the unconscious state?"

"Not in her case."

"But Dr. Sewell, isn't that exactly what happened to you? I've read your book, sir. Your own doctors were preparing to turn off your life support when you suddenly blinked your eyes and came back. Couldn't that have happened with Ms. Turkenov?"

"No. Like I said, her brain-stem had altogether ceased to function. Breathing, which is dependent on brain-stem functioning, had irreversibly ceased. The medical records will prove this beyond all doubt."

"What about in your own case? Had your brain stem function ceased?"

"That was never a certainty in my own case. However, my physicians were prepared to counsel my family that, given the length of time I had been away, my condition was irreversible."

"So how does your case differ from her case?"

"How? I came back. She did not. I was out a week or less. She had been out a month or more. So long that bedsores were a problem."

"So if a person has bedsores, we should pull the plug? Is that your standard?"

"I was merely illustrating."

"So the length of time of unconsciousness is your standard?"

"That and the complete absence of brain stem activity. That is measurable and definable. It is a scientific standard that is verifiable and consistent with good medical science. It is a standard by which families around the world are counseled by their loved one's physicians to pull the plug, as you put it."

"Brainstem."

"Absence of."

"So you really believe you didn't commit murder?"

"I really believe I didn't kill anyone if that's what murder requires. The woman was already dead when I found her."

"Nothing further."

"Mr. Murfee?"

"Nothing further, Your Honor."

"You wish to be heard, Mr. Murfee?"

"My motion says what I wanted to say. I would only be repeating myself."

"Mr. Sanders?"

Sanders again stood.

"Your Honor, it's ludicrous. I've never heard of such a defense as Mr. Murfee is trying to get the court to fall for today."

"Hold it, Counsel. That's argument. Do you have any law for me?"

"Not yet, Judge."

"Well, you've had this motion since early this morning, according to the time stamp. Why no law for me?"

"I really haven't had time to brief it."

"Then you don't know whether Mr. Murfee's position is right or wrong, correct? It seems to be you're just reacting as any prosecutor would where someone has died. Get me some law, Mr. Sanders, and we'll revisit my order here today if you make your motion. But in the meantime, the court is going to set bail at one million dollars. That is all."

Stunned, Thaddeus sat back, all but speechless.

"You did it, Thaddeus," said Dr. Sewell. "I don't know how, but it worked! Talk to my agent. He'll get the money for bail. Whatever we need."

"Uh-huh," muttered Thaddeus. Then he collected himself. "We should have you out of jail later tonight. I'll be over to see you."

At that point, the deputies accompanied the doctor out of the courtroom and headed back across the lawn to the jail.

District Attorney Sanders stood stuffing his file into his briefcase.

"Bullshit, Murfee. And you know it."

"No, I don't know it. The woman was gone."

"Hey, pal. Read your client's book. It's the exact same medical case. I'm going to shove that book up his ass if this thing ever goes to trial. You can count on it."

"Well, shove away, Jocko. Shove away."

"And up yours too, Murfee."

"We'll see about that, Gary."

38

Katy had reached the point where, without admitting it, she needed her husband with her. She was frightened and she knew he knew it. So she no longer pushed at him to continue with a normal life. He wouldn't leave Katy even for one night, so Christine came to him.

While Katy's nurse was helping her with lunch in the study, Thaddeus and Christine met in Thaddeus' home office. There were two security men in each of their rooms; Thaddeus and Katy trusted the agents implicitly; they were all XFBI; they knew how to keep a secret and the couple's privacy would be protected while their well-being was also under protection.

"Your plan is to do what about Mascari?" Christine wanted to know. "If you do nothing, he will eventually kill you. Or your family. Or one of the little guys. This man is desperate and capable, Thad. You should have seen how he's living and how well-protected he is."

Thaddeus, sitting at his desk with his feet up, nodded slowly.

"It couldn't be worse timing for me," Thaddeus said. "I won't leave Katy as she is. I just can't do that."

Christine nodded.

"I know and I don't blame you."

"And I don't want you going after him. It's too much for one person. So, what do I do?"

They sat and made eye contact and then looked away. For the first time since they had come together back in Orbit, the silence between them was an uncomfortable one. There was something else between them, a dynamic that neither wished to acknowledge. Finally, Thaddeus broke the silence.

"You know, in my life, I have sometimes had to do things I hated. Everyone goes through times like that."

"Sure."

"I think I don't have the choice of staying here with Katy and hoping for peace. Mascari is not going to allow that."

"True."

He sighed a long, full sigh. It was a sound of resignation. Then he stood and moved to the window that framed the mountains a few miles away. It was an endless kaleidoscope of clouds, sunlight, rain, snow, and perfect change that Thaddeus had come to attribute to more than nature. What it was, he couldn't say, but what happened outside that window, since he had been spending his days in that room, was breathtaking and sometimes kept him watching for hours. Outside his window was alive. That's the best explanation he could come up with. And he felt a part of it. He was inside the dream himself though he watched it all through the glass. His vision, his eyes, projected him into the scenes that came and went, turned and twisted, and made him one with the world he saw. It had been a long time, coming to believe that observation equals creation, the stuff of the quantum physicists. But deep down, he had bought in. It had happened while he was driving into town and Christine had called with the news of BAT's death. Thaddeus had cried out; he had finally reached the point where he could no longer handle his life on his own. He didn't consider himself religious and never would; he just knew he needed help and at that time he was feeling abandoned and the hope offered by Dr. Sewell and his book and the science well…for the first time, he saw a way to cling to something more powerful than his own inner strength. He didn't have a word for it yet, but he knew it involved belief without proof. And that was far, far beyond anything he'd ever tried on for size.

And if the physicists were right, then some part of him—some part of Katy—was eternal. He would always be inside the scene, and millions of other scenes, for eternity. The name for his new belief system, he didn't know. His long afternoons reading and watching scientists expound on YouTube while Katy dozed, had only left him with more questions. But of one thing he was sure: he would see her again. In fact, there would never be a time when he wouldn't see her.

The thought of his forever connection to Katy made him turn away from the vista outside. He met Christine's eyes.

"I'm going after him. My family needs me to protect them. It's that simple."

Christine stood and gave him a hug.

"Then I'm going with you."

Thaddeus leaned away and looked deep into her eyes.

"Ordinarily I would insist not. But this time, I know I need you."

"Then it's done. We'll get this guy together."

"How long will it take?" asked Thaddeus, returning to his seat at the desk. "Will we be gone more than a few days?"

"Unknown. Probably. He's surrounded by security every minute of the day."

Thaddeus' demeanor suddenly fell. The sadness pierced him like a spike.

"She could die while I'm away."

"I know. She could."

"But she has told me herself. Now it's about more than just she and I. There are children at risk today. Their safety is greater than what Katy and I have."

"I know."

"So what do we do?"

Christine sat down and crossed her legs.

"First, you're not going. I am."

"But I thought—"

"No. Not up for discussion. You're staying here."

"Why?"

"For openers, my people have a line on the money. We're maybe two transfers away from his stash."

"How long will it take to locate?"

"A week at the most. We're very close."

Thaddeus nodded. "And him personally. What do we know?"

"Let's start with a map of the area where he spends his nights and most of his days. It's a seaside villa."

"Google Earth."

"Exactly."

Christine pulled her chair up to the desk and swung Thaddeus' laptop around. "Let me do this."

She located Mascari's city, street, and enclave and resized them so the key area filled the screen.

"Here's his home, right here."

"All right. What kind of security on the perimeter?"

"BAT and I had decided it's an electric fence."

"With armed sensors, of course."

"Of course. Any breach and he's immediately alerted."

"So entry will be difficult if not impossible."

"Pretty much."

"And when he leaves there?"

"He caravans. Two or three groups of three or four vehicles will suddenly come pouring out, heading different directions, blackout windows in the cars. It's pretty damn impressive."

"I'm sure. But he has a favorite vehicle?"

"I think so."

"You need to be sure. You'll only get one chance at this. Hey, an idea. Where does he go every day?"

"He goes—he goes to Dista Fiencci's for lunch."

"What's that?"

"Continental cuisine. BAT and I cased it once. Hold it. That's it. Okay, you can cross Mascari off your death watch."

"What's that mean?"

She tapped the side of her head. "It means the wheels are turning. We're done here."

"Is it safe? Do you come home?"

"Hell, yes. I'm not laying down my life for some effing loser like Mascari."

"You're sure?"

She gave him a hard stare. It was her *Bet Me* stare. You didn't cross her after that look.

Thaddeus slowly nodded.

"Okay, then. I couldn't do this without you."

"That's why I'm here. You couldn't."

"You are—"

"I'm your friend," she said, and laughed. "Always have been. Always will be."

"I'll toast to that," said Thaddeus, raising his coffee cup.

Christine made an air toast.

"Time for me to check on Katy."

"Of course. I'll come with."

"She'd like that. She's crazy about you. Which brings me to something else she said about you. And me."

Christine shook her head violently.

"No. Let's go see her. That's all we can do at this time."

"Right, then."

"Right."

39

The District Attorney's investigator was a man named Herbert Constance. Lieutenant Constance was a slight man, angular face, who moved with the grace and confidence of a Spanish bullfighter. Watching him, those around him would find themselves marveling at the energy he brought into any room or meeting, for it was boundless and he refused to rest or back away from a problem until he had the resolution he thought was the correct one. He was thin-lipped and his aquiline nose fit his face perfectly. Hair was a brush cut with long, out-of-style sideburns that reached his jawline, his only nod to a personal grooming tic. Otherwise, he was neutral in his dress, the color of his shirts and ties, the style of shoes and suits he wore—everything was thought out to draw the least bit of attention possible to himself. Anonymity was his aim and he pulled it off quite well.

He called a meeting of the key players in Nadia Turkenov's conservatorship, those who had taken an active role in her situation while she was alive. In attendance were her brother Roy and her two children Albert and Anastasia. Anastasia was, as usual, accompanied by her husband Jack Millerton, complete with the CPA's case full of documents he thought might be important to the investigator. Never mind that they hadn't been requested; Jack brought them all along anyway.

They met on the second floor of the Coconino County Courthouse, inside the investigator's office that connected with the office of the District Attorney himself, Gary Sanders. Constance sat at his desk while the threesome pulled up chairs and waited for whatever it was he had to say to them.

"Thanks for coming. And my condolences on your loss. The taking of your mother's—and sister's—life is something that can't go unpunished. Dr. Sewell is going away to prison for a long, long time. That I promise you."

"What about the death penalty?" said Millerton, anger boiling in his words. "Is that still on the table?"

"Unknown right now. Sometimes we don't know until the last minute when the judge is settling jury instructions with the attorneys right before the case goes to the jury. At that time, the judge decides if there will be a capital murder jury instruction or not."

"There damn well oughta be," said Roy. He looked at his niece and nephew and they nodded their agreement.

"Here's our plan for the prosecution. We need the family's buy-in. First, put on your loved one's treating physician. He will testify that the decision hadn't been made to remove heroic measures. Meaning life support. I've talked to him at length. He's prepared to testify that he has seen patients come back, regain consciousness, who were unconscious as long as Ms. Turkenov."

"Damn!" exclaimed Roy. "That bastard *did* kill her!"

"Well, the downside is, according to your mother's neurologist, the fact there was no brain stem activity. In many medical circles that meant she was brain dead and that means legally dead. So there's that."

"But do *all* doctors believe that to be the case?" asked Anastasia. "In my studies, I see huge disagreements all the time on medical theories and procedures. Medicine is known for that."

Constance clasped his hands together as if washing them. "That I don't know. I'm sure the defendant will have a very attractive doctor who disagrees with our doctor. That's why we have trials."

"Can Dr. Sewell be a witness too?" Roy asked.

"He can and probably will, at least on the issue of legal death. He's a dangerous witness, too, because of his top-notch medical education and postgrad training. You can't attend a finer medical school than Harvard. So, there's that."

"What do you see our role as?" asked Jack, whose wife immediately made eye contact with him. Jack looked away, refusing to meet her gaze. They had talked about this already and it was her opinion that Jack shouldn't be introduced into the case or made known to the jury in any way. She wanted it that way because she felt her husband was always overreaching and always about me me me. She had told him so just that morning.

"That's something I want to talk about, Mr. Millerton. So I'm glad you brought it up."

"See?" said Jack's look back at his wife. "Thank you. I'm trying."

"Since your loved one was admitted to the hospital, it's my understanding Jack and Roy have been in charge of her estate? Her money?"

"Yes," said the uncle and son-in-law in unison.

"And have her funds been properly accounted for? No expenditures made that could be questioned?"

"Absolutely," said Millerton. "All above-board."

"Well, you did pay yourselves out of my mother's estate," said Anastasia. "Don't forget to tell Lieutenant Constance about that."

At just that moment, Albert Turkenov was shown into the room by the receptionist Constance shared with the District Attorney. Nadia's son looked distressed, which he was, having driven twenty above the speed limit across town to make the meeting.

"Sorry," he said, catching his breath as he took a seat on the couch. "Just closed a sale."

"I'm Constance," said the investigator. "You must be Albert?"

"I am. I'm one of the conservators of my mother's estate."

"We were just talking about that. Are you, Albert, aware of any expenditures made by the estate that weren't on the up and up since you've been a co-conservator?"

"Nothing. We're squeaky clean."

"What about what you geniuses paid yourselves?" Anastasia retorted to her brother. She was still angry about their having paid money to themselves for looking after her mother's funds.

"Whoa, what's this about?" Constance asked. His gray eyes had widened and he looked in alarm at the three men. "You paid her money to yourselves? Well, there must have been a court order allowing it, so it'll pass muster."

"No court order," Anastasia exclaimed. "That's what I'm so pissed off about. They just took my mother's money and haven't even told the judge about it."

Now Constance stood and paced east to west behind his desk.

"Let me get this straight. You three gentlemen paid yourselves money out of Nadia Turkenov's funds? How much was paid?"

"I got five thousand," said Uncle Roy.

"I got five thousand," said Albert. "But I earned it."

"I received an equal amount," said Jack. But Anastasia leaned and bumped hard into him with her shoulder.

"Tell the whole truth," she hissed at her husband.

"Well, there's been quite a bit of professional expenditure of time on my behalf. I'm a certified public accountant, you know."

"Never mind that. How much did you get?"

"Almost twenty-five hundred."

"Plus the five thousand?"

"Plus the five thousand."

Constance's pace increased behind his desk. He opened his mouth and bit his fist, an old habit he was trying to break. He repeated. It was better than shouting in frustration.

"You've taken over seventeen thousand dollars for overseeing a million bucks in CD's? Are you serious? What the hell could CD's require?"

"Well, I had to prepare an accounting," said Millerton, puffing his chest out. "Plus there was an entire weekend of paperwork, reviewing bank statements, going over a year's worth of expenditures."

"She'd only been unconscious for two weeks!" exclaimed Anastasia. "I told you it was stupid to go over the past year's expenditures. But oh, no, you had to make a big deal out of it like you were looking for money she shouldn't have spent. It was her money, goddammit!" she cried. "You just robbed her, Jack Millerton, and I'm seeing a lawyer and divorcing you!"

"Honey," said Millerton. "Let's save this for later. Let's go for coffee, cool down, and talk it through. I'll go over my time sheet with—"

"You and your time sheets can go straight to hell. I want my mother's money replaced by all of you or I'm calling the judge myself."

Constance ceased his pacing and pointed at Millerton. "You know, sir, this borders on theft. In fact, maybe it is outright theft. Any idiot knows you can't take money from a ward of the court without a court order. I'm going to have to take this to the D.A. At this point, I have to advise you not to discuss it further with me. It's not in your best interests to keep talking."

"You're telling us we're in trouble?" said Uncle Roy. He, for one, was ready to return to his store and the fifth of Wild Turkey he kept in the supply cabinet. It was past noon so it was allowed.

"I'm saying this is technically theft, what you're telling me. You have the right to remain silent, and you should. You have the right to an attorney, and you should see one right away."

Constance then continued with the balance of the Miranda statement.

The four family members managed to escape his office before he had concluded.

It was time to lawyer-up, said Albert in the hallway.

No one disagreed.

40

Getting past XFBI was simple. The Peak Home Health ID and his own picture ID—a brand new Arizona driver's license obtained just for the ruse—waltzed him right through the front door. He was shown all around by the on-duty aide and his duties explained.

He was introduced to Katy Murfee, who saw him through a haze of heavy narcotics but struggled nevertheless to make him feel welcome. The house and laundry, bathroom, and supply facilities were explained and presented so that he would feel comfortable and competent when he appeared for his first shift. Luchesi shadowed the on-duty aide over the final two hours of her shift, as planned, and he became comfortable with the job. He had never actually done any form of health care in his life, but he also didn't plan to be around all that long. It almost made him laugh out loud like he was in some kind of horror movie as he was taken through the house and saw the children and the parents: he had a fleeting moment with each one where he saw them riddled with bullet holes and bleeding. No, he wouldn't be around all that long. But neither would they. Not even the little boy with his trucks and trains. He just might be the first to go.

XFBI had searched his nursing bag. But they said very little about the medications he was bringing in. Nursing staff that showed up with re-supply was common enough; the drugs that Luchesi brought along were passed through without comment.

At the end of her shift, the on-duty aide re-introduced Luchesi to Katy, who this time understood she had a new helper.

"Katy, this is Diego. He'll be taking the next shift."

Katy smiled wanly. "Good to make your acquaintance. Welcome to my little house of horrors," she said, indicating all the medical gear and hospital bed and carts and cabinet stuffed with supplies and medications.

"Good to meet you," said Diego. "Thank you for allowing me to help."

Katy scootched up in bed with her arms. "So. Where did you train?"

"East Valley Community College. North L.A. County."

"I might have heard of that. And maybe I haven't. My mind is a bit foggy, as you'll see."

"That's all right. I'll try to keep you from having to think so much."

"That sounds good. Seriously, most of the time I get along pretty good on my own. Except for the stuff I have no control over."

"You're talking toilet."

"Exactly. That needs help."

Luchesi looked down and didn't meet her eyes. Katy caught this lack of eye contact and pursed her lips. What was that all about? she wondered. The topic was a sensitive one to any bed-ridden patient. Home health aides were trained to be very accommodating in that regard. But he had looked away. Well, she frowned.

But then she quickly forgot about it.

"Are you a one-nighter or will you have midnights for awhile?"

"I'm perm. I'm going to school in the daytime."

"What classes are you taking?"

"Oh..." his voice trailed off. Then, "something to do with nursing. I want to get my degree."

"Are you going for your BSN?"

"I don't think so. I'm going for my nursing degree."

Katy looked at the first aide, who was busily packing her bag to leave. The aide shrugged. Some people...her look said. There was no explaining. But still, he didn't know what the BSN degree was? Katy had referred to the bachelor of science in nursing, the standard bachelor's degree in nursing, and the man said he wasn't going for the BSN, that he was going for the nursing degree? What? She sat back, just a little ruffled, but she quickly attributed her feelings to the drugs they were giving her. She was paranoid, she told herself. Let it go.

Katy smiled. "Yes, the nursing degree is a great one to have."

"I hear you're a doctor?"

"I am."

"What kind of doctor?"

"What board certification? Family practice."

"Oh. Then you know more about my job than I do, I'll bet."

Katy nodded and said, "Maybe I do. I might at that."

The 4pm-12am aide finished her packing and came to Katy's bedside. She leaned down and pecked Katy on the forehead with her lips. "Have a good night."

"I will. Diego and I are going to get to know one another."

"We are," said Diego. "And I'm going to ask all kinds of questions about being a doctor. I might even go for that someday."

"Sure," said Katy. "We can talk all you like."

"By the way, Diego. We've got a pretty good bedsore on the coccyx. Take precautions."

"Will do," said Luchesi, though he hadn't the faintest idea what that meant. But he nodded graciously and assured the departing aide that he would do whatever was necessary.

Katy waited to see just what those precautions would consist of.

It would be interesting.

41

Physicians' Mountain Mutual Insurance decided to deny coverage to Dr. Sewell. They sent a certified letter both to Dr. Sewell and to Thaddeus. In it, they said that they had originally begun the civil case for medical malpractice with a reservation of rights, meaning they wouldn't confirm insurance coverage for Dr. Sewell until they were sure that what had happened was a factual situation that was covered by the insurance policy. Now they had completed their investigation and decided against coverage. They were very sorry, but their hands were tied by the terms of the contract.

Thaddeus was angry and decided they wouldn't just walk away like that. He made some calls and flew to L.A. and met with the claims manager in Irvine.

Stanis Vonocur was a man who smiled and whistled through his days as the claims manager at PMMI, but who, inside, was in turmoil as he blocked payment of claims at every turn. His job was to avoid paying out the insurance company's money and he had gotten very good at it over the years. He sat on the insurance company's mountain of money like it was his own. Screwing policyholders right and left, he continued to smile and whistle. He grudgingly agreed to meet with Thaddeus when the lawyer had called to complain about the coverage denial.

They met for lunch at Felix's, where the Cuban food was all the rave.

Sure enough, as self-described, Thaddeus found the balding, smiling man in the lounge, waiting for a table. He looked up as Thaddeus approached. Introductions were made and the men settled around the small table. Thaddeus ordered a coffee and Vonocur requested another scotch.

"So," said Thaddeus, "you've denied coverage to my client and I want to find out, for the record, just what your thinking is."

The smiling man licked a drip of scotch from his thumb. "Sorry. Uh, we just don't feel that writing a book and appearing on a TV show establishes a physician-patient relationship that would be covered by a medical malpractice policy, Mr. Murfee. The whole notion is really stretching it and we've tried to be forthright about that from the gate. If the woman wasn't a patient, there isn't any coverage for what happened to her. Especially where it was her own wrongful act. But that's just an aside."

"You have a point, and I'm the first to admit it from my side of the street. But there's a rising theory of liability for doctors who give medical advice on TV. All the doctor shows have contributed to this, as people have tried to follow Dr. Oz and Dr. Phil and apply some of their methods. Lawsuits have been filed against the TV medics and settlements have been made. There is a growing consensus among plaintiffs' lawyers that this is a very legitimate and very ripe area of the law. You're just going to see more of it, Mr. Vonocur. My suggestion is that you become a leader and honor the trend."

"Of course, you would suggest that. You're looking for a deep pocket for your client in case the civil suit goes ass over teakettle on you. Speaking of, what about the homicide charges? Thank God we're not in on that. Isn't that case pretty open and closed?"

"Some might think so. It gets into a very technical area of medicine."

"I'm all ears. Enlighten me."

Thaddeus' coffee arrived, with the claims manager's scotch. They both sipped.

"Well, there can be no murder without a living human being whose life is terminated by an illegal act. We're arguing there was no living human, that she was already deceased when Dr. Sewell withdrew the life support."

The claims manager smacked his lips. "Surely no judge is going to go for that. Are they?"

"Unknown. We're trying."

"What's the medical definition of death nowadays?"

"In this case, it's the cessation of brain stem activity that qualifies the patient's status as medically dead."

"Is that the same as legally dead?"

"The law will take its lead from medicine. Always a question of fact."

"Sounds like an uphill battle, to me."

"It sure is, and there's no denying that. But we're always prepared for battle around my office. Even in cases like this, bad faith insurance cases where the carrier is denying coverage. I came here to tell you that I'm prepared to file a bad faith action against your insurance company on Monday if you don't reverse your decision. Not only that, but there will be no settlement ever. I will take you to trial, I will hit you for millions of dollars, and I'll drag your name through the mud with every newspaper and TV station that will listen to me. Plus I'll let the American Medical Association know that they should decline your advertising in any of their journals to their membership. In short, you screw with my client and I will screw with you. Now, where were we?"

Vonocur grappled with the open collar of his shirt. He pulled it open wider and tried to appear relaxed, but clearly he was in panic mode.

Said Vonocur, "We're learning more from you about the underlying claim. You've raised some factual issues that we weren't aware of. It seems to me," he said, licking his thumb free of scotch, "you should allow me a week to discuss with my superiors. As I sit here I am more inclined to agree with your position, given the nationwide trending you've observed. I would like our in-house counsel to review those kinds of cases and try to give us a trend line. If it's as you say, that more and more of these cases are being filed, then PMMI should be among the first to rally and carry the fight. We should be among the frontrunners to declare coverage where our physician is sued for something he or she said on TV."

"That's what I call 'sweetly reasonable,'," said Thaddeus. He checked his watch.

"In a hurry?"

"My plane leaves at three. Any later and the runways are packed with late afternoon departures."

"What airline?"

"Thaddeus Murfee Airways. I have my own jet."

"Of course, you would."

Thaddeus leaned forward on the table, tipping it slightly so that Mr. Vanocur's scotch sloshed.

"Let me remind you. I'm speaking off the record now. You change your decision or I will trash you. With every dime I have I will outspend you and drag you into court and there I will trash you. Call me no later than Monday noon with good news. At twelve-oh-one p.m. I am going to file my lawsuit against you. Your job is to make sure that doesn't happen."

"Got it. Well, then, Mr. Murfee—"

But Thaddeus was already on his feet, turning on his heel and leaving before the man could respond.

As far as Thaddeus was concerned, it had all been said.

42

So now he had a civil case *and* a criminal case charging ahead at the same time against Dr. Sewell. The civil case was the lesser of two evils, so Thaddeus began concentrating almost solely on the criminal case.

There had been an indictment, so the preliminary hearing was unnecessary. The indictment charged a murder with premeditation, an offense punishable by death in Arizona with certain circumstances. Thaddeus knew that death penalty cases in Arizona came in all stripes and colors. In May of 2015, there was an appeal from a Maricopa County Superior Court death penalty case because twenty-nine pending first-degree murder cases combined to claim that state laws did not clearly limit which murders could result in death penalties. Under law established by U.S. Supreme Court decisions, death was supposed to be reserved for the worst of the worst murders, and statutes were supposed to define those cases. The Arizona appellate attorneys argued that Arizona law contained so many "aggravating factors"—circumstances that made the murder serious enough to warrant the death penalty—that virtually any murder qualified. Knowing this and knowing the ambiguity of Arizona's death penalty, Thaddeus feared for his client when the judge ordered a jury trial in the case to begin on October nine, the same date that discovery in the civil case was to be concluded.

The two cases running on the calendar in parallel actually helped Thaddeus. Ordinarily in criminal cases, discovery is severely limited and consists of little more than document exchange between prosecutor and defense counsel, plus a list of witnesses. However, the civil case breathed new life into the criminal case because the civil case offered the chance to take depositions ostensibly for the civil case but that really would be used in the criminal case in order to (1) put a freeze on witness testimony so that it became known, and (2) provide a platform—the deposition—to impeach the witness who tried to change his or her testimony at trial from what he or she had already sworn to in deposition. This being the case, Thaddeus and Shep made a list of all witnesses they would depose and set the plan in motion.

They made a file folder for each witness and spread the folders out on the conference room table in Thaddeus' office. It was a twenty-foot-long table with rounded ends, surrounded by five chairs per side and one chair per end, and hewn out of the same ponderosa pine that surrounded Flagstaff and left to its natural color. Thaddeus had had the table specially built and it allowed room to arrange the witness files three down and five across, for openers. There was a file for Warren Winnzing, the investigator on Nadia's civil case; Franklin Parsons, M.D., Nadia's personal physician; Jack Millerton, Nadia's son-in-law/conservator; Anastasia Millerton, Nadia's daughter; Albert Turkenov, Nadia's son/conservator of the person; Roy Underwood, Nadia's brother/conservator; Herbert Constance, City of Flagstaff homicide detective; Eleanor M. Hemenway, City of Flagstaff detective; Francis G. Ellis, M.D., Coconino County Medical Examiner; Louis Rachmanoff, M.D., the anesthesiologist/psychologist hired by Thaddeus to give expert testimony on consciousness; and Emerick Sewell, M.D., physician and defendant in the murder case. Twelve of the files were marked accordingly; three were unmarked, to be added as witness names surfaced.

They started with the detectives' report of investigation or ROI, as it was known in the Flagstaff Police Department. The ROI was a chronological listing of everything detectives Constance and Hemenway had done since first being assigned to the case. Shep knew the two detectives and told Thaddeus that Constance was the plodder, the mule pulling the plow down track after track; he was known for never giving up. To Constance, there was no such thing as a cold case. There were only cases in varying stages of being solved and closed out. Hemenway was a relative newcomer. She had started life as a patrolman doing traffic surveillance and answering emergency calls. She had had to use her firearm on duty once: a jealous husband had trapped his wife's lover nude inside the husband's bathroom and was threatening to shoot him with his hunting rifle. When Hemenway inched down the hallway to talk to the husband, the man suddenly pointed the rifle at Hemenway and worked the bolt action. Hemenway, who had qualified as Expert on the shooting range, fired one round, striking the husband in the right shoulder, disabling the trigger hand and finger. She was awarded the department's Citation of Merit for her actions and later was sent a spray of flowers by the husband as he recovered in the hospital from his wound. "Thanks for not killing me," the note said simply. Hemenway made her spurs that day and was now one of "the boys" in the detective bureau. Hemenway and Constance were partners and, as Shep and Thaddeus reviewed their chronology of the detectives' actions, it became clear that Hemenway took the lead on interacting with the citizenry while Constance took the lead on interaction with physicians, other police agencies, and the crime lab and medical examiner. It looked to be working well and all witnesses had been contacted by the duo and their statements taken.

The two lawyers then reviewed the crime scene pictures. Unlike most crime scenes, there was only one room under investigation—the ICU suite where Nadia Turkenov had spent the final days of her life. Photographs were taken of her bed. The two lawyers only glanced at these and found nothing remarkable. Photographs of Nadia herself were taken, head to toe, with special close-ups of the trachea wound where the ventilator had been inserted into her throat to pump life-giving oxygen to her lungs. The margins of the wound were fresh with blood where the plastic unit had been abruptly pulled free of flesh.

"I think this means nothing to us," Thaddeus said of the wound pictures.

"Judgment reserved," said Shep, scratching his head. "You never know in these cases."

"I'll put it in the TBD pile then," Thaddeus said, and he started a stack of photographs that would be returned to as the case developed.

Photographs of her telemetry monitors were taken as they appeared at bedside after her death. The nurses and staff remembered their training in such cases and had touched nothing. Thaddeus and Shep carefully reviewed the instruments. FMC's telemetry equipment were set up to monitor Nadia's vital signs including pulse and oxygen saturation levels. The lawyers studied the bundle of wires that had been attached to the patient. They hired an ICU nurse to come into the office and explain what they were looking at.

"Here, she said, are the colored lines. We monitor these at bedside and at the nurses' station."

"What machines are these?" asked Thaddeus.

"All right," she said, using her ballpoint as a pointer over the photographs. "This unit is the ventilator. A ventilator is a large machine that breathes for the patient. Sometimes it is used because the patient is not breathing well enough on their own and other times it is needed because the patient has been given drugs that suppress the breathing. You may have heard the term of a drug-induced coma."

"Our patient had a self-induced coma."

"You mean she OD'd?"

"Yes, on purpose."

"Oh, well. We get those every day. Usually require ventilator support. Now," moving along with her pen, "there are the IV's. There are multiple IV's and they were providing fluids and medications. I can't say what without seeing her chart. These are two IV pumps here, used to meter the flow of medications. The alarm, right here, is one noise we hear a lot around the ICU as these things are ridiculously inconsistent in their delivery."

"So the machine comes and you flick the tube with your fingernail."

The nurse nodded. "Something like that, yes. This independent tube down here is the NG tube. Its real name is Nasogastric tube, which was inserted in the patient's nose because they were feeding her liquid nutrition. Very common as well where the patient is comatose. Without food, they lose weight and eventually starve."

"And this? What's this?"

"Notice it's further down the bed. That's your urinary cath. The tube connects down here, like in this next photograph, to this bag hung on the bed frame. This carries urine from the patient to the bag. Continuous delivery."

"Blood pressure this one?"

"Exactly. That's the new style of blood pressure cuff that's left on continuously and then the machine kicks on at regular intervals to take the blood pressure automatically. The results at FMC are displayed on the telemetry monitor. Also, they're recorded and become part of her electronic chart."

Shep sat back and lit one of his Winston cigarettes.

"Please," said Thaddeus. "You know we don't have smoking in here."

Shep shook his head. "Well, partner, you have me, so you have smoking. If one of us goes, we both go."

"OMG," said Thaddeus. He folded his arms and shook his head. "Whatever."

"Now, Miss," said Shep through a cloud of smoke. "I need to know what kinds of problems can develop in these patients."

"You mean other things that can kill them?"

"Yep."

"Why is that important? Your client withdrew a patient's life support. That's what killed her."

"Humor me, please," said Shep. He didn't want to possibly tip-off the prosecutor by telling the nurse that he was going to prove the woman was dead already when Dr. Sewell took action. All processes that might have ended her life, besides the infection ravaging her brain, would need to be sorted. "I just want a full discussion with you. That's what I'm paying you for."

The nurse sighed. "All right. Well, a brain infection or injury leaves a person open to some complications. Some are the result of the patient being immobile. Others are because the brain's control of bodily functions has been compromised."

"Which might include what?"

"DVT's or blood clots. The lack of movement leaves the brain injured patient susceptible to Deep Vein Thrombosis, commonly referred to as DVT's. These are blood clots like I said. The major concern here is that these clots will travel in the body and cause a pulmonary embolism which can be fatal. In this patient's case, the hospital was using pneumatic compression boots and compression stockings to try to prevent their formation. There's also a Greenfield Vena Cava Filter that can be surgically inserted into the vein to catch the clots before they travel to the lungs."

"Whoa. Hold on. Greenfield what?"

"Greenfield Vena Cava Filter. It's a medical device that is basically a filter. It traps blood clots before they can do damage."

"All right. Well. Was that used with Ms. Turkenov?"

"No. Evidently it wasn't necessary. Does the autopsy mention pulmonary embolism?"

"No, it doesn't."

"So that wasn't even an issue. Should I go on?"

"Please do."

"Seizures are common following a brain injury or disease. So seizure medication is often given prophylactically. The problem is, these have a sedative effect. While you want your patient to wake up, you're giving them sedatives. Not a good medical scenario at all."

"What else?"

"Pneumonia. Many brain disease patients on ventilators end up with pneumonia. That's what kills them. The staff is expecting it as they look out for symptoms and treat it quickly. It can be stopped if caught in time."

"Go on."

"Minor stuff—minor regarding life-threatening: ulcers or bed sores. Drop foot. Autonomic functions can disrupt the body's ability to manage its autonomic functions. Very high temperatures might bring this on."

"Anything else?"

"Not really, at least not that I'm aware of. I'm an ICU nurse and these are the common disease processes we have to be aware of."

Thaddeus spread his hands and looked the nurse in the eye.

"So what killed Nadia Turkenov, in your opinion?"

"None of what I've been mentioning killed her. She died because she couldn't breathe without the ventilator. Open and shut."

"All right. If we called you to testify, that would be your testimony?"

"Please don't call me to testify. You haven't paid me for that and I haven't agreed to it. Won't agree to it."

"We won't," said Thaddeus. "Not if you really feel that way."

"I really feel that way."

"Well, those are all the questions I think we have. Shep, any other?"

Shep scanned over his notes and slowly shook his head. "Not that I can see. Can we call you if we remember something or find something else?"

"Of course. Just remember my hourly rate."

Both lawyers smiled.

"Of course," said Shep. "You have to be compensated for your time."

"Don't we all?" she said.

"Yep. All right, thanks for coming by."

"That's what you paid me for. But you're welcome. I hope I've helped."

"Definitely."

The nurse stood and gathered her things.

When she was gone, Shep said to Thaddeus, "Let's put this in context. None of what she just talked about killed the victim. What our client did is what killed her."

"Agree. And he's saying he had Ms. Turkenov's permission—in fact, was directed—to withdraw the life support."

"That's just downright crazy. Hearing voices, bullshit! Can you sell that to a jury?"

"Probably not. We're going to need experts in the field to do that."

"Experts in what field? The Hearing Voices Field?"

"No. I'm thinking consciousness studies. Have you read Dr. Sewell's book?"

"Started to. Then threw it aside. I ain't buying it."

"I know. It's very different. But that's the same thing they said to the first doctor who said germs are what cause infection. Everyone looked at him like he was crazy."

"You actually believe these people like Sewell are on the verge of some new discovery here, don't you? I knew it!"

"I am keeping an open mind. On the one hand, I've agreed to defend the guy. On the other hand, the whole inquiry is giving my wife some hope. That's enough for me to buy-in right there."

"Well, I can't be examining witnesses in court on this one. The jury would see right through me."

"You can handle the legal arguments outside of the jury's hearing. That was our deal. I'll do the witnesses."

Shep lit up another cigarette and blew a plume of smoke at the ceiling.

"All right. I'm in on that basis."

"Good. Now the next thing we need to do is have someone review the brain scans. We're going to have to prove there was no brain stem activity. If there's no brain stem activity, the patient is medically dead."

"Who do we get for that?"

"I've got feelers out to a couple of local neurologists. One of them looks promising."

"Name?"

"Jack Fielder. He's new, out of the University of Arizona med school, just spent four years at the Barrow's Neurological center in Phoenix."

"Where they treat brain injuries."

"And brain disease."

"Right. Sounds good. Well, let's break for now and then get him in here."

"Her. Jack is a her. Jacqueline."

"So be it. Let's get her in here."

"I'm on it. She's meeting with me later this afternoon."

"You're on it. That's excellent."

"We've already sent her the scans. We'll know in a couple of hours if she can help us."

"Fingers crossed, Thaddeus, my boy."

43

Jacqueline Field was, in fact, writing an article for *The Atlantic* explaining how doctors test for brain death. So, she told Thaddeus, his timing was perfect. Thaddeus was meeting with her after his meeting with Shep and the ICU nurse. She met him in her office on North San Francisco Street and told him she could give him fifteen minutes. When they were introduced, he was struck by her bright, cheerful manner, and her short blonde hair which she wore pulled to one side and held in place by a daisy barrette. "My dad always called me 'Daisy,'" she laughed when Thaddeus mentioned that he liked the barrette. "It's a family thing."

He didn't waste any time. "So tell me, Doc," he said, "how do you decide when a patient is brain dead?"

"Brain dead," she told Thaddeus, "is now a legal term as well as a medical term. When a person is brain dead, there can be the withdrawal of life support which, if done properly, does not result in legal consequences."

"What is the difference between someone in a coma, who may or may not improve, and someone who is truly brain dead?"

"Brain death is the irreversible cessation of all functions of the entire brain, including the all-important brain stem that houses the tiny brain function that keeps us awake and alert. It's called the RAS and it's the little thing that wakes us up in the morning. The brain stem is the mechanism that controls our breathing. Dead is dead. Brain death isn't a different type of death, and patients who meet the criteria of brain death are legally dead."

Thaddeus related the facts of the case, putting into context what Dr. Sewell had done. Then he asked, "Was he medically correct in doing this? I'm not asking is he legally correct, just medically."

"The EEGs showed no brain stem activity at all. Look, how about I do this. How about I tell you how I, as a neurologist, handle these cases when I'm called in to consult."

"Please do."

"There are strict criteria for brain death. These are carefully followed before a patient becomes an organ donor or their ventilator is unplugged. First, they must be in a coma with no brain stem or pupillary reflexes. That's what you had with Ms. Turkenov."

"Okay."

"But a formal brain death evaluation takes about twenty minutes. First, I pinch the patient to see if there's any flinch. Any reflex. Next, I will make sure there are no brain stem reflexes. Maybe I shine a light in their eyes to determine whether there's pupillary reaction. Last, I might disconnect the ventilator and check to see whether rising carbon dioxide levels in the blood stimulate the brain. If none of these three findings is present, I pronounce brain death. It's pretty straightforward, Thaddeus."

"What about the electroencephalogram?"

"Right. The EEG will record a complete absence of brain activity where there's brain death."

"So that's all it takes?"

"Yes. As you can see, it's a combination of factors. In your case I've reviewed the EEG. Your Ms. Turkenov had zero brain activity, zero brain stem activity. The woman was medically and legally dead."

"And you'll testify to this at Dr. Sewell's trial?"

"Sure I will. I testify all the time and rather enjoy it."

"Now that's refreshing."

"What about you, Thaddeus? Do you like to go to trial?"

"Absolutely. It's the scariest thing I do and the most rewarding thing I do. After my family, of course."

"You have a family, then?"

"Yes, four children. And one very sick wife."

"Oh, I'm sorry to hear that."

"Metastatic breast cancer. She doesn't have much time left."

"Oh, well you have my condolences. It must be very hard."

Thaddeus looked down at the desk. "It is."

"Okay, well," the doctor said with a flounce, "have I answered your questions today?"

"You really have. I can't thank you enough. And Dr. Sewell thanks you too."

"What about that? Are you going to be able to get him off?"

"You know, it depends on the jury we end up with. That's always a crap shoot, as they say."

"Is 'crap shoot' a legal term?"

Thaddeus laughed and the dark moment of Katy's impending death was dispelled.

He found that he liked the young doctor. Admired her.

And the blonde hair with the daisy barrette—that really sealed the deal.

She was adorable. But he didn't allow himself to think that. Not more than a thought he immediately drove from his mind. His thoughts turned to Katy and his adoration of her. He was loyal, he belonged to her and he always would.

He doubted there would ever be another for him. In fact, he was sure of it.

Walking down the street to his car, he noticed the light playing off the leaves of the trees in a glimmer and dance that he had noticed before, whenever he was happy. Which meant, because he hadn't noticed its absence for months now, he hadn't been really happy. But who would be? How could he be?

But for a moment, he was.

Now what was that all about?

44

"How did it go today?" Katy asked Thaddeus. "It was man-overboard around here today."

"What happened?"

"Diego changed my sheets."

"While you were in the bed?"

"Of course, while I was in the bed."

"So, what happened?"

"He had zero idea how it's done. He tried to change them the normal way you do when there's no one in the bed. I laughed so hard I peed on myself."

"Uh-oh. So tell me."

Katy swallowed down a laugh. "I'm lying there and he rolls me to my side and untucks that half of the sheet. So far so good. Then roll the other way, untuck again. But then goes down to the end and tries to drag the sheet out from under me, moving from head to toes. Disaster!"

"Lord, help us."

"Right? He dragged the sheet with me on it so I'm on my back, I get torqued and now I'm lying with my head off one side of the bed. So he comes around and straightens me out, apologizing the whole time, of course. Then he repeats and my head goes off the other side. This time my shoulders too, so I'm about to fall out of bed except I catch myself with my hand on the floor. And this bed is high off the floor. Just look."

"What the hell? Has he ever done this before?"

"Evidently not. But it gets better. He finally gets the bottom sheet off and the top sheet off and now he wants to put a clean bottom sheet on—with me in the bed. Now the way this is done, if you've ever been in the hospital, is they roll you onto your side and roll the sheet into a roll and unroll it as they put you onto your other side. When it's done, *voila*! You've got the sheet underneath and then you just tuck it in. But oh, no, not our Diego. He goes to the head of the bed and sits me up, holds me with his arm behind my back while he takes his other hand and tries to arrange the bottom sheet behind me. He satisfies himself that that's all good, then lays down my top half. Now what to do? You can see the gears turning in his head. He's got my top half on the new sheet and my bottom half on the mattress. This might have worked if he had rolled the sheet, lifted my bottom half and unrolled it waist to toes. But did he? Oh, no."

"Good grief. I'm firing this guy right now!"

"No, silly, don't you get it? This is the biggest laugh I've had since I got sick. Now he's lifting me around the waist and reaching up under me trying to snag the sheet and pull it down. Except I'm lying on it and I don't bend that way. Now he's stumped. So he excuses himself and goes into the kitchen. I can hear him talking on his cell phone. Come to find out, he called Peak Home Health and they told him how to do it."

"So he starts over?"

"No. He turns me crosswise on the bed—swear to God—and rolls me onto my side and pulls the sheet down. *That's* how he finished the job. Thaddeus, changing sheets is the first thing they teach new CNA's. But the comic relief was worth every penny we're paying those people. I've never laughed so hard!"

Thaddeus sat down in the chair beside her head.

He said, "It's funny, but it's also disturbing. He's not who he says he is. Is he?"

"I don't know. There're lots of other things too—little things. Maybe he's not."

"I'm calling Peak. I'm finding out how well they know this guy."

"All I can say is, this must be his first job. That and someone wasn't paying attention in school on sheet changing day. Good grief!"

Thaddeus stood up and walked to the window.

"I'm not convinced we should be laughing. I don't like this, given someone is shooting at us."

Katy's voice grew worried. "You know what about that? I've wanted to ask you. I think I'd like a gun."

"What? What on earth for?"

She pulled herself upright in the bed. "For safety. So I can defend myself. Or you or the kids."

Thaddeus turned away from the window and came to sit down beside her again.

"We can do that. Where would you keep it?"

"Under my pillow."

"Oh, you really are serious about this!"

She didn't smile. "Dead serious. Now that you mention it, what if this guy Diego isn't who he says he is?"

"I know. I'll be checking that out."

"I mean any of those aides or nurses they send out could be someone we don't want inside our home."

"Let me call Peak. Hold on, Biscuit."

Thaddeus put his cell phone to his ear.

The Director of Nursing answered her own number.

"Thaddeus Murfee calling. We want to ask about this Diego Luchesi you hired out for midnights. How well do you know this guy? I mean, do you have someone run backgrounds on these people?"

"Why, is there a problem?"

"Let's just say we're hyper-cautious. We had an incident out here."

She cleared her throat. "Basically, what we do is have them fill out an app. Then we check with the state Department of Nursing to verify licensure and status. That's about it."

"Seriously? You don't have anyone running background checks?"

"Not really. We've never had a problem, Mr. Murfee."

"Okay, well that answers that question. Thanks for the info."

"Is there anything else I can do for you?"

"No, thanks."

He hung up and shrugged. "Nada. No background check whatsoever."

"All the more reason to give me a gun. They're all going to be unvetted."

Thaddeus nodded. His lips were pursed and he was deep in thought. Then, "You've got your gun."

"It's for the best, Thad."

"I hate to say it, but you're right. I'm going to drop by Peak and get a printout on all the aides and nurses working here. I'll have the pros run backgrounds."

"XFBI?"

"Sure. We should be doing that anyway."

"Thank you."

45

Christine had learned enough of the language during her stay in Sicily with BAT that she was able to communicate with the young waitress. Her name was Monni and she was nineteen and wanted to attend art school in Italy.

In her primitive Sicilian dialect, Christine asked, "If I paid you ten thousand dollars American would you leave your job?"

The young waitress looked confused. In her native tongue, she asked, "You paying me not to work?"

"Yes, that's it. If you quit your job tonight, I will give you this money."

Christine dug in her backpack and withdrew an envelope stuffed with hundred-dollar bills. She spread the flap then riffled the bills before the girl's eyes. "See? Ten thousand USD."

"Give me. I do it, miss."

Christine had followed Monni after she came off her evening shift at Dista Fiencci's. A half block away was a coffee shop and the girl had turned when passing the window and Christine beckoned. "Me?" the girl indicated by pointing to herself outside on the sidewalk. Christine nodded excitedly. "Yes, you!"

The girl came inside and Christine had invited her to sit with her.

The coffee shop waitress was waved off. This wouldn't take long and Christine would leave a good tip.

Now the waitress, Monni, sat with her hand outstretched.

"You will walk back over before they close and you will tell them you quit, effectively immediately?"

"Yes. Give it now, please."

"I'm trusting you. And I know where you live."

"It is not a problem. I will tell them now."

"Tell you what. You go tell them and then come back here. I will wait."

"No, money first."

Christine grinned. "Don't blame you. All right," she said, passing the envelope to the anxious young woman, "and where will you go?"

"To Rome for school. I study art."

"Fantastic. So it's a win-win for both of us."

"It is."

"All right. I'll wait here and you go do it."

The girl stuffed the envelope inside her blouse and the deal was struck.

Twenty minutes later she was back, passing by the same coffee shop window and she turned and gave Christine the universal thumbs up as she went by.

Christine, wearing black jeans and a black turtleneck, and having pulled her hair back off her face, looked younger than her actual years. Her purse was woven fabric and cheap. Her makeup bordered on garish as a young girl might have it to make an impression when she was unsure of herself. Her nails were a hip Jamberry *Friday Flannel*, sure to draw the eye of the more astute hiring manager and sure to peg her age as much younger than her thirty-some years.

She put a ten-dollar bill on her tab and left the coffee shop. Without hesitation she made her way back up the street to Dista Fiencci's. Her presentation was that her roommate Monni told her she was quitting her job and Christine would like to know if she could apply for the opening.

The hiring manager looked her up and down.

"You waitress before?"

"I did. During high school in New York," she said.

"You are American. How good is your Sicilian?"

"I'm talking to you all right, aren't I? You know why I'm here, don't you?"

The hiring manager smiled. She said, "All right. Start tomorrow. Four p.m. But if it's four-oh-one you are fired before you begin."

"Can I get a noon shift too?"

"My, we are hungry for euros, no?"

"I am. I need money for my rent."

"Come in at ten o'clock tomorrow morning. But it will be a long day for you. Black slacks and starched white shirt open at the throat. Comfortable shoes, kitten. Black ones."

"All right."

Christine extended her hand and the manager flashed on the Friday Flannel Jamberry nails. She shook her head, reconciled to the folly of some youth.

"Good. Thank you for coming in, Christine."

"Thank *you*," Christine gushed. She clapped her hands and dashed from the restaurant.

~

As was his habit—the only habit she had been able to establish for him—he arrived at Dista Fiencci's just after 12:30 p.m. the next day. This time, 100€ saw to it that she would get to serve his table. Wearing all black except for the starched white shirt, Christine approached Mascari's table. She knew his previous face; the new one still resembled it, but was more Asian in appearance around the eyes. Maybe that was his aim, she thought, a look that was as generic as possible, as the rest of his features were definitely European. She had to admit that, had she merely been passing him on the street, she would have missed him. The new and improved Lincoln Mascari was finely crafted, a testament to the finest steel blades in the most talented Swiss hands.

He was speaking to a larger man, seated at his right, at their enclosed booth. When she approached, the larger man leaned away, hiding his head behind the demi-curtain that covered the top one-third of the booth. The curtain was damask rose and blood red with black stitchery. Christine brightly smiled and held her order tablet in both hands. She began punching keys on its face, inputting table and auto-timing the order, and she greeted them in her best accent.

"You look absolutely lovely today," said Mascari, leaning back against the booth and tapping his cigar against the gold-rimmed ashtray. He turned his head to the side so as not to blow smoke directly at her as he spoke.

"Thank you," she cooed, touching her hair. "I did it just for you," she smiled and laughed the laugh of a college coed.

He smiled broadly. "Well now. What are you recommending for us today?"

She knew exactly what she was recommending for the man, recommending because it was a dish glazed with sugar around the edges.

"I would strongly suggest the *Cassatelle alla Trapanese.*"

"Enlighten me, please."

"These are soft crescents of dough filled with sweet sheep milk, ricotta, and chocolate chips. We sprinkle them with icing sugar and you eat them while they're hot, when the chocolate melts into the creamy ricotta."

"Is it less than two thousand calories?"

"I think so. I can ask to be sure."

The mobster exploded with laughter. "I am only joking! My doctor says I must limit my intake to two thousand calories. But that's for a whole day. It's a joke!"

"It is!" she cried, feigning laughter as if he were the funniest man on earth. "So can I put in your order?"

"Absolutely, my winsome little waitress," he said. "And I would like your number, as well."

She batted her eyes and looked down. "I will bring that with your order. Just please don't tell the manager!"

"Of course not."

He reached, seized her hand, and pressed his lips to the back of her hand.

"Oooomph!" he said emphatically. "Such soft crescents of dough indeed!"

She took the other's orders and backed away from the table, smiling and scraping as she went.

The order was cooked and ready for delivery eleven minutes later. She had already brought their drinks and attended to their other nagging whimsies. Of course there had been more flirting and suggestive language and Christine had played right along. The man was half in the bag over her, she could see. He was excited, turned on, and kept asking when he would get her number. "When I bring the food," she told him several times. "You'll see."

Her tablet buzzed, indicating the order was up.

She ducked into the kitchen—right-hand door going in—and found the waiting tray of food. From her short waist pocket, she extracted what appeared to be a packet of sugar and heavily dusted the crescent of dough nearest the edge of the plate. She would need to make sure that morsel was closest to him and would likely be the first eaten. But even if not, even just one bite at any point in the meal would do it. Her hand shook with excitement. She was *so* close.

The chemist's assistant had told her, "Cyanide interferes with the enzymes controlling the oxidative process. This means his red blood cells won't absorb oxygen. Cyanide ingestion has been called 'internal asphyxia.' Swallowing a dose of cyanide as a salt will cause immediate unconsciousness, convulsions, and death within one to fifteen minutes."

With great pride in the chef's mastery of all things Sicilian, she bore the brimming tray to Mascari's table. Carefully she distributed the food per the orders. Last to be served was Mascari himself, whose food arrived with a flourish and a folded note that said, on the outside, *Only open when you've cleaned your plate!*

He read the outside of the note and she cautioned him with a wagging finger. "Only when you've been good and eaten everything.

Then you can open it. Promise?" she asked, her hand on the note as if to take it away.

"Promise," he said and made the Scout's Salute.

"All right, then, enjoy. And if you need anything, I'll be right over there."

"Thank you again, Miss."

She ducked away and found her shift manager. "I'm up for break. Restroom. Back in five."

The manager nodded and paid her little attention. She had no patience for the wait staff and viewed them as the problem and not the solution around her firmament.

Without missing a beat, Christine turned back to the hallway that led to the bathroom, strode right past it, and out the locked door at the far end.

Immediately she was standing in the alley behind the bistro and unlocking her waiting car.

Inside, Mascari forked up an entire crescent, the morsel treated specially by Christine. He paused to respond to the larger man before shoveling it into his gaping mouth.

Then he did the next worst thing possible: he gasped and frantically lifted his wine glass and swallowed down a purple bolus preceded by a toxic crescent of cyanide.

Attempting to stand up out of his booth and flee to the hospital, he instead plunged to the floor, where he writhed in paroxysms similar to a fish out of water. His mouth flapped open and closed, open and closed, and he tore at his throat with his hands until muscle lay bare beneath his snatching fingers and nails. But no matter what, he still could take in no air. Then convulsions took over, thrusting his body to the carved ceiling frescoes of the restaurant and then slamming his back hard against the tile floor. This manner of dying proceeded for another three minutes when, in the last gallant thrust, he fell back to the floor and foam issued down both sides of his mouth, streaking his face in a hue that just did complement the damask rose of the demi-curtain above him now. His eyes remained open.

Two blocks away, Christine dialed the main number of the restaurant on her cell phone.

"Mari, please," she said.

"Oh my God," cried the voice on the line. "Is this the emergency truck?"

"No, this is Christine. I won't be back. Did the gentleman enjoy his meal?"

In the background, she could hear emergency sirens converging on the restaurant. She casually tossed the cell phone out the window and the sirens could now be heard through the clear afternoon air. She brushed the hair from her face, removed the pins from the sides, and allowed her black mane to flutter in the breeze as she raced to the airport.

When the body had been removed from Dista Fiencci's, the large man, Mascari's driver, snatched up the note and read: *Sugar from your baby girl. Enjoy with me!*

Aloft in her Gulfstream and sailing northwest at 575 kph, Christine studied her fingernails.

She was sure of it: the *Friday Flannel* Jamberry had sealed the deal.

46

In selecting the criminal jury for the murder trial on the first day, Thaddeus and Shep Aberdeen were focused on placing as many healthcare workers on the panel as possible. Judge Herbert Hoover led things off by asking questions by himself for the first three hours. These were demographic questions: name, age, address, marital status, employment, children, and so forth, and really accomplished very little that the Clerk's jury list handout hadn't already done. Finally, Judge Hoover ran out of questions and took a late morning recess, following which he turned the panel over to the lawyers for questions.

Thaddeus and Shep found themselves looking at a nurse, a male CNA, a clinical psychologist, and a medical claims examiner who worked in Phoenix and commuted every day. It wasn't what they wanted, but it was what they were given.

When court reconvened, District Attorney Sanders sauntered up to the lectern. He smiled at the jury and smiled at the judge. He ignored the defendant and his lawyers, indicating that the jury should ignore them by his example.

He then began pursuing the rabbit down the hole.

"Ms. Robin, you indicated earlier that you are a supervisor with Dulles Corporation?"

"Yes, I am."

"Do you participate in the hiring process?"

"Yes, I have final authority on new hires."

"Can you describe the procedure for the jury?"

"Well, resumes are solicited with applications. Rejections are made based on qualifications and experience. Interviews are requested based on qualifications and experience. I then conduct a second interview, if the first team likes what they've seen and heard. Following my interview, I meet with the unit supervisor and go over three names. He or she then indicates to me his or her preference. I then make the hire."

"Do you always follow the supervisor's requested hire?"

"No, I have the right to hire as I see fit."

"How long does the entire process take?"

"Four to six weeks."

"Wow. That's quite a process."

"It's an important job."

"Yes, and it's similar to what we're trying to do here. We're trying to hire or select a jury that can appropriately decide this case. Only we don't get weeks like your company does. You understand that this case is just as important to the people of the State of Arizona as your hiring decisions are to you? Can you appreciate how difficult our job is? That's why we need your help. That's why it's so important for each and every one of you to actively participate in this process. Can you all do this? Can you team up with the people of the State of Arizona?"

He looked from face to face, presumably giving everyone a chance to address their ability to team up with the state in the process, as he had asked.

Thaddeus and Shep weren't fooled. It was an old prosecutor's trick and it was used to get buy-in, the line of questioning just presented. It was done to make the jury feel it had joined with the prosecutor in doing important work for the State of Arizona. The

State of Arizona also happened to be the complaining party, as the case was entitled the *State of Arizona, Plaintiff vs. Emerick Sewell, Defendant*. How neat and tidy it would be if all the jurors jumped on that team. It was up to the defense attorneys to make sure that didn't happen.

"Your Honor," said Shep slowly, while the moment hung in the air, "it would seem to me that the District Attorney is asking the jury to join his team. We would object to this maneuver, based on the requirements of due process that the defendant be tried by an unbiased jury. A jury that's sworn to function on the District Attorney's team hardly seems what the framers of the Constitution had in mind."

"Yes," said Judge Hoover to Sanders, "Mr. Sanders, I was okay with the question you were posing up until you asked the jury to join your team. The objection is sustained; the question is stricken. Please move along in your questioning now."

Without a flinch or a facial expression, Sanders asked the jury generally, "The judge makes a good point. Everyone knows that the defendant has a right to a fair trial. Do you understand that the people of the state of Arizona also have the right to a fair trial?"

No one blinked. All were in agreement the jury should be fair to the state as well as the defendant.

So Sanders continued, "It's my burden to prove the defendant guilty beyond a reasonable doubt, a burden I willingly accept. Mrs. Martinez, let's suppose I bring you two boxes of evidence and three witnesses. You look at all of the evidence; you listen carefully to the witnesses. You don't believe any of it. What's your verdict?"

"Not guilty, I think."

"Okay. Now let's suppose I bring you a hundred boxes of evidence and parade in a thousand witnesses."

"Oh, heavens!"

"Relax, I promise that's not going to happen. We'll get out of here during our lifetimes. But let's suppose we had all the time in the world and I spent one year presenting you with truckloads of materials. Let's say you didn't believe any of it. What would your verdict be?"

"Not guilty. And mad at you for keeping me a year."

"Understood. Let's change things a bit. Let's suppose I bring in only one witness. You listen carefully to that witness. You know that the witness is telling the truth. You believe the witness beyond a reasonable doubt. What would your verdict be?"

"Guilty."

"All right. Does everyone here agree that just one witness could possibly be enough to convict Dr. Sewell of the crime he's charged with?"

Again, waiting, giving the jury a chance to consider the point.

No hands were raised, so the prosecutor continued for another ninety minutes with this line of questioning. Then they broke for lunch, scattered to their favorite haunts around the courthouse, and reconvened at two o'clock, having run past noon for the first session.

When everyone had returned, Dr. Sewell, sitting between Thaddeus and Shep, uncomfortably shuffled his feet.

"No physicians?" Sewell said in a hushed voice. "I thought I would get a jury of my peers." His affect was almost depressed, Thaddeus observed. The guy was really frightened by now.

"That's the language we use," Shep answered. "The reality is different, however. As you can see."

"Well, there should be at least *one* doctor on the jury. Can't we make a motion or something?"

"It would be futile to even try. No, we get what the Clerk of the Court sends us from the voters' roll. The names are drawn all over the county randomly. Your chance of scoring a physician reflects the same ratio of physicians to civilians in the general population of the community. Not great odds at all."

"Well let's get rid of the psychologist. Can we do that?"

Thaddeus replied, "What's your thinking on that? Why get rid of someone whose main area of study is consciousness?"

Dr. Sewell leaned back and closed his eyes. "Psychologists are trained in classical psychological methods and theory. The notion that consciousness exists independent of the brain would be laughable to them."

Shep said, "Plus she would tend to hold great sway with the jury because of her credentials."

"Okay, I'm following you, Doc," Thaddeus said and put a check beside her name on his notepad. "We'll strike her."

When court resumed, it was Shep's turn to address the jurors. He focused right on the psychologist in an attempt to find and reveal bias to the judge, so that the defense could get her dismissed for cause rather than having to use a peremptory strike on her. Peremptory challenges were limited in number and you wanted to use one of them only where absolutely necessary.

"Dr. Ramziki, you practice psychology here in Flagstaff?"

The young woman brushed a wisp of hair from her forehead. "I do. I'm in the building next to the medical center."

"Your practice would be clinical psychology?"

She smiled and folded her hands in her lap. "Yes. Adolescents, mainly."

"Meaning teens?"

"Primarily."

"This case will involve a good bit of testimony about human consciousness. Would you already hold strong opinions in this area?"

"I would hold strong opinions. Would I be able to set those aside in favor of keeping an open mind? Yes, I could keep an open mind. I'm a scientist, sir. I'm always open to new learning."

She had backed him off with that answer. Bias would be difficult to show after she had just cut him off at the knees, evidently aware of what it was he was going after. Shep stepped to his table and whispered to Thaddeus, "Damned if she doesn't want to serve on our jury."

"Do you trust her?" Thaddeus whispered back. "I guess that's the real issue here."

Shep looked at Dr. Sewell. "Doc? You getting any kind of read on her?"

Dr. Sewell nodded slowly. "I'm probably the wrong one to ask, Shep. I tend to take people at their word."

Shep returned to the lectern.

"Dr. Ramziki, if the testimony presented in court was so very contrary to your training and your own beliefs, would you be inclined to reject it in favor of your own training and thinking and experience?"

"That's hard to say. But in all honesty, maybe so. I've been a practicing psychologist for nearly twenty years, sir. My opinions are pretty well formed by now."

"Such that, for example, if a physician testified that consciousness survives brain death? Would that be rejected out of hand by you?"

"Objection!" Sanders said smoothly so as not to tip his hand. "Seeks to pre-qualify the juror."

Shep coolly responded. "Your Honor, jury examination serves the dual purpose of enabling the court to select an impartial jury and assisting counsel in exercising peremptory challenges. *MuMin v Virginia*, 500 U.S. 415, 431 (1991). Moreover, where an adversary wishes to exclude a juror because of bias, it is the adversary seeking exclusion who must demonstrate, *through questioning*, that the potential juror lacks impartiality. Quoting *Wainwright v. Witt*, 469 U.S. at 423. Accordingly, I should be given considerable leeway in these types of questions."

But the judge wasn't buying it.

Judge Hoover looked from the juror back to Shep. "Sustained. Move along, Mr. Aberdeen, please."

"Please allow me to restate the question so that our prosecutor doesn't try to quiet you."

"Objection. Improper commentary."

"Mr. Aberdeen," said the judge.

"Moving along, Your Honor, yes. Dr. Ramziki, if testimony were presented in court that varied greatly from your own professional beliefs and if that testimony were supported by current concepts of, let's say, quantum physics, is there anything about that area of medicine that you would find off-putting to the degree that you would reject it in favor of your own beliefs?"

"I think I know where you're going with this, sir," the psychologist said. "That particular area is developing and new theories are propounded almost every week. My inclination is to keep an open mind—no pun intended—where I don't have the training and expertise to disagree. What I'm saying is, this area of thought is so new I really don't have any opinions about it. I'm sure I could keep an open mind."

"Very well," said Shep. He knew that it wouldn't get any better than that. She had just bought herself a first class ticket on the jury. Shep had been unable to dismiss her based on bias, but maybe something better had developed: he had found an expert in the field of human psychology who had just committed to keeping an open mind about the testimony that Shep knew the defense doctors were going to present. In the end, he knew, you really couldn't hope for much more than that. He decided to back off and suggest to Thaddeus and Dr. Sewell that they accept the psychologist on the jury.

He then decided to educate the jury just a bit concerning the defense's most difficult area of testimony. He could use any juror for this: what the juror said would be immaterial; it would be the questions asked by Shep that actually mattered. He glanced down his list of witnesses and settled on Mona Harwick, a college student who had said she was studying computer programming. He saw a potential opening there.

"Miss Harwick—it is Miss?"

The student smiled nervously. "It is."

"You're a student of computer programming?"

"Yes, sir. I'm getting my associates in Java programming."

"So you have a background in the theory of artificial intelligence, I'm thinking. Would I be wrong?"

"No, sir, you wouldn't be wrong. I've had two semesters of AI theory. I know a little bit about it."

"Are you one of those computer scientists who believes the human mind will eventually be replicated by computers?"

The student put her hand to her chin and considered her reply. Then, "Can I just say that my teachers have taught me that binary systems, ones and ohs, can produce systems of artificial intelligence.

Can computers eventually equal the human brain? I don't think anyone knows."

"Do you have an opinion?"

"Yes, I think computers will eventually be able to do the thinking of humans."

"Such that computers can maintain a conscious state just like people can?"

She sat back in her chair. "Well, it depends on what you mean by a conscious state."

"Consciousness, according to the defendant's doctors, is a state of awareness. Maybe this best describes what is meant. Computers can now defeat any human alive at the game of chess. However, computers don't know what chess is. Humans know. But computers don't. This is an example of consciousness as our case will present it. Do you have any preconceived notions about this kind of thing?"

"Yes. I believe that computers will someday know what chess is. And what flowers are. And what death means."

Shep was surprised at the last part of her answer.

"Will the computers you have in mind fear death like humans fear death? In other words, will they know the emotion of fear?"

"Now that, I wouldn't know."

"But wouldn't you agree that feelings are one aspect of consciousness? That feelings are part of what make us human and the lack of feelings is what makes computers machines?"

"You've got me there. I don't know."

Shep smiled his warmest smile. "I'm sorry. I'm not trying to 'get you.' I'm just trying to determine how you actually think about human consciousness and what bias, if any, you might have."

"Put it this way. If your doctors tell me that computers will never be able to do everything the human mind can do, I will have to disagree. But the area of consciousness as you describe it—well, that's something I would have to be open-minded about. We haven't studied that in school at all."

"I appreciate your candor, Miss Harwick. I truly do."

47

JUST BEFORE LUNCH, the jury was sworn in and sent away for an early lunch. Thaddeus watched them file out and he knew they would be discussing their own demographics over sandwiches and drinks, but that the focus of their conversations would edge more and more toward the evidence and testimony in the case as the days went by.

After the noon recess, Judge Hoover went straight ahead with testimony, telling District Attorney Sanders to call his first witness.

Sanders wanted to give the jury the twenty-thousand-foot view of the case, so he called Eleanor M. Hemenway, City of Flagstaff detective. Hemenway was dressed in tight-fitting black slacks with a black belt and gray houndstooth sport coat with a plain black tie. As she moved in front of the lawyers' tables, making her way to the witness stand, the jury was treated to a view of the heavy gold detective's shield on her belt on her left hip and her Glock 17 on the other hip. She walked confidently and cast an all-business aura. There was no nonsense about her, no gratuitous smiles or nods at the jury—none of the usual body and facial language so many witnesses use to ingratiate themselves to the jury. She wasn't standoffish; she was simply officious, there to do a job.

The Clerk swore her in and she took a seat.

Sanders stood and strode up to the lectern, a red file in one hand, his reading glasses and ballpoint in the other. He settled the reading glasses on the end of his long nose and began searching his notes. The jury saw his finger come to rest at the top of the page and they sat forward, anxious to get the testimony underway.

"State your name."

"Eleanor M. Hemenway."

"Your occupation?"

"Detective, Flagstaff Police Department."

"Have you been involved in the investigation into the death of one Nadia Turkenov?"

"I have."

"Tell us about your role in that case."

The witness leaned back in her chair. She took her time, coolly assembling her thoughts.

"I was assigned to the case by our Chief of Detectives. My partner is Herbert Constance and he worked the case with me. Actually, he's the lead detective on the case but he isn't here. His mother is very ill in Ohio."

"All right. What was the first thing you and Mr. Constance did regarding investigating this case?"

"We were told there had been an incident at the Flagstaff Medical Center. A death had occurred and certain statements had been made to hospital security personnel and nursing staff. So we proceeded to the hospital to begin our investigation. Upon arriving there, we contacted Francis C. Hickenlooper, the head of security services for the hospital. She told us that two members of the security staff had been in the room of Nadia Turkenov when the defendant Dr. Sewell made several statements about the patient's death."

"What did you do upon learning these things?"

"We made contact with C.S. Adamson, a security officer on the afternoon shift and Elin Montanez, another security officer on the afternoon shift."

"Where did this contact take place?"

"In the security conference room at the hospital."

"Did you speak to both officers at the same time?"

"We did."

"What did you learn?"

"Objection!" said Thaddeus. "Calls for hearsay."

"Your Honor," said Sanders, "I'm not offering any such statements to prove the truth of the matter asserted, but only that certain things were said. The veracity of those statements will be addressed through later witnesses."

Judge Hoover rubbed his chin with the back of his hand. "Well, it is preliminary. You may proceed. Objection overruled."

"Again," said Sanders, "when you spoke to the security personnel, what did you learn?"

"We learned that Nadia Turkenov had died shortly after her life support was withdrawn. We learned that Dr. Sewell had admitted he withdrew the life support."

"He admitted doing it?"

"Evidently so. Both security officers presented their separate incident report and the words were identical in each report."

"What did the words say?"

"Charlotte Mendoza was the duty nurse. She came into the patient's room after the monitor activated. She talked to the defendant and accused him of turning off the life support. At that time, he is reported to have said, 'I did. But she's free now. She asked me to set her free! You'll just have to trust me.'"

"So he admitted to shutting off the life support?"

"He did."

"Did you speak to the defendant doctor yourselves?"

"By the time we received the file, he was already lodged in the Coconino County Jail. The jailers made clear to us that his attorney had gagged him. No interviews allowed. So we didn't go there."

"Your Honor, that's all I have at this time. However, I reserve the right to recall the witness."

"Very well. Mr. Murfee, you may cross-examine."

Thaddeus waited while Sanders took his place at counsel table and finally stopped rattling papers. Then he turned to the witness and addressed her.

"Ms. Hemenway, did you review the circumstances surrounding Ms. Turkenov's death with anyone besides your partner Mr. Constance?"

"Did I what?"

"You know, have you discussed this case with anyone besides your partner?"

"I might have—wait, I spoke with the medical examiner. And I spoke with Nancy Stoudemire, the physician who spoke with Dr. Sewell at the jail."

"Did Dr. Stoudemire discuss with you any comments made by my client, Dr. Sewell?"

"No. She said she was serving him in a physician-patient manner and whatever he said to her was confidential."

"So you have no statements my client made at the jail?"

"No, sir."

"Did the medical examiner ever speak to my client, Dr. Sewell?"

"I don't know that I asked him that."

"Would it be important if he had?"

"I don't know. Depends on what was said, I suppose."

"What was the time of the death of Ms. Turkenov?"

"You'd have to ask the medical examiner for that."

"Please refer to your police report. The chronology pages."

Thaddeus handed the witness a copy of her own report. She began turning pages.

The witness nodded. "Okay. We talked to the medical examiner. He put the time of death at between noon and two p.m."

"Do you have any reason to think that might not be true?"

"No."

"Here's what our jury needs to know: Did turning off the life support kill Nadia Turkenov? Or was she already dead before Dr. Sewell did that?"

The witness came upright in her chair. She drummed her fingers against the file folder containing her report. She looked at Sanders, who was busying himself with a yellow legal pad.

"All I know is what the medical examiner told me."

"So you're putting the time of death between noon and two because the medical examiner told you that?"

"Yes."

"Did you ever talk to Ms. Turkenov's doctor?"

"Yes."

"Did you ever think to ask him whether Ms. Turkenov was alive at the moment Dr. Sewell withdrew her life support?"

"No. The medical examiner already told me—"

"I know what the M.E. told you. I want to know what the treating physician told you"

"I didn't ask whether she was alive. Of course not. Why else would she be hooked up?"

Thaddeus smiled and pointed at the witness. "That is exactly what we're here to find out. Why *was* she hooked up? Especially if she was already medically dead?"

"Objection!" cried Sanders, coming to his feet. "We're not here to find out when she was medically dead. We're here to find out whether the defendant contributed to her death!"

"Your Honor," said Thaddeus, "the jury has a right to know whether she was medically dead when the ventilator was turned off. That's the whole case for them to decide."

"Mr. Murfee, please refrain from instructing on what the jury has a right to know. That is my role. But for the record, I will overrule the objection as it's cross-examination and I don't want to limit you needlessly."

"Thank you, Judge."

Thaddeus paused and thumbed through his papers.

"So you didn't ask her doctor whether she was alive when the life support was turned off?"

"No."

"That is all. Thank you."

Sanders then attempted to rehabilitate on the issue of living versus already dead, but, without the expertise of a physician to fall back on, there was little he could do. The witness left the witness stand on a decided note of counter-climax, and, more important, left the jury wondering whether Dr. Sewell had actually killed Nadia Turkenov. Their faces were perplexed and their body language unsettled. What had seemed at first to be open and shut had taken on a sudden turn. When did the patient die? They asked themselves.

D.A. Sanders called his next witness.

Angus Wainwright, M.D., next took the witness stand. He was a mid-sized lanky man with a full beard and light-sensitive eyeglasses that still hadn't cleared up from the bright sunshine outside, which blocked any eye contact he might have attempted to have with the jury. He testified that he had served as the Medical Examiner of Coconino County for twelve years, that he was supported by a full laboratory staff and two other physicians who shared on-calls with him, and that he was married, had two sons at NAU, and had attended forensics training both in the U.S. and in Switzerland.

"She died between noon and two p.m."

"What time did you make this judgment," Sanders asked the doctor on direct.

"I arrived at the scene just after five o'clock that same day. The room was taped off with yellow police tape and nobody was being allowed in and out. The body remained on the bed as it had been when the patient died. I took her temperature, examined her, and wrote in my notes that the time of death was sometime between noon and two."

"Was there anything remarkable about the body?"

"A trachea wound in her throat where the ventilator had been inserted. Various IV tubes and telemetry wires still in place. I instructed the police photographers on certain additional photographs I wanted and they complied. Then I spoke with the decedent's treating physician."

"What did he tell you?"

The M.E.'s busy eyebrows closed together and he said, "He told me she had been in that same state as that afternoon when she died for about a month. There had been no change."

"But she was alive?"

The doctor chewed his lip. "Yes, she was alive. The machine was breathing for her and she had a pulse. I checked all of her vitals on the monitor later that evening."

"So she was alive?"

"Definitely, she was alive."

Sanders then proceeded through the autopsy, which had actually been performed by an associate physician. Photographs were entered into evidence, the autopsy report was entered, and Thaddeus made his notes. There was nothing remarkable in any of the exhibits so he would ignore those on cross-examination. Finally, his turn with the witness came.

"Dr. Wainwright, you've told the jury she was alive when Dr. Sewell removed her life support?"

"I did. She was."

"Tell us what indicated to you that she had been alive."

"Well, according to the monitor, her heart was beating, her body temperature was well within normal limits, her respiration rate was steady—"

"She was breathing?"

"She was breathing."

"But?"

"Well, the machine was doing her breathing for her. She was alive, however, no doubt about that."

"What about her brain activity?"

"The brain activity was difficult to assess."

"Well, are you a neurologist trained in the medicine of neurology?"

"No, I'm a trained forensic pathologist."

"You're a death expert?"

"Yes."

"Was there brain stem activity in the patient?"

"Yes and no."

"What does that mean, 'yes and no.'?"

"There were artifacts but I'm not the one to interpret their meaning for you. Again, I am not a neurologist or neurosurgeon."

Thaddeus nodded, then said slowly, "So on the issue of brain stem activity, you would defer to the neurologists and neurosurgeons for their expertise?"

"Yes, it would be inappropriate for me to offer expert testimony on brain stem monitoring."

"Thank you, Doctor."

The medical examiner stepped down from the witness stand and Judge Hoover recessed for the day.

Next up, Sanders told the court and jury, Nadia's own physician.

48

Dr. Sylvan Glissandos kept the jury waiting thirty minutes while she finished up with an emergency admit at the Medical Center. When she finally arrived, she flounced furiously down the aisle, her long dress flowing, stethoscope still firmly around her neck where she had left it and forgotten to remove it, white lab coat buttoned down the front, and her granny glasses looking at the jury as she came, clearly interested in her surroundings and the players involved. It was quite evident to Thaddeus that the woman was a pure scientist and gave little thought—or less of a damn—how she dressed and looked. As Detective Hemenway had been all-business, so was Dr. Glissandos.

She had been to court many times and waited for no one to tell her to climb up on the witness stand and be sworn. She breezed across the floor in front of the judge and stepped up the one small step, turning abruptly and raising her hand while she waited for the anointment of the magical witness words so she could launch into why she was there.

Sworn and smoothing her dress as she sat, the doctor looked from Shep to Sanders. She had recently spoken to both lawyers and wasn't clear which one had wanted her there.

But Sanders wasted no time.

"Dr. Glissandos, what was your admitting diagnosis for Nadia Turkenov?"

"Drug overdose. She was loaded on pain killers."

"What treatment was undertaken on admission?"

"Two things, initially. First there we did a gastric lavage. What you would call stomach pumping. This mechanically removes unabsorbed drugs from the stomach. Secondary was the administration of activated charcoal. This was forced into the stomach to help bind the drugs and keep them in the stomach and intestines to reduce the amount absorbed into the blood. Followed up with a cathartic to quickly evacuate stool from her bowels."

"Was she conscious?"

"Never was conscious. She had thrown up in her throat and her air supply was cut off. We cleaned that out in the ER but I think the damage was done. She had been without oxygen and her brain had shut down."

"Was she alive when she came in? Or was she shocked back to life?"

"I don't quite follow you."

"Did you have to give her shocks to get her heart started?"

"No, her heart never stopped beating. Not at any time."

"So she was alive?"

"She was what you would probably call alive."

"What would you call it?"

"Well, I would say she was alive or we wouldn't have taken such extraordinary measures as we took. Upon admission, it remained to be seen whether brain function would be restored."

"Did she have brain function on admission?"

"You know, we weren't doing EEGs on admission. We were too busy passing tubes, opening an airway, and getting her hooked up to a ventilator. The EEGs came later, on a consult with a staff neurologist."

"Who would that be?"

"Jacqueline Childs. She was in the hospital that night on an accident case. So she looked in on my patient, Ms. Turkenov."

"She ordered the EEG?"

"I ordered it. She recommended, of course, after we talked for a few minutes."

"Did she read the EEG?"

"She examined the patient. I don't know if she ever read the EEG. But I did. I am board certified in neurology as well as emergency medicine."

"What were your findings?"

"Abnormal."

"There has been talk of brain death in this courtroom and I want to set that issue to rest. Was she brain dead?"

The doctor drew a deep breath. "Brain death is referred to as the complete, irreversible, and permanent loss of all brain and brainstem functions. Brain death implies the termination of a human's life; correspondingly, the diagnosis of brain death is very important. Was she brain dead? We ran certain tests."

"What tests did you do?"

"Typically, isoelectric EEG recording is required at least thirty minutes and may last three to twenty-four hours. I thought three hours sufficient with this patient. The positive response of EEG tests suggests functioning of the brain. Consequently, the patient in deep coma might show some EEG electroactivity, while the brain-dead patient will not."

"Did she show electroactivity?"

"Yes and no. Let me answer that by explaining how I broadened the scope of my inquiry just a little bit. Nowadays, the standard diagnosis procedure depends on three cardinal neurological features: coma, absent brainstem reflexes, and apnea. These were the three features I was investigating."

"We will want to hear about how these were investigated. But first tell us what you're talking about in terms we can understand."

"Well, brainstem is the lower portion of the brain between the cerebrum and the spinal cord. The brainstem controls breathing, swallowing, seeing, hearing, and other vital functions. The examination of brainstem functions in clinical practice and in my approach included pupillary response to light, fixed or variation pupils, corneal reflex, gag reflex, cough reflex, irrigating the ears with cold water, presenting painful stimuli, and I think that was it. The examination of the absence of spinal reflexes included the test of ocular movement, facial sensation and facial motor response, pharyngeal and tracheal reflexes. These tests were corroborated, over time, by the several EEGs I ran."

"And your findings."

"You should know that I'm a little slow to pronounce brain death, maybe, compared to some physicians."

"You are a little slow, why?"

The doctor shrugged and her face lit up momentarily. "Because I have seen my share of miracles."

"You have seen brain dead patients revive?"

"I have. Remember, however, that medicine, particularly this area of medicine, is more art than science. We're talking here about physical tests, many of which are subjectively analyzed. Dilation, reflex, sensation—all of these are measured by the physician's five senses. They are not measured on a machine that gives numerical readings. So it is an art. When I say I have seen, as you put it, the brain dead revive, I am saying that based on my many subjective tests I have seen such phenomena. Now. What about this patient's case? It finally became evident to me, after several weeks of observing her vegetative state, that she wasn't going to revive. She wasn't coming back."

"Did you ever pronounce her brain dead?"

"Not in so many words. Not in her chart. Although in my own mind, I was deciding. But I was waiting to discuss with the family when the actions of Dr. Sewell suddenly intervened."

"And what was your decision?"

"My decision was to give it another forty-eight hours. Don't ask me why, but often when you give a patient another forty-eight hours a condition will suddenly resolve. It's an old wives' tale. Or old doctors' tale or something. I don't know. But it works sometimes."

"So you weren't saying yes or no to brain death when Dr. Sewell intervened? You were giving it two more days?"

"Yes. Two more days. Then I would pronounce if there was no change."

"And of course, we'll never know, now that he ended her life."

The doctor grimaced. "I don't know that I would put it quite that way."

"Did he end her life?"

"Well, that's the question isn't it?"

"What is your answer, doctor?"

The doctor leaned back and slid the stethoscope around her neck. Thinking better of what she had been about to say, she said, simply, "I needed another forty-eight to say. That's as far as I can go. I can't give you more than that, Mr. Sanders. I'm sorry."

"You can't say she was brain dead or not."

"Can't or won't. Probably the latter. You need certain findings from me for your law case. I'm sorry but medicine doesn't work that way with such clear lines between this and that. You want science; I can only offer art. I'm sorry."

"Well, thank you for coming."

"I had to. You served me with a subpoena. My lawyer told me I had no choice but to appear."

"Thank you for that."

The doctor shrugged. She appeared ready to get up and leave until Thaddeus strode up to the lectern. He gave her his best smile and she relaxed back into the chair.

He began, "Dr. Glissandos, you've been getting pressure from Mr. Sanders to testify that Dr. Sewell ended the patient's life, haven't you?"

Dr. Glissandos looked from Sanders and then up to the judge. "Should I answer?" she said quietly to the judge. "Do I have to discuss what we said?"

"Please answer, Doctor," said Judge Hoover.

"He has asked me many times whether I can testify that Dr.

Sewell murdered my patient. Meaning ended her life illegally. Yes, at times he has pressed me on that point."

"Is it too much to say he has pressured you?"

"I think 'pressed' better describes our interaction."

Thaddeus thumbed through his notes. Then, "Doctor, on a scale of one to ten, what was the number you would give to indicate how likely it would have been for Mrs. Turkenov to regain consciousness?"

"Two."

"That is all, thank you."

Sanders leaped to his feet.

"But you could just as easily have said five, couldn't you? I mean you needed two more days, so wouldn't it be fairer to say there was a spread, something like two-to-five?"

She again looked at the judge imploringly. He turned away, nodding to indicate she should answer.

"I feel like we're playing with words here," she said. "That's not my forte."

"Sorry if you feel that way. But you could have said five or you could have said two. There was more likely spread between those numbers than an absolute number, yes?"

The doctor looked at Thaddeus and smiled. "See what I mean by being pressed? This is the kind of conversation we have had on several occasions now. I say one thing and the District Attorney tries to get me to fudge it into something else. I cannot do that."

"Objection!" cried Sanders, his voice resembling the voice of some wounded animal. "Request that commentary be stricken and the jury told to disregard."

Judge Hoover looked down his stubby nose at the physician. Then he lifted his eyes to the jury.

"The jury will disregard the doctor's last comments. Doctor, please try to play by our rules here, simple as they may seem to you to be."

"Sorry, Judge."

"Doctor," Sanders came back, "you have mentioned that there are such things as miracles. There could have been a miracle here in Ms. Turkenov's case, correct?"

The doctor nodded. "That is why I gave it a two rather than a zero. In my heart, I knew it was a zero."

The jury could see the reality cross Sanders' face. There was nothing more to be gained with the witness. She might not be a word mechanic, but she had proved her mettle by avoiding his attempts to get her to say something not in line with her beliefs. He quietly folded the pages closed on his legal pad.

"Nothing further," said Sanders.

"No more questions, Your Honor," Thaddeus added.

The doctor was excused and she left the courtroom with the same determined gait—arms flailing the air and upper body thrust forward—with which she had arrived.

"That left a hole in the air," Shep whispered to Thaddeus.

Thaddeus only smiled.

49

ANASTASIA TURKENOV WAS a fourth-year student in medical school, she told the jury. She wasn't a doctor—yet—she said. But she was very close.

Sanders had called her to testify. She would serve as the family's representative before the jury. She had half-heartedly agreed. The family—being her brother, her uncle, and her husband—were of a different mind than her. But she would try to avoid revealing that, she had told Sanders early that next morning before testifying.

"Now you've discussed your mother's physical dilemma with your other family members, isn't that correct?" Sanders asked. He was going slowly with the witness, inviting her to tell things from her perspective, not trying to put words in her mouth. His tone had changed since yesterday when he had tried to force Dr. Glissandos into supporting his theory of criminal responsibility. It had changed because Detective Hemenway had dressed him down after court, telling him that he had come across as pushy and mean. As if he was out to nail someone for personal reasons.

"I discussed my mother with my brother, my uncle, my husband, and her other siblings, yes."

"At any point during her hospital stay was it decided to withdraw life support?"

"Did I decide that you mean?"

"I mean did the family come together as one mind, deciding to withdraw life support or not?"

"No. We hadn't reached that point."

"Had there been a discussion?"

"Of course. We were waiting for Dr. Glissando's lead. So far she hadn't made a recommendation to withdraw life support. So we hadn't voted."

"Voted?"

The medical student sighed. "We had gotten to the point where we were voting on things."

Sanders rattled his papers. The jury could tell from his furrowed forehead that he and the witness hadn't discussed any kind of voting on things. He quickly sidestepped, attempting to lead the jury elsewhere.

"As a fourth-year medical student, were you personally prepared to withdraw life support?"

"No. I'm not a neurologist and don't know that much about the art of neurology, as Dr. Glissando put it."

"In sum total, then, the decision was basically still up in the air?"

"Yes."

Sanders turned the witness over to Thaddeus, who took his place at the lectern and gave the witness a friendly smile.

"Back to the vote," he began. "Tell us more about the vote."

Out the corner of his eye, Thaddeus could see the air go out of Sanders. Thaddeus hadn't been led astray. Sanders, underestimating the community IQ of the jury, would have been disappointed to learn the jury hadn't been led astray either. Everyone in the courtroom wanted to hear about the vote.

"We voted on things because my husband and brother and uncle weren't agreeing on things."

"Now you're talking about your brother, Albert, your husband Jack Millerton, and your uncle, Roy Underwood?"

"Yes."

"And those three gentlemen are the conservators of your mother's estate and person, am I correct?"

"Yes. They were appointed by the judge."

"So they were in charge of your mother's money?"

"Correct."

"Did you have any say-so about your mother's money?"

"No, I didn't."

"Were you ever consulted by the threesome?"

"No, I wasn't."

"Did you ever interject your opinion?"

"Yes, I did."

"When would that have been?"

She looked at Sanders, who sat with head bowed, making notes as she spoke.

"There came a time when the three men wanted to pay themselves. I objected."

"Did they pay themselves?"

"Yes."

"How much?

"Uncle Roy got five; Albert got five; my husband got seventy-five."

"Five hundred?"

"Five thousand."

Thaddeus' head jerked up. "Hold it. You're saying your Uncle Roy has been paid five thousand dollars from your mother's money?"

"Yes, I am saying that."

"And your brother Albert received five thousand dollars of your mother's money?"

"Yes."

"And your own husband received seventy-five hundred dollars from your mother?"

"Yes."

"All told, they've taken over seventeen thousand dollars from her?"

Anastasia took a deep breath and nodded. Her face was tight and her mouth white around the edges.

"Yes, that's what's happened."

"Please tell the jury what the money was taken for."

"I don't know, exactly. They talked to the conservators' lawyer, Mr. Wang. It was agreed they would all be paid for services they rendered."

"What services were those?"

"Well, my husband went over bank statements."

"Your husband the CPA?"

"Correct."

"So he reviewed bank statements. Were these voluminous?"

"I don't know what you mean by that."

"Well, did they fill the giant size briefcase CPA's are fond of? That many checks?"

"No. More like a shoebox full."

"And he charged your mother over seven thousand dollars for going through those?"

"Umm. Yes."

"But of course the court allowed this? There was a court order that authorized these payments?"

"No."

Thaddeus was sincerely stunned. He closed his mouth into a grim line and allowed the jury to assimilate what they had just heard.

"So I understand," he slowly came back, "Judge Raul Mendoza hasn't signed an order authorizing payment of any of your mother's money?"

"Not that I know. I'm sure he hasn't."

"Have you told this to the District Attorney, Mr. Sanders there?"

"I haven't, no."

"Did you receive money too?"

"No. I'm angry about it."

"Who have you told?"

"Detective Constance knows."

"That would be Detective Hemenway's partner, the officer who's in Ohio with a sick family member?"

"Yes. He found out."

"What did he say about it when he found out?"

"We were sitting in an office here at the courthouse. He advised the guys they had the right to remain silent and they shouldn't say anymore."

"Because they were in trouble."

"Because they were in trouble."

Thaddeus nodded.

"Ms. Millerton, did your mother have a last will and testament?"

"She did."

"And who did that will leave her money to?"

"To a nursing scholarship at NAU."

"And to you and your family?"

"Nothing. She was fed up with us. Not with me, but with Roy and Albert."

"So if your mother died, the money went to the nursing scholarship. But if she were alive, then the three men could keep billing her estate."

"Yes. That's how it was."

"So your family had a financial interest in keeping your mother alive?"

"You could say that."

"Did that fact influence the family's decision to keep her on life support?"

"Not me."

"What about the conservators? Were they influenced?"

"You'd have to ask them."

"I'm asking you. I'm asking you what you saw and observed."

"I saw them influenced by my mother's money, yes."

"So much so that they wanted her alive, yes?"

"Yes."

"That is all, Your Honor. Thank you, Ms. Millerton."

Sanders immediately tried to rehabilitate.

"But there was also the question of whether she might still make a recovery, isn't that true?" he asked.

"Yes, there was that question."

"So in a way you agreed with the conservators' position, except maybe for different reasons? Would that be fair to say?"

Anastasia looked away.

"You want the truth?"

"Yes, we want the truth."

"I was so mad at my husband for taking my mother's money that I went to see a divorce lawyer."

"I see. But putting your feelings about your husband aside, there was still the chance your mother might recover?"

"There's always a chance in medicine, I suppose. Like Dr. Glissando said, it's an art, not a science."

Sanders backed away from the lectern and took his seat. Then, remembering himself, told the judge he had no further questions.

The witness was excused and the courtroom remained silent.

Thaddeus whispered to Shep, "The cat is definitely out of the bag, Colorado."

Shep's eyes met Thaddeus' eyes.

The cat was definitely on the prowl.

∽

DISTRICT ATTORNEY SANDERS buttonholed Thaddeus and Shep as they were making their way down the front steps of the courthouse.

"Guys!" he called. "Hang on one sec!"

They turned and set down their briefcases.

"Here it comes," Shep said out of the side of his mouth.

Sanders caught up to them.

"Some family, eh?" he said. He moved nearer the two defense attorneys, his bullish form making two of them.

"Different," Thaddeus said. "Interesting bunch you've got yourself there, Counselor."

"Definitely jumped the fence today," Shep said, unable to hide a smile.

"You old cattle rustler," Sanders said to Shep, placing his hand fondly on the lawyer's shoulder. Shep moved away.

"So what gives?" Thaddeus said. "You're here to tell us you're dismissing the charges?"

"Ha! Don't you wish! Actually, I'm throwing your guy a lifeline. Second degree, fifteen years minimum."

Thaddeus reached down and lifted his briefcase. "Get serious, Sanders. This is the case where you were going to shove my client's book up my ass, remember?"

"I was pissed he got bail. So what? Law is fluid, Thaddeus, you know that. So that's my offer. Aren't you going to respond?"

"I'm going to relay it to my client," Thaddeus said, "which I'm required to do. And I'm going to insist he tell you to go to hell."

Sanders shook his head wildly. "You're *miss*ing it, Murfee. The jury's ready to convict right now."

"Sure," said Shep, "and cow pies taste yummy. Don't kid yourself, Gary, you've got a dog of a case and he's about to take a whiz up your leg."

Sanders moved back a full step.

"You guys are starting to piss me off."

"Easy, big fellow," said Thaddeus. "We don't need any drama out here."

"Murfee—"

"I know, I know. The book up my ass and all that. Got it, big guy. Shall we move on, Shep?"

"We shall," said Shep, who lifted his briefcase and continued down the steps.

"You're a good guy, Gary," said Thaddeus. "But this case needs to be dismissed. Justice cries out."

"Your ass."

"There you go again, fixated on my ass."

"See you in court, Murfee."

"Got that. Okay."

50

THE DISTRICT ATTORNEY and the lead detective finally made contact that night at nine. Herb Constance was still in Ohio but was fine with Sanders calling him even though he was on personal leave. He knew the job back home went on 24/7.

"Herb," said Sanders, who was at home in his recliner, wearing blue jeans and a T-shirt and house shoes. He had a stiff bourbon on the table beside him, half-drained off. He was feeling no pain. "Herb, when were you going to tell me about the three musketeers taking money out of Ms. Turkenov's account without a court order?"

Constance was sitting in the guest room at his mother's house. Just returned from the hospital, he was pulling off his shoes when he picked up the cell.

"I sent you a memo," the detective said in his dull voice. He was tired, his mother was very ill, and the D.A. was not one of his favorite people.

"You should have come to me personally. Memos get lost. You know better, Connie."

"Maybe I do. Is that why you called me?"

"I'm trying to figure out how to make this murder one charge stick. I've got premeditation and bad act, but I don't think I've got a living victim."

"Come again?"

"It's turning out she might have been brain dead when the doctor unplugged her."

"That's bullshit. She was sure as hell alive. Her heart was beating and she was breathing."

"The machine was breathing for her. But you're right, her heart was beating."

"That's enough to get to the jury. I say go for it. Argue that this Dr. Sewell himself came back from the dead. I read his book on the plane. It's pretty damn interesting, by the way."

"They're making a big production out of brain death versus brain activity."

"Yeah, he goes over that in his book, too. He was definitely brain dead and he definitely came back to life."

"No shit? I better read that tonight."

"Download it from Amazon. It's only about nine bucks. Take you all of three hours to get through. But be sure to look at the medical records in the back of the book. He's got his EEG there. Shows very clearly there was no brain activity when he suddenly opened his eyes and said hello to the family."

An electric shock pulsed up the D.A.'s broad back. "Shit, Connie, that's exactly my case here!"

The detective said, thoughtfully, "Then I suppose that makes the defendant your best witness. You can ask him about what happened to him."

"But only if they allow him to testify."

"They have to allow him to testify. Or have you forgotten he says that the reason he did all this was because her spirit asked him to set her free?"

"Yes, that's true. He has to get up on the stand and explain that. Otherwise he looks like a rank killer."

"Exactly. I don't want to tell you how to do your job or anything, but you can also cross-examine Dr. Sewell's expert witness, the neurologist, by using Sewell's own book. Don't forget that."

"Connie, you're brilliant," said Sanders, taking a huge slug of bourbon. "I'm really glad we talked."

"You hadn't come up with this shit on your own?"

"Of course I had. I just wanted to see if there was anything else you hadn't told me besides the money they voted to themselves."

"We're back on that? Turns out I did tell you. Read the fucking memo, Gary."

"All right. Well, look, how's your sister?"

"My mom? Not good."

"Well, give her my best."

"I would, but she's unconscious. Is that all you had?"

"Guess so. Thanks for picking up."

"Goes with the job, Mr. D.A."

"Right. So long."

51

BILL BERNHARDT from L.A. XFBI flew over to Flagstaff. He wanted to deliver the news personally and help take action before it was too late.

He caught Thaddeus at the office, just before he left for home.

"Bill," said Thaddeus, and extended his hand to shake.

"Not now," muttered Bernhardt anxiously, and flopped into a chair across from Thaddeus. "This can't wait. Your man we backgrounded? Straight from Mascari's nest in Termini, Sicily."

"No way."

"I've got men swarming him but he doesn't know it. We've intercepted his cell calls. Hopefully we'll learn how far this thing spreads."

"Meaning?"

"Meaning it's very likely he's not here in the U.S. alone. That's our fear."

"So we're not taking him down yet. How do we protect Katy?"

"We're having Peak reassign him to the office for special training. So far he's going along with it. He's been told it will only take about a week and then he's out in the field again."

"So we've got a week of holding our breath at home, hoping he doesn't shoot out our windows again."

"I can promise you that won't happen. He's swarmed and he doesn't have a clue."

"I wouldn't count on that."

"We're not counting on it either. But we're not going to turn him out. Not yet, Thaddeus."

"I can tell you, Bill, you don't have my support in this. When I see a roach I step on it. He's pure roach, as far as I'm concerned."

"We're thinking bigger than that, Thad. You're just going to have to trust me this time. Don't ever forget: Mascari has still got a small army of thugs operating in Chicago. Luchesi has their full support. We are certain of that."

"Why? Has he been in contact with them?"

"He's been in contact with several numbers we've located on the ground. So far, Chicago and its environs are not included."

"What is?"

"Local stuff, mostly. Pizza deliveries. Call girls. That sort of thing."

"Sounds like a hell of a guy. Well, let me tell you this. If I see him loose before you see him, it's over. He's dead on the spot. I can promise you that."

"Thaddeus, if you see him on the loose and we're not one step behind, you have my permission. Do what you will if that's the case. But it won't be."

"You don't have my vote, but you have my assent. That's as good as it gets right now."

"That's good enough. I don't need your vote. I've got eleven ex-FBI agents on the ground here. This guy's toast."

"So be it."

Thaddeus shuddered as the men sat staring at one another.

The guy had actually been inside his house, alone with Katy.

His breath caught in his throat and he coughed and uncapped a water bottle.

Inside his house. That wasn't going to happen again.

The guy should be so lucky XFBI got to him first. Had it been Thaddeus it would all be over. He checked his watch. He wondered what the guy's hours were inside Peak's office.

Maybe he would pay a visit there.

Bernhardt abruptly brought him back to the moment.

"I know what you're thinking, Thad. Do not go there. Stay the hell away from Peak."

Thaddeus grimaced. His world-class poker face wasn't so world-class.

He would remember that for the next time.

~

THE CPA LUGGED into the courtroom a CPA briefcase as big as a dishwasher. It was tall, wide, deep and black and featured brass hinges on the top where the loading door opened up. Jack Millerton's shoulder ached from the weight of the documents and books he had brought along just in case—just in case Thaddeus Murfee threw him a curveball and he needed documentary proof of his mother-in-law's accounting workup he had performed. To the tune of twenty-five hundred dollars. In fact, there was another twenty-five hundred dollars owed now, for a year before the prior year which he had already audited.

"It's not cheap, asking a CPA to perform these cash flow analyses, Mr. Murfee," he told Thaddeus during the examination.

"But that's my point, Mr. Middleton: who asked you to do it? Certainly not Ms. Turkenov—she was unconscious. And not her daughter, your wife: she's told the jury she plans to sue you for taking her mother's money. And not Mr. Wang, the lawyer for the conservatorship. So I can't find who or why you even performed the so-called cash flow analysis. Except you did it and you got paid. Paid, of course, being an ambiguous term, since the only legal payments a conservator can make are under a court order, which never existed in your case. So maybe we should be saying you took the money without legal justification. Or, to be blunter, maybe we should call a spade a spade and just say you stole the money from your grievously ill mother-in-law. Does theft sound about right to you?"

The CPA twisted nervously in the witness chair. He all but bit his own fist as he brushed his hands over his face and tried to slow his racing mind. He would need to be very careful about what he said. That much, he knew for damn sure.

"You know, Mr. Murfee, with you making such accusations, I'm going to take the nickel."

"Meaning what?"

"You know, the Fifth Amendment. I have a right not to testify against myself."

"So now you're taking the Fifth Amendment? You're afraid of theft charges being filed against you?"

The witness looked up at Judge Hoover. "I took the Fifth, Judge. Do I have to keep answering now? Am I protected now?"

"You really should talk to an attorney," said the judge. "We'll take the morning recess so you can call someone."

And so the morning recess of the third trial day began. Before that, midway through yesterday, the state had rested and the defense had moved for dismissal of all charges, based on the fact that all the evidence, even if taken in the light most favorable to the prosecution, wouldn't be enough to convict the defendant. The judge had regretfully had to disagree, hanging his hat on the fact that there was a twenty percent chance the victim might have recovered, as testified by Dr. Glissandos when she scored that possibility a two on a scale of one to ten.

And so the trial continued. Today, Thaddeus had called Jack Millerton as the first witness for the defense. Discussing the witness order with Shep, the lawyers had agreed to take another bite of the apple, putting the key mover and shaker of the dead woman's relatives on the witness stand to once again point out their vested interest in keeping her alive even though she was legally and medically dead. Millerton had played right into that, admitting that there was a will and that his wife—and, indirectly, he—would receive nothing if the money was turned over to the nursing scholarship.

"First," Thaddeus had said, "before you let her go, you wanted to milk the estate for ten or twenty thousand dollars each of you, am I right?"

Millerton had turned white. "Not right."

"But you were well on your way. You had received seventy-five hundred and now you tell us you had another twenty-five hundred coming down the pike. So you make ten thousand and never leave the privacy of your home office. You don't deny that, do you?"

"I fail to see what difference it makes where I work."

"It doesn't. But what does make the difference is just who, exactly, you're working for, Mr. Millerton. Near as I can figure out, nobody asked you to do these audits. You just did them without being asked. And now you've been paid for doing a bunch of work nobody asked for and nobody needed."

"Well—"

"Can you produce a court order that gives you money from the estate?"

"Not yet. Mr. Wang says that will be forthcoming."

"But you paid yourself without a court order."

"I didn't act alone."

"So the others got money too?"

"Yes."

"That would be Roy and Albert? Five grand each?"

"Yes."

Several questions later, they were on break, while Millerton discussed his plight with counsel of his own choosing. He hadn't heard back from Detective Constance since their meeting when he had been warned not to say anymore, and he had felt justified in coming into court that morning and, despite the detective's admonitions to shut the hell up, talk about the money he received and try to explain the whys and wherefores. Bottom line, the wool he had pulled over his own eyes left him feeling self-righteous in asking to be paid for work he had done fair and square.

"You don't expect a CPA to work for no pay," he told Thaddeus at one point.

"I might if I'm unconscious in the hospital and have no one to rely on except my CPA son-in-law. Maybe."

"Well, in my family we get paid, even if it's for a family member."

"Not to put too fine a point on it, Mr. Millerton, but family rules don't usually control how courts see things. You acted here without a court order and that makes what you did a crime."

"I have to disagree."

"And that's why we have trials and courthouses and juries. You will get your chance to experience all that, I'm sure of it."

Sanders had at that point jumped up and down at the closing argument Thaddeus was attempting to make in the middle of the trial and the judge had sustained his objection.

Following the break it went quickly downhill. Millerton had been instructed by an attorney to say no more, and, for once, he followed the rules. And so he was dismissed and it was with great relief and sagging shoulders he lugged his enormous CPA briefcase back up the aisle and out of Judge Hoover's court.

The damage had been done. He paused outside the courtroom and speed-dialed Anastasia's cell. No answer. And he knew there wouldn't be. She had seen her own lawyer and it was getting ugly at home, with no one speaking and great care being made to avoid all touching even when passing in the hallway or bathroom.

He wondered if it was too late to return the money he'd been paid.

He dialed his new attorney. Time to find out.

52

THE SICILIAN DROVE down to Prescott and walked into Iron Mountain Guns and Ammo. He told the clerk he needed a gun, something small that could be carried concealed in a pocket. But the magazine must hold at least fourteen rounds.

The clerk pulled three semi-automatic pistols from the display case and spread them on the wide velvet mat that half-covered the far side of the case.

"Here is a favorite. The Glock twenty-six."

"How many bullets will it carry?"

"That's just it. You have several magazine capacities to choose from."

"What's the most it can hold?"

"Well, that's where you get into concealing it or not. In theory, you can get a magazine that holds thirty-three rounds. But that isn't concealable, not like you're talking in a pocket. You're looking at probably ten rounds. Maybe fifteen at the most."

Luchesi did the math in his head. Four kids plus the mother plus Murfee himself? Six in all. Add six wasted shots if they're moving. He'd feel safest with fifteen rounds on board.

"Give me a fifteen round magazine. I'll take the gun and magazine right now. And Arizona has no waiting period to buy a gun?"

"Correctamundo. No waiting period. If you've got six hundred and forty dollars plus change, you're leaving here fully armed."

Which he had and which he did.

Never mind that XFBI sat across the street and recorded the entire drop-in on video. Never mind that two agents entered the store and watched the purchase from nearby.

Luchesi saw the men come in and he had noticed the van across the street. It pulled in just after he had parked and exited his car. He was no dummy and instantly knew he was being followed. Well, so be it. When the moment presented itself, he would bypass them altogether and show up for work. The gun would already be waiting.

∽

SUPPLIES WERE DELIVERED from Peak Home Health to the Murfee residence. Among them was a large box of 4x4 sponges, critical in the nursing care of cancer patients. The box had been steamed over and then resealed. In the bottom of that box, unnoticed lay the Glock 26 and its 15 round magazine. The box went into the supply cabinet and was pushed behind the already-opened 4x4 sponge dispensing box.

Now he was ready.

53

THADDEUS HAD FOUND neurologist Jacqueline Field very attractive and he knew he would have to make doubly sure that didn't come across when he put her on the witness stand as his first expert witness in Dr. Sewell's defense. But it was difficult: she was again wearing the daisy barrette in her blonde hair, pulled to the side, lending her face a scrubbed, cherubic look that said it was way too young to actually hold the degree of medical doctor.

But she did.

He didn't waste any time. "So tell me, Doc," he said, "how do you decide when a patient is brain dead?"

"The EEGs showed no brain stem activity at all. Look, how about I do this. How about I tell you what I did here."

"Please do."

"First, I pinched the patient to see if there was any flinch. Any reflex. Next, I made sure there were no brain stem reflexes. I shined a light in her eyes to determine whether there was pupillary reaction. Last, I disconnected the ventilator and checked to see whether rising carbon dioxide levels in the blood stimulated the brain. None of these three findings was present. I declared brain death to Dr. Glissandos. It was pretty straightforward, Mr. Murfee."

"What about the electroencephalogram?"

"Never saw it at the time I examined her. But I have since. The EEG recorded a complete absence of brain activity. She was brain dead."

"So that's all it took?"

"Yes. As you can see, it's a combination of factors. In this case, I've reviewed the EEG. Ms. Turkenov had no brain activity at all, zero brain stem activity. The woman was medically dead."

"Can you tell us about the state of medicine in the United States regarding brain death?"

"I can. In the United States and many other countries, a person is legally dead if he or she permanently loses all brain activity or all breathing and circulatory functions. However, the heart's intrinsic electrical system can keep the organ beating for a short time after a person becomes brain-dead—in fact, the heart can even beat outside the body. But without a ventilator to keep blood and oxygen moving, this beating would stop very quickly, usually in less than an hour."

"Which is what happened when Dr. Sewell turned off the life support."

"I suppose. With just a ventilator, some biological processes—including kidney and gastric functions—can continue for about a week. But it is extremely important to understand that such functions do not mean the person is alive. If you're brain-dead, you're dead, but with technology we can make the body do some of the things it used to do when you were alive."

"Tell us what is missing when the brain is dead."

"Well, without the brain, the body does not secrete important hormones needed to keep biological processes—including gastric, kidney and immune functions—running for periods longer than about a week. For example, thyroid hormone is important for regulating body metabolism, and vasopressin is needed for the kidneys to retain water. Normal blood pressure, which is also critical for bodily functions, often cannot be maintained without blood-pressure medications in a brain-dead person. Also, a brain-dead person cannot maintain her own body temperature, so the body is kept warm with blankets, a high room temperature and, sometimes, warm IV fluids. That was happening with Ms. Turkenov, especially the high room temperature. It was stifling in her suite."

"How long can brain dead people be kept going?"

"There is very little research on just how long the body of a brain-dead person can be maintained. Today, with ventilators, blood pressure augmentation, and hormones, the body of a brain-dead person could, in theory, be kept functioning for a long time, perhaps indefinitely. But with time, the body of a brain-dead person becomes increasingly difficult to maintain, and the tissue is at high risk for infection. Terri Schiavo's family, who fought to keep their brain-damaged daughter on life support for fifteen years, has said Terri Schiavo was not brain dead, but in a vegetative state in which she had some brain activity. That's a different scenario than Ms. Turkenov."

"That is all?"

"That's all I can think of that might be helpful to the jury."

Thaddeus started to turn away, then paused. Here it came.

"Doctor, did you review the medical records, in particular, the brain scans, while Dr. Sewell was a patient and comatose."

She straightened herself in her chair and smiled over at the jury. "I did."

"Tell us about those brain scans."

"Nothing," she said. "No brain stem activity. Dr. Sewell was legally dead for several days."

Thaddeus paused at the lectern, allowing it to fully settle in the juror's minds.

Then, "That is all," he said.

The witness was passed to the prosecutor for cross-examination.

"Dr. Fields, have you been paid to testify here today?"

"Yes, I have."

"Who paid you?"

"Mr. Murfee."

"How much?"

"I reviewed the case and agreed to come to court and testify for a flat fee of thirty-five hundred dollars."

"Isn't that low?"

"There wasn't that much to do. Dead is dead, any way you slice it."

"I see."

"Besides, Dr. Sewell was in the right, in my opinion. I would have come in and testified for nothing. That woman was dead and her kids were keeping her alive out of self-interest, I am told."

"Who told you that?"

"The daughter, Anastasia. The medical student. She called me and told me she wanted me to tell the truth."

"Why was she afraid you wouldn't?"

The doctor smiled before she inserted the knife.

"No, she was afraid you would try to get me to tell something untrue. She said you had tried that with Dr. Glissando and she was calling me to warn me. Then she told me about her family and how they went for her mother's money. She's actually standing up for Dr. Sewell, you know."

Sanders flipped through page after page of medical records, saw nothing helpful through the haze of the bomb that had just exploded in his face, and abruptly sat down.

Judge Hoover cocked his head at him. "Mr. Sanders? Were you finished?"

"Finished, Your Honor," said Sanders, springing to his feet. "Lost in thought there."

"The witness is excused, unless you had more, Mr. Murfee?"

"Nothing further. Thank you, Dr. Fields."

"You're welcome."

At noon, the judge excused the jury. He and the attorneys would settle jury instructions that afternoon, he told them, so their services wouldn't be needed until nine in the morning. He reminded them to avoid news accounts of the trial, to avoid all discussions of the trial, and to let him know immediately if anyone tried to discuss the trial with them. They all nodded their assent and filed out of the courtroom.

It took until five-thirty that day to finish up with jury instructions. Judge Hoover made it very clear: there would be no time wasted after closing arguments. The jury would get the case immediately and, based on what he had seen thus far, he didn't expect them to be out discussing the case for too long after.

"I'm betting one hour," said Judge Hoover.

The lawyers packed up and left.

"You thinking what I'm thinking?" Shep asked Thaddeus on the elevator when they were alone.

"Plea negotiations?"

Shep nodded. He had worn his Stetson hat that day and now put it on his head, smoothing his hair back with his hand as he did so. "Seems to me this case is all but over. But I'm concerned with our guy touching the patient without the treating physician's okay. That's assault and battery where I went to school."

"I hear that. So how do we work around that?"

"Let me chew that over. I'll get back to you, Thad, my boy."

54

THURSDAY MORNING, before court, found Thaddeus with his feet up on his desk, laptop balanced precariously in his lap, reading assault and battery cases from the Arizona appellate courts. It wasn't looking good for Dr. Sewell. No living person had given him permission to touch the unconscious Nadia Turkenov. His only permission, as he would have it, came directly from her when her consciousness asked his consciousness to set her free. But would a jury believe that? And what about the question of brain death? What if they decided she wasn't brain dead? Might they believe that she had nonetheless in another form given Dr. Sewell permission to unplug her?

Thaddeus smiled. He, for one, wasn't buying it. Consciousness talking to consciousness? *Not on my watch*, he thought. *That's just about the last thing I'll ever believe.* Of course, there was Katy, who more and more did believe in such things. *Necessity being the mother of invention*, Thaddeus thought. *She needs something like that to believe in, in extremis as she is.* He punched the keys on his laptop again, flipping over to the next case. *How on earth was he ever going to get the jury to buy into spirits talking to each other when he didn't even believe it? Didn't all the trial manuals and trial experts tell you that if you didn't believe in your client's cause the jury would know it and see right through you for the fraud you were?*

He closed his eyes and tried to still his fear—the fear that he would be found out. That he would be seen for the hypocrite that he was, selling snake oil to the citizens of the jury. He wondered, then, what he really did believe in. Did he believe he would ever see Katy again after she was gone? His eyes immediately teared over with the thought of losing her. "But she's going, Thaddeus," he reminded himself. "You need to make some kind of peace with that." He listened to his whispered words and found himself looking up at the ceiling for answers. Why was it, he wondered, that people always looked up whenever they were looking for God? And why was he doing it just now? The tears ran down his face and he backhanded them away. He knew the jury would wonder at his bloodshot eyes if he kept it up, so he swallowed hard and forced himself to think of something other than Katy, something other than losing Katy.

He touched the thin recorder in his jacket pocket. It would be triggered by the spoken voice just as soon as he switched it on. The witness today was someone he wanted Katy to hear, if only on the recording. He was going to testify about incredible things and Thaddeus was excited to record his testimony and tear home with it and play it for Katy. The kind of science Dr. Rachmanoff was going to present in the courtroom was rare and it was supported by some pretty remarkable studies and theories. If it went over with the jury, Dr. Sewell would walk out a free man and Katy could pass on knowing that the end wasn't the end, that the end was really a beginning.

He brushed back tears and closed his laptop. He stood up and went to the window in his office and stared out at the San Francisco Peaks, rearing up in the near north, snow-capped and certain in their place on the earth.

One hour later, he was back in court, back at his familiar defense table, surrounded by Dr. Sewell and Shep, the jury assembled and settled in, the judge having just told Thaddeus that he could call his next witness.

"Defense calls Louis Rachmanoff," said Thaddeus. He reached inside his jacket and flipped the recorder into RECORD. *This one's for Katy*, he thought.

The bailiff headed up the courtroom aisle to retrieve the witness from the bench outside the courtroom. He returned moments later, followed by a slight, bald man with a goatee. As he came closer to the jury they saw the man looked very fit and at peace. He gave the judge a slight nod and whispered, "Good morning," and crossed to the witness stand. He had no notebook, no papers, no notes that the jury could see. They flipped open their notebooks and poised their court-issue pencils to make their notes.

Thaddeus moved to the lectern and, without use of notes either, began with his questions.

"State your name."

"Louis M. Rachmanoff, M.D."

"You're a medical doctor?"

"I am."

"What is your specialty?"

"Two, actually. Anesthesiology and psychology. I teach both at the University of Southern California."

"Where did you go to school?"

"Undergraduate and medical school at Harvard University. Followed by internship and residency. Board certified in anesthesiology."

"Doctor I have asked you to do certain things in preparation for your testimony here today. Would you tell the jury what those were?"

"Essentially I've been asked to review the medical records and the narrative of Dr. Emerick Sewell and to be prepared to comment on his near-death experience and the death of Nadia Turkenov, and offer opinions."

"Did you make those preparations?"

"I did."

"And do you have an opinion regarding Dr. Sewell's near death experience?"

"I do."

"State that opinion?"

"Objection!" Gary Sanders swept to his feet, a firm tone in his voice. He appeared comfortable in the courtroom that day, knowing that this strange testimony was coming and that he would have all day to deride it. One thing was certain in Thaddeus' mind: he wasn't going to be able to run over Sanders with Dr. Rachmanoff.

"Sustained," said the judge. "Please lay your foundation, Mr. Murfee."

Unbowed, Thaddeus rolled along.

"Doctor, what records did you review before coming here today?"

"The medical records of Dr. Emerick Sewell from the illness that hospitalized him and rendered him comatose. That illness forms the basis for the book he wrote, which is the book Nadia Turkenov said she relied on in overdosing herself in an effort to copycat the doctor's near death experience."

"What else did you review?"

"Well, I talked to Dr. Sewell himself, at some length. We had two sessions, each lasting about three hours."

"Where was that done?"

"In my office in Los Angeles."

"That would be the Keck School of Medicine at USC?"

"Yes, in my office at 1975 Zonal Ave, Los Angeles, CA 90033."

"Who attended those two meetings?"

"Just Dr. Sewell and myself."

"What if anything did you learn from those meetings?"

"Well, let's see. Dr. Emerick Sewell was forty-four when he woke up one morning before dawn. This occurred in his house in San Diego. He awoke with a terrible headache. And his back hurt as well. He got up, went into the bathroom, and fell off the toilet onto the Spanish tile floor. He says he lost consciousness. He finally came around and crawled back to his bed. His wife heard none of this. He pulled himself up and sat on the edge of his bed, trying to stop the room from spinning. When it wouldn't stop, he stretched out on the bed and immediately fell back asleep."

"Was that it? What happened next?"

"He was awakened forty-five minutes later with increased pain. He went back into the bathroom and vomited several times. Thinking he was coming down with the flu, he went back into his bedroom and dialed his service on his cell phone. He told his office to cancel all appointments for that day and to get cover on his cases. Then he went back to bed, where he began shivering and shaking so hard that it woke his wife up. She took his temperature and found he was burning up. Her words."

"Did she call anyone?"

"Eventually, she took him to the hospital where he did most of his neurosurgeries. He was admitted. He lapsed into unconsciousness and was comatose for about six days. On the seventh—I believe it was the seventh—he regained consciousness. All faculties were intact though it was several months before his perfect speech returned. There was some speech deficit at first."

Thaddeus nodded and paused, allowing the jurors to make their notes. To aid in this, he went to counsel table and retrieved a glass of water, which he took back to the lectern.

"Now, doctor. What exactly was wrong with Dr. Sewell?"

"In laymen's terms, he was eventually diagnosed with an infection of the tissue that covers the brain. Within hours of being admitted to the hospital, his entire cortex—the part of the brain that controls thought and emotion and that in essence makes us human—had shut down."

"Is this a common occurrence in humans?"

"Extremely rare."

"Tell us about Dr. Sewell's brain activity while he was unconscious."

"Yes, well, the neurons of his cortex were stopped, period. There was complete inactivity due to the bacteria that had attacked his brain."

"What happened during this time?"

The doctor smiled. "While he was absolutely without any meaningful brain function, his consciousness journeyed to another, larger dimension of the universe."

Thaddeus smiled and watched the jury. Several were stopped, pencils poised, staring open-mouthed at Dr. Rachmanoff. Others were furiously making their notes. But the courtroom was silent. No one was moving. Everyone was waiting to hear what came next.

"Doctor, is what you have described as a journey to another dimension medically possible?"

"Yes, it is."

"Please explain."

The doctor nodded and made eye contact with the jury. "This is my area of study, the consciousness. My theory, called the ORCH-OR theory, believes that when we die, we remain who we are, in consciousness."

"That says a lot."

"Yes, it does," the small doctor said. He smoothed down his goatee with two fingers. He uncrossed his legs and sat back comfortably in the witness chair.

"Tell us about consciousness leaving the body."

"In my laboratory, I have studied brain neurons. Each neuron has microtubules. Here is where many of my colleagues and I believe consciousness resides."

"Inside the microtubules?"

"Yes, and when death occurs, the consciousness leaves the microtubules and journeys into the universe. But the consciousness is still gathered together and connected because of entanglement."

"What is entanglement?"

"It is a law of quantum mechanics that states very small things can stay connected to each other even over great distances."

"Now there are spiritual implications to entanglement?"

"Yes. I'm not a religious person. But know this. At death, the microtubules give up consciousness and it dissipates into the universe but remains entangled as a soul. If there is cardiac arrest, the consciousness or soul can leave and then come back with resuscitation. This is what I believe happened to Dr. Sewell, your client."

"So his book is based on scientific knowledge?"

"Objection! It's only a theory at this point!"

"Sustained."

"His book is based on scientific theory?"

"Yes. It is one theory and entanglement is based on scientific laws. There are divergent views, of course."

"In your opinion, is Dr. Sewell's book based on commonly accepted scientific laws?"

"Yes."

"One last question. If Dr. Sewell says that Nadia Turkenov's consciousness communicated with him, is that possible?"

Dr. Rachmanoff leaned back and smiled. "It's not impossible. There's much about the consciousness that we don't know. And much that we do know that some in the know are simply refusing to accept."

"Did they communicate?" he went back at it again. He realized that he was asking as much for himself and Katy as for Nadia and Dr. Sewell. He wanted more than anything to hear this doctor say there was hope for him, hope that he would communicate with his love again.

"Did they communicate? Why not? I would ask. Why not? Simply because you haven't done it? It reminds me of that old song by John Denver that goes, 'How do you know the animals don't speak just because they haven't spoken to you?'"

"That is all, thank you doctor."

DA Sanders was immediately on his feet and crossing to the lectern.

"Doctor, there are other explanations for near-death experiences besides yours, correct?"

"Yes."

"In fact, some experts believe that the so-called near death experiences are really just the brain flashing up images under great stress, correct?"

"There is some theory something like that, yes."

"So isn't it equally possible that Dr. Sewell's brain was just starving for oxygen and it created this so-called near death experience out of thin air?"

"No, because that would require brain activity. There was no brain activity during the six days Dr. Sewell was brain dead. All the chief arguments against near-death experiences suggest that these experiences are the results of minimal, transient, or partial malfunctioning of the cortex. Dr. Sewell's near-death experience, however, took place not while his cortex was malfunctioning, but while it was simply off. This is clear from the severity and duration of his meningitis, and from the global cortical involvement documented by CT scans and neurological examinations. According to current medical understanding of the brain and mind, there is absolutely no way that he could have experienced even a dim and limited consciousness during his time in the coma, much less the hyper-vivid and completely coherent odyssey he underwent."

Again, the courtroom was soundless.

Then Sanders began riffling through the papers he had brought to the lectern. He appeared to read from his notes or other documents. During this time the jury sat, as one, staring at Dr. Rachmanoff. Their approval of the man was evident on their faces.

"Nothing further." Sanders went back to his table and said something to Hemenway. They both smiled derisively.

But Thaddeus caught the jury out of the corner of his eye. They were watching every move the doctor made. In that moment, Thaddeus felt that he had brought the best defense case to them possible. And he was very grateful for Dr. Sewell leading him to Dr. Rachmanoff. Grateful for his case, certainly, but most of all grateful for Katy.

He patted the recorder in his pocket, patiently poised to get it all down.

55

THADDEUS NEXT CALLED to the stand the attorney who had set the original lawsuit against Dr. Sewell in motion. Thaddeus had one end of the string and he was about to unwind the whole ball. It was Milbanks Wang's turn to give it all up to the jury.

"Mr. Wang, who do you represent in the Nadia Turkenov conservatorship case?"

"I represent the conservators, Roy Underwood, and Jack Middleton."

"And they represent the estate? Meaning, the money?"

"Yes."

"Who represents the conservatee, Nadia Turkenov herself?"

"That would be Albert Turkenov, her son."

"Who is Albert's lawyer?"

"That would be the public defender. He had to have a lawyer to get a bond. The court appointed the public defender for that purpose so that Nadia—Ms. Turkenov—wouldn't have to spend money on a lawyer of her own."

"Was that a wise thing for the court to do?"

"Well, she hasn't had to spend any of her money on a lawyer for herself."

"Speaking of which, who pays you?"

"The estate. I'm paid out of estate funds."

"How much have you been paid so far?"

"Five thousand dollars."

"And that's by order of the court?"

"Well...I'm working on that. Judge Mendoza has a form of order that I've prepared and given him to consider."

"But he hasn't signed that order yet?"

"No."

"And yet you've already been paid?"

"Yes."

"Without the court authorizing it?"

"Yes."

Thaddeus saw Judge Hoover leaning down toward the witness so as not to miss a word. His face was calm, but Thaddeus knew Judge Hoover well enough to know that his calm exterior could often bely the raging storm inside the man.

"Has anyone else been paid out of Ms. Turkenov's money?"

"Yes. Both conservators of the estate. And the conservator of the person."

"How much so far?"

"Seventeen thousand and five hundred dollars."

"Has Judge Mendoza authorized the money they received?"

"No, he hasn't."

"But there's an order pending that you've prepared."

"Yes. It hasn't been signed. But I expect it will be."

At just that moment, Judge Hoover raised his hand, shutting Thaddeus off. He adjusted the spectacles on his short nose and fixed the witness with his stare.

"Just so the court understands," said Judge Hoover, "I would like to follow up with my questions."

"Certainly," said Thaddeus. He turned and took his seat.

The judge went on for five minutes or more, eliciting the names and addresses of the persons paid, the dates of payment, the names and addresses of the persons writing the checks, and other facts that would assist him in understanding what exactly had been transpiring with Ms. Turkenov's money. At least, that's why Thaddeus imagined he was doing it. But then came the shock.

"Bailiff," said the Judge, "Go downstairs and return with six deputies."

The bailiff left on the run and everyone stared into space until he returned five minutes later with six armed, uniformed, burly deputy sheriffs.

"The clerk has made up a list of three names and addresses. I am issuing a bench warrant for each of these gentlemen. You are to go out two-by-two, arrest them, and bring them before me without delay. Do you understand me?"

The deputies all confirmed their understanding.

"Now, go!"

"Ladies and gentlemen of the jury, I ask your forgiveness for that little detour, but the court just couldn't continue with this trial knowing that a felony had very likely been committed by the names you just heard me give to the deputy sheriffs. And as for you," he said to Attorney Wang, turning his full attention to him, "I would suggest you carefully consider whether you too might have committed larceny during your dealings with the money that belonged to Ms. Turkenov. You have testified that you received five thousand dollars without an order of the court. Here inside these four walls," the judge said, indicating the walls of his courtroom, "that amounts to theft. As far as the bar association is concerned, those facts also amount to the commingling of your personal funds with a client's funds. Lawyers get disbarred for such inappropriate acts every day. You, sir, should see a criminal lawyer. Which you, obviously, are not. Bailiff, I hereby order you to take this witness to jail and hold him there until charges can be brought against him."

"Now, ladies and gentlemen, being without a bailiff, the court is going to recess until our bailiff returns."

He slammed his gavel down twice against its pad and abruptly stood to his full height and soared from the bench to his chambers.

"Not a sound could be heard all through the house, not even a mouse," Shep said to Thaddeus.

Both men laughed.

Dr. Sewell stood and looked around, dumbfounded.

"What?" he said.

"Let's just say, the jury is out," Thaddeus told him. "Come on back to the office. I'll explain it all to you there."

56

SHE KNEW SHE WAS GOING. It felt like fingers losing their grip one by one on the sheer face of a granite cliff. It was a dream, a dream about falling, but it wasn't. It was real and the drugs were what made it surreal, dreamy, almost wistful.

It occurred to her one afternoon: the world no longer needs my thoughts. At just that moment she felt the pain move its fist up along her spine, twisting the tortured ligaments and nerves there one more time until they cried out, "Too much! End this!" Ignoring her body's wracking cries just one more time, she said to herself, again, *the world no longer needs my thoughts. I won't be missed by the world. It will survive without me. My kids will survive without me. My family. Thaddeus will survive without me.*

She realized what all people must learn: the world will survive them. There is no rule to keep them above ground and doing for the world. No rule whatsoever.

So she could afford to relax her grip. Could afford to let go.

They had replaced the oral medications with a pump, the plunger to which was gripped in her hand. With a poke of her index finger, she could release the strongest pain reliever known to medicine directly into her bloodstream. Then—Sweet Jesus!—the relief would come, instantly and remarkably suppressing the pain in its path. Of course, it made her lose consciousness each time she self-dosed. Her consciousness, as she saw it, stepped aside briefly to allow the medicine to do its job.

Her consciousness would survive. She had read the doctor's story. The book, *The Doctor Is In...Heaven* was all but committed to memory. And she had heard the recorded testimony of Dr. Rachmanoff from the Consciousness Institute and USC School of Medicine. Thaddeus had provided it to her. Dr. Rachmanoff had provided the science she so desperately needed to give her the only kind of hope she could countenance. The religious kind of hope was based on faith; her world of thought and ideas and feelings were based on science, on measurability, on experiment and notation, of inquiry and testing. Her hope was rational where the other was faith-based. It was the same difference that existed between binary computational systems and quantum physics. The one was measurable going in, the other was measurable only coming out. Did that make sense to her? Going in and coming out? She had to admit: it did.

Now she had her science of a consciousness that survives death. Now she had the hope that she would meet her children again. Meet her Thaddeus again.

So when he came home that night, she told him.

It was time to go up on the mountain.

He held her in his arms, lying beside her on the hospital bed, rocking with her.

He said nothing more.

He had brought to her all he could find to offer.

∽

AFTER DINNER, served in the room where Katy passed her days and nights, Thaddeus maneuvered the kids to their mother, one by one, kissing her good night. "Tell mama something sweet tonight," he encouraged the little ones. "Tell her your most secret secret."

"I love you, Big Mama," whispered Parkus. "Come tuck me in when you can."

"G'night, Mommy," whispered Sarai. "God loves you, don't forget."

Celena leaned up and cupped her hands. She couldn't be heard, but Katy began nodding her head and turned to kiss the little girl. "Yes, love you back, my precious," Katy said.

And Katy was strong, Thaddeus saw, my God, she was strong. She never cried nor flinched. Gave no clue that she wouldn't be there for them in the morning.

Not a clue.

He watched the ten o'clock news as he did most nights when he was home. She—lying on her side, a rare enough event—watched with him. The weather predicted snow by the end of the week. The NAU Lumberjack football team lost to the Arizona Wildcats by forty points. An Amber Alert was abandoned after the missing girl was found upstairs asleep in her closet. And *Pet Parade* had a serious Schnauzer puppy up for adoption.

At ten-thirty, he went to the front closet and shrugged into his barn jacket. Then he came back to Katy and pulled a blanket from her closet and wrapped it around her.

Without a word, he lifted her from the bed. She had double-dosed for what she knew was coming: the unbearable pain of being lifted and pulled from the bed. She was unconscious as he carried her silently out the back door of the house and came around front, heading for the mountainside two miles away.

"When Diego shows up for his shift," Thaddeus told the two XFBI agents out front, "put him in your backseat and wait for me to come back."

"Yes, he's back on tonight?"

"Yes, he is. Do it. He gets no closer to my house than we are right here."

"Done, Thaddeus."

"It will be done when it's actually done."

They looked from Katy to Thaddeus. But they didn't say anything. His intention was clear.

Like a trail horse, he knew the way even in the dark. There was only a brief stumble as he carried her in his arms, bearing her up and up onto the side of the mountain that she loved and that her tribe reverenced. It was a holy place to her people, Thaddeus knew, a place of spirits. Good spirits. A place where she could safely go to meet them.

He was still climbing a half hour later and still hadn't broken a sweat. She had lost thirty-five pounds during her illness and weighed less in his arms than the hay bales he tossed easily around the barn when servicing the horses that stood stamping and blowing below the loft. She was light and she was mostly unconscious, until the last several hundred yards when he realized her eyes were open and she was studying his face. She was reading his face, actually. She was memorizing every detail, every pore, every hair, his look. And for him, he wordlessly allowed her to come that close.

The final one hundred yards were realized through her gasps of breath as his footsteps jolted her with unimaginable pain. She turned her face to his chest and clenched her fists. Finally, when they came to her tree, she wept because she could hold it back no longer. So he sat with her at the foot of her tree, a hundred foot ponderosa that marked the edge of the invisible circle where the trees ran out and the shale and volcanic pumice began. He sat at the base of the tree and arranged her across his lap. He was cradling her as if a small child.

"Cold?"

She shook her head.

"Good."

He pulled her ever closer to him. Together they breathed. Their breath, coming forth in white clouds, mingled and boiled before blowing sidewise off into the night. A puff, still air, another puff, still air, puff.

Thaddeus watched the air move and move. He felt her heart against his own. He leaned forward and kissed her head. He kissed her cheeks. She moved and he kissed her mouth.

"Now," she whispered.

He reached into the pocket of his barn jacket and withdrew the small clear plastic bag that she had prepared. It contained twenty white pills. Then he withdrew the small water bottle and unscrewed its cap.

"Shall I pass them to you?"

She nodded and opened her mouth.

One by one he fed the pills into her open, warm mouth. Not until she had all twenty on her tongue did she move her mouth toward the water bottle. He held it to her lips and tilted. She swallowed hard one time. Then less hard. Then easily. "Ahhh," she said and closed her eyes.

"You swallowed them all at one time?"

Her eyes opened. "You should mind your own beeswax."

She turned her face to his chest.

He pulled her ever tighter against his body.

Then he told her about the night sky, the constellations he could make out through the trees, the two satellites that crawled across the panorama, the owl he heard less than twenty feet away, the sound of a doe galloping past to a water hole. He described the children, back down the mountain, safe and asleep in their beds. He told her about their dreams, about their lives as they would grow up, who they would marry, where they would live, what her grandchildren would look like and how they would love her. He told her all the things he saw that she could no longer see for herself.

Because the world, at last, no longer needed her thoughts.

And she, in the end, no longer felt the need to visit her thoughts upon the world.

They were even.

At four o'clock a.m. his back was aching from not moving. Using his back and thighs, he moved upright against the tree. She was still clutched to him, still warm on the side pressed against his body. But cold where their warmth wasn't shared, him to her.

Tears streaming, he carried her back down the mountain. Carried her back down the mountain and crept back inside the large ranch house with her in his arms. He placed her on her bed, reattached the long tube that ran from the medication rack into the connection in the back of her hand, then drew the sheet up over her. He arranged her long, black hair on the pillow so that she looked as lovely there as she would have wanted when they came for her.

The people he called removed her body before daybreak.

He would be able to pick up the urn at five p.m., they told him.

He went into the kitchen and made coffee. He went out back and stood on the porch, looking off across the meadow at the forest beyond.

Then he went back inside and refilled his mug and sat down at the kitchen table. He switched on the flat panel TV that she had insisted be installed in her kitchen. At six o'clock the local news came on and the dream—he knew by now it was all a dream—continued.

Five o'clock, he reminded himself. He could pick her up at five.

It would be a long day without her. But he knew he could make it, because by now he too had read the book and he had heard the doctor's testimony and he had accepted that the science had it right.

He would join her again. No idea when or how, but it would happen.

He would settle for no less.

~

AT HALF PAST SIX, he remembered.

Diego Luchesi.

Thaddeus went out the front door of his house, stood on the deck and stretched. The two north side agents were parked forty yards apart, listening with their electronic gear for any movement. Their heads turned and they stared at Thaddeus when they heard him come out. The agent on the east side of the property reached out his driver's window and pointed at his rooftop.

Fine, that would be where Luchesi was being held.

Thaddeus went back inside, reached beneath Katy's pillow, and withdrew the Glock 26 he had left with her. He stuffed it in the front pocket of his jeans. The man who'd sold him the gun had specifically told him it was not a pocket gun. As Thaddeus walked toward the agent's vehicle, he slapped the pocket containing the gun. Not a pocket gun, hell, he thought. What do you call this?

At the passenger's window, rear, Thaddeus motioned Luchesi to exit the vehicle. The agent popped the lock, allowing Luchesi to comply. The man stood up, slightly bent from being cuffed behind, and stood to face Thaddeus. He shivered in the cold, as they had removed his winter coat and searched him before placing him in the vehicle.

"So," Thaddeus said to the man. "You have come here to kill me. Or my wife. Or my children."

"Not so!" cried the man. "I have only come to help."

"Is that what Mascari told you to say if we caught you?" Thaddeus asked. "Tell us you were only here to help?"

"Who is that? I know no Mascari."

"Right, pal. Well, I have it on good authority that you were the guy who threw gasoline on my friend and set him on fire. You don't have to answer that; I already know what you'll say."

"I didn't—I didn't—"

"No, of course you didn't. Now. Do you know what a dry well is, Mr. Luchesi?"

"No."

"Well, let's go then, you and I. You are going to learn something this morning."

Together they went to the tool barn and Thaddeus opened the door to his Ram 3500 and placed the handcuffed man into the passenger seat. Then he backed out and drove them several minutes south until they came to the south end of the ranch. Ahead was open, flat plain that fell away to Sedona to the south, and, off to the west, sparkling desert sand sizzling in the morning sun where the snow ended downslope.

"Right about here," Thaddeus said. He stopped the truck at the point in the barbed wire fence where the natural gas pipeline right-of-way marched through, bisecting his property south to north.

"These fellows were drilling for water out here one afternoon,"

Thaddeus told him. "It's used in the pumping stations. They didn't find water here and so that's why there's no station here. But right here—" Thaddeus stepped ahead of the truck and pointed down, "right here is where they drilled." He pushed the Sicilian ahead of him and they both peered down into a hole.

"That, sir, is a dry hole."

Luchesi took a step away. "No."

"Yes. You can jump in or I can shoot you right here. Now if you jump in, I might not let you die down there. But if I shoot you right here, I'm going to throw you in any way. No one will find you, either way, unless I say so. Now, which is it?"

He stood back and extended his arm, placing the muzzle of the 9mm against the man's forehead.

"I—I—"

"Can't decide? Tell you what, I'll decide for you."

Thaddeus stepped around the man before he could resist and shoved him toward the hole. Luchesi dug in the heels of his running shoes but Thaddeus had the leverage on him. Luchesi found himself skidding up to the opening. Without a word, Thaddeus swept the captive's legs out from under him and the man plunged into the dry hole.

Down, down, down, he remembered falling when he regained consciousness. Above him was a disk of light the size of a dime. He was still handcuffed and his claustrophobia set in as he stood there, thirty feet below the surface, unable to bend or even turn. His breath came in gasps until he thankfully blacked out.

Thaddeus climbed back inside his truck and started the Cummins Diesel. It loped along in neutral, pleasant enough in its powerful sound.

Without another thought about the dry hole and the man it held he drove back to his home.

The school bus was coming down the gravel road just as Thaddeus arrived.

"Not today," he told them, and waved the school bus on by.

"Why not" said Parkus, the youngest. "Snow day?"

"No, we're going to go inside and have some hot chocolate. Then we're going to talk about Mommy."

"We went to kiss her and she was gone. Back to the hospital, Dad?" said Sarai, the middle child of the three young ones.

"Nope. We'll talk inside."

"Dad, I'll race you," said Parkus. Without a word Thaddeus broke into a loping, losing run for the house.

Parkus looked down at him from the deck, having won the race by a good ten yards.

"You know I'm getting too old for that trick, Dad?" said Parkus. "Letting me win? Really?"

The girls climbed up onto the deck and went inside.

Parkus and Thaddeus followed.

Thaddeus closed the door behind them and gathered everyone around the table.

"Who wants hot chocolate?" he said.

"Dad, what's in your pocket?" asked Parkus.

"Nothing. Keys, I think," said Thaddeus. He remembered he hadn't taken the Glock 26 out of his pocket since XFBI found it in with the 4x4 sponges. It was the same gun that Luchesi had purchased, according to XFBI's copy of the paperwork created from the purchase at Iron Mountain in Prescott.

He thought of Luchesi caught down inside the dry hole and he thought of the gun and fifteen rounds he had brought into Thaddeus' and Katy's home.

XFBI would take the gun and dispose of it.

Mother earth would take the killer and dispose of him.

57

It was a week after the ashes and the mountainside ceremony. Then, court resumed again. Judge Hoover had, without asking, continued Dr. Sewell's trial a full seven days.

Thaddeus called his last witness, Dr. Sewell himself.

Dr. Sewell testified that while he was in Nadia's room before he turned off the ventilator, Nadia came to him and asked him to set her free. She asked him to act as her doctor and remove the ventilator so she could go. He told the jury that he had only done what she asked. Thaddeus tried to read the juror's faces, but they were mostly impassive. Which made it difficult if not impossible to know how well the first words cast toward them were received.

So he continued asking the doctor more questions. Sewell said that, following his own near death experience, it had taken him months to accept what had happened to him. For one thing, it was medically impossible that he had been conscious during his coma—but there you were: he had been. Which paled in comparison to the scenarios he had experienced while away. He told the jury that in the beginning there were clouds around him. Just like some of the *New Yorker* cartoons depicted heaven: clouds and angelic figures talking. As he rose among the clouds, his vision stretched out and he became aware that there were gigantic beings shimmering above the clouds—beings with wings and voices that were filling the universe, casting down the song that played on and on. It was coming from them as they sang music unlike anything on earth. This music was his best self stretched across the entire sky and being set to music. It was the best of him and it was singing glory. When asked by Thaddeus, he said simply the beings above were more complex creatures than we knew on earth. They were a new level of consciousness and he wanted to join them. But he did not.

Seeing and hearing were not separate in this place where he journeyed. He could hear the visual beauty of the silvery bodies of those gleaming beings above, and he could see the surging, joyful perfection of what they sang. Seeing and hearing were transposed until they both became the same sense. It seemed that you could not look at or listen to anything in this world without becoming a part of it—without joining with it in some mysterious way. Again, from his present perspective, he would suggest that you couldn't look at anything in that world at all, for the word "at" itself implied a separation that did not exist there. Everything was distinct, yet everything was also a part of everything else, like the rich and intermingled designs on a Persian carpet...or an exotic bird's face.

Thaddeus saw that the jury was rapt. Pens and pencils were set aside as they hung on every word.

The doctor continued, saying it got stranger still. A three-part message began flowing through his body. The message—and he had to translate it into earthly language—ran something like this:

"You are loved and cherished, dearly, forever."

"You have nothing to fear."

"There is nothing you can do wrong."

The message flooded him with a vast and crazy sensation of relief. It was like being handed the rules to a game he'd been playing all his life without ever fully understanding it.

"We will show you many things here," the message said, without actually using these words but by driving their conceptual essence directly into him. "But eventually, you will go back."

To this, he had only one question.

Back where?

Which was as far as Thaddeus had permission to go. There were certain spiritual moments that the doctor demanded to be kept quiet. He had purposely left them out of his book as they were intended only for him. All he would say is, "All is well. All is more well than you can ever begin to imagine."

Then came the cross-examination.

"Doctor," D.A. Sanders began, his voice already bordering on mimicry, "you are asking this jury to believe that a dead woman spoke to you, correct?"

"No."

Ignoring the answer, Sanders continued.

"In other words, your witnesses have said she was brain dead and therefore legally and medically dead. And now you come in here and say even so, 'she spoke to me.' Isn't that what you're asking the jury to believe, that the dead speak?"

Unflustered, the doctor's mouth formed a polite smile. "No. While the body is dead, the consciousness continues. That's all I'm saying."

Which caused Sanders to come fully upright in his bullish manner.

"So we die but we don't all parts die?"

"That's definitely one way of putting it."

"If she were still alive and you withdrew her life support then you killed her, wouldn't you agree?"

"I wouldn't disagree since you base your question on her being alive."

"Then you tell us that you were likewise brain dead during your own illness but that you came back. Came back with this terrific story you just told the jury, correct?"

"I definitely came back. Whether her condition and mine were the same is impossible to say. As other physicians have testified, there is no instrument that pegs brain death at one, five, or ten. It is a phenomenon that is more subject to a physician's interpretation than some instrument's reading."

"You always do that—always say it can't be measured. Don't you think you're weaseling when you do that?"

"I'm not making the rules about this. The whole field of medicine has made these rules. I simply accept them and play by them."

"Well, to whatever degree, your condition and Ms. Turkenov's condition were very similar, yes?"

"Yes."

"But you got a get out of jail free card and came back and she didn't get one."

"That's not how I would put it. But if you need to, go ahead."

"Thank you, I will. Point being, you got a miracle and came back to life. How do you know she wouldn't have been granted the same miracle?"

"I don't. I only know what she told me."

"There we go again. The dead speaking to the living. I dare say, doctor, that no one in this room has ever had a dead person speak to them."

Thaddeus watched the jury. He wasn't certain they all agreed with the prosecutor on that point. Many were sitting back, arms folded on their chests.

Looking directly at the jury, Dr. Sewell answered, "Like Dr. Rachmanoff said, how do you know the animals don't speak just because they haven't spoken to you? Look, Mr. Sanders, I'm not here to convince anyone of anything. I'm simply telling you what happened to me. I am a vital, forty-something physician trained at the finest medical school in the world and acknowledged by my peers with all the licenses and board certifications that a neurosurgeon can achieve. I have no reason to come here and tell you fairy tales. I am telling you what happened to me, both in my own case and in Ms. Turkenov's case. That's the best I have to offer. You can agree or disagree until they turn out the lights and force us to go home, but my story isn't going to change and neither is your skepticism. Whether you're a skeptic because your job demands it for this case or because you hold certain lack of evidence as a kind of truth for your life, I can't say. I only know my own truth. So ask away, but nothing is going to change what I know."

Sanders appealed to Judge Hoover. "Your Honor, that was a nice closing argument to the jury, but it was unresponsive to any pending question. I would ask you to tell the jury to disregard everything the defendant just said."

"No," said Judge Hoover without hesitation, "I believe that what has just been said was a hundred percent responsive to the argument you were making. In fact, it was quite well done. Please continue, sir."

Flustered, Sanders cried out, "But you claim the dead speak!"

"I claim that someone's consciousness communicated with my own."

The air went out of the D.A. "Then we'll have to agree to disagree."

"I expect so."

"That is all," said the District Attorney, throwing up his hands in feigned dismay.

Again, Thaddeus made a judgment about the jury. That judgment was simple. They had heard all they needed to hear and they had heard all they were going to listen to. But trials always came down to that: at some point, the jury's patience was exhausted. At that moment, it was time to pack up and go home.

"No further questions," Thaddeus said. "The defense rests its case."

Closing arguments and jury instructions followed. The jury seemed to pay little attention to either until Thaddeus hammered home the fact of Nadia Turkenov's conservators taking her money without a court order and the fact of them keeping her alive to keep taking her money. That was real and tangible and they could make of it what they would. The rest of it was argument—tenuous, far-fetched, faith-based although predicated on scientific theory, and the two sides totally inconsistent. Ordinarily in criminal cases, there is a general set of facts that remains after all the testimony and all the exhibits, and the jury can pick among those pieces and reconstruct the most compelling view of the evidence. But not here.

In Dr. Sewell's case, the evidence was diametrically opposed, one side saying the dead are silent, the other side saying the dead can speak. There was no middle ground, no half-dead, no half-speaking. You either believed one way or the other. It worried Thaddeus; his entire case was bizarre. It was with great discomfit he finally turned the case over to the jury and sat down from his closing argument.

As Thaddeus sat down, for the first time in his career he had to admit he had no feel whatsoever for which way the jury was leaning. Even after the jury was taken out to deliberate and he discussed their strengths and weaknesses with Shep and Dr. Sewell, he had little to offer regarding predictions. He simply did not know what was coming.

So they walked back across the street to wait for the verdict.

YEARS later he would remember every detail of the dream. Shep had gone around the corner to his office to wait for the verdict; Dr. Sewell had faded into the shops along West Aspen Street to shop for gifts to take home to San Diego.

Thaddeus, alone and missing Katy with every fiber in his being, told Katrina he wasn't to be disturbed unless the court called, and he shut his office door, laid down on his couch, crossed his ankles, and folded his hands behind his head. He thought of her and couldn't quit thinking of her. For a moment he thought he could smell the shampoo she used. He thought he could feel her fingers touch his face.

Then he was asleep.

She appeared as a young girl, a child. There was a beach and when he first saw her she was on her knees, wearing her swimming suit, digging in the sand with her sand shovel and packing the wet sand into her sand bucket. The sand bucket was very distinct when he saw it: it featured a whale blowing bubbles, and a yellow beach and blue sky. It occurred to him that the bucket was exactly the bucket she should have had. It was what he had known all along it would be.

He walked up to her and leaned down, his hands on his knees.

"Want to go in the water?" he asked.

"I do."

She stood up and, without being asked, placed her hand in his. Together they approached the foamy surf and stepped into its ebb and flow. She danced from foot to foot, shivering. "Cold!" she cried.

But it was a cry of joy. The day was a day of joy. There was no sun in the sky but there was a brilliant light all around. There were people everywhere but no one spoke yet there were no strangers. She and he were part of them and yet separate. They were themselves.

She stretched out in the water and he pushed her by her feet. She crumpled and turned under and came up laughing and splashing water at him. She did a good job of it too, soaking his face and his glasses. Always the glasses. Even there.

"I'm hungry," she said.

"What do you want, Biscuit? A biscuit?"

"You always call me Biscuit. Why do you call me that?"

"Because you're my biscuit. Do you want a burger?"

"Yes. And a day-long sucker."

Together they trudged across the sand to the green sandwich shop with its hinged shutters pinned in the open position. There was no line; the smell of burgers and onions wafted through the air as they drew near. They hurried the last thirty yards as the sand was hot on their feet. Quickly they made the shade of the burger stand and she bellied up to the counter and planted her elbows on the green wood surface.

"I want a day-long sucker," she told the young man.

He plucked a large pinwheel of a sucker from a display. "This one good?"

"Perfect," she said.

"You, sir?"

"I'll have a burger with fries and a cherry Coke."

"I'll have the same thing," she said.

While they waited, he watched her turn cartwheels in the sand, coming up each time and dusting her hands off, complaining about the hot sand. Hot sand or no, she persisted. Each time she came around she looked up from her upside-down position, making sure he was watching. He was. He applauded. He whistled. She stood up and bowed.

Food and drink in hand, they walked back to her bucket, shovel, and a hole in the sand. Water had filled the hole and she kicked at it in disgust with her size five foot. He arranged two towels for them to sit on and they both sat and opened their brown bags. The fries were hot, not greasy, and salty enough. "Shall I pass them to you?" he said, indicating the fries. "Please do," she said and opened her mouth. He placed several fries on her tongue and she took a sip of Coke and washed them down.

"You should chew your food better," he told her.

"You should mind your own beeswax," she told him.

His heart moved in his chest then, and he felt the unbearable love he had for her.

But she ignored his gasp, chewing dramatically and looking out at the ocean.

"What would you be if you weren't a man?" she asked.

"I'd be a whale on the side of your bucket."

"I'd be a doctor for horses," she said. "That's what."

They chewed and drank, drank and chewed.

They flew a beach kite and laughed when it dipped and caught the waves. Finally, she pulled it in and kissed the thin paper. "I like you!" she cried to the kite

She laid back on the sand and made sand angels. He sprawled back on his towel and put his arm across his eyes.

They dug in the sand and made a sand castle. She told him all about her life. She told him what it was like, where she lived. She told him about the music.

Then the light blinked as the lights in a theater calling back the audience. She stood and took his hands in hers.

"Time to go," she said with an ancient smile that came as no surprise.

She turned and walked down to the surf, this time without him. He stood up and waved but she didn't turn around again. She walked directly into the surf, into the crash of the waves, and disappeared.

He waited and waited but she was gone and the light was trailing away as he swam to the surface of his—

"The Clerk called! Thaddeus, wake up."

Sleep! He commanded himself. *She might return. Don't move!*

"Thaddeus, are you going to wake up? Judge Hoover says the jury has a question."

58

They had sent out a handwritten note. The judge read it to the lawyers and Dr. Sewell: "Can we find Attorney Wang and Jack Middleton CPA guilty of theft?"

Judge Hoover looked across his office desk at the lawyers. "Well?"

Thaddeus wasted no time. "I say give them a 'yes.'"

"Funny man," said Sanders. "The question requires a 'no,' of course, Your Honor."

"Agree," said Judge Hoover. "And there was a second question. More of a request, actually."

He looked at his visitors. Then he shook his head. "They have asked for a copy of Dr. Sewell's book, *The Doctor Is In...Heaven*."

"I see no harm in them having the book," Thaddeus immediately said. "Maybe they want to compare Dr. Sewell's medical records in the back of his book with the medical records of Nadia Turkenov. No harm in that."

Sanders violently shook his head. "No, no, no! The book isn't in evidence. It would be gross error to provide it to them during deliberations."

Thaddeus continued, "But you made such a big deal out of Dr. Sewell's illness compared to Nadia's illness. Now they want to follow up on your comparison. It might be error but it's harmless error. And it's helpful error."

"Show my continuing objection," Sanders said. "My strong objection."

"I wasn't going to provide it," said the judge. "But I am required to provide any such communication from the jury, to you. It might indicate to you this would be a good time to enter into a plea agreement."

"Voluntary manslaughter," Sanders immediately said. "No less."

"Complete dismissal of the charges and we'll agree not to sue the D.A.'s office for malicious prosecution," Thaddeus shot back.

The judge sighed. "So. We're that far apart, are we? Then I'll send a 'No' to the jury on both questions. That's all for now, gentlemen. Thank you for coming in."

The attorneys and Dr. Sewell trudged back into the courtroom and took the chairs along the rail, the padded ones. Thaddeus crossed his ankle over his knee and began keeping time to an interior melody with his foot. Shep sat beside him, poking his smartphone over and over. Dr. Sewell was on his other side, looking exhausted and shell-shocked and wondering when it would all be over with. His own cell phone erupted with the Grateful Dead's "Touch of Grey," and he answered it. "No, we're still waiting. All right, honey. I will."

At 4:45 the bailiff strode into the courtroom. "We have a verdict," he announced.

Judge Hoover, again robed up, took his seat on the bench and nodded at the bailiff. The bailiff went down the hall and retrieved the jury. They followed him back into the courtroom and took their places in the jury box.

"Ladies and gentlemen, have you reached a verdict?"

The computer programmer spoke up, "Yes, we have, Your Honor."

"Please pass the form of verdict to the bailiff."

The paper changed hands and the bailiff held it up to the judge, who read it once through.

"Very well. Is this your verdict, ladies and gentlemen?"

They all answered affirmatively.

"Very well. The clerk will read the verdict."

The clerk took the verdict in hand and read, "We, the jury duly impaneled in the case of *State of Arizona vs. Emerick Sewell* do find the defendant not guilty. Signed, Mona Harwick, Foreperson."

The defense table immediately erupted in handshakes and whispered congratulations. Dr. Sewell threw his head back and silently mouthed words at the ceiling. Then he whipped out his cell phone and began punching numbers.

"We're in recess," said the judge, and he thanked and excused the jury.

∽

CHRISTINE HAD FLOWN in six days ago, and the next day the two adults and four children had taken Katy's ashes to the mountain and the ceremony was held and words said and the ashes spread. Thaddeus remembered all of it as he drove home to the ranch that night. As his windshield wipers swatted at the falling snow, he remembered the dream. The little girl and the sand and the ocean. A chill ran down his spine, a good chill. "Thanks, Biscuit," he said in the dark cab of the Ram.

∽

DR. SEWELL WENT HOME to San Diego, "A free man for the second time in my life," he told anyone who asked. He was writing a new book, one about his most cherished conversations in heaven. His publisher was frantic for the new volume, since the finding of not guilty had spurred a hundred thousand new orders for the original title. *The Doctor Is In...Heaven* was number one on the best-seller lists and looked to remain there for weeks if not months to come. His dream of touching others with his journey had come true.

Shep went back to his office and purchased 160 acres that joined his ranch on the north side. New cattle would soon take over the grassy slopes and the project would enlarge and become the dream he had always envisioned.

District Attorney Sanders, all but crippled from his rodeo days, walked clumsily around his office and stared out his window at the cloudy, snow-heavy skies. He was intent on prosecuting the three conservators and Milbanks Wang. Herbert Constance, the lead detective, was putting together the case, while each of the four defendants hurried up to say they would testify against the other three in return for grants of immunity. Sanders was angry but wasn't carrying a grudge. He was too professional for grudges. But he fully intended to see all four of the *Four Horsemen of the CD's* (his name for them) do some time in jail for their theft. "It's a dream case," he told everyone. "They might as well start packing."

∽

ON FRIDAY, Thaddeus finished up in the office just before noon. Christine drove in from the ranch, where she was staying, helping the smaller children adjust. Together they walked down to Kathy's Kafe for lunch. As they strolled along on the snow, Christine passed her hand into Thaddeus' hand and gave it a squeeze. Then she withdrew it.

"You're all going to be fine," she said.

It was snowing again, the sun was hidden, and the girl was a memory from a dream.

He shivered hard and hot tears burned his eyes. They stopped at the red light and he swiped a backhand across his face.

"What?"

"Beeswax," he said.

She slipped her hand beneath his arm and kept it there.

Across the street they went and then up over the curb.

At the sidewalk sign with the damask rose, they stepped inside the cafe.

Christine smiled and Thaddeus looked at her.

She shook her head. "Nothing."

They ordered and passed the bound menus back to the waitress.

Thaddeus ran his hands up and down his face. "Hey," he said, "remember that meadow a week ago? Where we spread her ashes?"

"Sure."

He blurted it out, unable to keep it inside any longer.

"Here's the deal. She told me I should go there with you in six months and marry you. But she told me not to tell you."

Christine leaned forward and took his hands in hers.

"You didn't," she said. "She told me the exact same thing."

"Is the jury still out?"

"No, the jury's back."

"And you're still here."

"I'm still here."

THE END

UP NEXT: FLAGSTAFF STATION

"Wonderful book as I expected, as all of Mr. Ellsworth's books have been."

"I love the character of Thaddeus Murfee and John Ellsworth has an imagination that brings life to his characters."

"What a book fast paced thrilling story. You need to pay close attention as it's so intertwined with the drug cartels mob and FBI ."

"If you like fast paced mesmerizing mystery novels is author's work is definitely worth reading."

Read Flagstaff Station: CLICK HERE

ALSO BY JOHN ELLSWORTH

THADDEUS MURFEE PREQUEL

A Young Lawyer's Story

THADDEUS MURFEE SERIES

The Defendants

Beyond a Reasonable Death

Attorney at Large

Chase, the Bad Baby

Defending Turquoise

The Mental Case

The Girl Who Wrote The New York Times Bestseller

The Trial Lawyer

The Near Death Experience

Flagstaff Station

The Crime

La Jolla Law

The Post office

The Contract Lawyer

SISTERS IN LAW SERIES

Frat Party: Sisters In Law

Hellfire: Sisters In Law

MICHAEL GRESHAM PREQUEL

Lies She Never Told Me

MICHAEL GRESHAM SERIES

The Lawyer

The Defendant's Father

The Law Partners

Carlos the Ant

Sakharov the Bear

Annie's Verdict

Dead Lawyer on Aisle 11

30 Days of Justis

The Fifth Justice

STANDALONE THRILLERS

Girl, Under Oath

The Empty Place at the Table

HISTORICAL THRILLERS

The Point Of Light

Lies She Never Told Me

Unspeakable Prayers

No Trivial Pursuit

God Save The Spy

LETTIE PORTMAN SERIES

Please Wait For Me

AFTERWORD

My sources are Stuart Hameroff, M.D., of the University of Arizona School of Medicine, who posits the ORCH-OR theory of human consciousness, with the incredible collaboration of Roger Penrose of Oxford. That would be *the* Roger Penrose, the one who received the 1988 Wolf Prize for physics, which he shared with Stephen Hawking for their contribution to our understanding of the universe. If you have an interest in this stuff, suggest a jumping off place for you might be YouTube's video interviews with Stuart Hameroff, a series of five or six thirty minute interviews that will bring you up to speed.

The scientific method and the legal method of our judicial system have much in common. No assumptions, testing of veracity, and eventual laws that will emerge because they overwhelm us with their truth.

This novel is a work of fiction. Names, characters, businesses, places, events and incidents are either the products of the author's imagination or used in a fictitious manner. Any resemblance to actual persons, living or dead, or actual events is purely coincidental.

EMAIL SIGNUP

Click here to subscribe to my newsletter: https://www.subscribepage.com/b5c8a0

Copyright © 2015 by John Ellsworth

All rights reserved.

No part of this book may be reproduced in any form or by any electronic or mechanical means, including information storage and retrieval systems, without written permission from the author, except for the use of brief quotations in a book review.

ABOUT THE AUTHOR

For thirty years John defended criminal clients across the United States. He defended cases ranging from shoplifting to First Degree Murder to RICO to Tax Evasion, and has gone to jury trial on hundreds. His first book, *The Defendants*, was published in January, 2014. John is presently at work on his 31st thriller.

Reception to John's books have been phenomenal; more than 4,000,000 have been downloaded in 6 years! Every one of them are Amazon best-sellers. He is an Amazon All-Star every month and is a *U.S.A Today* bestseller.

John Ellsworth lives in the Arizona region with three dogs that ignore him but worship his wife, and bark day and night until another home must be abandoned in yet another move.

ellsworthbooks.com

John@ellsworthbooks.com

Manufactured by Amazon.ca
Bolton, ON